Michael

Enjoy

To Vancouver's

# 1 Security Information

market.

Kathy

12/15/00

# THE VOYAGE

## OF THE ENCOUNTER

# THE VOYAGE
## OF THE ENCOUNTER

### SHELDON BURTON WEBSTER

Rutledge Books, Inc.    Danbury, CT

This is a work of fiction. While, as in all fiction, the literary per-
ceptions and insights are based on experience, all names, charac-
ters, places and incidents are either products of the author's imag-
ination or are used fictitiously. No reference to any real person is
intended or should be inferred.

Rutledge Books, Inc.
107 Mill Plain Road, Danbury, CT 06811
1-800-278-8533

Manufactured in the United States of America

**Cataloging in Publication Data**
Webster, Sheldon Burton
   The Voyage of the encounter

   ISBN: 1-887750-86-X

   1.  Fiction 20th Century.

810                                        97-76074

# Dedication

To Alice Helms

# Prologue

He stood on the mezzanine of the lobby staring down at the black marble floor twenty feet below, holding a coil of half-inch rope. How fortunate he was to have found the rope in the janitor's closet, he was thinking. This is my lucky day.

*Is there anything left unattended? Forgotten? My will is in order in the safe deposit box along with my life insurance policies. Easy to find. I've written the note — stupid note — should have been longer. Oh God! Please forgive me! Damn it, my obituary; I forgot to write that.*

*This damn rope! I hope it's strong enough. What kind of a knot do I tie? This should do. NO! There should be something better than a simple slipknot. How the hell do you tie a hangman's noose anyhow? I once heard it was illegal. Jesus Christ, I can't go through with it. What will people think? Screw 'em, I'll never have to worry about it. They will, the rotten bastards. I hope those two rot in hell.*

*"Umph." That should hold. God forbid, what if it doesn't? Now let's tie it over here. Yes, that should be secure. "Umph." Yes, nicely done; that will hold me.*

*Dear Heavenly Father, forgive me. I have no other choice. I believe in the Father and the Holy Ghost and I repent for my past transgressions. I have tried, oh Lord, how I have tried to repent from my past and now I beg for your merciful forgiveness. Take care of my loved ones and give them the strength to live with this terrible deed. I ask in the name of Jesus Christ, my Savior. Amen.*

*What time is it? A quarter 'til six, OH GOD!, I.., I just can't do this! The janitor will be coming any minute now. Climb up there! Is that enough slack? Have you got enough goddamn slack? At least for Christ's sake make it painless and don't fuck it up....*

*What have I forgotten? OH GOD!, forgive me!* "OOMPH."

*"Aaauch...GOoucch..!" I've got.. to.. pull myself back......up. Come on, damn it, pull. Yes, just another foot. That's it. Get a hold of the ledge with your hand. Good going. OH God, that hurts...., rest for a second! Loosen it up. Now the other hand......., "OOMPH."*

The body struggled briefly, right leg twitching, spinning it counterclockwise. It swung slowly, very slowly now, until it hung very still.

# Chapter 1

## Brooklyn
### Labor Day, 1985

Flynn O'Grady stood on the East River Promenade overlooking the skyline of Manhattan. The Securities and Exchange Commission agent leaned on the railing, smoking a Camel and staring smugly across the river at the world's financial center. Insider trading on Wall Street was an epidemic and he had just arrested Peter M. Slade.

The tall slim man took a drag off his unfiltered cigarette, pondering the arrest of the Chief of Mergers and Acquisitions at Porterfield Hartley & Co. It was O'Grady's second arrest of a top executive from Wall Street's most prestigious investment bank that year. 'I have an ironclad case against Slade,' O'Grady was thinking, 'for trading on insider nonpublic information for personal gain. Same thing his partner, Herb Gidwitz, pleaded guilty to after making millions. I put that guy away for ten years in the federal pen.'

It was the time in the early 1980s when flagrant and indiscriminate securities fraud ravaged Wall Street, putting great pressure on the S.E.C. The Reagan Administration passed new legislation, the Insider Trading Sanctions Act of August 1984, which imposed fines of up to three times the profits gained or losses avoided for those convicted. Even with the new legislation, it seemed an unsolvable problem for the S.E.C. agent. Wall Street's greed was out of control and rapidly eroding international confidence in the United States financial markets.

It was Flynn O'Grady's job to stop it. The securities market was being protected by less than two hundred investigators in the S.E.C.'s Division of Enforcement. It was an impossible task to police billions of dollars and millions of shares traded each day. 'Yes, an impossible job,' thought Flynn O'Grady, smoking his Camel, knowing he was the last of the old guard, considered technically obsolete by the younger high-tech agents.

O'Grady was still riding a high after accompanying his only friend, FBI Agent Oden Terry, to arrest Peter Slade in his plush Porterfield Hartley offices on Exchange Place the previous Monday afternoon. At exactly four-thirty on August 26, 1985, the FBI agent had read Slade his rights. The athletic banker was marched handcuffed through his offices in front of his dazed staff to their outcries of disbelief. "This will get their attention, Ode," O'Grady had said once they were out on Wall Street.

The arrest had gone as planned. O'Grady checked his watch before they made the arrest after receiving the commissioner's instructions when he signed Peter Slade's arrest warrant. "Don't serve Mr. Slade until after the bell Monday, gentlemen. I don't want every goddamn congressman on the Hill calling me when the market has a sell-off like it did when you arrested Gidwitz before the market closed."

Within minutes after Peter Slade's arrest, the news hit the

airways. Rumors spread like wildfire in the financial district. A CNN television crew recorded Slade being taken into the Jacob K. Javits Federal Building in Manhattan. The coverage of the handsome executive in his early forties, wearing a tailored, $2,000 dark blue pin-striped suit was flashed around the world on CNN Business Report. Tuesday morning brought front page headlines of Slade's arrest in the *Wall Street Journal, New York Times* and *Barons*. The news had Wall Street buzzing about who would be arrested next.

Tokyo's Nikkei 225 stock index and the London markets had soared the next day when institutional investors, shaken by the securities fraud, transferred billions into the global markets. President Reagan had summoned the S.E.C. commissioner to the White House for an urgent meeting with his Treasury Secretary to solve the crisis. Investor confidence had continued to crumble, driving the Dow Jones Industrials to close down over thirty points that week.

O'Grady lit a cigarette and slowly walked back to the St. George Hotel along the street lined with maples. It was a tranquil neighborhood of fashionable brownstones across the East River from Manhattan where the hotel was a landmark. When completed in 1930, it became the city's largest and finest hotel. It was at its prime before World War II, but by the early eighties it had fallen into disgrace from old age and neglect.

Flynn O'Grady entered the deserted lobby and took the creaky elevator to the eighth floor to Suite 8813. He looked out his window while talking to himself, accompanied by a bottle of Four Roses bourbon, chain smoking. "I'm a securities cop, Commissioner, and one of the last of the old-time agents who's gotta natural sense for routing out the crooks. Your young smart-ass attorneys, Certified

Public Accountants and analysts with big name MBAs from Harvard and Yale are just a bunch of yuppies trying to make a name for themselves, doctoring up their resumes so they can land a six-figure salary on the Street after they spend a few years with the S.E.C. No sir, Commissioner, not Flynn O'Grady. I'm the last of a dying breed of real securities cops, and I've just proved it. You listen to me, Commissioner, sitting down in Washington on your fat ass behind that big mahogany desk. O'Grady's the best!"

He stopped to light another Camel, exhaling the smoke that floated slowly out the open window. "Yeah, took me twenty years, Commissioner, but I knew that some time the almighty Peter Slade would screw up. Now I got him nailed for insider trading, just like Gidwitz. Don't let my case get screwed up by those Justice Department lawyers!"

He took a drink of Four Roses, swirling the whiskey and ice in the glass, methodically smoking his cigarette, worrying about just that. At nine o'clock next Wednesday morning, Slade's preliminary hearing would be held before the federal magistrate in Manhattan. Too damn close for comfort, O'Grady was thinking, to meet the ten-day time limit under criminal proceedings procedures or the case would be dismissed. "Better not let the U.S. Attorney screw this up, Commissioner," he said to himself.

He chuckled, recalling Peter Slade's expression when Ode Terry read him his rights. He had stood stone-faced, unemotional, his ice blue eyes staring out of the fortieth floor window at the Statue of Liberty. "Call my attorney and tell him I need to see him immediately," he had instructed his secretary as he walked down the hall.

"Where?" his secretary asked, crying.

"At the Manhattan Federal Building on Federal Plaza, lady," O'Grady had said with a smirk.

A large crowd had gathered in front of the Jacob K. Javits Federal Building on Broadway in the short time it had taken them to arrive. The arresting officers pushed Slade through the screaming reporters and camera crews, and thirty minutes later he stood before the federal magistrate, the Honorable Judge Norman Goodwin. His bail was set for five million dollars, an amount he easily arranged the next morning, after spending a miserable night in the nearby Metropolitan Correctional Center. John Moffett had arrived from Florida and apologized.

"Well, Commissioner, I put Slade in jail for one night, anyway," O'Grady was saying, recalling the last twenty years of investigating Slade's activities on Wall Street. "Those yuppies you're hiring these days with all their fancy computers could never have caught him, Commissioner, for damn sure!" He took another drink, and admitted that he was glad to have had these guys and their technology that could track a stock transaction in any global market anywhere in the world in a split second. Even old securities cops need those computers, but O'Grady would never admit it aloud.

Slade still might get off, O'Grady worried. What if Slade's arrest warrant didn't show probable cause? A technical matter certainly to be challenged by his lawyer. 'I'll shoot myself if it does,' he was thinking, 'after all those years of investigation.'

Peter Slade's attorney, John Moffett, was one of the most brilliant defense attorneys in America, a master at manipulating the judicial system. O'Grady knew and respected the abilities of this renowned criminal attorney from Providence, Rhode Island. In his twenty-four years with the Securities and Exchange Commission, he had seen Moffett successfully defend four of his major open-and-shut security fraud cases, letting his white-collar criminal clients walk scot-free.

O'Grady went to the bathroom and looked in the mirror above the commode at the man pulling on the cigarette dangling from the corner of a lopsided mouth, warped from years of speaking confidentially. He examined his nicotine-stained teeth hiding behind thin blue lips, overshadowed by a nose reddened by spider-webbed varicose veins from years of heavy drinking. A three-day growth of reddish graying whiskers sprouted on a face that had never stood out in a crowd. "Piss on you, Slade!" he snarled when he flushed the toilet.

Now in his early fifties, O'Grady was the last of the old-line investigators, an infantryman in the S.E.C.'s attack on criminal abuse in Wall Street's financial markets. His job was patronizing the commissioner's bureaucracy by catching big-time white-collar criminals. Flynn O'Grady had waged a personal war in the process, unknown to his enemy for the past twenty years. Bitterly he had watched as Slade became one of the most powerful investment bankers on Wall Street.

O'Grady downplayed his arrest of the Porterfield Hartley executives involved in the latest Wall Street scandal. It was a textbook case that showcased the corruption and greed of a powerful few who had manipulated the nation's financial markets for personal gain. No one knew that this was the beginning of the S.E.C. investigation that caused the arrest of Dennis Levine a year later. Levine rolled over and exposed Ivan Boesky and Drexel Burnham Lambert and others. It was the beginning of the cleanup of Wall Street.

O'Grady's vendetta against Slade was personal, a deep hatred that no one knew, for he was a man without a family or friends except Oden Terry.

In all of this chaos on Wall Street, Flynn O'Grady's name was never mentioned by the press. The S.E.C. commissioner, U.S. Attorney, U.S. Marshal, FBI and Porterfield Hartley & Co. had made headlines. "I'm just a skinny securities cop on the staff of the S.E.C.'s Division of Enforcement, so let the commissioner have the headlines. Who cares? I finally got what I was after. Peter Slade is headed for jail."

His weak, bloodshot gray eyes gazed aimlessly out the window of the St. George at the fashionable brownstones and apartment buildings where he used to live. The white smoke curled upward, drifting lazily out the open window, vanishing in the light breeze off the East River. His thoughts were interrupted by the rumble of the West Side Seventh Avenue Subway as it pulled into the Clark Street Station in the hotel's basement. Soon the passengers would troop from the elevator into the lobby to the once grand twin-pillared staircase that led to the closed front desk. He waited patiently for his verbal ambush of the passengers as they spilled out onto the street below.

He drank heavily while waiting, the Camel choking his lungs with unfiltered nicotine, aggravating his emphysema. Coughing from deep inside his chest cavity brought up yellow mucus, which he spit into the trash basket, requiring a slug of Four Roses to suppress the pain. He stared out across the East River to Manhattan at the World Trade Center, home of the Northeastern Regional Office of the Securities and Exchange Commission. Tomorrow morning would be the first time in twenty-four years that he had not dreaded to go to work, he thought, while waiting patiently for the passenger to arrive.

Now his wait was almost over. The shadows of the apartment buildings crept slowly across Court Street in the late afternoon sun. He watched the passengers fan out on the street, many decked out in Mets paraphernalia, as they returned from Shea Stadium. 'Stupid fools, spending hard-earned money to see a bunch of over-paid ballplayers,' he thought, yelling from the window, "Hey, schmucks! Youse guys should of saved your money and stayed home and watched the jerks lose on TV!"

"Shut de hell up, mudder-fucker. I'm tryin' to sleep, man!" an irritated voice came through the open window back up to him, as he hid from the crowd on the worn-out blue corduroy couch in the shabby two-room hotel suite that he called home.

"Yeah, yeah, I hear you, brother!" O'Grady shouted back out the window, laughing his head off at the voice he recognized without a face. He reached for another whiskey, knocking the empty Four Roses bottle off the cluttered coffee table. "The Mets stink," he muttered, remembering the good old days of watching the Brooklyn Dodgers before they left for Los Angeles.

"To hell with baseball, Commissioner, I'm going to the deli. I'm out of smokes," he groaned, lifting his lean one hundred and sixty pound, six-foot-three frame. Lighting another cigarette, he rummaged around on the table for the room key.

The shadows of the buildings covered Clark Street as he walked outside into the cool freshness of the late summer breeze. This was Brooklyn Heights, all right: very clean with its deserted tree-lined streets, quiet and peaceful in the late afternoon of Labor Day, 1985. He turned, looked up at the majestic old landmark hotel and saw that, much like Flynn O'Grady, it was old and running out of time.

The St. George Hotel was part of an eight-building complex with 2,632 rooms. It had once been among the most elegant and exclusive hotels in the city. It had boasted the world's largest indoor saltwater swimming pool, grand ballrooms, restaurants and bars with aristocratic atmosphere. Now its once-fashionable shop windows were boarded over. Its rooms were filled with sophisticated guests from around the world escaping the hassle of Manhattan, just across the East River. These were only lingering memories. Over the last two decades four of the buildings that comprised the hotel were closed. The grand ballroom was turned into the 'Pussy Cat Club.' Three of the remaining four buildings surrounding a courtyard were condemned, leaving but one serving about eighty residents, half of whom were permanent and the rest welfare recipients housed by the city welfare agencies. Flynn O'Grady had been a guest in Suite Number 8813 on the eighth floor since his divorce in 1969.

Towne's Liquor Store anchored the corner of Court and Henry and was one of only a few remaining shops on the ground floor of the St. George. O'Grady staggered in and bought a fifth of Four Roses before crossing the street to Finocchio's Deli. He stopped outside long enough to smash out his cigarette, clutching his bottle tightly with one hand.

Glancing up from the New York Times, Mr. Finocchio watched the profile of the freckle faced, balding Irishman, framed by the St. George deteriorating in the background. The old Italian automatically reached for a carton of Camels and laid it on the counter. O'Grady entered and handed Mr. Finocchio a rumpled up twenty-dollar bill. Neither man spoke. O'Grady took the cigarettes and carefully counted the change. His weak gray eyes met the Italian's quick dark ones, neither blinking as he turned and headed for the door. The old man was thinking, as he thought each time O'Grady had left for nearly twenty years now, 'that guy's a weird son-of-a-bitcha.' He watched him through the window of the deli, passing back across the street into the St. George lobby. 'The Irishman, he's-a crazee,' he shrugged, returning to the paper.

Back at the St. George, O'Grady opened a fresh pack of Camels and poured a stiff drink. He stared again out the window at the skyline of Manhattan, thinking now, as he often did, of his ex-wife, Julie, whom he had divorced twenty years ago. The image of Julie's long red hair blowing in the wind was painted in the brilliant colors of the sunset that covered the western sky and approaching thunderstorm. His eyes, blurry now from the whiskey, fell on the brownstone across Henry Street where he once lived with his beautiful young bride, twelve years his junior. "Yeah, she was a real beauty, Julie, and a no-good, rotten whore. Damn you to hell, Peter Slade," O'Grady swore, hating the two of them. He stood at the window, looking out, getting drunk.

"I GOT SLADE, COMMISSIONER!" O'Grady suddenly shouted at the top of his voice, breaking into hysterical drunken laughter. He could picture Slade in his million-dollar condo on Fifth Avenue, scared to death after his arrest. His lean body shook as tears ran down his cheeks, laughing so hard he coughed violently, dropping cigarette ashes on the dirty carpet. "I GOT SLADE, COMMISSIONER!"

"MUDDER-fucker! WILL YOU SHUT DE HELL UP, MAN! You gone fuckin' nuts talkin' trash, or what, man?" came the same angry black voice from below.

"You shut de hell up," O'Grady barked back angrily, coughing, putting out the Camel and reaching for the pack. Yeah, over twenty years to nail Slade, he nodded, lighting up before laying down on the sofa, smoking, drinking Four Roses and thinking how rotten his life had been.

He thought about Hell's Kitchen, the old Irish neighborhood on West 20th Street where he grew up, a tough address in 1934 when he was born. He thought about his dead father, a hard-drinking

Irish emigrant who was a plumber and a member of the Marine Pipe Fitters Union and who worked for years repairing ships on the East River piers off the Brooklyn Heights Promenade. O'Grady's father had passed his blue-collar mentality and racial prejudice on to his two sons. Joseph, the older son, got killed in Korea, leaving Flynn the sole survivor, deferred from the draft during Vietnam.

O'Grady was taught at an early age to never trust WASPs or Jews. Blacks, Orientals or Puerto Ricans were no problem in the neighborhood in the early days, but Flynn had learned to hate them too.

He had joined the S.E.C. because it was the only job he could find after graduating at the bottom of New York University's 1960 economics class. He often wondered why his twenty-five years with the S.E.C. had gotten him nowhere. But it didn't really matter, now that he had arrested Peter Slade. That was what was important. Screw his lack of self-assertiveness and the bureaucratic political correctness that kept popping up in the annual evaluation reports of his work. To hell with them. He knew he had become envious of the wealth generated by Wall Street investment bankers, brokers and lawyers who manipulated the financial markets as corrupt power brokers. Sadly, getting a conviction in court was almost impossible in an industry protected by big New York law firms whose former partners were now the federal judges.

Tonight, the man Flynn O'Grady had arrested last week was a long way from his plush Fifth Avenue condo in Manhattan. Peter Slade admired the view as he stood alone at Benton Point State Park on the outskirts of Newport, Rhode Island. The winds from the smoky sou'wester had died down as yachtsmen dashed for the safety of Newport Harbor. Driven by the approaching night, they raced the setting sun that ended the Labor Day weekend and the worst week of Peter Slade's life.

Their magnificent white sails were more pronounced on the water by a brilliant orange sun that settled in an immense, jagged, fragmented wall of clouds in the western sky. The sun quickly plunged below the horizon, painting brilliant reds and purples, blues and golds in its mirrored silvery reflections off the ocean. The silent profiles of the boats sailed quickly past him and up the East Passage of Narragansett Bay, kicking white spray in their wakes. Their bows split the currents of the running tide for safe harbor.

Sounds of the Atlantic breaking on the rocky shore left Slade dark and depressed as he stood looking out at the Brenton Light. The Labor Day crowd was leaving and a fine cold salty spray blew across the abandoned parking lot. The roar of the building surf left an uneasy, empty feeling in his guts. He glanced down at his Rolex. 'I'm a damn fool, he thought, standing out here for another hour waiting for Charlotte Cocknell, another man's wife. Why in the hell didn't I just go back to New York?'

'I'll just have to wait now.' He thought back on the weekend he had spent with John Moffett and his wife, Anna, at their home in Providence. John would be having a Scotch on his patio about now, lighting the barbecue grill. 'Here I am, stranded in the middle of nowhere, starving for a drink, waiting for a woman who is probably a no-show anyhow!'

Earlier that afternoon, Moffett had dropped him off at the Providence train station to catch the 6:13 Mount Vernon for New York. Twenty-three minutes later he jumped off the train in Kingston, Rhode Island, and caught a cab back across the Newport Bridge through downtown Newport to Brenton Point, arriving a little after 7:00 p.m.

He could still vividly hear John's Harvard-educated voice, deep and powerful like the breakers, "Peter, I know you have had one hell of a stressful weekend helping me prepare for your hearing next Wednesday."

"I've had less stressful Labor Days, but you did all the laboring, Johnny. I greatly appreciate you and Anna inviting me up for the weekend."

"No problem. Now we're ready for Wednesday's preliminary hearing."

"Do I have to be there?"

"Damn bet'ya."

"What do you think, Johnny? What are our chances of getting the charges dismissed?"

"Slim to none, I'm afraid."

"I understand."

"Now don't get your hopes up, Pete, but from what I have learned this weekend, I'm fairly confident of our chances for a plea arrangement once I discuss your case with the U.S. Attorney."

"When do you think that will be?"

"Don't know, but I want to do it before your case goes to the Grand Jury. Can't rush those guys, but we're better off not to get the additional publicity after the Grand Jury convenes if we can help it. Hope to plea bargain with the U.S. Attorney before they indict you."

"What time frame? Week? Months?"

"Depends on what his caseload looks like and how much importance—or should I say how much pressure—the S.E.C. commissioner and Investigator O'Grady place on your case . . . "

"That son-of-a-bitch! Will he be at the preliminary hearing Wednesday?"

"You bet. He's the fed's prime witness."

"What's with that skinny guy? Why is he after me? I've never done anything wrong. You know that!"

"Now don't take it personal, Pete! He's just some bureaucrat trying to make a name for himself, I guess. He's gotten a little cocky since he nailed your partner."

"Convicting the ole' mastermind behind corporate takeovers of major Fortune 500 companies must have gotten him lined up for a promotion or something. I guess his success has gone to his head," Slade replied.

"Been up against this guy O'Grady before, Pete, batting a thousand against him. He's one of those mavericks held over from the old days, been at the bottom of the investigators staff for a long time, over twenty years or more, but he is shrewd, crude and smart as hell."

"Yeah, well Gidwitz, by God, should have gone to jail! He pleaded guilty to insider trading, the dumb shit. I haven't done one damn thing wrong, Johnny, unless you call working with Gidwitz at Porterfield Hartley a crime!"

"I believe you, Pete! As your best friend and attorney, I really do believe it! Now just calm down and don't take it personally. . . "

"Don't take it personally! A lot easier for you to say, John. That. . . that redheaded O'Grady arrested me in front of the whole office! What in the hell did I ever do to him? Man, I'm innocent as hell!"

"I know, it's nothing personal. He's just doing his job. Now take it easy and don't get all worked up. Want a drink?"

"Yeah, I'll have a Scotch, Johnny. . . And you say, 'Don't let it get to me.' That's easy for you to say, but you're not about to go on trial in Federal Court for securities fraud. Hell no, your life's not ruined, you still have your criminal law practice, your big fine home, lovely family, the *Encounter*." Slade zipped up his jacket against the cold, recalling their conversation on the sailboat that afternoon.

"Just take it easy, now. I'll be in New York tomorrow to take O'Grady's deposition down at the Securities and Exchange Commission office in Manhattan before the hearing on Wednesday. No need for you to be there. I will meet you at the Federal Court on Wednesday morning. I want to depose Porterfield Hartley guys that afternoon to see if we have a case of wrongful dismissal. They fired you before you had your day in court."

"The firm's gun-shy, that's why," Slade chuckled. "Second major arrest of their M&A chief this year! Bad publicity for them."

"Pete, hope the barbecue last night and our sail this morning eased your mind some."

Slade nodded. "Great party last night; enjoyed meeting Charlotte. You didn't tell me she was your first cousin."

"Yeah, I saw you making a move on her, man."

"Naw, I wouldn't do that, Johnny. That new boat of yours is really something!"

"God, isn't she great! Man, that's the best legal fee I ever collected. Now remember, keep a low profile and don't discuss your case with anyone, especially the press. Stay close by the phone in case I need to talk to you tomorrow."

"You bet, buddy."

"Where do you want to have dinner on Wednesday night?"

"What about a steak at Smith & Wollensky's on East 49th around eight? It's a cigar-friendly place...."

"Smith & Wollensky's it is," Moffett replied, thinking of the old-time waiters amid a sea of suits, serving a great cut of aged beef.

"Thanks for a great weekend, John," Peter replied, shaking hands with his close friend. "It's been a Labor Day weekend to be remembered, all right, and I hope to hell I don't spend the next one in the cell with Herb at that so-called 'country club' of a federal prison in Lewisburg, PA."

"Minimum security, yes, but I'll tell you, it's no country club. You got money, Peter?"

"Enough to last me to Wednesday, Dad!" Slade laughed, getting out of John's car and disappearing into the train station.

It was dusk now and Slade was wondering what he was doing in Newport. 'Will she, or won't she show up?' Perhaps he should have gone on back to New York. Serious second thoughts ran through his mind. He removed the folded piece of expensive white stationery from his pocket. Written in impeccable handwriting in blue ink, he read for the third time, "Peter, meet me at the overlook at Brenton Point State Park in Newport tomorrow night at 8:00 p.m. If you can't make it, please discreetly call 433-3477. Signed 'C'."

He folded the note and put it back in his pocket, listening to the powerful breakers crashing on the rocky shore. His thoughts of the stunning beauty of the woman he had met last night made him feel like a silly teenager inside. Her electrifying charm had been wonderful therapy for his destroyed ego, bringing back the sense of humor and charisma that he had lost last week. He wanted to see her warm, sincere smile on that beautiful aristocratic face, her intelligent eyes sparkling blue. He wanted to see that short blond hair and those ample breasts that stood firmly in her tight sweater, tapering down to a narrow waist and shapely hips. God, it had been a long time since Peter Slade had met a woman who really turned him on.

The fury of the ocean reminded him of how angry at and

embarrassed she had been by her drunk husband, Robert Cocknell. Why in hell was a beautiful woman like Charlotte married to that old silver-haired drunk? He laughed at the thought of Robert staggering around, pulling up the pants that kept riding down on his belly, and pushing up his horn-rimmed glasses while sipping his martini and smoking a cigarette. What a typically nasty, blue-blooded, trust-funded snob that guy was.

He was no fool, drunk or not. Seeing his wife enjoying handsome Peter Slade's company he had staggered over to where they were standing. "Robert, this is Peter Slade. . . "

"Peter Slade? And who are you? Some New York stockbroker who's after my wife's money?"

Slade smiled politely, thinking, 'no, her pussy, asshole,' before replying, "Nice to meet you, Robert. I'm John's college roommate and house guest for the weekend. . . "

"No. You're a New York stockbroker? John told me. . ."

"Please, Robert, don't be obnoxious, darling." Charlotte had said, taking her husband by the arm and leading him away.

Later, after all the guests had left, Peter and John helped put Robert in the back seat of her new red Bentley. Charlotte returned to the house to get her purse, discreetly handing him the note and saying, "Thank you, darling, for helping me get him out of here."

'So now you're standing, Peter Slade, out in the middle of no-damn-where. What a man won't do for a strange piece of ass, you fool, waiting for a married woman that didn't exist yesterday. Of all the women to get mixed up with, it had to be John's first cousin! If he finds out, I hope he doesn't get mad.' He glanced at his watch: eight o'clock. 'I'll give her another fifteen minutes and then try to get a ride back to town,' he thought, when the last of the Labor Day sun disappeared below the horizon.

Slade took a deep breath of the crisp salt air and reached in his pocket for his last cigar. Turning his back to the wind, he bit off the end. He licked the Macanudo carefully, making sure the wrapper was moist. He then lit his lighter, turning the cigar slowly just above the flame until a radiant orange glow appeared in the weak light. He pulled on the black-brown maduro whose aroma of coffee and spice was tantalizingly good. The smoke drifted with the wind. 'Thank God, I have one last Macanudo left in my life,' he thought, savoring each draw of the maduro and waiting.

Slade stood smoking. Then it hit him, not that he hadn't realized it before: his days as a hotshot investment banker on Wall Street making millions were over, finished forever. 'It's a hell of a note,' he thought, smoking the cigar whose savory smoke lifted his crippled spirits. 'So what if the IRS has frozen my checking account and all my assets, forcing me to borrow money from John to live on? Now I'm broke? That's a joke,' he thought, thinking of the ten million dollars he had stashed in his secret trust account in the Bank of Bermuda Limited.

# Chapter II

## Sunny Meadows
### Labor Day Night, 1985

The rush from the Macanudo gave Peter Slade a nicotine high, momentarily removing the loneliness he felt deep inside. He knew the loneliness would only disappear temporarily then return stronger than before, leaving an empty, sick, guilty feeling in his guts. He had been feeling that way since his arrest and it was hard to remember feeling different now that a week had almost passed.

Slade slowly smoked his cigar, regretting that he had made this big mistake, exercising bad judgment that had ruined his life. He was not about to confess his mistake to anyone, including John Moffett. Was he man enough to face the consequences? Five to ten years in federal prison was a long time. Even if he got lucky and wasn't convicted, the penalty had already been harsh. He would never forget the humiliation of being fired by the board last Friday, his appearance before the federal magistrate, the night in jail, and the horror of watching himself on CNN while reading about his arrest in the newspapers. His reputation, whether he was found guilty or not, was ruined, and for the first time he wondered what Jackie was thinking about all of this.

That was strange, he hadn't thought of Jackie Slade after his arrest or throughout the turmoil of the past week. She had not called, and that seemed strange after being married to the woman for fifteen years. Well, at least he would not have to tell his son, David, who would be twelve if he had lived. 'Sad miracle that is,' he thought. Their marriage had died with him, although neither was really willing to admit it at the time. Losing a child does that to marriages, and it would have been extremely difficult to tell David that his father had been arrested for insider trading and securities fraud.

When he felt loneliness during the past week, it was not for Jackie or any other woman, but the disgusting feeling that he had somehow gotten caught. 'That O'Grady must be one smart son-of-a-bitch,' he thought, wondering how in the hell the S.E.C. uncovered his foolproof system. Now with the cold wind to his back, he tried to drive away the loneliness by thinking again of the woman he had met last night in Providence. She could damn well keep the loneliness away for a little while if she ever showed up. He leaned against a sign post, waiting, and the crashing of the surf let the brutalizing loneliness crawl back in, and along with it came the dark.

From a distance the oversized headlights of the approaching car on Ocean Drive could possibly be a Bentley, Slade thought, as it came closer along the ocean. At the last minute, when he thought it would pass him by, the odd-sized lights suddenly took a sharp turn into the overlook to the sounds of squalling tires at the near-missed turn. Was this the same red Bentley that he had loaded drunk Robert Cocknell into last night? 'Thank God,' Slade sighed, as the mammoth car came to a quick, easy stop and the driver's electric window slid silently down.

"Peter! Jump in quickly!" ordered the rich, wonderful voice of the woman he had been waiting for as his heart pounded in his chest. He hurried around and opened the passenger door to the rich smell of new car leather and the elegant fragrance of Joy perfume. The interior lights revealed a woman much more beautiful than his memory of the night before.

"Have you been waiting long, darling?" Charlotte Cocknell's aristocratic New England voice silenced the wind in his ears as he struggled to find his.

"Only an hour or so, lady," he managed to say, still standing, admiring her short golden blond hair that glistened against her tanned face. She crossed her shapely legs as the deep leather power seat silently adjusted her body upward, and extended her hand.

"Come on, get in before someone sees us!" she ordered again, glancing nervously around the overlook. "Were you afraid I wasn't coming, darling?"

"Never!" Peter replied. "But, it was getting a little lonely out here in the dark, Charlotte. Well worth the wait, though. Let me get rid of this cigar," he added, flashing his warm, charming smile. He grasped her outstretched hand, which sparkled with a two-carat, pear-shaped diamond ring.

"No! Don't throw it away!"

"Are you sure?"

"Yes, it's OK, get in. I love the smell of a good cigar. It reminds me of Grandfather, who smoked Havanas. Partagas Havanas, before Castro. I remember as a little girl the rich fragrance that reminded me of chestnuts and cinnamon. What is that you're smoking?"

"A Macanudo Prince Philip. You sure as hell know more about cigars than any woman I've ever seen," Peter replied. 'Hope she knows just as much about making love,' he was thinking. He slid his bag into the back seat and shut the handcrafted door as the Bentley's V-8 turbo, in a pure expression of power, carried them down Ocean Drive into the night.

"Peter, you don't have to go back to New York tonight, do you?"

"Or tomorrow, either," Peter laughed, thinking, what the hell for? I have no job, no money, no wife: only the damn loneliness and good ole George.'

"I'll just need to call George and let him know how to get in touch with me," he said.

"Sure, no problem. There's a phone where we're going, or here, use the car phone."

"No. There's no rush, and besides, you don't need my home phone number on your telephone bill."

"George? Is he one of your colleagues at work?"

Peter laughed, "Hardly!"

"Who's George, then, may I ask, darling?"

"George Washington Henley. He's this old black man who has been part of my family since before I was born. Showed up from South Carolina during the war. Dad put him to work as a dishwasher at our restaurant in Baltimore. Worked his way up to bartender and when Dad died I somehow inherited a chef, butler, bartender, confidant. You name it, my man George can do it. George Washington Henley, he's one helluva guy."

"No kidding! That's a great story. I hope he has a better sense of humor than my mother's stuffy old English butler at Beach Mont, Thomas Terrell. She also inherited Thomas from my grandfather who left a stipulation in his will that he was to remain the butler until he either died or wanted to retire."

They were both laughing now and, God, it was good to be laughing again, Peter Slade thought as he cracked the window, drafting out the cigar smoke.

"Peter, this is one of the craziest things I've ever done, driving out here and picking up a man I only met last night. I feel like I'm a college freshman slipping out of the girls' dorm, or a harlot or something," said Charlotte, glancing over at the Roman features of the handsome man enjoying his cigar.

"Charlotte, I hope you aren't getting yourself into trouble."

"What do you mean, darling?"

"Husbands have a tendency to get a little upset when they find their wives in a situation like this."

"Oh, really? And how would you know, Mr. Slade?"

"Yes, really. I found out the hard way years ago when this guy caught me with his wife in an apartment in Brooklyn Heights."

"Naughty boy, Mr. Slade! For heaven's sake, don't worry about Robert."

"Where... where did you tell him you were going to be tonight? Or should I ask?"

"Don't worry," Charlotte replied, placing her hand on Peter's arm, "Robert's so damned hung over he won't even know I'm gone until noon tomorrow, if then. He's on one of his binges that will last for a couple of days."

"You're driving, lady. I've got enough problems without getting shot by a jealous husband. That's for damn sure."

"What kind of problems, Peter? John mentioned that you were divorced."

"Yes, that's right. Sometimes it works and sometime it doesn't," Peter replied, taking a long draw on his cigar, thinking, 'I wonder if John has told her about my arrest?'

"Was it a messy affair?"

"Not really. She just got up one morning about four or five years ago and signed the papers. Went back home to Atlanta, where I send her alimony check each month. No fights; never hear from her anymore."

"Do you have any children, Peter?"

"Had a son, David, once. Wonderful boy. Got struck by a car in front of our home when we lived in Arlington."

"Oh, God. I'm terribly sorry, Peter." Charlotte's voice dropped, as she glanced now at her stone-faced passenger.

"It's tough, still tough, something you never quite get over, but that's the sad reality of life and you have to go on with it. What about you, Charlotte? Any kids?"

"No, but I have always wanted children . . . we were unable to have any . . . Robert's damn fault," she replied with a sigh, so Peter Slade let it drop at that.

"My marriage has been a nightmare for years," Charlotte continued as though she needed to justify why she was driving a stranger through the rural Rhode Island countryside. "Living with an alcoholic is a living hell. You only saw his good side last night. God, it's embarrassing. Especially after the drunk passed out at John's barbecue and the two of you had to carry him out to the car. I'm at the end of my wits with him." Charlotte's voice bitterly tapered off, as she reached over and changed the station on the car stereo.

24

Beethoven's Fifth Symphony came on with its powerful music sounding superb on the stereo. This was like being in Carnegie Hall, with the wonderful music playing. The elegant smooth suspension of the car whisked them along on a cushion of air. "And what are you thinking?" he asked the woman.

"How brash it was of me to write you that note last night. Do you think I am awful?"

"Why did you do it then?"

"Because you are one of the most handsome, interesting men I have met in a long time. That's why."

Peter chuckled. "Come on now, really, that's very flattering of you to say."

"Really. I took one look at you, Mr. Slade, and decided for the first time in my life, what the hell: I like this man."

"Thank you. You're very flattering."

"It's not as though I don't really know you. John confirmed that you're quite a guy when I phoned to apologize this morning for Robert's grand performance last night."

They crossed the Sakonnet River Bridge on Rhode Island's eastern shore, turning south onto State Route 77. At Tiverton the sign pointed to Little Compton, eight miles ahead. As she drove along the shore and rounded a curve, the high beams of the oversized headlights fell on a 'FOR SALE' sign in front of an old abandoned New England inn. In passing, Slade got a glimpse of the ghostly white structure standing in the moonlight, like a haunted ghost of its past splendor. Slade's head snapped around as it faded in the red glow of the taillights.

"Charlotte! What's that place we just passed?"

"What, the old Inn?"

"Yeah. What was it?"

"That's the Stone Bridge Inn, Peter. Isn't it sad? It was my favorite place when I was a little girl, growing up. I would come every Sunday with my mother and grandparents for Sunday lunch after church. God, those are fond memories, darling. I've attended many wonderful wedding receptions there on Saturday afternoons over the years. The old man that owned it finally died a few years ago and it's been up for sale now for some time and is about to fall down."

"Damn, what I couldn't do with that place! Would you mind turning around and going back for a second?"

"What? You want to go back to the Stone Bridge, Peter?"

"Yes. Please, let's go back, if you don't mind. My family was in the restaurant business in Baltimore for years, and I've always wanted to have my own place. A quaint, quality establishment like this where I could be my own boss, serve quality fare to an elite clientele and, of course, to a beautiful lady who drives a red Bentley."

Charlotte laughed as she whipped the car around. "Sounds like my kind of place, Mr. Slade. Let's have a look."

They stood arm-in-arm now in the littered, overgrown parking lot, Peter marveling at the Inn looming in the moonlight. The once splendid three-story structure with its veranda overlooking the water, and a large porch that ran the length of one side, stood haunted before them in sad disrepair. 'How grand it would be to renovate this 1700s historical treasure,' he thought, saying, "God, isn't it magnificent? I bet it was a wonderful place in its time."

"It was wonderful, Peter, and it's so sad to see it fall into ruin. I do hope someone will buy and restore it soon."

"It would definitely qualify for an historical restoration income tax credit for some lucky investors who wanted to do just that."

"Really! With the damned income taxes I have to pay, I could use some tax credits for darn sure," Charlotte laughed.

"Well, then," Peter Slade replied, lowering his voice to sound very business-like. "Call this organizational meeting of the Stone Bridge Inn Corporation to order, Madam Chairman, and I, Peter Slade, as Chief Executive Officer of the finest inn in all of New England, do hereby make a motion that renovations begin immediately, if not sooner!"

Charlotte giggled, squeezing him around the waist. "I second that motion, Chief Executive Slade. John did say that you were a financial wizard, Peter, and I believe him," she replied.

Their lips met for the first time in a wet, passionate kiss, bringing hot steamy breaths. Slade felt an instant erection rising. "Stop! Oh, stop it," she purred as she caught her breath, pushing Slade away. She grabbed his hand and tugged him toward the car. "Let's go."

The car headed south in quiet luxury on the two-lane highway. The silent passengers were each thinking their own thoughts, listening to the classical music. Charlotte broke the silence, "I mentioned I had a long phone conversation with John this morning about you, Peter."

"Well, the two of you must be hard-up for something to talk about then."

"Hardly, darling," Charlotte replied. "John thinks a helluva lot of you, Peter. He told me about all the things you guys have been through together at the University of Maryland, the fraternity, even serving in Vietnam together. I got the feeling he's representing you on some legal matter, but he didn't say that."

"That's right, met Moffett in the athletic dorm at the University of Maryland during the Fall of 1964. We came from very different backgrounds, John from a wealthy... well hell, you know that, but we hit it off together from the very start," Peter replied, not mentioning the war.

"Were you a baseball player?"

"No, John was the baseball player, and a damn fine one. I always expected he would make it to the major leagues. He could have if he had chosen to."

"What about you?"

"I went to Maryland on a football scholarship."

"You look the part. What position did you play, Peter?"

"I was a defensive back, but that was in the days before all the fast black athletes came on the scene."

"Interesting. You're John's best friend, Peter. He didn't say, but is he representing you now?"

"You're right, Charlotte. John is my best friend and lawyer and, thank God, one of the best criminal defense attorneys in the country," Peter replied as the Bentley slowed and turned off the highway onto a gravel country lane lined with mature maple trees that led down to a quaint old New England farmhouse. "Where are we?" he asked.

"Welcome to Sunny Meadows, my grandfather's farm, Peter," Charlotte replied, turning off the engine and getting out of the car.

Peter stepped into a world bathed in moonlight, glanced up at the star-studded galaxies, inhaled the fresh autumn air and admired his surroundings. 'Sunny Meadows, this is the way the really rich live,' he thought, admiring the quaint seventeenth-century brick farmhouse with white columns, surrounded by manicured grounds, traced in the moonlight by white fences that ran along the lane and crisscrossed the meadows to the large red barn off to one side. Suddenly, galloping hoofs of thoroughbreds broke the tranquility as they raced across the meadow, summoned now by the sound of the car doors closing. Their hoofbeats resounded as their dark silhouettes abruptly stopped at the fence, neighing, frolicking, prancing, permeating the air with the smell of horses that carried in the crisp cool breeze. "Aren't they beautiful, Peter?" Charlotte asked, as they walked over to the fence to admire them.

"Yes, and so is Sunny Meadows, Charlotte!"

"Wait until you see it in the daylight, darling, especially at this time of year, with the beginning of the red and gold of the changing maple leaves," she replied, opening the trunk, handing Peter two large paper sacks of groceries and, to his pleasure, her Louis Vuitton overnight bag. Silently he followed her up the sidewalk to the front door, watching the movements of her hips in the moonlight, thinking to himself, 'God, Slade, life doesn't get better than this.'

Inside, Charlotte turned on a lamp before lighting candles on the massive hand-carved mantel over the fireplace. She opened the windows to let in the fresh country air as the closed-up musty smell quickly vanished from the room. "Please make me a dry gin martini, darling, while I get things organized," she said as he followed her into the large modern kitchen and placed the groceries on the island that ran for seventeen feet through the middle. He watched her fill the sterling silver ice bucket from the ice maker. "Straight up or on the rocks, lady?" he asked.

Taking the ice, Slade returned to the living room and placed it on the polished bar that ran across one side of the spacious room with heavy overhead beams. 'This is a man's room if ever I've seen one,' he was thinking, mixing the martini as he admired the furnishings: antique Persian rugs, accented by various pieces of English Renaissance furniture, framed in rich mahogany paneling on which hung fine equestrian art. A heavy leather sofa flanked by two wingback chairs, aged and formed by countless guests who had left their indentations worn in the leather cushions, sat in front of the fireplace. Behind the bar was an antique humidor which he opened and, sure enough, there were still a dozen or so aged Cuban cigars, the tobacco hard as a rock. Slade got a napkin and returned to the kitchen with Charlotte's martini.

"Find some music and make yourself at home, Peter. There's some Port or Scotch in the bar. Fix a drink and I'll be right with you," Charlotte said, as Peter handed her the gin martini. She picked up her overnight bag and disappeared down the hallway. He heard the bathroom door shut and soon the sounds of the water in the shower and, as he imagined her sexy naked body, he felt his manhood rising.

Peter poured Scotch from a heavy crystal canister and tuned in WKLZ FM, Providence, as the soft classical music filled the room. He sipped his Scotch and admired his surroundings before wandering over to inspect the volumes of leather-bound books that lined the bookshelves on either side of the candled mantel. Besides the classics, there were volumes of outdated medical journals as he scanned the titles. He reached for one of them, opened the cover and read the name, Harriman Harris, Columbia Medical School, 1922, signed in faded blue ink. Charlotte slipped silently into the room, unnoticed.

'God, he looks wonderful,' Charlotte thought, admiring the back of Peter's six-foot athletic body as he stood at the bookshelves browsing the titles. Wearing a flowing black robe and high heel slippers she tiptoed up behind him. The shower had hardened her dark nipples and they jutted against the sheer gown, swaying firmly as she came. She reached her arms around him, hugging him tightly, feeling his back muscles tighten with surprise, kissing him on the back of his neck. "Fix me another martini, darling."

Startled, Peter swung around to one of the loveliest sights his eyes could remember. Standing there in the candlelight was the most beautiful woman he had ever seen. He lightly kissed her forehead, took her empty glass and returned to the bar. "You look absolutely stunning, Charlotte," was all that he could say.

"Thank you, darling," she replied, looking up fondly at the books. "This was my grandfather's medical library, Peter. He was a physician in New York and a part-time professor at Columbia University College of Physicians and Surgeons. He was also one of the country's first radiologists, practicing in New York and spending holidays and summers here at Sunny Meadows."

"Was your father from Newport?"

"No. New York City. He met my mother in New York in the thirties when she was visiting some of her college friends."

"What about your mother, Charlotte? She still lives in Newport?"

"Yes, all of her life. She was a Harrington before she married my father."

"I see," Slade replied, thinking, 'Harrington, like from the shipping magnate's family you heard about . . . like the Harrington Steamship Lines in New York, one of the world's largest shipping companies before World War I. Jesus Christ, Slade, you are way out of your class here, son, you lucky son-of-a-bitch,' he was thinking, remaining cool at being in the company of the granddaughter of such turn-of-the-century wealth.

"My great-grandfather built his summer home in Newport, Beach Mont, around the turn of the century. Mother still lives there and is always complaining about Thomas Terrell, poor fellow. But Grandfather loved this farm, spending most of his later years here working every day with the horses, and probably staying out of Mother and Grandmother's way. He loved his cigars and horses, taught me to ride at a very early age. He loved to sit on the veranda of the Stone Bridge Inn on Sundays after lunch and smoke his cigars, watch the sailboats and chat with their friends. Oh, darling, I so well remember those days."

"You were very close to your grandfather, weren't you, Charlotte?" Peter asked, handing Charlotte her martini with an unsteady hand as she leaned forward on the couch and crossed her jet-black nylon-clad legs. He stared up at the portrait of the late Dr. Harris above the mantel. "He must have been an exceptional man," Peter added, joining her on the couch.

"Yes, he was, like a father, Peter, since my father was an infantry officer killed in the invasion of Normandy during World War II, and I never really knew him."

The soft FM music floated down on the couple as Peter set his drink on the end table and put his arm around her shoulder, drawing her to him as they both snuggled down on the cool leather. Their lips met in heated passion and he felt her hand on his thigh. He leaned back on the couch, turning her toward him, slipping off her robe. "My God," he gasped at the strapless black stretch-satin, lace bodysuit that barely covered her ample breasts. He massaged her shoulders, skillfully slipping down her top as his moist lips sucked lightly on her erect nipples, his tongue flickering, his heart pounding in his chest.

"This is FM WKLZ, Providence. The time is now 11:00 p.m.," the announcer's voice faded as Slade unzipped the back of her bodysuit. She slipped it off, pushing his head backward, her tongue thrust down his throat as she ran her fingers though his thinning hair. 'To hell with this,' he thought, lifting her in his strong arms and walking down the hall to the bedroom, laying her gently on the magnificent Elizabethan four-poster walnut bed.

Two hours later the bed's headboard, inlaid with some long-forgotten Englishman's family crest, was in Peter Slade's sweaty face as he slowly began making passionate love for the third time.

When she awoke the next morning, she knew the whole Peter Slade story and was appalled that the government had arrested this wonderful self-made, innocent man. After breakfast in bed, they strolled casually around Sunny Meadows, admiring the horses that frolicked in the brilliant sun of the autumn day.

# Chapter III

## Manhattan
### Monday, December 9, 1985

Т he doorman's shrill whistle pierced the cold air. The driver of the passing taxi hit his brakes and made a U-turn in the street before coming to a jerky stop under the porte cochere of the prestigious Fifth Avenue high-rise condominium. Wearing a General Charles de Gaulle French-style hat and long cape, the white-gloved doorman promptly opened the rear door, bowing slightly as the passenger got in. "Have a very good day, Mr. Slade, and Merry Christmas to you, sir," he said smiling, conscious of his annual Christmas gratuity.

"Merry Christmas to you, Walter. Please remind George not to forget the Scotch when he comes down to do his shopping," Peter Slade replied, aware that George was getting a little forgetful in his old age.

"Yes, sir, Mr. Slade. 'Tis the Season to be jolly!"

The beady-eyed driver was slumped behind the wheel, staring

at his passenger in his rearview mirror, waiting impatiently for his destination. As Slade got in, the doorman took notice that he was dressed down from his usual expensive Fioravanti attire, wearing instead an inexpensive Brooks Brothers trench coat and plain, gray suit that he had purchased from Goodwill. "Where to, Mister?" the driver asked in a muddled voice.

"Federal Building at 26 Broadway. Take the FDR, if you would please, driver," Slade replied, unfolding the Wall Street Journal and glancing down the center column.

"What's wrong with takin' Broadway?" the driver growled in his surly Bronx accent, simultaneously hitting the meter and stepping on the gas as the cab shot out into the traffic.

"Nothing, but I want to take the FDR!" Peter snapped, putting down his paper, thinking, 'what a hell of a way to start this cold, miserable day, arguing with this idiot.' He glanced out at the New York skyline, blanketed with heavy, gray skies that threatened snow or rain. He hated going downtown to meet John Moffett at the U.S. Attorney's office. He hoped Flynn O'Grady wouldn't be there.

The cabby leaned forward in his seat, gripping the wheel. 'This nasty bastard ain't even from New York,' he thought, wondering, 'what de hell's eatin' dis guy anyhows?'

The cab darted through the rush hour traffic on East 79th Street toward the Franklin D. Roosevelt Drive. 'At least the jerk is going the right way now,' Slade thought, returning to his paper.

Slade could see the beady eyes staring at him in the rearview mirror. "He must be thinking us rich guys stink," Slade muttered as the obnoxious driver kept blowing his horn just for the hell of it.

Peter Slade ignored him, searching the paper for any news on the insider trading scandal on Wall Street. He rapidly scanned the pages until he finished and laid the paper on the seat. 'Thank God, there is nothing in the *Journal* today about me,' he thought. The cab took a traffic jolt from a pothole just as it began to rain.

"Hey, take it easy, cabby!"

"Sorry, buddy. Don't blame me, blame de damn mayor. He's de guy what 'pose to be fixin' deese streets, you know."

Slade remained silent, thinking, 'if I don't wind up in the federal prison, I've got to get the hell out New York before I become as screwed-up as this jerk. Damn it, I knew I should have caught the Lex Express downtown,' he thought, looking ahead at the snarled traffic.

Stopped at a traffic light, Slade watched the windshield wipers flapping monotonously, and wished he was having coffee with Charlotte this morning at Sunny Meadows. He smiled, remembering the Thanksgiving weekend he had spent with her in the country. He had rented a car and driven from New York, arriving by late afternoon to a wonderful feast of turkey and dressing and bottles of superb French white Burgundy, Montrachet '66, which had flowed freely. They had made wonderful love on the old leather couch before the open fire in the great room. The sturdy wooden beams overhead had given him a very secure feeling at the time that everything would be fine. He wished to hell he could have stayed at the old brick farmhouse in the peaceful Rhode Island countryside forever. Outside the first snow of the winter had turned the landscape white and pure that night. He wished he were there now, far away from the rat-race and congestion of New York as he waited for the light to change.

The wipers seemed to be playing that old Roberta Flack tune from the early '70s, "The First Time Ever I Saw Your Face." The words evoked the beautiful face of the woman he had fallen in love with. He could hear Charlotte's rich New England voice saying as they sat before the fire, "Poor Robert. The poor, pitiful man followed me all the way to John's law office, crying like a baby. When I went in to sign the divorce papers, he was still begging me not to leave him . . . "

'Oh, how pathetic,' Slade had thought at the time of Robert Cocknell, the man whose wife he had been having an affair with for the last three months. He felt no remorse about taking her away from him.

Slade thought of last weekend. How wonderful it had been having Charlotte in New York for the first time. She had arrived on the 12:40 Patriot from Providence on Friday, looking fresh and relaxed, as though the divorce had been a great burden lifted from her.

He had rushed to meet her at Penn Station on a pale blue winter day, bringing George along to take care of her luggage. After his brief introduction, George had given an approving nod and left with the luggage.

They had taken a cab to the Ritz Carlton on Central Park South for lunch at the Jockey Club. "Here's to your freedom and happiness, my love," Slade toasted as they sipped a bottle of Dom Perignon '71 champagne in the exclusive finery.

"Without you, darling, I would have spent the rest of my life with that miserable drunk," Charlotte had said.

Slade shrugged his shoulders.

"Honestly, I would never have divorced him if I hadn't fallen in love with you, darling." She filled him in again on all the latest details of how Robert had threatened suicide.

They had eaten a vanilla-scented rack of veal for two served with roasted vegetables, uncorked a second bottle of champagne, and so fine was the setting that it almost brought tears to

Charlotte's eyes. After coffee and cheesecake, they strolled through Central Park under a cloudless sky, inhaling the cool, crisp winter air. Crossing the Sheep Meadow with beige grass crunching under foot, the lovers lingered at the lake watching the green-headed mallards and gadwalls swimming complacently in the yet unfrozen water. "The ducks will be flying south soon," he had said suddenly.

Charlotte had held him tight, looking lovingly into his eyes, knowing that he was feeling a sudden urge to flee southward with them to escape prosecution. 'My case always seems to return at the wrong damn time,' he was thinking, 'I hate to spoil Charlotte's day.'

'Oh, how happy I am,' Charlotte had thought, hoping that Peter would forget his troubles, at least for the moment. The winter sun's warmth was radiant on her black suede jacket. They walked arm-in-arm again, squeezing each other as they went. She suddenly stopped and kissed him, her mouth hot and moist, sweet with the taste of champagne, sending them scampering back to the condo in a heat of passion. From the twelfth floor bedroom they had raw savage sex in the bright sunlight, turned on by the beauty of their handsome bodies. Staring deeply into each other's eyes, they reached a perfect climax, and then, collapsing into their warm nakedness, they quickly fell into a deep, sound sleep.

When Peter awoke it was after four and Charlotte was gone. He got up and looked out the window at the sun hanging low over Central Park, wondering where she was. He had just gotten out of the shower and put on his robe when he heard the key in the door. "Charlotte, that you?" he shouted, knowing George had gone to visit friends in Baltimore for the weekend.

"Yes, darling, I'm back," she had replied, standing in the foyer with a box of Peter's favorite Macanudo Prince Philip cigars from Nat Sherman's wrapped with a big red Christmas bow.

He had come to her, dropping his robe, sweeping her off her feet and made love to her all over again on the sofa as she screamed in passionate delight, "Harder! Harder! Don't you dare stop now . . . darling. Damn you!"

They were dressed for an evening on Broadway when Peter had opened his new box of Macanudos and lit one, tasting the rich aroma of the fine tobacco. With a broad grin, he began, "What a wonderful Christmas present, dear. Thank you for being so thoughtful," he said, leaning over and lightly kissing her on the forehead.

"You're welcome, darling," she had replied, thinking, should I tell him about his real Christmas present, or wait?' She waited, sitting back and smiling at her lover dressed in his black tailored tuxedo. 'He looks absolutely charming,' she thought, thinking dinner would be the best time for her surprise. She happily watched Slade smoking his cigar, exhaling the thick blue smoke. They continued drinking their cocktails, watching the winter sun sliding quickly off the horizon, leaving Central Park dark in the cold winter dusk below as Perry Como sang "Silent Night" in the background. 'What a wonderful day this had been,' she thought, snuggling next to her man. Her eyes beamed with excitement. She sipped her gin martini, almost blurting out her grand surprise.

In the grandeur of the Rainbow Room, high atop Rockefeller Center, they had admired the skyline of New York through the two story-high windows, listening to the orchestra playing sounds of the big bands and an occasional Latin tune. She finally knew it was the right moment. "Peter, darling, what a wonderful surprise I have for your real Christmas gift this year."

"Real? The box of cigars was quite real, thank you."

"No, really, I have something very special that will be for both of us on this, the happiest Christmas of my life!"

"Wel-l-l-l," he had replied, sensing her excitement as the satin-gowned singer began a swing tune, "what is it? Or do I have to wait for Santa, Christmas morning?" he laughed, leaning forward to grasp her hand.

"I've decided, darling, to make an offer on the old Stone Bridge Inn, the one we looked at on the way to the farm that night! Do you remember, darling, on the Sakonnet River?"

"Yes, of course I remember."

"I'm going to do it Monday afternoon, now that my divorce is final," Charlotte had grinned, searching his face for approval.

"Wonderful, Charlotte, but what in the world are we going to do with it if they take your offer?"

"We will renovate it, of course, and you, Mr. Peter Slade, are going to be my new business partner and the innkeeper of the Stone Bridge Inn, New England's very finest!"

Peter had smiled weakly, shutting his eyes and shaking his head sadly as the music ended. "Charlotte, what a wonderful idea, but it's going to be damn difficult for me to be an innkeeper if I wind up in federal prison."

"Stop worrying about that, Peter. John's a judicial wizard . . . "

"Easy to say, dear, but I'm worried as hell about it even though, damn it, I'm innocent. After all, I have been indicted by the Grand Jury and was arraigned last week. Remember . . . "

"Yes, and you pleaded 'not guilty'! Everything will be just fine, darling. Justice will prevail. Even by the slim chance you get convicted, John said you would only have to serve a year to eighteen months and then be out on probation."

'Year to eighteen months,' the words made Slade shudder as the cab slowly crept forward again.

The cab picked up speed. Peter Slade recalled how difficult it had been to tell Charlotte goodbye for possibly the last time this morning when she had left in tears. If his plea bargain was unsuccessful with the U.S. Attorney, he would not put her through the embarrassment and humiliations of his trial. No matter how much she loved him, it just wouldn't work, and their love affair would have to end in a bittersweet farewell. He loved her desperately, and leaving her would be one of the hardest things he had ever done. That terrible thought weighed heavily on his troubled mind.

He reflected back on the whole ordeal now to the Monday afternoon in late August when his career rise to the pinnacle of Wall Street's elite was shattered in nothing flat. The words of the FBI agent's voice, "You have the right to remain silent . . . " were vividly etched in his mind forever as was the cold steel of the handcuffs locked tightly around his wrists. Never would he forget the smirk on Flynn O'Grady's face as he had led him through the halls of his office on their way to jail.

His carefully orchestrated plan of concealing his trades had unbelievably failed, its secrecy veil pierced, and for the life of Peter Slade he could not figure out how the Feds had done it. Perhaps it had somehow happened when he quit trading, running scared after his former boss, Herb Gidwitz, was arrested in a ring of attorneys, brokers and arbitrage specialists. He had thought long and hard about that at the time, but if his plan had worked it wouldn't have made any difference.

'You really screwed up this time,' Slade told himself, 'you stupid ass.' 'No,' he rationalized, 'you just had bad luck that dealt you a rotten hand, and now you've got to play it out. My system is perfect, nobody can figure it out, nobody except maybe God. Flynn O'Grady is only speculating based on the facts in the Gidwitz case, making assumptions and playing a poker hand with no aces, the rotten bastard. No hard evidence,' Slade was thinking, evaluating his insider trading scheme for the thousandth time for any possible weaknesses. 'I'll go over it one last time before my plea-bargain conference with John Moffett and the Federal District Attorney.

'God, should I have told John Moffett the truth?' Slade asked himself for a starter.

His confidential trust account in the prestigious Bank of Bermuda Limited in Hamilton had accumulated nearly ten million U.S. dollars since he had opened it in 1981 with fifty thousand, all profits from illegal trades on insider information that he had made until last year when Herb got caught, when Slade lost his inside source of information.

Slade had decided to stick by his plan from the very beginning to tell no one, not even John Moffett. Neither his ex-wife, Jackie, nor certainly the IRS knew about his Bermuda trust account. Only God and Bank of Bermuda Limited knew. Slade had thought more than once about fleeing the country and starting all over somewhere with the millions he had stashed.

It seemed like yesterday now, yet five years had passed since it began by accident late one night in his office. The senior merger and acquisition specialist for Porterfield Heartley at the time, Slade was in the heat of battle, another one of those ninety-hour weeks working on Tireron's takeover of Felsing, a billion-dollar junk bond deal, when his computer went haywire. He had walked next door and borrowed Herb Gidwitz's computer to run a financial analysis spreadsheet, hoping as he went that he could remember Herb's password.

He had flipped the computer on to the chirping, moaning sounds as the hard drive booted up. He entered 'PLUTO' on the screen and then hit return, waiting anxiously for the menu. Much to his relief, it appeared, black letters on a green screen. He dropped the cursor to LOTUS, casually checked Herb's index file on the neon-green screen before starting. 'What the hell's this 'Lexus' file,' he wondered. He had overheard Herb using it from time to time on the telephone in a hushed voice, and Slade put the cursor on 'Lexus' and hit return. 'What the hell is this,' he thought, reviewing the screen on data containing strange dates and a column of trading symbols of companies, none of which were on the New York, American or NASDAQ exchanges. The dates and symbols were followed by three columns of figures, the third of which showed either a debit or a credit with those at the bottom mostly left blank. He wasn't sure what Gidwitz was up to, but it looked suspicious as hell. He quickly got to work before Herb walked in.

Needing a present value table, Peter had taken a statistics book off the cluttered bookshelf and opened to a piece of coded paper in Herb's handwriting. It was an inverted alphabet, with 'A' being 'Z', along with the inverted numbers one through nine in the same fashion. Hearing someone in the hall now, he quickly found his present value numbers and placed the book back on the shelf, making sure the slip of paper was in place. He quickly finished his spreadsheet and copied it down along with the Lexus file onto a blank diskette. Making sure everything was just as he found it, he took the diskette and turned out Gidwitz's light.

At home that night, Slade had worked until four in the morning decoding the Lexus file, recording each trading symbol on his home computer. The first entry turned out to be the Parthenon merger! RAP was deciphered to the call sign for PAR, Parthenon! Bought March 21st, '79, ten thousand shares at 16-1/8, sold April 14th for 28-1/4! 'Jesus,' Slade thought, 'the bastard must have made one hundred and twenty thousand dollars on one of Smith Barney's client's mergers. How the hell did he get the inside information?' As the decoding continued, to his utter astonishment the list grew into insider trading transactions of top merger stocks on Wall Street, none of which were clients of the firm. 'Over the last four years, Herb Gidwitz has made millions of dollars in illegal profits, that crooked little bastard.'

After work the next day, Slade was at Delmonico's bar, the popular hangout on the apex of the triangle of Williams and Beaver streets, in the heart of New York's financial district. He sat on the wooden bar stool on the corner facing the door, drinking single malt Scotch with a splash. It was early in the afternoon before the markets closed, before the power brokers came in to drink their martinis and manhattans, gloating over their financial brilliance in a time of junk bond financing of take-over targets that made it one of the most turbulent times in corporate history.

'What in the hell do I do now?' he had asked himself, seeking advice from the Scotch.

Gidwitz was stupid to leave such detailed records of his insider trading transactions, and what should he do now that he had found the evidence? 'Do I go to Porterfield's board with the fact that their fair-haired boy, Herb Gidwitz, is trading on insider info? Using privy information and purchasing stock in targeted companies before their announced merger, selling the stock at a big profit after the merger was announced when the stocks run up for a handsome profit? That would set really well with the board, wouldn't it? Ratting on their leading merger specialist, the nationally recognized Herb Gidwitz, who is making them millions. They would just love the hell out of that,' he thought. 'Probably fire me, who the hell knows? The members of the board might just very well be part of this insider trading scheme, too.'

Should he go directly to the Securities and Exchange Commission and report it? That would be the safest and most honorable thing to do. Then what? Get branded as a snitch and never work on Wall Street again, and besides, he would still get canned at Porterfield and wind up having to testify for the Feds.

He drank his Scotch and was thinking, 'I'm a man of honor, by God. I know the difference between right and wrong. I'm an officer in the Army of the United States, having lived by the military code and led soldiers into battle. I'm an Eagle Scout with thirty-one merit badges, God and country, kindness for helping little old ladies crossing the streets of Baltimore, for God's sake! What about my dead father, a man who had worked hard in life, served with the marines in the Pacific, who would turn over in his grave at the thought of my even considering doing something illegal?'

He felt sick when he finally, after four drinks, had decided to use his opportunity to make just a few illegal trades. 'Everyone else must be doing it,' he rationalized, 'or else the stocks would not run up as soon as the news went public. It's not stealing from anyone, it's the market, and besides, I'll do it just long enough to build up some capital and buy a nice quiet inn now that my marriage with Jackie is breaking up.'

He had another Scotch. So this was the only alternative: no way to rat on Herb, just take advantage of the Lexus file and make a killing undetected by piggy-backing Herb's trades. Why not? Who in the hell would ever find out? Here he was knocking down a measly two hundred grand while Porterfield Hartiley's directors were making hundreds of millions. The thought of pirating Herb's Lexus file made sense now to Peter Slade.

The process had been simple enough: one flight to Bermuda, a night at the Hamilton Princess Hotel, a short walk to the Bank of Bermuda Limited on Alouby's Point the next morning for a two-hour meeting with the bank's trust department. "Mr. Slade, under Bermuda status there are no disclosure provisions for a trust to be established. No bank references or other personal information need to be supplied. As settlor, your trust establishment fee will be US $1,000 plus legal costs for the trust documents," the young trust officer assigned to Slade had said.

"What is the annual trust fee?" Slade had asked.

"That, of course, Mr. Slade, depends on the service required and complexity of the trust which will include accounting costs. It is either negotiated or on a sliding scale based on the trust assets, etc."

"Can I stipulate in the trust document instructions on how the investments are to be handled?"

"Most certainly, sir."

"Can you open a trading account for the trust in an offshore secret account in the Bahamas?"

"If you so desire, sir."

And so was established the Peter M. Slade Discretionary Trust under Bermuda law of confidentiality. It was for a perpetuity period with the beneficiary being an offshore Cayman Islands Corporation whose shares were owned by Peter Slade. The dormant corporation was over a thousand miles away and consisted of an inconspicuous brass plaque on the entrance of a law office on that remote island.

Slade then had given specific instructions never to contact him in any way by telephone or mail in New York.

In the ensuing months and years, Peter Slade had watched Herb Gidwitz like a hawk, developing a pattern of knowing by the change in his daily routine when a merger was about to happen. He would then work very late at night and pull up the Lexus file on Herb's computer, taking every precaution not to get caught. Using his resources at Porterfield he would research the pending merger stock and hedge against any possible loss by making sure that if the merger did not proceed he would be covered on the value of his risk in the market. Slade would then take the insider trading tip of a yet unannounced merger and place a buy order with a collect call from a pay phone to the Bank of Bermuda Limited trust officer, who would in turn place an order via its secret trust account in the Bahamian subsidiary of Bank Lou, Switzerland's oldest. Bank Lou would place the order with one of many brokerage houses in New York and charge the trustee secret bank account for the trade. The Bahamian bank would then transfer the securities to the confidential trust portfolio in Bermuda. Peter had monitored his portfolio on the firm's stock quote terminal and sold at the time he thought the stock had run up to its highest price, using Porterfield's resources and the Lexus file to assist him. A quick collect call using a pay phone made sure that no record would be made when it was time to sell.

Slade's duplicate Gidwitz trades on the next soon-to-be-announced merger were hidden by his confidential Bermuda trust. The trust placed the trades through a Bahamian bank whose secrecy laws would protect him even further. How could this have failed?

Now the cab slowed in traffic as the most dreadful day yet of the ordeal was about to begin. 'I'll get at least five years if they can prove it,' he thought, remembering his last trip to the U.S.

Attorney's office in lower Manhattan where he had been arraigned. His thoughts turned once again to Charlotte, the woman he loved.

# Chapter IV

Pussy Cat Club
Friday, December 5, 1985

The grand ballroom of the St. George Hotel, where once New York's elite had waltzed to the sounds of the Benny Goodman and Tommy Dorsey bands, was submerged in a thick cloud of cigarette smoke. It was a far cry now from the old days when Perry Como broadcast his radio show from the St. George as celebrities, politicians and wealthy, fashionable New Yorkers danced and partied at black-tie benefits and galas. Tonight it was the sounds of bump and grind blasting over a powerful sound system into the once splendid hall as Flynn O'Grady watched from his favorite bar stool in the pink Pussy Cat Club, drinking Four Roses whiskey at five dollars a shot. It was his entertainment for the weekend: Friday night at the Pussy Cat, drinking, smoking, watching the stripper's tassels twirling, asses twisting and hunching against the brass poles that lined the stage.

The middle-aged man looked out of place in a crowd of

younger men. White-collar professionals, their ties undone, were among sailors in dress blues on shore leave, joined by the working class of blue-collar workers who had come down from Brooklyn to gawk at some skin. But this was the St. George Hotel, where Flynn O'Grady lived in a run-down suite on the eighth floor. He lit another Camel as he waited for his girlfriend, Vixen, to perform.

As he waited, he mulled over the Peter Slade case once more in his head, the case that the goddamned U.S. Attorney was trying to plea bargain away next week. "To hell with a plea bargain! Send the son-of-a-bitch Slade to jail," he suddenly shouted out of the side of his mouth, his voice unnoticed and drowned out by the loud music and the crowd.

Yes, it was a fact that Slade's partner, Herb Gidwitz, had gotten convicted on an anonymous tip from the Merrill Lynch office in Caracas, Venezuela, that two of their brokers were duplicating suspicious trades. This started his investigation that disclosed that the trades piggy-backed much larger trades made by Herb Gidwitz. An investigation of Gidwitz disclosed that he had organized a sophisticated ring of professionals that had accumulated and assimilated insider trading information among themselves and others using offshore secret Bahamian bank accounts and leaving a huge trading pattern that the computers had traced.

It was a fact that the Justice Department had used strong-arm tactics on the Bahamian government and the officers of The Bank of the Bahamas who were granted immunity against prosecution by disclosing the names of the secret bank accounts of the defendants, of whom Gidwitz was the ringleader. 'Must have cost the U.S. taxpayers millions to bribe those unscrupulous Bahamian officials to get the names,' O'Grady thought, as he took another drink.

The fact was that Peter Slade's name had not come up in the trading pattern with Gidwitz and the others. There were two identical trades, however, that had been very profitable to the tune of over a million dollars made through the secret Bahamian bank by the Bank of Bermuda Limited.

Peter Slade didn't have a secret bank account in The Bank of the Bahamas and it was O'Grady's deep suspicion that there was a secret account trading for him by Bank of Bermuda Limited Trust Department. The funds were then transferred back to a confidential trust account in the Bank of Bermuda Limited in Hamilton which he controlled.

The Bank of the Bahamas was as far as his investigation could trace the two identical transactions he associated with Slade. The Justice Department had tried and failed to get the Bank of Bermuda Limited to cooperate in its investigation of Slade by requesting the identity of the trust account. They refused on the grounds of protecting confidential client information and the Justice Department knew the Bermuda bank officials, unlike the Bahamian officials, were unbribable and held client confidentiality as their highest professional standards.

The music was louder and the crowd larger than usual for a Friday night as a very young dancer with a tremendous peach-skin body, stripped stark naked, danced in front of O'Grady at the bar. The eighteen-year-old-redhead whirled around and around on the brass pole, leaning back as her long hair glowed in the spotlight. Then, with a grand finale of a drum roll, she finished her act by bending over at the waist, shaking her perfect ass in front of O'Grady's face as her long red hair fanned down touching the stage. "Let's hear it for Melissa, the Pussy Cat's newest talent, gents! Let's give her a big hand," the announcer's voice rose in an unmistakable fusion of Brooklyn brogue and sinus congestion to the catcalls and whistles from the excited crowd of men.

Flynn O'Grady peered into the hazel eyes of the upside-down face that was staring back at him through long, shapely legs topped by a mound of reddish pubic hair. His jaw went slack in disbelief at the spittin' image of his ex-wife, Julie, whom he had divorced eighteen years ago. "Hey, Melissa! What's your last name, babe?" he shouted. Melissa pranced off the stage to a roaring crowd.

"And now, gents, let's hear it for our next dancer, Vixen, who's going to do her Rudolph Christmas routine..." The announcer's voice spiraled as a tall dark-skinned Jamaican wearing a blond wig and Santa outfit, black high-heeled boots and a red Santa hat whose tail trailed down to her buttocks sashayed on stage. She pranced about like Dancer, like Prancer and, yes, like Vixen, to the accompaniment of "Rudolph the Red-Nosed Reindeer" blasting over the speakers. The crowd went wild as she peeled off her Santa jacket and squatted down and started wiping O'Grady's balding head with her long-nailed fingers. Her white teeth and the whites of her eyes were flashing a sexy smile all the time. "You want some of this black pussy tonight, Flynnie?" she purred, as the tassels on her rock-hard silicone tits whirled like propeller blades to the crowd's delight.

"Yeah! You goin' to give it to me, Vixie?"

"For the usual three hundred bucks, baby, I'll fuck you all night!"

"Who's this new girl Melissa you got here?"

"Don't you be fooling with no white bitch," Vixie scolded, slowly rising, propellers still whirling, "or I'll cut your nuts out...."

That was about all Flynn O'Grady remembered about last

weekend, after waking up Sunday morning in his hotel room hungover and stone broke. It was now Monday morning and he was trying to piece back together the weekend as he drank coffee with trembling hands waiting for the U. S. Attorney in the attorney's office at the Jacob K. Javits Federal Building in Manhattan. Damn, he felt bad and hated like hell to see his case against Peter Slade plea-bargained away.

The image of the young redhead stripper named Melissa kept reappearing in his aching head. 'Damn, she's the spittin' image of Julie,' he kept thinking, with the return of his bitterness and hatred for Peter Slade stronger than ever now.

Outside, Slade's taxi was snarled in traffic as it got off the FDR at the Brooklyn Bridge exit. 'Damn it,' Slade thought, as the bottom fell out of the dark gray skies and the rain pounded on the roof of the cab, running in rivulets down the fogged windows. Peter glanced nervously at his watch: '9:45. Just in time to meet John in the lobby,' he thought, as the cab turned onto Broadway. When they stopped in front of the federal building, he shoved ten dollars through the partition, not waiting for change.

Slade splashed through puddles and leaned against the cold north wind as he made a dash across the long, gray granite Federal Plaza to the Federal Building. The revolving doors flapped as he passed and proceeded through security. He wiped his face with his handkerchief and eagerly searched for John Moffett in the crowd.

"Pete!" John shouted, as he suddenly appeared from the men's restroom. The old friends shook hands and exchanged greetings.

"Pete, now just remember to stay calm, man. They will try to play on your emotions. You let me do all the talking."

"You mean I'm going to be in the meeting?"

"You bet you are! It's a bit unusual, but I feel your presence will throw them off guard in what I have to say."

"OK, you do the talking then," Peter nervously grinned, "that's why the hell I'm paying you two hundred bucks an hour!"

"Don't answer any questions if you are asked. As I said, I'll do all the talking; you're not on trial this morning. We are only trying to keep from going through that process and, hopefully, if I feel it is in your best interest, we will change your plea to nolo contendere and get a plea agreement. Pay attention, and if you've got a problem with anything they are saying, jot me a note and we can recess and discuss it. Confer with me whenever: we got plenty of time. These bastards make about sixty grand a year, Peter, and they love nothing better than nailing Wall Street investment bankers."

"Former Wall Streeter, John. I understand what you are saying."

"Pete, one last time. As your lawyer, is there anything you have failed to tell me about your case?"

"No, John, nothing," Peter replied, shaking his head as they got on the elevator and John punched the fourth floor button.

On the fourth floor of the Federal Building they were seated by an apathetic black receptionist who was reading a romance novel and drinking a cup of coffee out of a styrofoam cup. Peter looked across the waiting room at his lawyer thinking, 'damn it, should I have lied to John about having my Bermuda trust account?' He sat pondering the point, watching John's broad granite face with eyes that appeared sleepy but could easily be merry or mean. Now forty-one, it seemed like only yesterday that John was on the pitcher's mound at the University of Maryland. 'He practices law in the same manner that he used to deliver his fastball in college,' Peter thought, 'ninety plus miles an hour, in the strike zone, retiring his opposition.' His broad shoulders and athletic waist formed a powerful profile that persuaded juries that there remained a shadow of doubt as to whether his clients were guilty.

In the U. S. Attorney's office on St. Andrews Plaza, the secretary reminded the young Ron DiLorenzo that he was running late for his meeting with John Moffett at the Javits Federal Building. DiLorenzo grabbed his briefcase and ran across the tiny plot of pavement behind Manhattan's towering Municipal Building to the federal courthouse where he was to meet Flynn O'Grady and an attorney from the S.E.C., Jack Mullins.

The doors to the waiting room burst open, startling the defendant, when Ron DiLorenzo rushed in. Slade felt sweat forming in the palms of his hands as he and John Moffett stood up.

"Good morning, gentlemen. Follow me, Counselor," directed Ron DiLorenzo. The cocky young U. S. Attorney assigned to Peter Slade's case started walking.

"Mr. DiLorenzo. I want my client in the meeting..."

"What?"

"Yes."

"That's a bit unusual, but, OK, let's go."

They followed the short, prematurely balding attorney down a long corridor, passing numerous doors along the hallway, until they reached the end where there were massive double wood doors through which they entered.

Inside the dark-paneled conference room sat the all-too-familiar face of Flynn O'Grady smoking a Camel cigarette. "Mr. Slade? What you doing here?" he asked abruptly out of the corner of his mouth while still seated. "Are you aware that the charges against you fall under the RICO Act as well as the Insider Trading Sanctions Act of '84?"

Slade flinched, watching O'Grady's cold noncongenial gray eyes piercing him like daggers through half-moon glasses. He cringed at the brashness of the question. The two men stared at each other. O'Grady took a long drag off the Camel, blowing smoke out his nostrils, waiting for an answer.

"Just a damn minute, Mister," John Moffett snarled. "You're not going to intimidate my client with that question! Who the hell do you think you are talking to anyhow?"

"My name's O'Grady, Flynn O'Grady. I'm an agent for the Enforcement Division of the Securities and Exchange Commission," O'Grady interrupted in a raspy combative voice from deep in his smoker's throat. Now standing, he flipped out his credentials. "I've had the pleasure of investigating your client, Peter Slade, Mr. Moffett."

"I know who the hell you are, O'Grady..."

"Be seated, gentlemen," the U. S. Attorney interceded, closing the door. "Jack Mullins, the S.E.C.'s attorney from Washington called from Penn Station and will be here any minute so that we can proceed. While we are waiting, Mr. Moffett, are you sure you want your client to sit in on this meeting?"

"Absolutely. He doesn't have anything to hide."

"We will see about that, but fine. Now....Oh, here's Jack Mullins now," DiLorenzo said as the S.E.C.'s attorney entered.

"Good morning, gentlemen, sorry I am late," replied the tall lawyer from Washington as the men were introduced.

"Gentlemen, now that we've all gotten acquainted, shall we proceed? Mr. Moffett requested this meeting and asked for his client to be present. As you know, any agreement will have to be approved by Judge Goodwin."

The two camps sat opposite each other across a large conference table as DiLorenzo began, "We got your client dead to rights on the two felony counts of insider trading. That's Section (b) and rule 10b-5 of the '34 Securities Act and..."

"You're wrong," Moffett interrupted.

"The anti-fraud provision to prevent insider trading..."

"Look, DiLorenzo, we know the charges, so can we skip..."

"Just formality,.....but OK, Counselor, you're on my turf now and we're doing things my way this morning. You understand?" he snapped, recoiling like some fat, relentless snake, coiled to strike.

"I do understand, Mr. DiLorenzo. But let's get this straight. We are willing to cooperate with the government in this case, but I'm not going to allow my client to be intimidated by you or O'Grady's terror tactics. OK?"

O'Grady's face reddened, preparing to make his point as he lit another Camel. "The RICO Act, Mr. Slade—or Racketeer Influenced and Corrupt Organizations Act—allows the government to seize all your assets and carries twenty years in prison for each count. It's going to be my testimony that you should be made an example of so the rest of you Wall Street hotshot investment bankers will know what happens when they breach the public trust. I want it perfectly clear from the onset, that from the S.E.C.'s position, there will be no plea bargaining in your case."

"Mr. O'Grady, we're here to discuss Mr. Slade's case with the Justice Department. Mr. Slade is now under indictment by the Justice Department, not the S.E.C. You're not involved with the case now as far as I am concerned, so, upon my insistence, please excuse yourself so we lawyers can proceed and get this worked out..."

"Beg pardon? Mr. Moffett!" Jack Mullins, the S.E.C. attorney snapped. Mr. O'Grady and I are here to insure that the Securities and Exchange Commission is represented in any plea that the Justice Department enters into. Mr. Slade was arrested on security fraud statutes, you know."

"O'Grady is not going to badger my client, I'll file a complaint on this unethical conduct with my former classmate at Harvard Law, the Honorable Judge Norman Goodwin, United States Justice for New York. I think you guys have all heard of him!" John Moffett snapped in a sharp voice.

DiLorenzo cringed at the thought of Moffett having the federal judge assigned to the case interceding, causing him a lot of trouble with the S.E.C. Not wanting to run the risk of not settling the case because of this jerk, O'Grady, with whom he had to work, he held up his hands. "Gentlemen, please, all this won't be necessary. Jack, I feel that the S.E.C. can gain more from Mr. Slade's cooperation than by putting him in prison. That's what you are here to help me decide today, so let's get down to business."

"We got this guy nailed red-handed for insider trading and the U. S. Attorney wants to negotiate a plea bargain?" muttered O'Grady to Jack Mullins, crushing his cigarette in the ashtray.

John lunged across the table at him. "Like hell you've got him nailed! You got to prove your case beyond a reasonable doubt, Mister, so get a guilty verdict from the jury then, by God!" John shouted as he stood up and began packing up his files.

"Ahem, gentlemen, please. Mr. O'Grady, I must insist that we proceed without your interference or you're out of here and I'm by God not kidding. Now, if you and I need to consult one another, I will recess until we can agree on a mutual point of law or facts in this case."

The freckled-faced O'Grady retreated. Slumping down in his

chair, he took out a handkerchief and blew his red nose in short repulsive snorts. 'I'd love to slap that skinny bastard shitless,' Slade thought, as sweat ran down his flanks.

Ron DiLorenzo nodded. "Mr. Slade, you have been arrested on two counts of using confidential, privileged information to trade securities for personal gain. Let's see, the first on the indictment was a transaction in January of 1983 whereby you bought and sold twenty thousand shares of Southern Natural Resources at a gain of approximately six hundred thousand dollars. In March of last year you made another stock trade in which you acquired and sold thirty thousand shares of Dataflex stock at a four hundred and fifty thousand dollar gain. Both of these companies were being pursued in LBOs for hostile takeovers at the time you purchased them and then sold for healthy gains soon after the buyout was concluded and the stock had risen significantly. You did this through an offshore bank using a Bermuda trust account in the Bank of Bermuda Limited."

Peter Slade's heart stopped at the U.S. Attorney's words, "Bank of Bermuda Limited." He never flinched a muscle, however, remaining composed. The Bank of Bermuda Limited! 'How in the hell did they find out about that,' he wondered as his guts began to turn.

"What's this Bank of Bermuda Limited bit?" John asked, cutting his eyes quickly at Peter. "My client doesn't have an account in Bermuda."

"Are you sure, Counselor? We think he does. These two major trades are identical to his former associate, Herb Gidwitz, who confessed to the same two identical transactions made through Merrill Lynch, Caracas. We traced the two trades to a Bank of Bermuda Limited's Trust Department trading account from the

Bank of the Bahamas. It only stands to reason to us that Mr. Peter Slade's illegal activities are being sheltered by a confidential bank account in Bank of Bermuda Limited."

Peter Slade could feel his pulse quicken as the hair on the top of his head tingled. He reminded poker faced and silent.

"Show me evidence that my client has a Bermuda bank account in the Bank of Bermuda Limited, then," John demanded.

"We're still getting the Bank of Bermuda's cooperation on that, but we'll get it," the U. S. Attorney replied as Flynn O'Grady agreed.

"For the record, Mr. DiLorenzo, neither one of these companies was represented by Mr. Slade's firm, Porterfield Hartley. Smith Barney was the investment banking firm in the Southern Natural transaction, and Kidder Peabody was the underwriter on Dataflex. My client has never worked for either firm nor does he have any close friends or associates that do. I can prove that in a court of law."

"Your client, Mr. Slade, did work for and in the next office to Herb Gidwitz, who has pleaded guilty to making these specific stock transactions based on illegal insider information. Correct?"

"Mr. Slade was on the staff of Porterfield Hartley and a partner of Mr. Gidwitz, yes. He was not implicated or charged at the time Mr. Gidwitz was. Did he consult with Mr. Gidwitz to obtain inside information? No, he did not."

"The two stock transactions for which your client is indicted are identical to two trades Mr. Gidwitz has already admitted were made with insider confidential information that also corresponds to two transactions that we traced to the Bank of Bermuda's trust trading account from the Bahamian secret account. Now, since the two worked together, it's my opinion that a prudent jury will convict Mr. Slade of insider trading, using the foreign Bahamian bank as a shield against his confidential trust account in Bermuda!" DiLorenzo countered in a fast nervous voice, nodding his head wildly while painting his Italian face with a shit-eating grin.

"Only circumstantial evidence! Most piss-poor evidence I have ever heard of. Let me see a bank document with my client's name on it from your so-called Bank of Bermuda Limited trust account."

O'Grady's skinny body shook with a sadistic chuckle. "We'll get it, just you wait and see! I'll by God get it!"

Peter Slade's muscular jaw tightened. 'I wonder if the skinny bastards really can get hold of my trust account in Bermuda?'

"Mr. Slade, did you or did you not fly to Hamilton, Bermuda, in November 1981?"

"DON'T answer that, Pete," John ordered. He took three copies of a thick document out of his briefcase and threw them on the table. "Perhaps you gentlemen would like to read Mr. Gidwitz's sworn affidavit regarding his involvement with Mr. Slade at Porterfield before you make any further accusations."

"What's this, DiLorenzo?" snorted Jack Mullins, darting his eyes first at DiLorenzo and then at John Moffett, who sat back in his chair and crossed his arms. O'Grady crushed his empty Camel pack with his hand, then opened a fresh one.

"As you know, Mr. DiLorenzo, I got a sworn affidavit from Gidwitz last Thursday in Lewisburg. He has sworn under oath that he at no time had any involvement with my client concerning insider information—I repeat—on any occasion or in any manner, nor was Mr. Slade in any form or fashion part of his ring. No discussions with Slade regarding any tip on any leveraged buyout. Provided no, nor in any way shared, information that he, Gidwitz, used in his insider trading activities, especially these two transactions in question, about which he has confessed."

The blood drained out of Flynn O'Grady's face. His breathing became uneven and heavy.

'I hope the skinny sucker has a heart attack and dies,' Slade thought. He fought hard to wipe a smile off his face as he watched O'Grady beginning to hyperventilate.

The three men read the lengthy affidavit in silence while John Moffett tapped out an irritating cadence of defiance with his fingernails on the conference table. Standing up, DiLorenzo looked out the window at the rain turning to snow. He turned to face the table with a sheepish grin on his face. "OK, Mr. Moffett, this testimony by Gidwitz does weaken the government's case, but there's still the question of the Bermuda trust account and we know trades were made on these dates that we are assuming to be in Mr. Slade's name. It only stands to reason that Mr. Slade traded on inside info and has hidden his transactions via secret accounts in Bahama before transferring them to Bermuda."

"Peter Slade is a damned astute investment banker, a graduate of Wharton Business School, and was an executive in Porterfield Hartley until you guys got him fired with your reckless and illegal investigation based upon assumptions. You have no evidence to convict my client! Furthermore, this meeting proves that if you were not protected by a grant of governmental immunity, I would have good cause to file a civil action for false accusations, slander, and defamation of character against the Securities and Exchange Commission. I am still thinking about going after Porterfield for firing my client," John Moffett shouted, as he let loose his fastball, taking the government agents by surprise. He stood up and once again began to pack his files.

"Please, Mr. Moffett, hear me out on this now."

John Moffett's sleepy eyes never looked meaner as he sat back down, punching Peter under the table with his knee. "What I am saying..." began DiLorenzo.

"What I am saying," Moffett fired back, "is that Mr. Slade is a damned outstanding citizen, a decorated army officer who has never received so much as a parking ticket on his record, and you guys have assassinated his character and reputation along with his career! By God, somebody is going to pay for it. Just because he works at the same firm and in the next office to Gidwitz is not a crime or a reason for you goddamn people to crucify an innocent man!"

"Bullshit!" shouted O'Grady. "He's like all the rest, he's an insider trader ...."

"Mr. O'Grady, do you know Senator Starlings of Rhode Island?"

"Yeah, he's the Chairman of the Senate Finance and Banking Committee. So what?"

"The so what, Mr. O'Grady, is that Mr. Slade served with the senator, and very courageously so, in Vietnam. When I leave this meeting, the senator will be very interested that you, a lightweight GS 9 S.E.C. investigator, accused the man who saved the senator's life in Vietnam of insider trading, having deemed yourself prosecutor, jury and judge in his case, Mr. O'Grady."

'Jesus,' thought Slade, 'I don't know Senator Starlings,' as he thrust forward with a snarl on his face at O'Grady.

"Gentlemen, let's take a break. I need to confer with Mr. O'Grady and Mr. Mullins. The men's room is down the hall on your left; if you would like a cup of coffee, it's down at the reception room. We'll be back in fifteen minutes and if you would like to propose a proffer for your client, Mr. Moffett, I think it would be appropriate at this time," DiLorenzo stated as he left the room with the other two men.

"Damn it, John, what the hell's a 'proffer'?"

John Moffett shook his head, held his fingers up to his lips and pointed to the table spelling 'bugged' with his lips.

Peter nodded his head and the two men sat and waited.

Later, DiLorenzo reentered ahead of Mullins and O'Grady, who was gasping for air from his brisk walk down the corridor. The three men sat down meekly at the conference table beside each other, DiLorenzo grasping his hands. "OK, Mr. Moffett, the three of us are in agreement that our case has been weakened, but still there's a good chance that we can convict Mr. Slade. We feel, however, that the government's interest can best be served if we use your client's contacts and knowledge of the investment banking industry, securities transactions, international banking contacts, etc. and that he change his plea from innocent to nolo contendere. We want you to provide us with a proffer to give us an indication of Mr. Slade's value to the Justice Department and the S.E.C. if he cooperates with us."

"What did you have in mind, Mr. DiLorenzo?"

"You can petition the court and agree to have Mr. Slade cooperate with the government's fight on white-collar crime and security fraud on Wall Street."

"Now you're making sense, Mr. DiLorenzo. What did you have in mind?"

"We'll drop the indictments on insider trading if Mr. Slade will agree to cooperate for a period of years with our intelligence agents, investigating white-collar criminals on the Street or wherever else they need his expertise on undercover work."

"You're too vague, Mr. DiLorenzo. I want to know what, when, where, and especially for how long we are committing Mr. Slade's services and what are his likely risks of receiving any personal injury."

"Say, over a five-year period Mr. Slade agrees to work under-cover, at our expense, for either the Securities and Exchange Commission, Justice Department, or the Intelligence Division of the Internal Revenue Service to infiltrate or assist in investigating securities fraud."

"Oh no. No more than one investigation, and we must have my client vindicated from any civil liability in his performance as an undercover agent for the government, in addition to being vin-dicated on these securities charges."

"Fair enough, but only after the five years are up. During that time he will be on probation, will not leave the country and will refrain from taking a position, unless we so direct him to, as an investment banker involved in the underwriting of securities."

"Three years. Three years is enough."

"No. We need five years if you are going to work only on one investigation."

"All right then. Four and a half years, but just one undercover assignment."

"Agreed."

"What about my client's frozen assets with the IRS?"

"They will be returned and interest paid in accordance with the IRS Code. The Special Agent handling the case has audited the returns, and has only minor issues to be resolved. Mr. Slade will be cleared with the commissioner if the judge goes along with our plea agreement. You were very astute to pay your taxes, Mr. Slade."

"WHAT? Are you implying that my client's a tax evader?

"No! Sorry, nothing like that."

"I would like to confer with my client, if you will excuse us, gentlemen," John said, as he and Peter walked down the hall toward the men's room.

"What in hell's this Bermuda bank account all about, Pete?" John asked in a low voice as they walked. "No. No, don't answer that."

"Beats the shit out of me," Peter quickly lied at the water fountain.

"You call it then, Pete. Heads or tails. Do you want to go to trial, or take the U. S. Attorney's offer?"

"You're my lawyer, what do you recommend?" Peter asked as Moffett drank. "I'm paying you two hundred an hour."

"A guy who lives in a plush apartment overlooking Central Park and makes a million bucks a year won't get much sympathy from a jury of twelve, mostly poor blacks and Hispanics, especially when tainted by your association with Herb Gidwitz and the rest of the insider trading publicity, and now this Bermuda bank question. That's a hell of a challenge for your lawyer, Pete, and a risk to consider since you're walking almost free today."

"Let's go with DiLorenzo's deal then," Peter said, holding back his excitement of wanting to rush out and call Charlotte with the wonderful news.

"You've always been a decision maker, buddy."

The two men reentered the conference room as heavy snow fell outside. "Mr. Slade has agreed to your terms, Mr. DiLorenzo. I'll prepare a written proffer and get it over to you first thing in the morning, if that will suffice."

"That's fine. I'll take a look at it and submit it to Judge Goodwin for approval."

"As soon as you can get the documents drawn up, please give me a call and we'll come over and sign it."

"I do hope I have the opportunity to work with you, Mr. Slade," said Flynn O'Grady in a vindictive voice.

Peter Slade spoke for the first time, "I hope we don't, Mr. O'Grady. Four years is a long time. Better stop smoking those damn cigarettes and start eating or I'm afraid your time will expire before mine. Good day, gentlemen, and thank you for your time."

Peter Slade was formally enrolled as an agent of the S.E.C. on the following Wednesday, December 10, 1985, when, with John Moffett looking over his shoulder, he signed the settlement agreement with the Securities and Exchange Commission along with his plea agreement with the Justice Department in the Municipal Building at St. Andrews Plaza.

Besides the provision for the plea to cooperate on one undercover assignment and be banned from practicing as an investment banker, broker or consultant to the securities industry, the agreement was totally specific in its language:

> Peter M. Slade, a citizen of the United States, must at all times give complete, accurate and truthful information and participate as a government undercover agent on one assignment prior to the termination of this agreement at midnight, Saturday, June 30, 1990. Should Carolina Barrington commit any further such crimes, or should it be determined by this Office that Slade has intentionally failed to give complete, accurate and truthful information and testimony, or has otherwise failed to cooperate as a witness or agent for the United States Justice Department, then Slade shall therefore be subject to prosecution for any federal crime violation of which this Office has knowledge, including but not limited to perjury and obstruction of justice.

"You have a typo here," John Moffett pointed out with a lightening stroke of the pen, circling Carolina Barrington's name.

The embarrassed U.S. Attorney corrected and initialed it on the document and threw down his pen, "Goddamn word processors...I am terribly sorry, Counselor," was all that he said.

# Chapter V

## Stone Bridge Inn
### Thursday Morning, June 14, 1990

The inn was built on the highest knoll and on the narrowest point of the Sakonnet River's eastern shore before it opens into Mt. Hope Bay to the north. The wide blue river flows southward in a very wide passage to the Atlantic Ocean and beyond. Across the river from the inn lay the emerald shores of Aquidneck Island, home of historic Newport, Rhode Island, twenty miles to the southwest. Sakonnet is an Indian name, meaning 'a place for the black geese to light', and is a sportsman paradise for hunters and sailors alike.

The Sakonnet is usually white-capped in the summer from the prevailing southwesterly winds that blow fresh and fair in the afternoons. From the inn on the knoll you look down on a small pleasant cove formed by the remaining abutment of the old stone bridge for which the inn was named.

Sitting on the veranda of the Stone Bridge Inn, Peter Slade

inhaled the rich aroma of his morning coffee that he poured with an unsteady hand. Above, seagulls soared in a cloudless sky. He grasped the mug with both hands, steadying it now, with the fresh breeze off the Sakonnet ruffling his blond thinning hair. He watched the FBI agent's car leave to the sounds of crunching shells in the parking lot. He looked down at the brown envelope lying on the table. "You rotten bastards...," he swore darkly, letting his voice trail off as though leaving it up to fate to fill in the rest.

Where had all the time gone, Slade wondered. It seemed like an eternity since that miserable December morning at the Federal Building in Manhattan, when he had been enrolled as an agent of the S.E.C. as part of his plea agreement. In just sixteen days his commitment would expire and he would be a free man. They had just called their marker and had picked the worst time in doing so.

Slade's concerns about his pending undercover work for the Justice Department had faded over the years. Hopefully his file had been lost in the bureaucratic shuffle, he had thought until just now.

In the pit of his stomach, Slade cringed, knowing his Bermuda trust account was accruing interest daily, accumulating well over fourteen million dollars by now, tax free. His worst nightmare was having it discovered by the Feds someday, somehow. He had become so paranoid that he had dared not contact Bank of Bermuda Limited since his arrest, not even by pay phone. He had often wondered if the bank thought he was dead or had disappeared. Not one penny of federal income tax had ever been paid on the illegal profits that he had amassed during his insider trading days.

Over the years he had often wondered what had happened to Flynn O'Grady. The persistent bastard wouldn't have given up so easily, and it was more than Slade could bear to think of now. What a naive fool he had been to think for one minute that all his past would just disappear, vanish like the cries of the seagulls overhead. How could he have let the changing of the seasons and the passing years since Wall Street fade into the back of his mind? The forgotten terms of his plea agreement were now very real.

Peter Slade managed a weak smile, thinking now of his fairy-tale life since his Wall Street days as an investment banker with Porterfield Hartley. Life had been too good to be true until just recently.

His romance with Charlotte had blossomed in the following spring after his agreement with the government was signed. On a warm beautiful Saturday in May, Charlotte Cocknell had become Mrs. Peter M. Slade. The wedding ceremony was held in a rustic little Episcopal Church in the countryside near Sunny Meadows. "Do you, Peter Slade, take this woman..." the rector had said in a private ceremony witnessed only by Charlotte's elderly mother and Mr. and Mrs. John Moffett when the holy vows of "until death do we part" were exchanged. Afterwards the new bride had presented her husband with his wedding gift, the four million dollar renovated Stone Bridge Inn which had required the contractor to work two shifts to complete.

Their wedding reception had been attended by four hundred of Newport's and Providence's socially elite. The guests drank cases of Dom Perignon '75 champagne and marveled at the wedding cake, six tiers high. Music was a three-piece combo from the remains of Tony Dorsey's band from New York. The stuffy old Englishman, Thomas Terrell, drank champagne with his first black man, George Washington Henley, and they had a wonderful time.

The Stone Bridge Inn had held its grand opening on the first day of July 1986 in time for the Fourth of July weekend. It was an instant financial success and had been ever since, making a quarter of a million dollars in profit the first year. The Inn's reputation for fine dining and as a weekend retreat flourished under Peter Slade's meticulous management. His charismatic personality directed a select staff of highly trained and well-paid professionals. The guests were pampered with the attentiveness of European royalty in the Inn's plush surroundings. No cost had been spared during the renovations, right down to the finest china and silverware.

Living in the magnificent old Beach Mont mansion was like a journey back in time. The newlyweds moved in after Charlotte's mother died that fall. It was a journey back to the turn of the century when the nation's wealthiest families spent their summers on Bellevue Avenue. Peter awoke each morning to a panoramic view of the Atlantic. Breakfast was served at eight in the sun parlor by the white-haired English butler, Thomas Terrell. They would then stroll through the manicured lawn and flower gardens before Peter left for the Inn at ten.

The social acceptance Peter Slade had received by his marriage to the beautiful New England socialite was wonderful and excellent for business at the Stone Bridge Inn. He had become a real hit with Charlotte's friends and family after her disastrous marriage to the drunk and abusive Robert Cocknell. Surprisingly, never a word had been mentioned about Slade's past and his dismissal from Porterfield Hartley. No one seemed to remember that he had once been arrested for securities fraud.

Five years later, something was now terribly wrong between Peter Slade and his wife. It had been a slow deterioration of the marriage, small arguments now and then, kisses to make up, then more arguments, larger and louder ones, over the silliest things, worse each time than last, leaving damaged egos and resentment in their path. Charlotte had wanted to have a child but she was past forty. Peter was unable to even discuss it after David's death fifteen years ago. She became depressed, passing her time alone at Beach Mont or occasionally riding horses at Sunny Meadows. On Wednesdays she played tennis with girlfriends at the Newport Casino.

Peter Slade spent seven days a week at the Inn working to develop New England's premier country inn. He had wanted Charlotte to join in and become part of the management team. She had flatly refused, out of jealously and spite, he assumed.

The Inn became Peter Slade's mistress, demanding long hours, or so he had rationalized, using it for an excuse to stay away from Beach Mont. This only further deteriorated his relationship with his wife. His micro-management style for attending to details left Charlotte alone managing martinis at night. He returned home after midnight, exhausted, to a drunken wife. Then all hell broke loose if Charlotte hadn't passedout or gone to bed.

"We had another record day, Charlotte," he would try to explain, only to be drawn into a fight by Charlotte's jealousy that grew more disgusting each day. Oh, how she hated the time he spent with his new mistress, the Stone Bridge Inn.

Slade poured another cup of coffee, his hand steadier now. The envelope lying on the table brought back memories of Wall Street. The eighties had passed into history, leaving behind one of the most turbulent times in American business and he had played a major role in the early part of it. The junk bond financing of leveraged buy-outs of Fortune 500 corporations had soured. The 1986 Tax Reform Act had created a real estate market collapse that resulted in the Savings and Loan scandals that rocked the financial markets and forced Washington to form the Resolution Trust Corporation to try and straighten it all out.

Slade's old firm, Porterfield Hartley & Co., had fallen through arrogance, mismanagement and greed. When he read about the firm's demise in the *Wall Street Journal*, he was heavenly thankful that he had gotten fired in time. Porterfield Hartley was dead all right, he spitefully thought, its doors closed forever, and a number of its top executives in federal prison. The government had stepped up its attack on white-collar crime and it had been successful.

'Life deals you strange hands,' Slade was thinking, still looking back and staring blankly out across the Sakonnet River. His life ran before him like the changing tide. After receiving his MBA from Wharton Business School on the GI Bill he had married Jackie Reynolds, a beautiful Delta stewardess from Atlanta. He had accepted a position with E.F. Hutton in Washington D.C. in their Pennsylvania Avenue office close to his home in Baltimore. Hutton, the brokerage firm, 'that made people listen,' introduced him to Wall Street through its training program for new stockbrokers in the fall of 1968.

Peter Slade had been captured by the wealth and power of Wall Street from the moment he first arrived. He knew he was destined to return to work there someday. Manhattan's financial district, Wall Street, the New York Stock Exchange was where the action was. The towering skyscrapers, traffic congestion, confusion, noise, and passion for the Big Apple made him fall in love. He was intrigued by the bars and restaurants filled with power brokers drinking with their colleagues and secretaries, boasting about their fat commissions after the bell or sulking over martinis if the markets closed down for the day. New York was the place Peter Slade was going to be.

A long time before Hutton was acquired by American Express in the early eighties, Slade had decided it was time to seek his fortune in New York. He contacted an old classmate from Wharton who got him an interview with Porterfield Hartley, a very prestigious old firm that had developed quite a reputation by enraging powerful CEOs and their boards of directors by its hostile tender offers financed by junk grade bonds.

Porterfield Hartley was difficult at first for an outsider to break into. It was an institution controlled by Ivy Leaguers, judgmental of social connections rather than personal merit. Slade's career timing had been perfect, what with the deregulation of the investment banking industry and the growth of corporate acquisitions which had forced the firm to relax its snobbish attitudes and recognize that this young man from Baltimore had savvy street sense and a special charm. In the ensuing years, Slade had become a master of alerting Porterfield Hartley top brass of pending mergers and takeover opportunities through watching the Dow Jones ticker and by listening to Wall Street gossip in Delmonico's or other bars he frequented daily in the financial district. All of this, along with hard work and luck, had gotten him to the top rung of the corporate ladder at a very young age.

Suddenly a familiar, cheerful, "Morning, Boss," brought Peter back from Wall Street as the French doors opened and George Washington Henley began preparing the Marble Bar for the day. "Want a shooter in that coffee, Boss?" chuckled the gray-haired black man who had shadowed Peter for forty-five years of his life. Sensing his boss's troubles, he walked out onto the veranda and began spreading the crisp white linen tablecloths on the tables. Vases of red and white carnations which had just arrived from the florist awaited their placement from a serving cart.

"George, you're my man of the hour and thanks for asking, but never before noon except on Sunday, my birthday and before duck hunting," Peter replied with a forced laugh.

"Boss, what did that man want? We don't have more of that ole trouble that's followed us up here from New York City, do we?"

Peter shook his head slightly, not wanting to lie or face the truth.

George frowned. "Must be this boat race to Bermuda what's bothering you, then. Bothers me, too, Mr. Pete, you goin' way out there in the ocean and all. Sailing out in the Sakonnet River here's one thing, but that ocean, now that's somethin' else, Boss."

Peter turned and shook his head, removing the envelope from the table and placing it out of George's sight.

"Why don't you just tell Mr. Moffett you gotta stay here and run the Stone Bridge Inn? Forget that tom-fool Bermuda race!"

"George, please, this is the famous Newport-Bermuda Ocean Race that has tested yachtsmen's seamanship since 1906. Everything will be just fine, and don't you worry."

"No sir. It's hard to keep from worrying, and besides, who's going to run this place, Mr. Pete?" he sighed.

"You will, of course. You run it now anyway, George."

Peter looked up and smiled at the tall, stately black man, dressed in his white bartender's jacket and sporting a red carnation in the lapel. His silver-white kinky hair contrasted well on his dark skin that glistened in the sun. Peter couldn't remember life without George, all the way back to his first memories of his father's McCormick & Slade Fish House & Bar in Baltimore where he had showed up one day from South Carolina after the war. Suddenly Peter realized that his lifelong and trusted chaperon was growing old.

"I'm not the least bit worried, George. Captain Moffett's the best skipper on Narragansett Bay and the *Encounter* is the fastest fifty-footer on the East Coast. Johnny's been training us for over a year now and you know I'm indebted to him, George."

"Yes sir. Man's got to do what he's got to do."

"Don't worry, George, when the *Encounter* crosses the Newport Brenton Reef Light starting line tomorrow afternoon, we're sure winners of the Bermuda Trophy."

George laughed, then his voice turned serious. "Peter," he always called him by his first name when he wanted to make a point, "I've been lookin' after you since you wore diapers and I know when you're not settin' easy on somethin'. No sir, you can't fool George Washington Henley, Mr. Slade. This race isn't what's bothering you; it's that government man what just left from here what's bothering you. Am I right?"

Peter rubbed his face with his hands, thinking, 'ole George reads me like a book ever since I was a kid. Wonder what those rotten bastards want me to do for them in Bermuda? What will happen if Charlotte shows up here drunk while I'm gone? Well, if she does, George can handle her. He's had experience handling drunks for years, and I'm damn lucky to have him to see that this place doesn't go to hell while I'm gone.'

"When is it you're leavin', Boss?"

"In the morning. I'll be departing here this afternoon around three, after the noon lunch crowd thins out. I've got some last minute details to take care of, then I've got to get down to the boat for a crew meeting with the skipper."

"And just what do you want me to do when Mrs. Slade comes down here ordering those double martinis?"

Peter thought before answering. "Just handle her," he replied, taking the envelope in hand. "I'll suggest she go to New York shopping on our way to the Race Committee's cocktail party at the Yacht Club tonight. Maybe she'll go to Europe or someplace."

Peter Slade hadn't slept well last night alone in his king-size bed after a terrible fight with Charlotte. 'Why do we get into it so,' he thought, and 'it's always after she has a half-dozen martinis too many. What the hell's wrong with that crazy woman? Always bitching about how much time I spend running this place, never a word about the handsome profit it's making or how much fun I'm having. Maybe I shouldn't have hired Melissa Jenkins without checking her out more and getting Charlotte's approval. Now I'm catching hell over this damn yacht race her cousin, John Moffett, got me roped into. And now the goddamn Feds!'

Peter was tired. He stood and stretched, loosening his shoulders by shaking out the tension. At six foot one and a hundred and eighty-five pounds, he was down to his old playing weight as a defensive back for the University of Maryland. He had never felt stronger, having spent an hour each day training for the race. He was physically prepared, but what was this lingering uneasy feeling deep in his gut? A deep inner-apprehension that something in his life was unraveling. Peter Slade knew one thing: after the visit from the FBI this morning, his debt with the Justice Department was about to be paid and he had a feeling that his life would never be the same.

John Moffett, the Managing Partner in the law firm of Moffett, Spencer and Grace in Providence, gave final instructions to his secretary before leaving his law office for two weeks. He drove to the Stone Bridge Inn on this beautiful June afternoon, wondering if Peter had gotten his passport back from the U.S. Attorney. Peter was the oldest and least experienced deep water sailor of the

*Encounter's* crew, never having sailed an ocean race. Moffett needed Peter's exceptional competitive spirit to inspire his crew to push themselves to their limits to win the internationally coveted Newport-Bermuda Ocean Race.

John smiled, remembering that cold February winter night when Peter had committed after his fourth Glenfiddich Scotch and the shared savored aroma of Macanudo cigars at the Marble Bar. "I'll serve on the *Encounter's* crew if the Justice Department will give me permission to leave the country," he had finally said.

The clink of fine bar crystal sounded the toast in the dim light. A cold bitter wind howled outside. George, who always kept his distance when Peter talked to his close friend, had been eavesdropping on their conversation and the dark man concealed his frown of disapproval. Lawyer Moffett for once in his life had been speechless, finally managing to say, "Thanks, buddy," while trying to control his emotions. He knew Peter's acceptance would greatly increase his chances for winning the race.

"I owe you this one, Counselor, in light of the legal brilliance you displayed in the federal courthouse in Manhattan back in '85. If you're as good a sailor as you are a lawyer, the *Encounter* will win this damn race hands down," Peter had said, thinking this might be a perfect time to check on his millions in the trust account at the Bank of Bermuda Limited.

"Pete, you owe me nothing. You paid my legal fee at your own persistence."

"Best damned twenty grand I ever invested."

"Here's to the Bermuda Trophy, and may you be in heaven thirty minutes before the devil knows you're dead."

"Mr. Slade, you're the only thing I know smoother than

Glenfiddich single malt scotch whiskey and Macanudo cigars! To the Trophy, my friend."

The smoky sou'wester lifted the seagull aloft from the piling on the pier. It flapped its white black-tipped wings. The gull's cries echoed off the water when it flew and carried in the prevailing wind which announced noon each day, turning the calm morning into the windy afternoon. The crowd would soon be arriving at the Stone Bridge Inn for lunch. The gull soared higher, looked down upon the wide blue Sakonnet River, the most beautiful part of the Narragansett Bay. Sailboats were moored below, protected by the remains of the abutments of the great stone bridge which had been washed away in the '38 hurricane that devastated New England. The bridge had once connected Aquidneck Island to the eastern shore of Rhode Island, before it was swept away by the storm.

The Stone Bridge Inn had been built in 1787 just after the American Revolution. The stately structure loomed magnificently below on a bluff. It was a large white wooden structure with dark green shutters, surrounded by manicured grounds, facing the remains of the bridge for which it was named on the highway south to Little Compton. The Marble Bar was of antique pink Italian marble and had been salvaged out of the McCormick & Slade in Baltimore when it was razed for the Baltimore waterfront development in the late 1970s. Peter had found it by accident when George was in Baltimore visiting, running into an old friend that worked for the salvage company.

The seagull set its strong white wings and dove earthward, catching sight of the innkeeper standing on the steps of the Inn, greeting his customers. Peter's smile was a charmer, warm, sincere, making strangers easy when they first met him. He shook hands with his guests, calling them by their names which he always remembered. His tailored navy blue, double-breasted blazer with rich antique gold buttons and white pants were his trademark in summer. He wore black loafers and a rich maroon and dark blue silk striped tie. His gold Rolex was the only jewelry he wore although he was married.

The luncheon crowd was a mixture of yachtsmen and businessmen from Newport, Providence and Fall River who were accompanied by their ladies, not always their wives. The sailors, dressed in yachting attire, mixed in at the Marble Bar with the businessmen who were dressed in two-button Brooks Brothers suits and wing-tipped shoes. George kept them all laughing with vodka martinis and gin and tonics, and by applying his special charm and masterful barmanship practiced for almost fifty years. The atmosphere was relaxing with the retired Boston Pops pianist, William McWaters, playing beautiful melodies on the Steinway grand piano. "The Days of Wine and Roses" floated out across the veranda on this fine summer afternoon.

Pierre Borochaner, the young French chef, entered from the kitchen and checked each table, making sure the dishes were to the guests' satisfaction. He had served his apprenticeship in Paris and after less than a year he had been featured in the *Boston Globe*. He ran one of the finest new restaurants in New England, featuring wonderful seafood cuisine. The Inn was bringing the chef culinary acclaim and preparing deserts was his passion.

It was two o'clock and the crowd was thinning out when John Moffett's black BMW wheeled into the parking lot. Peter caught a glimpse of the car and rushed to the door to greet him. "Steady as she goes, Skipper. How about some lunch? Pierre's clam chowder today will knock your socks off."

"Hello, Pete! Have you got your passport yet?"

Peter shook his head and led the way to an isolated table on the veranda. "John, an FBI agent from Boston came by this morning and left this, but no passport," he said, handing over the envelope.

"What's this?" John asked, opening the envelope, his eyes quickly scanning the document.

"Evidently I've got to do some undercover work for the Feds when we get to Bermuda. I've got to meet two agents at eight-thirty tomorrow morning before we cast off, down on Newport Beach."

"What did he say about your passport? It's not in here," John said, folding the paper after double checking the envelope. "These orders are in accordance with our plea bargain, Peter. It's been over four years now and I was hoping that they had forgotten about you. Bad damn timing for this shit to come up now."

"I'll say. Guess when I asked permission to leave the country it became the perfect opportunity for them to call in the marker."

"I wonder what the hell they want you to do in Bermuda?"

"Jesus Christ, I have no idea. I'm sure it's something that has to do with Wall Street and the securities business."

"No doubt."

"Sorry, Johnny. Hope it hasn't fouled things up for you."

"Hell no! Don't worry, Peter. We need to make a final inspection of the boat and equipment around five and have our final crew meeting. I'm going over to the *Encounter* after my three o'clock meeting with the race committee. Can you get there early?"

"Sorry, Skipper, I've got to hold a staff meeting here, run by home and pick up my duffel bag, but I'll be there by around five."

"Is Charlotte coming to the Yacht Club deal tonight?" John asked apprehensively.

"I think so, Johnny," Peter replied.


The mid-afternoon smoky sou'wester prevailing wind built to twenty knots. The sailboats on the river were having a grand time: white sails taut, heeling over as they kicked up white spray in their wakes. Peter sat on the veranda with his key staff. George, Pierre, and Melissa Jenkins, the Stone Bridge Inn's newly hired hostess, all had pencils and paper ready to take notes

"How long will you be gone, Mr. Slade?" Melissa asked in a whispering voice, crossing her long, sinuous legs and revealing a lot of thigh. She flipped her long sun-streaked red hair out of her face. 'God, what stemware,' Slade noticed for the first time. Melissa caught his glance and the twenty-two year old from New York smiled.

'This place is a hell of a lot better than New York,' she thought, remembering her days working for Carolina Barrington and the Pussy Cat Club in Brooklyn Heights. She had been working as a hostess and cocktail waitress, trying to get part-time assignments as a fashion model. The modeling agency wanted her to look as though she were anorexic and she had hated that. No one at the inn had bothered to check her references after she answered the ad in the *New York Times,* and that was good, for her checkered past was something Melissa Jenkins was not particularly proud of. This was a far cry from the old Sunset Park neighborhood in Brooklyn and P. S. 314 elementary school.

Peter Slade had hired her based on the picture she had enclosed with her resume. He knew very little about her except that he found her to be a very beautiful and charming young lady when she came for the interview and, after all, a hostess didn't need to have a top secret clearance for the job he wanted her to do. Slade had experienced a strange feeling about Melissa, though, when she arrived on the morning George met her train in Providence. Something that was hard to identify, eerie in a way, something that he had shrugged off as just a weird feeling he got for people sometimes. She had a great personality and was very quick. The fact that he had given her a suite at the Inn to live in as part of her compensation had not sat well with the Chairman of the Board of the Stone Bridge Corporation, Charlotte Slade.

"Let's go over some last minute details, please," Slade said. "The race should take three and a half to four days to Bermuda with good weather. Then we will celebrate the *Encounter*'s victory with five days of ceremony and partying before taking a leisurely sail back to Newport. I plan to be back on Friday, June 29th. The *Encounter* will be berthed at either the Royal Bermuda Yacht Club or somewhere close by, depending upon when we arrive. I am staying at the Glencoe Hotel in Salt Kettle Bay, just across the Hamilton Harbor from the Yacht Club and the Princess Hotel. The phone and fax number are on my desk if you need to get in touch with me."

"We won't need to bother you, Boss," George replied.

"Good. Now remember, John Legate's daughter's wedding reception starts at one on Saturday. Reservations are for two hundred. As always, let's do it up right. He's running for governor, so there will be a lot of important guests here that will be good for future business. Pierre, you have any questions about the menu? The dessert is vodka orange segments with snow eggs served with a nice Sauterne. They ordered a Beerenauslesen which we have plenty of in the cellar, George."

"I'll check the cellar and see if we need more."

"Good. The Culinary '92 Olympics are just ahead, Pierre, so let's show the future governor and his guests that the Stone Bridge has the finest French chef in New England."

A glowing grin came on Pierre Borochaner's thin face. He twisted his handlebar mustache. His dark eyes glowed with admiration for the man who had given him the opportunity to serve as the Inn's head chef at the young age of twenty-three. He sat erect, trying to disguise his shortness with the help of his white chef's hat. He spoke with a heavy French accent. "Monsieur Slade, I have telephoned my mentor from the Cordon Culinary School in Paris, Chef Barron, now the head chef at the Princess Hamilton. He wants to prepare you a wonderful dinner when you arrive in Bermuda, Monsieur."

"Thank you, Pierre. What a kind gesture. I'll be sure to give him a call.

"Now, George, when they toast the bride and groom, please present them with a bottle of the Dom Perignon Brute '57 beforehand, as they leave."

"They got it, boss."

"Does anyone have questions?"

"Good luck, Mr. Slade, and be very careful. We'll miss you," Melissa replied with a sad, lonely smile as their eyes met and lingered for a moment.

"Thank you, Melissa," Slade replied, thinking how strange he felt about her, not in a sensuous way, and he wondered why.

"Well, that's about it. George, let me see you for a moment alone, please."

Peter looked up fondly at George, adjusted the carnation in his lapel. He began in a firm voice, "When Mrs. Slade comes over here, try to make the best of it, try to keep her sober and away from Melissa. Remember she owns fifty-one percent of the Inn and I don't want to get us all three fired."

"Yes sir, Mr. Pete, I'll do my best. Lord God, she's a mighty powerful, strong-willed woman, that Miss Charlotte is," the old bartender replied with a tired but willing sigh.

"Yes, I know, George."

"That's it, isn't it Peter? That's what's been worryin' you so. It's not going good with you and Mrs. Slade these days, is it?"

Slade frowned and shook his head. "Everything will be all right, George. You take care, my friend," he said, reaching over and embracing the old man in a big bear hug. 'Now why in the hell did I do that,' he thought as he left.

Outside in the parking lot a lone passing seagull glided low across the parking lot. Its white wings were set against the strong southwesterly wind. Peter Slade stood by his Range Rover and waved goodbye to the staff. He hesitated for a moment, admiring the beauty of his Stone Bridge Inn, and for some strange reason he wondered if he would ever see it again.

# CHAPTER VI

## NEWPORT YACHT CLUB
### EVENING OF JUNE 14, 1990

John Moffett left the Captain's meeting at the Marriott on Goat Island and drove the short distance across the causeway to the Newport Yacht Club on Long Wharf. He loosened his tie as he hurried down the pier, admiring the elegant appearance of the blue-hulled *Encounter* as he approached her slip. His pulse quickened looking at her sleek beauty, while thinking now of the challenging race that lay ahead for both of them.

The *Encounter* and her sister yacht, the *Martinis*, were designed by the famous Newport naval architect and builder, James H. McLean of the firm of McLean & Rhodes. Built as a matched pair, they were identical in every respect except for their names and the color of their hulls.

The yachts had been ordered in 1978 by two wealthy Bostonians: an industrialist named Ross Williams and his close friend and fierce sailing competitor, Avery Garner, a real estate magnate. Both boats were built using embellished traditional design to create two of the fastest fifty-foot sloops of their time. When completed, the two yachtsmen could hold match races and eliminate any argument of boat design as a factor in their competition.

Mr. Garner had suddenly died in 1982 at the age of fifty-eight. Flint Firestone, a blue-blood, moneyed inheritor from Providence, was keenly aware of the boat's speed and reputation. He acquired the *Martinis* from the Garner estate for a fire-sale price of $700,000 to help pay Garner's estate taxes.

Flinton Ashton Firestone III was a very arrogant man. He had nothing better to do than to sail daily and he was extremely good at it. He pleasured in bullying the Class Four competition on Narragansett Bay with the *Martinis* and bragging obnoxiously at the prestigious Seawanhaka Corinthian Yacht Club of Oyster Bay and to John Moffett. His new boat won the New York Yacht Club Annual Regatta that year, sailing under the pennant of his club.

After the victory Firestone applied for membership to the New York Yacht Club but was rejected by the Board of Governors. It was not for lack of sailing experience or money, but his flawed personality. The NYYC commodore put it bluntly in the board meeting when Firestone's name came up by saying, "Mr. Flint Firestone, gentlemen, is a first-class son-of-a-bitch unworthy of our presence."

Flint was married to John Moffett's younger sister, Rosa, at the time, and the *Martinis'* reputation as the fastest yacht on Narragansett Bay was envied by his competitive brother-in-law. The two had never gotten along very well and Moffett could never understand why his kid sister had made such a poor choice, even if Flint Firestone did inherit millions.

After Mr. Garner's death, his long-time friend and sailing companion, Ross Williams, had lost interest in racing, but not his late friend's widow, a much younger woman named Patricia Isabelle Garner. At thirty-eight, Pat was a petite, beautiful brunette with a charming personality who had come from a modest family on Cape Cod. It was apropos that the yacht was named the *Encounter*, when the news broke that Ross and Patricia Garner had been indicted for the murder of Ross's wife of thirty years.

John Moffett had been in bed watching the ten o'clock news on the Boston channel when he heard of the indictments. "My God," he had cried, immediately telephoning Ross Williams' corporate attorney at his home.

"Hello, Roscoe; John Moffett here. I hope I didn't awaken you by calling you at your home at this late hour."

"No! No indeed, Johnny, my boy. Good to hear from you as always, what's on your mind, Counselor?"

"I hate to bother you, Roscoe, but I just heard about your client, Ross Williams' murder indictment and was..."

"Say no more, Johnny. I've already spoken with my client after arranging his bail this afternoon. We have an appointment tomorrow afternoon in my office to discuss his predicament and, as I told Ross, he needs the best damn criminal lawyer in New England. Can you join us?"

"I will be there, Roscoe. Thanks for the referral."

"Think nothing of it, Johnny. Ross Williams is one of our most important clients. If anyone can keep him out of jail, you can!"

"I'm deeply honored, Roscoe," John replied, hanging up and thinking, 'Flint Firestone' kiss my ass. Now, by God, I'll name the *Encounter* as my attorney fee and we'll just see who's the best damn yachtsman in this family.'

John Moffett had become the *Encounter*'s master in the summer of 1985 after taking Ross Williams' yacht as the fee for representing him in his wife's murder trial over much protest. "Your fee's inconceivable! It's robbery! The damn yacht's worth a million dollars or more," Ross had cried as he signed over the title.

"You can't sail the *Encounter* from the electric chair, Ross," Moffett had replied, "and you unfortunately have run out of cash."

The case turned out to be one of Moffett's rare defeats in court, although it was no fault of his professional skills or preparation of Ross Williams' defense. Patricia Garner got cold feet and blew the case wide open when she confessed to conspiring with Mr. Williams to kill his wife and pleading nolo contendere, hoping for a plea bargain and lenience from the court.

Her confession gave the grim details on how they had planned and committed the crime on board the *Encounter* by throwing Mrs. Williams overboard while underway with a rope tied to her right ankle. It had originally appeared as if she had accidentally gotten tangled in a line and fallen overboard. The yacht had received a tremendous amount of publicity during the so-called *"Encounter* trial" with the press capitalizing on its name as the details of the illicit love affair and murder brought national attention. The trial had dominated the news for nearly a month until Mrs. Garner's confession brought quick convictions. Moffett's client had received a life sentence while Patricia Garner got twenty years in the state prison for women.

John sailed his prize yacht to the Newport Yacht Club where fierce competition erupted between him and Flint Firestone of the competitive Seawanhaka Corinthian Yacht Club. The yachts were so identical in their performance that most weekend races ended in a dead heat at the finish line. Firestone, with nothing else to do but practice, held a slight advantage since he sailed daily. Bragging rights as to who was the best sailor came down to the captains entering their yachts in the 1990 Newport-Bermuda race after a heated argument at a family wedding in the summer of 1988. Both skippers put together experienced crews and took nearly two years for training and preparation. In the interim period, Firestone divorced Rosa, leaving the men at greater odds than ever before.

The yachts *Encounter* and *Martinis* were a sailor's dream. The fifty-footers were designed for open ocean racing yet had many of the amenities and comforts of a cruiser. The boats were equipped with the latest kevlar sails, but still required a minimum crew of five for offshore sailing since they were not equipped with roller furlings, electric power winches, or auto pilots. Jim McLean had been instructed to spare no cost in their design and construction. Using the latest in high-tech materials and the best hardware available, the racing/cruising sloops were considered McLean's greatest work and had cost close to a million dollars each to build.

Now settled on board the *Encounter*, John Moffett waited for his crew to arrive. It was warm in the afternoon sun as he changed into shorts and T-shirt before making another walk-through inspection on the deck, which was designed for ease of handling when cruising and efficiency when racing. He shaded his eyes and peered up at the triple spreader rigging that had just recently been replaced. 'This superb sailing machine will bring home the Bermuda Lighthouse Trophy,' he thought.

Moffett rested in the cockpit rereading the 1990 Newport-Bermuda Race Book including the Notice of Race and the Sailing Instructions. No detail was too small to be overlooked and he knew just one small item of faulty equipment or rules violations could cause a disaster once they were underway. A thousand last minute details rushed through his mind as he gathered his thoughts on his prerace address to his crew.

Within an hour his seven handpicked crew came on board and were each welcomed with a hearty handshake and slap on the back. He stood with his navigator and watch captains known as the afterguard in nautical terms, and said, "As captain and on behalf of the afterguard, it is with great honor and pleasure that I enter the most challenging race of my life with you guys. My personal thanks for serving on the crew."

Standing erect in the cockpit of the *Encounter*, John continued his prerace peptalk with the same degree of forcefulness he used in making his final argument to a jury in a murder case. "Let's go over the details of the race one final time. You know what we're after, gentlemen, the Bermuda Trophy, a trophy coveted by yachtsmen from around the world and especially our sister yacht, the *Martinis*, and Flint Firestone."

"What does the trophy look like?" someone asked.

"It's a tall, silver replica of the Mount Hill Light on St. David's Head in Bermuda which is where the finish line is. They present the trophy with all the pomp and circumstance available to the governor of Bermuda at ceremonies held at his mansion. The way you guys have been sailing, I am confident that we can beat our tough competition, especially Firestone, and bring the Bermuda Trophy back to the Newport Yacht Club."

"Hear! Hear!" came the chant from the crew, followed by a moment of silence, broken only by the lapping of the waves on the *Encounter*'s hull.

Gathered around the skipper, sitting or standing on the deck, their faces wore the tension and excitement that was building prior to the start of the competition. John's voice, calm but forceful in its rich New England brogue, held them in a trance; everyone except Slade that is, who was still thinking about the FBI and O'Grady.

John looked around proudly at his crew: experienced sailors from many different walks of life, committed to the Bermuda Race because of their strong loyalty and gratitude to their lawyer. A strange cohesion, all were clients that had been saved from prison by John Moffett. Slade looked around, too, thinking, 'what a bunch of criminals I'm sailing with, me included. Even this damn yacht's a murderess, drowning poor ole Ross Williams' wife before John stole it from the guy for his attorney fee. I bet Ross would like to kick John's ass now that he's serving life without parole. But what the hell, without Moffett's lawyering, we would all be in jail.'

Moffett paused for a moment, collecting his thoughts, then started talking like a lawyer. "We all know the thrill of ocean racing, endless tiring hours at sea, often in foul weather, always with the uncertainty of danger that lurks from the unforgiving ocean. We are sailing purely for the competitive spirit that lured us to the open sea; to satisfy our ego's conquest for the deep, burning desire of victory and the prestige it brings, especially when we beat Firestone."

'That's a bunch of bullshit, John,' Slade thought. His mind slowly drifted back to the orders that he had received that morning from the government and wondered what his assignment in Bermuda might be. 'I hope to hell I don't have to work for Flynn O'Grady.' Glancing around at his shipmates, he thought again, 'what a bunch of criminals. How in the name of hell did I let John talk me into this?'

"I can't overemphasize the importance of teamwork and how important it is to all of us for the *Encounter* to win the Bermuda

Trophy. You have trained extremely hard for almost two years now. We all know the risk. The ocean is unforgiving, especially if we hit a storm. If you have second thoughts about the race, for God's sake, speak up now."

Serious men all looked at John Moffett. He searched their faces for any signs of doubt. No one spoke as John hesitated. He put his arm around Tony Stevenson's shoulder, drawing him closer. "As you all know, the real key to winning the Bermuda Trophy lies with this sawed-off Englishman. The founders of this race, nearly ninety years ago, wanted the Bermuda Race to be a true test of seamanship and navigational skills that distinguished the winners as the best yachtsmen in the world. In this race, electronic navigation is banned by the rules except for radio directional finders which we will need if Bermuda is fogged in. Tony will have to find the island by celestial navigation, which is no easy task, being only a small island twenty-two miles long and surrounded by treacherous coral reefs. It's 635 miles out there in the middle of the vast Atlantic and will require precision navigation. This means that Tony will shoot the stars at dusk and daybreak, and the sun at noon each day...."

"Indeed I shall," the Englishman interrupted. "Make sure I am awake. The rest of the time I shall be dead reckoning as to where we are from the celestial fix I take at these times. Bloody damn important, this is."

"Everyone got that? OK, the watch captains and crew must respond immediately to course and sail changes. You must make your sail changes briskly, decisively. Many races have been lost because of tacking too sloppily; especially at night, when you can't see, and we run the risk of losing a man overboard. At night, remember, the strong and fast rule is to always wear safety harnesses.

When we enter the Gulf Stream, Tony will be plotting our position and watching the temperature. If we're fortunate enough to hit the Stream's deadly meander just right, we will need to keep close to our Bermuda rhumb line. Right, Tony?"

The Englishman, a small man with thick glasses, stood up and tipped his woolen, short-billed European sailor hat. The bankrupt physicist, who had filed false financial statements with his bank to keep his jewelry company afloat, was a favorite with the crew. They laughed at his good-natured jest. "Aye, Skipper," he said, pulling a loran out from under the seat. "I dare say that I have smuggled an extra loran (short for long-range aid to navigation) on board just in case the bloody sextant fails us!"

"The hell you say, you outlaw!" shouted Mel Swenson, the Scandinavian cook and Newport High history teacher John had defended in a sexual molestation charge. The crew roared in laughter.

"Put that damn thing up, Tony! We've got to play by the rules here and win this thing fair and square."

"Sorry, Captain."

"Let's go over the port and starboard alternating teams one last time, guys."

"Anyone want a beer?" Peter asked, getting bored with it all.

"Hold it a minute, Pete, we are almost through. OK. The port watch captain, Bob Ganloff, and his watch, Peter and Eric Dunlop, will start the race from 1400-1800 hours tomorrow afternoon. The starboard watch captain, Bill Jennings, and starboard crewmen, Doc Pearson and Voris LaFaye, will have the 1800-midnight watch. Then the port watch from midnight to 0400 hours and so forth every four hours for the rest of the race. This system will provide for an automatic rotation each 24-hours. It will be a grueling three and a half days, hopefully no more, so when you're off watch, let's get some rest and conserve our energy for the last few hours. This, gentlemen, is the most critical part of the race. Not only are we confronted with the coral reefs off Bermuda, but we will either win or lose by our performance in the homestretch, especially against Firestone's boat."

"How's the weather looking?"

"Looks good so far, and I hope we don't have any bad weather when we get to the Onion Patch. Now, we're fortunate to have an excellent cook on board. Mel Swenson has got plenty of grub on board."

'I wonder if that Swenson did really molest that Newport High cheerleader,' thought Slade, looking around at the rest of the crew. He caught Bob Ganloff's eye. Bob responded with a slight nod of his head, his face concealed by the thick brown beard that covered his ruddy face. Strings of wild hair danced on his bald head as the smoky sou'wester whipped the rigging in a musical chime.

Peter watched the serious-minded German, a Miller Beer distributor from Fall River, Massachusetts, who had inherited his father's business. A stern, no-nonsense man in his mid-forties, Bob was also a Vietnam combat veteran, an enlisted man in the Ninth Infantry Division in the Mekong Delta. 'Bob's a damned good man to have on board if we get into trouble,' Peter thought. 'He's a man who has nerves forged out of steel.'

"As I was saying, our preliminary weather report is excellent. No major depressions at the moment, with moderate southwesterly winds, and I hope it stays that way. Summer storms can develop instantly out on the northern Great Plains this time of year, turn nasty in a matter of hours. Then we have big trouble," John said, remembering Tony's account of serving the 1979 Fasnet Race in which fifteen sailors lost their lives in the Irish Sea.

"When will we get a copy of our latest satellite photo of the Gulf Stream?" Tony asked.

"Tomorrow morning, so you can plot our course to cross the Gulf Stream at the most advantageous point."

"How many boats have officially entered, Skipper, and how many are sailing in our class?" asked Eric Dunlop, Peter's watch mate on the port watch. The senior at Dartmouth had killed two classmates in an automobile accident and had been charged with vehicular homicide. His strong arms, from years on the oars with the skull crew, rippled with muscles as he polished one of the *Encounter*'s twelve Barient winches that run the backstays and mainsheets.

"There's a total of one hundred twenty-two boats officially entered, Eric, twenty-eight yachts in our racing division. We will be entered along with Firestone in the IMS (International Measurement System) Division of twenty-four boats and, as you all know, the race will be judged using the computerized Performance Curve Scoring Systems."

"And just what the hell does all that mean, John?" Peter asked.

"OK. There used to be two sets of rules for handicapping yachts in ocean racing. The older rules or IOR, International Offshore Rule, goes back for years before the computer age, and now we have the IMS rules. When the newer yachts were built in the late seventies their designers, using computers, had each yacht certified using a wide range of data such as hull, sail and rig measurement to develop a handicap system so that yachts of similar size can compete fairly. Each yacht is then given a handicap measured in time allowances in seconds per mile, 636.1 in the *Encounter*'s case."

"So, Skipper, shall I?" asked the physicist, feeling John

stumbling with his explanation. Talking very fast, he said, "What this means, Pete, is that the Performance Curve Scoring System is a further refinement of the IMS rules that determines the implied wind conditions separately for each boat on its elapsed time and, they say, eliminates the need to assign wind speed in handicapping. Bloody brilliant system. Bloody brilliant!"

"Sorry I asked the bloody goddamn question! Glad we got a physicist as a navigator to figure all that crap out!"

"What it all means, gentlemen, is that we will be left in the dark about relative handicaps with our competition during the race," Tony added.

"True to a certain degree, Tony," the skipper interrupted, "Offshore racing is somewhat different from what we are used to. But remember, our game plan is to sail like hell for Bermuda. A rule of thumb is that boats of our length generally are handicapped pretty much the same and, as you know, Firestone's boat is a sister to the *Encounter* so it is identical. The bottom line is let's go for the overall winner!"

"Are there any other questions?

"OK. Let's be here by ten o'clock tomorrow morning. Bring only the essentials that I listed in your poop sheet to keep down the weight and conserve space. For those of you who will be flying back, don't forget your airline ticket since Bermuda customs won't let you disembark without proof of return passage and your passports."

Peter Slade held up his hand. "What would you say, Skipper, about getting up a wager on the race with Firestone and those jerks on the *Martinis* tonight at the Yacht Club shindig?"

John Moffett smiled. "One hell of an idea, Peter. I'm putting you in charge of that."

"Youbetya! Tony, get some slips of paper and each man jot down the amount of money that you feel comfortable with betting. I'll take care of the rest tonight with Flint, if I don't punch out his lights!"

From her second floor master bedroom window, Charlotte Slade looked out across the manicured gardens of roses and lush green lawns of the Beach Mont estate. Out past Brenton Point she could see the open ocean of Rhode Island Sound. Ocean Drive meandered into the distant sinking sun. She sipped her third dry gin martini, the clear poison in Baccarat crystal harboring two large olives. With indecision she glanced back to the bed upon which four cocktail dresses were laid out. "What shall it be for the commodore's cocktail party, to bid farewell to that flamboyant husband of mine and his juvenile confidants, sailing away on their silly Bermuda yacht race?" Charlotte asked herself. She took another dress out of the closet and held it in front of the full-length mirror. Her blue eyes darted between the mirror and window, expecting any minute to see Peter's Range Rover drive through the massive entrance columns of sandstone topped with granite that guarded the noble estate.

Beach Mont, one of Newport's magnificent smaller mansions, was built at the turn of the century by Charlotte's great-grandfather Harrington. The wealthy New York shipping tycoon was seeking the prestige of a summer cottage, as they were then called, near the Belmonts, Vanderbilts, Astors and Berwinds on Newport's world renowned Bellevue Avenue. It had been Charlotte's inheritance from her mother who had just recently died. The magnificent three-story stone mansion had two entrances under circular porches located on its east and west sides, each supported by ten massive columns through which a circular brick drive passed. Upon entering either entrance, Beach Mont's lavish ballroom viewed the ocean to the south and west through wavelike windows and were detailed with panels depicting scenes from Greek mythology. It was no ordinary mansion and such craftsmanship could never be duplicated today. Thomas Terrell, the English butler who had been answering the door for many years, greeted Peter as he returned home from the Newport Yacht Club to get dressed.

"If it was not for John, I damned well would not attend this stupid party tonight, darling," pouted Charlotte, taking a sip of the martini as Peter arrived upstairs on the steep servant stairs from the kitchen.

"John will appreciate it that you did," replied Peter, undressing and getting into the shower. 'Spoiled bitch,' he thought, as the hot water relaxed his tense shoulder muscles. 'To hell with her. I don't give a damn if she goes or not,' he was thinking, as he lathered up. He finished quickly and dried off with a large white towel.

"Have you had a good day, dear?"

"As usual, boring."

"I thought you were going to the farm to check on the horses and drop by the Inn."

"Which of these dresses do you like, darling?" she asked, holding up a black and a blue one.

"The black one. You always look great in black."

"You didn't even look; you just say those things to try and placate me."

"No, really. I like the black one. Please hurry or we will be late," he said, walking into his closet to get a clean shirt. "I have everything squared away at the Inn for when I'm gone."

"I hate that goddamn inn!" Charlotte shouted, her voice raging, throwing the black dress down on the bed.

"Why the hell do you say that, Charlotte?" Peter asked sharply, gripped by instant anger.

"Because you spend all your damn time there, never leaving a minute for me...."

"I'm sorry. But it takes management to make it run right. When I get back from Bermuda, I'll hire a manager so we can spend more time together. I'll take you on a trip to India or China. Now hurry up and get dressed or we'll be late."

"To hell with India and being late! It's always a rat race with you, Peter Slade. I think I'll stay home," the influence of the martinis spoke as she teetered with her most effective form of defiance.

"Come on now, Charlotte, John's feelings will be hurt. How many of those have you had to drink?"

"To hell with John! And to hell with you, Peter Slade! I'll drink as many as I goddamn please, if it's any of your business...."

"Charlotte, I'm not arguing with a drunk. Stay home then if you like, you stupid bitch," he yelled, grabbing his jacket and taking the steep stairs down to the kitchen.

The Range Rover roared out of the drive and Charlotte began to cry. 'If only I had not been dumb enough to finance the Inn's restoration, this would never have happened to us. Peter would have time for me, like he did when I was married to Robert, instead of all that time he's spending with the Inn. I cannot believe the bastard's leaving me here for two weeks while he's in Bermuda, drinking, womanizing and having a grand old time while I just sit here. Sit? Like hell I will! Peter Slade, that bitch Melissa Jenkins better be staying in town while you are gone!'

Charlotte, standing in her bikini panties and bra, checked her profile in the mirror: her blond beauty, now fading, eyes puffed and face swollen, tummy pooching out a little too much from hard drinking, as spider webs were woven in the corner of her eyes by cruel Father Time. She lit a cigarette and fixed another martini. 'I'll go to New York shopping while the son-of-a-bitch is gone and stay at the Ritz. I'll pay for it with the Inn's checkbook, by God, I own the damn place. Yes, that will show Mr. Slade what management is.

Flynn O'Grady was on the phone in his World Trade Center office making final arrangements with FBI Agent Oden Terry for their trip to Newport in the morning. "What time do I meet you, Ode?" he asked, his voice shaky for a cigarette in the newly enacted smoke-free offices of the S.E.C.

"Be here at my office at five tomorrow morning. I have a van from the motor pool reserved."

"Will that give us enough time to get things squared away with Slade?"

"Hell yeah, but be here at five sharp."

"You got the cash from the U.S. Attorney's office?"

"Picked it up this afternoon. Everything's arranged, so don't worry."

O'Grady hung up the phone and hurried to clean off his desk and make sure Slade's file was secure and locked away. He now had decades of his life invested in getting Peter Slade behind bars and his calender was running out of time.

# Chapter VII

The siren's blast wailed across the open water, signaling a warning from the committee boat anchored four hundred yards off the starboard bow. The large white motor yacht, crowded with committeemen and press, flew the CCA burgee along with the race committee and alpha code flags from her halyard. Captain Moffett watched for the signal closely from the helm of the *Encounter*.

"OK! It's 1315 hours and that's our preparatory signal for Racing Division Class Three, gentlemen. Five minutes to the starting time," he shouted, as the blue shape dropped down the committee boat's halyard. The *Encounter* maneuvered with the competition to maintain her speed before crossing the starting line, jockeying for a favored position.

John Moffett was bare-headed and wearing sunglasses against the glare off the water. "The wind is light from the southwest. The committee boat is laying at right angles to Brenton Light and the wind. Our first heading is 185 degrees. What do you think, Tony?"

"Bloody good, Skipper. Keep a hundred yards off the committee boat so we will not be penalized."

"The breeze is coming and going, Skipper!"

"Right, Bob. You got everybody assigned?"

"Aye, aye, Skipper," shouted Ganloff as he made a quick visual inspection of the crew. His dark eyes darted upward to the sails and he said, "Everything's under control."

"That looks pretty good to me, too. Your sail selection looks good, Bob. What is the current, Tony?"

"The bugger's changing against us, Captain. I say, it's a little late from the bloody tables. You would be well advised to stay above the committee boat if possible."

"Right. Prepare to come about. Coming about," Moffett barked as he threw the helm hard to port, swinging the boom free to the luffing of the mainsail. Seconds later, the mainsail cracked, filling with wind as the boat responded quickly leeward to the whine of the sheets running through the winches.

"Captain, four minutes to the starting siren. Give the engine full throttle. We got to get her moving now. Talk to us, baby!" Bob shouted as the 65-horsepower Perkins diesel engine ceased blubbering in an idle, revving into a roar as it vibrated the deck and the boat shot forward. The *Encounter* and her eight member crew were under power, riding over light seas and under sun-dappled skies, their faces tense with excitement, adrenalin rushing through their veins.

"All right. Stand by to kill the engine."

"WATCH OUT FOR THE MARTINIS, Skipper!" Peter Slade screamed from the bow lookout.

"Come up now! Go above her and cut her wind!" John ordered. "Hey, Firestone, you got the five thousand dollars on board to cover your bet if you happen to make it to the Onion Patch?" John shouted at the passing yacht.

"I'm covered! YOU better make sure one of those criminals you got for a crew doesn't steal yours, Moffett!" Firestone barked back over nervous laughter from his crew.

"We're on the short end of the bloody starting line right here, Skipper," Tony yelled as he nervously watched the two large orange buoys, approximately 800 yards apart, marking the starting line ahead.

Moffett nodded. "Bob, listen. I'm putting her down on a reach. Let's go that way and keep her headway up, then we'll reach back."

"Right, Skipper, that starting line is biased 25 degrees with the current and there's only going to be room for one or two boats to be favored, so let's go for it."

"WATCH OUT FOR FIRESTONE!!!" Peter Slade screamed again from the bow as the competing yacht approached from astern. "HARD STARBOARD, QUICK!"

"Watch what the hell you're doing, Firestone," John shouted at the near-missed collision. "You were damn near in violation of 'a mast abeam', on that one, sport!"

'I'll file a protest with the Racing Committee and have him penalized on that one if he should luck up and beat us,' he thought.

"Two minutes to the starting gun, Skipper. I'll give you a countdown," said the navigator to the cries of a flock of passing seagulls.

"ONE AND A HALF MINUTES."

"Good position! Damned good position!" John said to Ganloff.

"FORTY-FIVE SECONDS."

"How about that main, Bob? Can your main come out a little?"

"There's the drop, Skipper," Bob said, pointing to the committee boat and counting out loud. "TEN, 9, 8, 7, 6, 5, 4, 3, 2, 1," and the siren blast screamed across the open water as they passed the committee boat quickly astern. The 1990 Newport-Bermuda Race had just begun and out there somewhere, John was thinking, across six hundred miles of open ocean lay the island of Bermuda and St. David's Head Light.

"Great start, gentlemen! Clear air, nobody near us."

"Let's get the weight out of the bow, Pete. Eric, trim the jib. Everybody to windward, let's make her move. Trim your main, Bob."

It had been only a few hours now since the sun burned away the fog on the abandoned Newport Beach and Peter Slade had been listening to the eight-thirty weather report in his Range Rover. He was thinking of Charlotte still asleep at Beach Mont as he looked at Cliff Walk, captured now by the early morning sun as the ocean rolled in and crashed against the rocks. 'Damn her,' he thought, frustrated at having to go to the party alone last night. 'And damn her again for not getting up this morning when I left,' he was thinking, 'too hung over, or she just doesn't give a damn.'

Slade had felt an anxiety attack coming on while waiting for the federal agents to arrive. He had felt that same sick nervousness settling in his guts many times before. Vietnam over twenty years ago, for example. That same damn sick feeling you get listening to the battalion CO giving his Operation Order for a search and destroy mission. It makes you so nervous you want to puke, break down and cry, or just jump up and knock the goddamn hell out of something. 'You have to stay cool, Slade, never let them see you sweat,' he thought when ever he felt this way. He inhaled deeply, holding his breath, counting slowly backwards from ten to chase the damn anxiety thing away.

He had seen the approaching van coming slowly down the road along the beach. It was a dark blue Ford panel job with two men that pulled into the spot next to the Range Rover. The driver killed his engine, sitting there for a moment before getting out. Peter switched off his key just as the 8:30 news announcer started on the half-hour news leaving him with the sounds of the surf. "Mr. Slade? Please get out," ordered a firm voice as Peter pocketed his keys and was joined by a short wiry man about his age and the tall skinny ugly face of S.E.C Investigator Flynn O'Grady.

"Mr. Slade, my name is Oden Terry, Special Agent, FBI," the shorter man said, flashing his credentials, then extending his hand. "You remember me and Flynn O'Grady from the Securities and Exchange Commission?"

"We've met, gentlemen," Peter had replied coolly, thinking of his arrest and not wanting to get off on the wrong foot with Oden Terry, while shooting O'Grady a dirty look. 'The bastard's skinnier and uglier than I remembered and looking a hundred years old,' he thought.

"Wouldn't miss our meeting this morning for anything, Slade. Guess you thought us guys forgot about you or somethin' after nearly five years?" O'Grady's words had shot out of the corner of his mouth as he lit a cigarette.

"Let's get in the back of the van, gentlemen. And how about putting out your cigarette, Flynn," the FBI agent had ordered, opening the side door, glancing up and down the deserted beach before the three men climbed inside.

"You ready for the race?" the FBI Agent had asked in a pleasant voice, clearing out a place for Peter to sit on a seat that ran the length of one side.

"As ready as I'm going to get, Mr. Terry. What is it that you want me to do for you guys?"

He hadn't answered. "Would you like a cup of coffee, Mr. Slade?" he had asked, opening a thermos and releasing the aroma of fresh brewed coffee. He handed Peter a styrofoam cup.

"Sure, thanks."

"Cream and sugar?"

"No, black's fine, thank you."

The agent had sipped his coffee. "We don't have much time, Mr. Slade, so I'll make this as brief as possible. By the way, I read our file on you and must say you had a damn impressive record in Vietnam with the Big Red One. I like working with ex-infantry officers, especially those with combat experience. I know how it is to get shot at; I've been there myself."

He had sipped his coffee again. "This assignment will be done, as we used to say in the infantry, Mr. Slade, 'by the numbers', one step at a time. We'll tell you what we want you to do and what we want you to know, step by step. Understand?"

"Yeah, I understand," Slade had replied.

O'Grady had grunted as he leaned over and pulled a blue canvas bag from under the seat and opened it. "Here, count it, Slade, you got to sign for it," he said, shoving the bag at Peter.

"Jesus!" Peter had exclaimed, staring down at the bag full of circulated one hundred dollar bills in wrappers of one hundred, bounded ten to a brick. "Jesus Christ, count it? Hell, it will take me to Christmas to count all this!"

"Just test count some of dem wrappers then, count the bricks, it will be quicker that way if you like," O'Grady had suggested.

Peter had removed the rubber bands off the first brick, his fingers counting quickly through the bills before replacing the rubber bands. Dumping the bag on the floor, he counted fifty bricks of ten thousand dollars each, stacking them on the seat. "I count a half million bucks," he said, stacking the bricks neatly next to the bag.

"Right. That's the count, half a mill. Here, sign for it on this hand receipt. Today's the fifteenth of June," O'Grady had said, handing Peter a black U. S. government ballpoint pen.

"Now what?"

"Mr. Slade, when you reach Bermuda your yacht will clear customs at the Royal Bermuda Yacht Club in Hamilton. I understand that you will be staying at the Glencoe Hotel across Hamilton Harbor in Salt Kettle."

"How did you know that?"

"Never mind. When the Bermuda Customs Officers come on board, do not declare — I say again — do not make declaration of the half million dollars on the customs form. Understand?"

"What the hell happens then if they catch me with it?"

"It's very unlikely, but if dem guys do, you might consider bribing dem, say for a hundred thousand bucks or so," O'Grady had smirked, putting his hand over his mouth. "But you got to pay us back, Slade," he cackled as the FBI agent frowned and shook his head.

"Bull shit! You think I woke up yesterday? You can't bribe one of those Bermuda Customs agents!"

"Don't worry, you're making too much out of all this, Mr. Slade. If you get caught, we'll sort it out with the American Consulate for you," Terry had replied.

"Hell yes, you will, after I spend half my life in jail!"

"Don't worry, we have our contact in Bermuda through the

State Department. So you can save yourself a lot of trouble by not getting caught," the FBI agent had firmly replied.

O'Grady had added, "Just stay cool, man, like the time we busted you in your big fancy office in New York..."

"After that, what do I do?"

"On Tuesday or Wednesday morning, June the nineteenth or twentieth, depending on your arrival time in Bermuda, take the money and go alone to the Hamilton Princess Hotel on Pitts Bay Road. It's next door to the Royal Bermuda Yacht Club, you can't miss it. Big pink hotel — I think you stayed there once. At ten a.m. sharp on your first day in Bermuda, you take the money and go to the lobby and use the house phone to ring Room 300, and, when the party answers, identify yourself, Mr. Slade."

O'Grady had handed Peter his passport. "Here's your papers," he said. "You no longer need it to enter Bermuda, but it makes things run smoother if you got it, especially with a half million of dem undeclared dollars."

Peter had flipped through the pages and doubled checked to make sure it had not expired.

"So you want me to launder some money in Bermuda. Right?"

"I said this mission was by the numbers, Mr. Slade," interrupted the FBI agent, whose eyes darted disapproval at O'Grady who had taken out his pack of Camels. "You will be further instructed by our contact in Bermuda. Go over my instructions for me, please."

"OK, I got it. Ten hundred hours, Room 300 at the Princess on Tuesday or Wednesday, the nineteenth or twentieth with the money," Peter had replied apprehensively. "Is there someone I can contact if things get fouled up?"

"I'll be your handler and know if it does. Just do as you have been instructed. Your progress will be monitored, so don't do nothin' you wouldn't want your mother to find out about, Slade," O'Grady had cracked.

"Thank you, Mr. O'Grady, I'm looking forward to working for you. Has anyone ever casually mentioned to you that you're an asshole?" Peter had asked, getting out of the van with the bag. He shot O'Grady a dirty look while shaking hands and smiling at the FBI agent who was trying hard not to laugh.

Below now, Tony Stevenson sat at the nav table which was located next to the aft hatch, plotting the *Encounter*'s course. Peering through his thick glasses at the boat's IMS certificate, he calculated on his slide rule the maximum sail efficiency based upon the current and the prevailing winds.

"Bet Firestone's navigator wishes to hell computers weren't banned by race rules, Tony. We're the only boat in the race with a navigator that's smart enough to plot our course and use all that damned data off the *Encounter*'s IMS certificate."

"Oh dear, bankrupt English physicist at that, Captain, I am bloody sad to report."

"You just caught on too quickly to the American entrepreneurial spirit. Every millionaire has got to go busted two or three times before they make their fortune. Next time, though, don't be giving false financial statements to your bank."

"Stupid move of me, wasn't it? Won't make that mistake again, old chap. I greatly appreciate your getting me out of it all, John. Prison would be dreadful, quite dreadful. Yes, quite a lawyer, you are. Don't know how the bloody hell I'll ever repay you."

"Start by getting this baby to Bermuda ahead of Firestone and the rest, will you?"

"Indeed I shall! I calculate our speed as a function of sailing condition, under the present wind velocity, taking into consideration the *Encounter*'s sailing trim, and we do indeed need to steer a heading of 165ˋ to catch the knuckle on the southbound meander of the Gulf Stream, my dear Captain."

With a quick burst of speed, the *Encounter* surged forward. Peter looked back across the water at Beach Mont, the white, majestic old mansion standing radiantly in the afternoon sun, fading slowly into the distance. "Goodbye, sweet Charlotte, I'll love you till I die," Peter sang in his rich baritone voice, still smarting from his bitter fight last night. A group of seagulls darted past just above the crest of the oncoming waves. Their cries seemed sadder than usual as they glided and Peter Slade hated it when they cried sadly that way.

From the Inn at Castle Hill on Ocean Avenue, the two agents were finishing a leisurely lunch on the patio, enjoying the magnificent view of the ocean after making sure Peter Slade had sailed on the *Encounter*. The sailboats were distant images under the sun-dappled skies. "Damn glad I'm taking Delta out, instead of one of dem sailboats," Flynn O'Grady chuckled, blowing Camel smoke out his nostrils in the breeze.

"When you leaving, you lucky bastard?" asked the FBI agent.

"Sunday afternoon. What about the Madam?" O'Grady asked.

"Sunday sometime...morning, I think. She's flying out of Boston."

"Good! Believe I've got Slade's ass setup good this time, Ode. What'ya think?"

"If everything goes as planned, you have finally got him, Flynn," Ode replied, taking a sip of his coffee. "For the life of me, I can't understand why the hell you're so goddamn determined to get this guy."

"Cause this guy's guilty as hell! I appreciate the help, Ode. Now let's pay out and get the hell back to New York; it's Friday, you know."

"Headed for the Pussy Cat tonight, are you?"

"It's Friday night, isn't it, buddy?" he laughed, feeling smug about his plan and knowing it was payday.

# Chapter VIII

## The Gulf Stream
### June 16, 1990

The *Encounter*, sailing in moderate seas, approached the Gulf Stream's powerful currents that flow northward out of the Straits of Florida, passing between the continental slope and the Sargasso Sea. The gargantuan seagoing river flows more water than all the rivers of the world combined, creating unpredictable zigzagging meanders up the eastern coast of the United States before its crossing of the Atlantic to Europe. The *Encounter*'s key to victory lay in its ability to aggressively manipulate the Gulf Stream, catching the knuckle of a southbound meander whose current would give the boat a two to three mile per hour speed advantage over the competition.

"Skipper, our last National Weather Service satellite chart you gave me shows the knuckle of the meander at approximately latitude 37 degrees 16.7 minutes North, 69 degrees 24.2 minutes West. We have been steering a heading of 185˚ south for over five hours, and from my last plotting, we should be entering the Gulf Stream at any time," Tony said. The two men drank black coffee and pondered over the charts on the nav table. Tony logged the *Encounter*'s position in the race book: 17/2000 latitude 37 degrees 37.5 minutes North, 69 degrees 18.4 minutes West. Wind moderate from southwest, seas moderate, four feet. Full moon.

"Bob!" John called to the watch captain at the helm. "We're closing on the Gulf Stream. Watch for the chop on the surface of the water where the two forces mesh. What's the water temperature?"

"Sixty-four degrees, Captain. I haven't noticed any differences in the water yet."

"It's ten o'clock. You still have a couple of hours on your watch. Chances are we will enter the stream very shortly now. Keep a close eye on that thermometer. When the temperature rises, we've got our work cut out for us."

Slade and Bob Ganloff sat in the *Encounter*'s cockpit, their faces barely visible in the dim glow of the cockpit lights. Ganloff constantly glanced up at the sails, which appeared ghostly in the moonlight, as the *Encounter* sailed silently across the expansive Atlantic.

"Keep your eyes peeled for running lights, guys. We don't want to get run down by a freighter," Bob ordered, thinking how easy it was for the *Encounter* to go undetected in the busy shipping lanes.

"Right," replied Slade, taking the binoculars and searching for other white sails on the dark surface of the ocean. "Firestone and the *Martinis* are out there somewhere," he said, just to hear his own voice.

The rhythmic smacking of the *Encounter*'s bow on the approaching seas chafed Peter's nerves as he felt his anger at

Charlotte returning. He had arrived home fairly late but halfway sober from the yacht club to find Charlotte staggering around in the great hall of Beach Mont, dog drunk and screaming, "Thisss is no way to live, being left alone. I'm going to sellll the goddamn Stone Bridge Inn, you bassstard!"

"Please, Charlotte, just settle down, I'm only going to be gone for a few days, and when I return we will go to Europe, like I said."

"Helll no we're not!"

"OK, if you want to fly to Bermuda, be my guest. Here, give me that drink; you've had enough for one night."

"Gibme...me back my drink, you bassstard!" her shrill voice had echoed off the twenty-four foot ceilings of the great hall, "I'm seeelling the Inn, you're damn riiight I am!"

Peter cringed as her piercing screams still vividly rang in his ears. He could feel his pulse rising as he tried to think of other things, an approaching ship, maybe, the ocean, anything. Last night's fight kept coming back. His anger grew hard in his heart and the feeling of guilt for the woman he loved tried to creep silently back inside at the same time.

Perhaps she was going through the change of life, or something. Menopause he didn't understand. Why be a bastard and not be more supportive and get her some help? 'Damn her,' he thought after a while, getting angry all over again. No, it wasn't menopause at all. He had to get her off the bottle, and he just hadn't faced up to that.

How could she have such violent animosity against the Inn? Something that was his pride and joy, livelihood, and wedding present, no less? Life without the Stone Bridge was unthinkable, and he had to get this all worked out with her when he got back from Bermuda. He was losing Charlotte. He felt it deep in his heart. As he began dozing, her screams pierced his unconscious, "....I'm seeeling the Stone Bridge...."

"LIKE HELL YOU ARE!" Peter bellowed, jerking awake to the sounds of the ocean rushing past the *Encounter*'s hull.

"Say again?" young Eric Dunlop shouted from his forward watch position.

"NOTHING. Nothing. Forget it, Eric," Peter, embarrassed replied, standing to wake up. He looked at Bob Ganloff at the wheel, who acted as though nothing had happened.

'This Bob is a strange fellow, very difficult to get close to, distant as if he has some great personal secret locked inside him. I wonder what the hell it is,' Slade was thinking. He always seemed preoccupied, yet keenly aware of his surroundings. 'Whatever it is that he carries from the past is heavy as hell.' Was it his wife's murder, or was it something else? Peter Slade was determined to find out.

Peter had known him for almost two years. On occasion, after an afternoon of sailing, he would drop by the Inn and drink a Miller Lite over some very stimulating conversations. Sometimes he would talk about Vietnam; they had that in common. He had received a Silver Star for heroism in combat with the 9th Infantry Division and he was proud of that. The German in him had made him a damn fine soldier, too. 'Those Germans are like that,' Slade thought, realizing now that he knew nothing about Bob's personal life except that he owned the Miller distributorship in Fall River and that John had represented him in his murder case. Trying to stay awake, Peter turned and asked, "Bob, you're married, aren't you?"

"Yeah, for the second time, and it doesn't seem to get any better," he responded flatly, his eyes traversing between the sails, compass and the horizon.

"I know what you mean, man," Peter chuckled, reflecting his frustration in his tone of voice, thinking again about Charlotte. Waiting for a response, Peter sighed, trying to keep the conversation alive, "My head bartender, George, at the Stone Bridge Inn, used to worked for my father in Baltimore when I was a kid. I'll never forget what George told me the night I broke up with my first love."

"What's that, Pete?" Bob asked curiously, his eyes glued on the horizon.

"He said, 'Boy, you can't figure them women out, cause women are all sprinkled with fucked-up dust, some of them more sprinkled than the others!'"

Bob laughed loudly, a rarity for him, as he pounded the helm with his gloved hand.

"I remember asking, 'What do you mean, George?' and he replied, 'Lord God, boy! You'll find out soon enough. Just remember what I said.'"

"Pete, George is a brilliant man, a philosopher, no doubt. It sounds like he's in the same league with Homer, the blind poet," Bob replied, still chuckling.

"What happened to your first marriage, if you don't mind my asking?"

Bob Ganloff's profile turned rigid, facing straight ahead at the horizon with his wool stocking hat pulled down over his ears to fight off the cold. The rolling waves spread out beyond him on the great expanse of the ocean in the moonlight. 'Jesus,' Ganloff thought, 'Slade doesn't realize that Johnny got me two hung juries for murdering my first wife.'

Then there was the silence that only the ocean transcends: the wind in the sails and the running sea. Bob glanced down at the compass, turning the helm slightly to the correct heading of 185 degrees and finally replied flatly, "It's something I don't talk about."

Slade let it go at that. He'd ask Moffett when they were drinking sometime. He suddenly noticed the thermometer on the dashboard. "Wait a second here, Bob! We got something happening. Hey, Skipper, the water temperature's rising, up to 67 degrees now. Better come topside and have a look."

John Moffett bolted up the companionway ladder into the cockpit. He grabbed the binoculars and studied the surface of the ocean in the moonlight, rechecking the thermometer several times. "We're entering the Gulf Steam, gentlemen." He watched the approaching fine chop of the surface glistening as the forceful current of the Gulf Stream met calmer waters. "Get the crew on deck; we got some serious sailing to do.

"Prepare to come about. Steer 270 degrees, hard right rudder... coming about," ordered the captain as he closely monitored the thermometer and the yacht tacked to starboard. "The warmer the water, the closer we are to the western edge of the southbound meander, where the current flows the fastest."

The moon rose higher, all hands except the Swede on deck. Seventy-two degrees and the water temperature continued to rise; two hours later the thermometer hit 80 after constant adjustments on the sheets and halyards to keep the luff out of the sail. "Prepare to come about to 165 degrees...Come about," the skipper ordered, presuming that they had hit the warmest water of the southbound meander. "OK, Bill, you and Doc and LaFaye got the starboard watch. Keep your eyes on the thermometer, gentlemen. If the water temperature starts falling off, tack to port till it rises. We hopefully will hold the southbound current for a hundred miles or more."

"Bloody fortunate to hit the Gulf Stream appropriately," the Englishman said, thinking, 'what fine weather."

Dr. Duane Pearson and his friend owned an old Victorian house in Newport that they had planned to make into a 'bed and breakfast' before he lost his job. He lived there after coming on weekends for a number of years to sail on Narragansett Bay. He was a New Yorker by birth and had been a psychiatrist at the Payne Whitney Clinic, Manhattan's premier private psychiatric hospital, for his entire career. Wealthy New Yorkers went there to repair their psyches, dry out, or regain their sanity.

The enormous whitebrick hospital on the East River was named for the reclusive financier, Payne Whitney, who willed millions for its construction. It was at the time the most prestigious psychiatry hospital in America, not only for its medical training but because it catered to the rich, providing its residents a wonderful accolade for starting their own practice later.

This strangely handsome man in his late thirties had dark, thick, wavy hair, smoked a pipe and wore horn-rimmed glasses, remindful of the typical movie psychiatrist. At times, out of frustration, he drank excessively, and when he became nervous his right eye twitched uncontrollably, forcing him to close it. His mannerisms were slightly feminine, along with his speech, but not overly so for the bachelor. In the past year he'd had plenty of time for sailing after surrendering his medical license and being forced to resign from Payne Whitney. The New York State Medical Board had suspended his license for a year after a hard and bitter fight by his lawyer.

Doc Pearson's thoughts returned to the long hallways and dark consulting rooms of the self-contained asylum where he had been accused by another physician of having homosexual relations with one of the patients. His accuser, Dr. Barbara Goldberg, who had once been romantically involved with Doc Pearson, had called off the relationship when she found out he was gay. He desperately missed the hospital where he had worked his entire career and was counting the days until he could return to his profession.

'I wonder if my reputation is too far shot to hell to get another clinical position,' he thought, staring out at the horizon. 'Well, with New York's gay community there shouldn't be any trouble making a living in my own practice if I have to. Heaven forbid, I could practice medicine in an AIDS clinic. Darn it, I miss being at Payne Whitney.'

"Why in the hell do we have to have that queer shrink from New York on the crew?" Slade had asked John Moffett one summer night over single malt Scotch at the Marble Bar.

"Why do you ask, Pete? You homophobic or something?"

"Hell no, it's just that the guy gives me the creeps, man."

"Well, for one thing, Pete, he's a physician and it is always good to have a doctor on board. Doc is an excellent sailor, having competed in a number of Stamford-Veneyad Races, and besides that, do you know for sure he's gay?"

"Well no, not personally, but... well, hell, remember that time you asked me to have lunch with him in New York after I got arrested? I'm telling you, that guy's as queer as a three dollar bill, Johnny."

"Come on, Pete! This is the 1990s, for Christ sake, stop queer-bashing. I can't think of a man more trusting," said the lawyer who had represented Dr. Pearson at the New York State Medical Board's inquiry. It had been a lengthy hearing in which Dr.

Goldberg had testified in explicit detail about catching the physician sodomizing a young man under his care. The board had been divided by Counselor Moffett's argument that Dr. Goldberg was lying and only retaliating against her former lover for calling off the romance. Dr. Pearson's license to practice was suspended, not revoked, on the grounds that there was a reasonable doubt that neither party was telling the truth. John had argued, "...Doctor Pearson knows that the profession does not sanction sexual involvement with patients. Dr. Goldberg has no other witness and the alleged patient also denies the allegation. There are no other confirmed homosexual activities by the accused..."

Doc Pearson was the only member of the crew besides John Moffett who knew about Peter Slade's termination from Porterfield Hartley or his indictment by the Feds. At the time, John had worried about Peter becoming suicidal after his arrest. He had asked Peter to see a psychiatrist.

"No way in hell I'm talking to a shrink!" was Peter Slade's response.

"Just have lunch with Dr. Duane Pearson from the Payne Whitney Clinic, Pete. He's an interesting young psychiatrist and a fine sailor. Just have a friendly chat over lunch, no couches. Won't do you any harm and it will be helpful in our case for wrongful dismissal against Porterfield Hartley if we decide to pursue it."

"Peter suffers from a sociopathic condition," Dr. Pearson had reported to John after their lunch where the details of Peter's arrest for insider trading were discussed. "Peter, I am afraid, apparently does not know the difference between right and wrong in his own mind, if he is, in fact, guilty of the charges brought against him. I don't know if he's an inside trader or not, but he's convinced himself that he did nothing wrong. He's naturally depressed at this point in time after losing his job and getting divorced, but by no means is Peter Slade suicidal."

The crew retired below. Doc took the helm, holding a course of 165 degrees, parallel to the rhumb line between Newport and Bermuda. His eyes shifted between the compass and the thermometer hovering now around 80. The *Encounter* was making excellent headway. It was midnight when John Moffett came up the companionway to the sweet smell of tobacco from Duane's pipe. "How's she doing, Doc?" he asked.

"She's just handling marvelously, Captain, a real princess this boat of yours," replied Duane's nurturing voice. "John, I've been wanting to tell you something, and now that we're alone, it's the perfect time in this beautiful moonlight."

"Shoot," John apprehensively replied.

"You know that your ex-brother-in-law, Flint, wanted me to have a drink with him before we left.'

"No, of course I didn't."

"Well, I must say, John, Flint Firestone has never been a problem to me, however, I know you two have bad blood..."

"Had! I don't particularly like the guy, never really did. Now he's pretty sour after we reamed him a new one in my sister's divorce."

"I didn't think your firm could represent Rosa..."

"We had an out of court settlement."

"Well, Captain Moffett, I politely declined his offer, didn't mean to offend him, but I was on your crew and I didn't want to compromise myself."

"Good, Doc, I appreciate that. I can't believe the bastard would stoop so low as to try and infiltrate my crew. What's wrong with the guy's ego that would make him want to do that from a professional standpoint?"

"Now, now, John! You know my licenses have been suspended, thanks to my former colleague at Payne Whitney. I can't give you any professional opinions, you know, or the buddies will get me good."

"Yeah, sorry about your licenses, Doc. I didn't do a very good job in representing you."

Duane Pearson limp-wristed his free hand off the helm in a gesture. "For heaven's sake, John, stop it! You saved my license to practice! I'm only suspended for a few more months now."

"Thanks, Doc, but I felt bad about it..."

"I said, stop it, Johnny! You are not being fair to yourself, and besides, heavens, you didn't even send me a bill!"

"You bet I did. You're paying for it right now, Doc, so hold her steady, I got to get some rest."

"Do you think I'm gay, John?"

'Jesus, how in the hell do you answer that,' John pondered. "Duane...uh, your sexual preference is..."

"Don't worry, John, because I'm not gay, just feminine. I know Peter and the rest of the crew think I am gay, and I hate that damn Goldberg for making up that lie. I'm considering suing her for slander."

"Your lawyer says don't bother, Duane. It would be almost impossible to get a judgment, especially since the medical board suspended your licenses."

"Well, isn't there anything I can do?"

"Yes, hold your course, sailor, and thanks for your loyalty."

Dr. Duane Pearson was now thinking, 'too bad those guys don't get along. Flint's such a nice, handsome man.'

Meanwhile, down below in the crowded main salon full of sails and equipment, Peter Slade lay exhausted in his berth. He slowly drifted into a deep sleep listening to the sounds of the ocean rushing past the hull. He dreamed of his wife, Charlotte, sitting with Flynn O'Grady on the veranda of the Stone Bridge Inn drinking Bombay gin martinis and smoking cigarettes.

*O'Grady, his red face glowing, wolfed down boiled jumbo shrimp, dipping them into the cocktail sauce that left a red trail across the white tablecloth and up his soiled tie. "More shrimp out here, bartender!" Charlotte yelled. "Hurry! We have a very important guest, George! Don't keep Mr. O'Grady waiting!"*

*George Washington Henley moved quickly for a man nearly seventy, returning with a fresh bowl of peeled shrimp. "Where in the hell's my martini?" Charlotte barked, seductively crossing her legs to Flynn O'Grady's sadistic chuckle.*

*"Yes'um, Miss Slade. Is there anything else what I can bring you and the gentleman?" George politely asked, setting her martini on the table.*

*"Yeah. Keep everyone off this veranda for the afternoon. Mr. O'Grady is an investigator with the Security and Exchange Commission and he's going to throw Peter Slade in jail and we don't want to be disturbed," she laughed.*

*"Miss Slade," George protested, "the veranda is reserved for a big wedding party this afternoon, Miss Slade. Mr. Legate's daughter, she's getting married and he's running for the governor of Rhode Island. Mr. Slade, he gave me special instructions ..."*

*"To hell with that spineless politician, Legate! I'm the owner of this goddamn place and not Peter Slade. You better get that straight or you're fired, George," Charlotte screamed.*

# Chapter IX

The Atlantic
June 17, 1990

The *Encounter* was beyond the Gulf Steam now, sailing with a steady northwesterly wind. Nothing happened that night except the movement of the full moon and the stars across the heavens as the yacht raced toward Bermuda. Much phosphorescence was in the ocean, churning in the wake like small white embers of fire. The wind dropped just before dawn and with it Peter Slade dropped out of his dream, into the reality of another day at sea. "Get off the veranda and out of the Stone Bridge Inn, Charlotte, you no-good worthless bitch or I'll kill you!" he screamed, bolting up in his berth, banging his head. "Jesus," he muttered groggily, rubbing his forehead and glancing around in the dark, hoping no one had heard him. He checked the blue canvas bag locked safely in the bottom of his seabag in the sail locker and then he laid back down again.

"You awake, Pete?" John Moffett asked, suddenly appearing through the aft passageway from the captain's cabin.

Slade grunted.

"How you feeling?"

"If I felt any better I just couldn't stand it, Johnny. What time is it?"

"Nearly four a.m. Time for the port watch change."

"You got any rack time yet, Skipper?" Peter asked, pulling on his pants.

"Not yet. We're making too much headway to be worrying about sleep, man. I hope this favorable northwesterly wind holds so that we can keep east of the rhumb line now that we're out of the tank. I hope we don't get stalled in the bottom of the meander or bogged down."

Peter yawned. "I feel like I slept in a tank," he replied, stretching after the short three and a half hours of sleep. 'I've got to be crazy for putting myself through this abuse,' he thought a little while later in the galley, pouring a cup of black coffee. Tying his Harken sailing shoes in the dim light, he said to John, "Go ahead, damn it, John, get some rest, man. We'll call you if we need you."

"Talk to me first," he said to Peter, putting his hand on his shoulder, lowering his voice and looking about to make sure they were alone. "What the hell do the Feds want you to do when we get to Bermuda? I'm concerned about it."

"I know. Thanks. Got to meet a contact at ten o'clock on either Tuesday or Wednesday in Hamilton, but don't tell anybody. It's a big-ass government secret, John! That's about all I know. I'm sorry if it interferes with our plans," Peter replied, thinking he dared not mention the half million dollars stashed below for fear of taking the skipper's mind off the race. Bermuda Customs would just have to catch him, and then he would have to deal with that.

John's sleepy-looking eyes were feeling heavier. "OK, I'll try to get a little rest now." He retired to his aft cabin.

Sleep would come easy, Moffett thought, lying fully dressed in his berth. He waited, exhausted, the anxiety and hype of the race keeping him awake. 'If only I can win the Bermuda Trophy, the tall silver replica of the St. David Lighthouse' and have it sitting in the lobby of my office for all the clients to see. No, that's crazy. In the trophy case at the Newport Yacht Club. Yes, of course. Yeah, that's it, so Firestone can eat his heart out with envy when he hears the Seawanhaka Corinthian members talking about how impressed they are when they visit.

'Firestone, you loser, now won't that be poetic justice to make you squirm, you son-of-a-bitch, weaned with a silver spoon in your mouth. God, why do I let him get to me, damn Yalie, never working a day in his life. We reamed him a new one when he divorced Rosa to marry that young girl from Boston. I've always despised the guy, not for leaving Rosa, but just the way he went about it after she was paralyzed in the automobile accident that was his fault. Poor dear. At least my partner, Jack Spencer, did a fabulous job handling her divorce and she won't have to worry about financial security after Jack got her four million of Firestone's trust fund in the settlement.' Turning, he sighed, smiling in the dark, remembering the look on Firestone's face when the judge made the award. Adding insult to injury, he had ordered Firestone to pay his ex-wife's attorney fees to Moffett, Spencer and Grace in the amount of one hundred thousand dollars.

Staring into the dark and wallowing about with the boat, he listened to the rush of the water against the *Encounter*'s hull, his body crying out for sleep as his mind raced wildly onward. 'I wonder what the Feds really want Peter to do when we hit Bermuda. Something to do with the securities industries or financial institutions, that's what Pete knows about; besides insider trading, of course. I have always thought he was lying to me about a foreign bank account after the U.S. Attorney mentioned it at his plea-bargaining conference. Damn sure hope he doesn't. Should it ever surfaces Pete Slade's ass is in deep trouble. What the hell's going on between him and Charlotte? She's always been very close to me, my favorite cousin, and not a bad paying client for the firm. Sure, she's spoiled and always had her way, but if Peter's smart he'll let her keep doing her thing. Especially with her fortune. He's got to get her some help. Poor girl, stayed married to Robert Cocknell until she's hooked on the sauce, I'm afraid. Whatever their problems are, I hope it gets worked out between them; it would be damn hard for me to take sides if they get divorced. His eyes shut as he drifted off into a light sleep to the sounds of his yacht and the ocean, hoping for dreams of victory.

Brilliant sunshine glistened off the Atlantic at noon. The ocean was the *Encounter*'s alone as she sailed gently onward in light seas. Tony Stevenson climbed out of the cockpit, shielding his eyes against the glare. It was time to take his noonday sighting of the sun, handing Duane the chronometer. The sextant felt like it weighed a ton when he held it up to the horizon. Thirty-six hours without sleep was taking its toll on the frail little Brit as he sang his usual trivial Englishman's song while sighting, "Oh, bring the sun down, my lad, bring the sun down." Peering through the horizon glass of the sextant, he waited for the exact instant the sun would be at its highest to determine the exact longitude of the boat. He adjusted the angle of the sun-mirror so that the image of the sun appeared to sit on the horizon. "STOP," he shouted as the arc of the sun kissed it. Doc Pearson stopped the chronometer, recording the time. Taking the chronometer, Tony scampered back down the companionway hatch to plot their position at the nav table.

"What's our position? How much water have we covered?" John Moffett eagerly asked two questions at once as he joined him. Tony smiled, then carefully began preparing his sight-reduction worksheet, referring to the tables and *Nautical Almanac*. Taking his parallel rules and dividers he plotted the *Encounter*'s position on the chart. The physicist double-checked his calculations and then turned to John with a smile. "There we are, sir, latitude 68 degrees 45 minutes, longitude 35 degrees 66 minutes," he said, shoving the chart over for the skipper to see. "Bloody well past the tank, and east of the rhumb line — perfect position, Skipper!"

"Brilliant! We're parallel and east of the rhumb line, two hundred miles from Bermuda all right. Look at the time we made in the Gulf Stream: we were making damn near thirteen knots ground speed. Now, if we are only lucky enough to hold this northwesterly wind we could damn well win this race. It's noon, gentlemen. What's for lunch, Swede?"

The crew took their corned beef sandwiches on rye and cold Miller beer up on deck. "How we doing, Skipper?" Peter asked.

"We're, in my opinion, ahead of our competition. Has anyone seen another sail?"

The Englishman jumped up, grabbed the binoculars and peered over the *Encounter*'s stern, "Aye, aye, sir! Astern, there, I say. Sail ahoy!" he shouted in jest.

"Where?!" John quickly cross-examined, as all eyes peered at the empty horizon.

"It's Firestone! Caught in the tank of the Gulf Stream!" Tony laughed, slapping his knee, receiving the jeers of his shipmates in return.

"There is a funnel off our starboard bow," Bob Ganloff said in his no-nonsense voice, pointing to a distant speck on the horizon he had spotted with his naked eye.

"Let me see," John replied, taking the binoculars from Tony as the crew quieted down and stared at the distant speck leaving a long thin trail of smoke across the cloudless horizon.

"It's a hell of a long way off. Just keep an eye on her and see which way she is headed," John said, putting down the glasses and returning to his lunch.

"Watch-end duties, starboard watch. Check the sheets and halyards to make sure there's no chaffing. Tony are you going to log us out?" Doc asked.

"Indeed I shall, Doctor," Tony replied, glancing to the horizon at the ship that was a little closer now. "Winds out of the southwest, at ten to twelve knots, I say."

"It's nap time, guys," Doc Pearson remarked, double checking the time. The port watch took over with Peter at the helm. "We're steering 172 degrees, Peter."

"With this wind, John, let's make a starboard tack, get up our No. 2 geona and sail her close-hauled for a while," suggested the mate.

"She's doing fine now. Let's wait a little while and see where that ship will be crossing before we make a sail change, Bob," he replied, taking his binoculars and focusing on the decreasing range of the approaching ship which was bearing down on the *Encounter*'s starboard bow.

"Looks like she's a supertanker. I can only see her superstructure and it looks like she's going to cross our bow well ahead of us," John said, putting down the binoculars.

Slade glanced down at the compass, correcting his heading, then looked out at the approaching ship. "I don't know, looks like it's going to be damned close."

"Look's like it to me, too," replied Bob Ganloff as he inspected the huge oil tanker riding high out of the water, closing rapidly. "Can you make out her identity?"

"Not yet," John muttered, wrapping a frown on his broad face. "I'd better get below and contact her by radio to make sure she knows we're here," he said, handing the binoculars back to the mate.

"She's a supertanker, all right. Unladen, riding high out of the water. Must be headed back to the Middle East. I didn't realize those badboys could move that fast when they're empty."

The squelch of the radio blared through the open hatch. "This is the sailing yacht *Encounter*, heading 165°. Acknowledge, eastbound oil tanker, over," he ordered, receiving only squelch in reply.

John adjusted the squelch on the radio before trying once more. "I say again, this is the sailing yacht *Encounter*, heading 165°. Please acknowledge, eastbound tanker, over...Do you read me, over?" his voice was almost pleading as he stuck his head through the companionway hatch for another look. "Can't raise her on the radio, guys. Tony, get a fix and plot her course."

"I'm already fast at it, Skipper."

"I think she's Iranian." Bob took the binoculars, studying the Arabic lettering on the tanker's bow. "I sure can't speak the language, and it's apparent they don't speak English either, or just don't give a good goddamn. I know damn well they see us."

"HEY! WE HAVE THE RIGHT OF WAY. DON'T YOU KNOW THE RULES OF THE ROAD?" Peter Slade yelled, his face red with anger as the other sailors gathered on deck and began shouting too.

"Skipper, I say, come below and look at the bloody crossing angles!" came the navigator's anxious voice from below.

"Should we tack to port, John?" Ganloff's tense voice asked, peering through the binoculars at the bow of the huge ship bearing directly down on the *Encounter* a mile and a half ahead.

"Hold what you got for right now. Let me check her course."

Slade took the binoculars back. "I don't see anyone on the bridge. They very well could be on automatic pilot."

"Jesus, Tony, are your calculations correct?" John asked, shocked at the tanker's collision course with the *Encounter*.

"Bloody to hell believe it, they are, I say."

"Goddamn it! Give me the radio. Let me try one more time to raise her on the radio. 'Eastbound tanker, you are on a collision course. I say again, on a collision course with the sailing yacht, *Encounter*, off your port bow. Do you acknowledge? Over'."

"HEY, JOHN! GODDAMN IT, GET TOPSIDE, MAN! THIS DAMN TANKER'S GETTING TOO CLOSE FOR COMFORT!" Bob yelled down to the nav station, sending the skipper scurrying up the ladder.

"Damn, I hate to tack to port. Every second counts and it could be costly at the end of the race," John muttered.

"John, YOU have no damn choice, mate. The bloody bastard's going to run us down if we don't tack, and NOW!" Tony yelled from the nav station. "Besides, if the bloke saw us now that ship's of such tonnage that it would not respond in time to alter it's course... I mean to say it is rubbish..."

"You're right, it couldn't respond..."

"The bastard's just being an ass, John, because we're

Americans," Slade interrupted, being able to see the rivets on the plates on the bow of the huge ship now. Higher than the *Encounter*'s mast hung two massive anchors, their rusting chains leeching out red rust that ran down the black hull like blood from the nose of a great sea monster.

"Will you guys make up your goddamn minds before we get killed? What the hell do we do if she cuts off our wind?" Bob said in an adamant but calm voice.

John Moffett looked over at the tanker, thinking for the first time that he had gravely erred. He read fear on his crew's faces as he took the helm from Peter. "Prepare to come about, hard port....Coming about," he ordered. The wind suddenly died, cut dead by the massive high-riding hull of the oncoming ship. The boat's sails luffed, hanging lifeless to the jingle of halyards in the rigging as she stalled and continued slowly into harm's way.

The tanker shadowed over them. "Holy shit! Start the engine!" Bob Ganloff ordered in a calm, precise but commanding voice, as he reached for the ignition switch on the cockpit instrument panel. "No, Bob!" John shouted without thinking, grabbing his hand. "It's against the rules!" It was the Fair Sailing Fundamental Rule C that flashed instantly through his mind, that would have to be entered in the logbook for running the engine, accessing hours to the boat's corrected time for the race in lieu of disqualification.

"Fuck the rules, John!" Ganloff said flatly, switching on the ignition as the low, lovely throb of the Perkins diesel erupted underneath them.

"I've got it!" John snapped, now realizing his stupid blunder, glancing up at the intimidating bow of the ship bearing down at two thousand yards and closing fast. He shoved the drive lever forward to engage the propeller. Nothing. Harder this time as the muscles bulged on his arm and he shouted out of anger and fear, "GODDAMN IT! IT'S STUCK!"

Blood vessels in his neck protruded as he strained to unlock the shift lever with brute force. The crew crowded around the cockpit, watching in terror. "Careful, John, don't break it off!" Bob calmly said, grabbing a hammer and a can of WD-40 lubricating oil out of the tool chest which was stowed under the cockpit cushions.

"Hurry! Get everyone on deck and start breaking out the life raft. Get your life jackets on, guys, goddamn it!" John ordered, having regained his composure as he watched Bob spray the base of the gear lever with the lubricant.

'What the hell do I do with O'Grady's half million?' The thought flashed through Peter's mind as he watched Bob pound the gear lever with his hammer. Peter grabbed the ARGOS transponder from its bracket to transmit an SOS signal and position by satellite to Maryland to be relayed to the race committee in Newport. 'To hell with the money,' he thought as he pulled on his life vest. Seconds seemed like hours as the churning of the tanker's screws were throbbing thunder. Her massive bow pushed the ocean with the roar of Niagara Falls.

Kawwack, kawwack, kawwack, the sound of the hammer echoed through the boat. The crew hastily inflated the life raft. "Should I send a distress signal????" Slade shouted, glancing up at the oncoming ship.

CLUNK. The *Encounter* shuddered as the propeller engaged and then throbbed under full power as John Moffett hit full throttle and full port rudder. "Standby, Peter, I think by God we're going to make it clear."

"GO BABY, GO!" Peter shouted in near panic as the *Encounter* slowly began to get underway. The bow of the supertanker, pushing a huge white foaming sea, passed within a hundred feet as the crew braced for the tremendous wake that lifted the *Encounter* violently upward when it collided from astern. The crew's faces, wiped clear of terror now, broke into broad smiles then hysterical laughter at their near brush with death. They braced for the next huge wake that followed from the tanker's stern passing with a deafening thunder from the propellers.

John Moffett, realizing how foolish he had been to threaten his yacht and crew for the dumb Bermuda Trophy, cut the engine in disgust, allowing the boat to drift as the sails filled again with the wind.

"Gentlemen, I apologize for putting you in harm's way. In doing so I have violated the most fundamental of yacht racing rules, Fair Sailing, by engaging the engine while underway and competing by the help of the engine. I will have to enter it in the logbook and the Racing Committee will more than likely disqualify us. Damn well penalize us for sure..."

"Bullshit, Skipper, that situation was not your fault!" Slade interrupted, as the crew just stood, stupefied, watching the stern of the tanker as it grew smaller. "That Iranian almost ran us down, the bastard! Not your fault at all."

"Thanks, Pete, but still I must take responsibility for what just happened. We have to log it. The Race Committee has to know we engaged the engine for whatever reason."

"Did any of you guys hear an engine?" Slade asked, standing now by his skipper's side. "I didn't hear any damn engine. Did any of you guys?"

Thinking he was joking, they laughed lightly. Slade's eyes stared them down and they all began to shake their heads, saying, "Hell no..heard no engine...naw, no engine..." They muttered amongst themselves, looking up at Peter Slade for an answer.

"Pete's right, John, who the hell will ever know if we keep our mouths shut? That goddamn Iranian almost killed us!" Bob Ganloff said, standing next to the captain and Pete. The crew's eyes fixed on the man they knew had saved them from a certain death.

Moffett looked up with his sad droopy eyes at his crew. He remembered that he had vindicated each and every one of them in a court of law for various crimes. Without him they would all more than likely have gone to prison. He knew they were for the most part good men, and had only made a mistake in judgment, much as he had done just now. Down deep in his guts he knew they were all guilty as hell, so why not let them lie for him now?

"Gentlemen," the mate began in a forceful voice, "as foreman of the jury then I want the crew of the *Encounter* to swear an oath of silence not to ever reveal what just happened. Will you swear on your mother's grave never to mention it again?

"Do you swear, Tony Stevenson..."

"I swear on my mother's grave never to mention this again," Tony replied, raising his right hand as did each and every one of the crew, including the captain, who was now feeling lousy as hell about it. John Moffett knew that Ganloff had saved them, perhaps saved the race, by having all the crew lie. The lawyer in him knew his clients and knew that he could trust them to keep their word... all except, perhaps, one man.

# Chapter X

Providence, Rhode Island
June 18, 1990

Jack Spencer watched from his twelfth floor office. The red Bentley stopped below and the old white-haired Englishman stepped out and opened the back door. It was her, the long lost love of his childhood, and for the likes of him he could not figure out why she had made the appointment. He watched as she easily and gracefully got out of the car as though she was doing the sidewalk a great favor by stepping on it.

The old man shut the door and tipped his hat as the Bentley drove off. The woman, dressed in a black, chic-streamlined suit hemmed above the knee, disappeared into the office building. Her high heels echoed off the marble floors as she approached the elevator and stepped in just as the door closed. Seconds later the elevator stopped on the twelfth floor and opened into a reception room of the prestigious law firm of Moffett, Spencer and Grace.

Charlotte Slade stepped out of the elevator into the formal reception area, bathed in soft light, and was greeted by the receptionist.

"I have a nine o'clock appointment to see Mr. Spencer," she said in a cold voice that felt a little shaky inside as it echoed back to her. She was thinking, not about her decision to be there, but whether she had selected the right lawyer.

Jack Spencer's office made a spectacular presentation with a panoramic view of the Seekonk River and the surrounding city of Providence from the two glass walls that formed his corner office. The floor was covered by an antique Persian rug. The furniture consisted of rare antiques, a mixture of French and English, blending into rich mahogany walls from which hung the works of several renowned nineteenth-century New England artists. Jack Spencer arose from behind a mammoth wooden desk and walked over and gave Charlotte a light kiss on the cheek while his secretary stood in the door awaiting further instructions.

"Good morning, Charlotte. You look splendid. Would you care for coffee?" he asked, as he ushered her toward the two Queen Anne wing-backed chairs where he joined her.

"Please, darling. Cream and sugar," she replied as Jack nodded to his secretary, who closed the door.

"Have you heard any news from the *Encounter*?"

"No. I have heard nothing, Jack," she replied flatly.

Jack Spencer was surprised. Being a keen lawyer, he quickly picked up on the bitterness in her voice. "What can I help you with this morning, Charlotte, that cannot wait for John's return? I'm not that familiar with your affairs, but you sounded urgent on the phone, and if it is necessary we can always contact John by phone in Bermuda for counsel."

"No, don't you dare bother John, darling. What I need is rather simple. As chairwoman and majority stockholder, I want to call a meeting of the Board of Directors of the Stone Bridge Corporation for the purpose of firing my husband, Peter Slade, as President and Chief Executive Officer. The corporation's year-end is June 30th, and I want to start the next fiscal year without Peter Slade as a business partner."

'What?' Jack Spencer thought, reading his client's face closely to see if there was any hint of her joking. The woman was angry and upset. He knew she was dead serious, and he was ready to listen.

His secretary reentered, setting the silver coffee tray on the coffee table. "Anne, get me the Stone Bridge Corporation's file, please," he directed.

As Jack Spencer stood up to pour the coffee, Charlotte admired the incredible shine of his English handmade Church shoes. A tall, slender man in his late forties with dark hair graying at the temples, he was impeccably dressed in a tailored gray suit, accented with a rich blue and red striped tie. His Harvard class ring and a Piaget wristwatch with leather band was the only jewelry he wore, she noticed as he handed her coffee.

"Just set the file on the conference table, Anne, and hold my calls," he instructed his secretary upon her reentering.

Jack took his cup of coffee and sat at the round conference table in the corner, joined by his client. He opened up the Stone Bridge file and pulled out the Articles of Incorporation dated July 1, 1986 and began to read. His eyes quickly came to Article VI of the document, INCORPORATORS: Charlotte Slade, 51 Shares of Class A Common Stock; Peter Slade, 48 Shares of Class A Common Stock; John Moffett, 1 Share of Class A Common Stock.

He made a note on a yellow legal pad and then turned to the

Corporate By-Laws and read aloud to his client: "Article III. Section 4. Special Meetings. Special meeting of the Board of Directors may be called at the request of the chairperson, president, or any two directors. Section 5. States the place of the meeting. Section 6. Notice. Notice of any special meeting shall be given at least ten days previously thereto by written notice delivered personally or mailed to each director at his business address, or by electronic device. If mailed..."

"Very well, Jack," Charlotte interrupted, "let's fax Peter and John in Bermuda then."

"It will have to be held on Friday the 29th of June to give proper notice. Where do you wish to hold it?"

"Send notices that we will hold it at ten o'clock on the morning of Friday, June 29th, at the Stone Bridge Inn, for the purpose of replacing Peter Slade as President and Chief Executive Officer of the Stone Bridge Corporation."

"John and Peter, I'm afraid, will not be back by then, Charlotte. You will need to..."

"Well, that will be fine with me."

"Charlotte, please, it's not that easy. If they're not present at the meeting, then you will not have a quorum, so no business can be legally conducted by your board."

"I have controlling interest," Charlotte barked, leaning forward with her arms resting on the table.

Jack, head of the firm's domestic practice, thought for a second. "Yes, that will work. The by-laws of the corporation state that a majority of the shares of common stock must be present. You are the majority, owning 51%, Charlotte..."

"You damn well better believe I am. I bought and renovated the goddamn place with my money."

"Yes, of course you did. We will have to send a fax. John's secretary has the address in Bermuda where he is staying. What about your husband?"

"Peter is at the Glencoe Hotel and here is the address," she replied, handing the attorney a piece of paper. "Please see to it then, Jack."

"Charlotte, I'm not aware of what all is going on between you and Peter, but have you given full consideration to the impact of all of this? Perhaps we should wait and let John meet with you first to try and..."

"Yes, I have, Jack. So, please, just do as I have requested."

Jack Spencer leaned back and put his hands behind his head. He looked at the woman he had known since early childhood, having been raised with her in the same elite Newport social circles. Those dreadful concerts on hot lazy summer afternoons at the Newport Casino before it became the International Tennis Hall of Fame. Charlotte, a pretty little girl with red rosy checks, always wearing white gloves, it seemed, came with her mother and grandparents, joining Jack's parents who dragged him along to the Boston Symphony or New York Philharmonic concerts. Oh, what a bore for a boy. Then suddenly one day, when she was about thirteen, he had noticed that Charlotte's breasts were developing nicely and he had begun to notice her more closely, as young men do.

The attorney sat in his office, remembering that hot summer night when Elvis was the king. He had run into Charlotte at the Newport Jazz Festival and asked her for a date the next night, only to be turned down. Charlotte's rejection had never left him.

Now he looked at the woman, still very attractive but fading, as she reached for an ashtray with a trembling hand. She lit a cigarette and, even though their business was over, Jack had a feeling she wanted to talk for a while longer. He started to say something, but she beat him to it.

"Why, Jack, has a successful, handsome lawyer like yourself never married?" she asked, her beautiful blue eyes penetrating through the cigarette smoke she exhaled.

'Damn, what a question,' Jack thought, jerking in his chair at its personal nature, even though he shouldn't have been surprised. After all, they had known each other all their lives. "I never got over your rejection for a Saturday date at the beach thirty years ago," he laughed. "Do you remember?"

"Ask me again in a few months, you might just get a different answer, if you would like," Charlotte smiled, putting out the cigarette and gathering up her purse. She walked to the door, displaying a profane movement in her hips, which along with her parting words, left the lawyer standing at the table, stunned.

Jack Spencer immediately canceled his afternoon golf game and dictated the notice of the Stone Bridge Corporation's shareholder meeting to his secretary, instructing her to fax the notices to Bermuda. Then he asked to see the estate file of Dr. and Mrs. Harriman Harris from the firm's archives along with that of Mrs. Sally Hilderbrand, Charlotte's mother.

It took several hours to review both estate tax returns and wills of the Harrises and Charlotte's mother, but the attorney took copious notes on a yellow legal pad. 'Jesus Christ, look at all of this,' Jack Spencer thought when he was finished. 'I had no earthly idea how much wealth these people have!' Leaving a living will for Mrs. Harris when Dr. Harris died had created a taxable estate of nearly fifty million when she passed away. Taking into consideration the vast fortune that had already been put into a generation-skipping trust for Charlotte since childhood, this was a real fine job of estate planning. He reviewed his notes of the deductions for an endowment to the Columbia Medical School for three million, the American Cancer Society, two million, various other charitable contributions for two million more.... His eyes scanned further down his notes. My God" he exclaimed out loud. "Charlotte inherited Beach Mont from her mother's estate, after her death in 1988, in addition to her trust fund, which must be in the millions and millions of dollars by now!"

Charlotte's phone rang later that same afternoon at Beach Mont. "It is a Mr. Jack Spencer calling, Madame," Thomas Terrell's English accent came over the intercom after taking the call.

"Hello, Charlotte. I had the notice of the shareholders' meeting faxed to Bermuda at two-thirty this afternoon. Would you like for me to drop your copy in the mail?" Jack asked, detecting a slight slur in her voice when she answered, even though it was only four in the afternoon.

"No, don't Jack. Would you mind dropping my copy off on your way into Newport this evening, darling, if it's convenient? Or do lawyers make house calls these days?" she giggled.

Jack jumped at the chance. "Why... why sure, Charlotte, we pride ourselves on client service! Around six then?"

"That will be fine. Thank you, Jack."

Charlotte was waiting outside for Jack Spencer by the massive door of the east entrance to Beach Mont. It was an overcast afternoon and the seagulls flew close to the shore, feeding as she looked out at the fog rolling in from the ocean. She wore a white linen tailored wrap dress, held in place by one gold button and curved above the knee hem along with red high heels. Tommy Terrell had conveniently been given permission to retire early to the carriage house and the maid had gone home as well. It was exactly six p.m. when Jack's black Jag rolled through the gates of the mansion and came to a stop under the entrance wing.

Jack Spencer's heart missed a beat when he got out and saw Charlotte standing at the top of the stairs holding a martini. Her head was thrown back, catching the southeasterly breeze in her blond hair, and there was a light rain that was beginning to fall. Her dark, oiled tan contrasted nicely against the white dress as he followed her into the large library on the back side of the mansion to classical music playing in the background. "What would you like, Jack?" she asked in her rich sinuous voice, her breath tainted by the smell of gin.

Charlotte poured the vodka strong based on the sounds of the bottle. She turned and handed him his vodka and tonic with a large wedge of lime. "Have a seat and make yourself comfortable. Here, let me help you with your jacket."

Jack fumbled in his breast pocket, pulling out an envelope containing the notice of the stockholders' meeting which he handed to her as he pulled off his jacket. Charlotte laid it face down on the table, her nimble fingers quickly reaching up and unloosening his tie, much to his surprise.

"God, how do you guys wear these things all day?"

"Like everything else, you just get used to it," he smiled, taking a sip of his drink, tasting the tartness of the tonic and inhaling the smell of lime. He sat down on the couch.

"Jack, who is the best damn divorce attorney in Providence besides you?"

"I wouldn't know. I've never needed one since I've never been married!" he laughed, looking at his client as she crossed her bare legs.

"Come on, Jack! I'm serious. You're a lawyer and know these things. You did a heck of a job for cousin Rosa when Flint Firestone filed for a divorce. What was it she got? Four million?"

Jack chuckled, touching her lightly on the arm. "You know I can't comment on that."

"Who is the best in your opinion?" she asked again, taking another drink of her martini and kicking off her red high heels.

Jack looked back at Charlotte. She was now sitting with her legs under her on the couch. He felt the beginning of an erection.

Charlotte continued as she straightened her legs, showing more of her thigh as Jack's embarrassment grew larger. "I've heard that Judy Ketchum is a damn good divorce lawyer," came her words, slightly slurred. "Know anything about her?"

Jack took a long drink of his vodka and tonic. He gawked, watching Charlotte bend over to get a rum cheese and cracker, exposing her breast to the nipples. "Jesus, Char...Charlotte... I have a conflict in all of this and don't want to make any recommendation. Look, your cousin is my law partner. He's Peter's best friend..., and, and, Peter's a client of the firm and has been for a number of years. You both are clients and you and Peter are married. We have known each other since we were kids. Our parents were the very best of friends. So, please, if you are considering divorcing Peter, just leave me out of it completely."

Charlotte swirled the olive in her Bombay martini with her finger, then sucked it seductively. "Look," she said angrily, "I was born in this place, married Robert Cocknell because it was the social thing according to my mother and grandmother. He was a bore and a drunk and when I finally had it up to here, then along came the charming Mr. Peter Slade out of the clear blue. Yes, Peter Slade, close friend of John's, football player, war hero, successful

Wall Street investment banker, was a charmer all right. A master bullshitter and mutilator, that's what he was. He caught me when I was very vulnerable, divorcing Robert, and I must say he swept me off my feet, or should I say out of my panties..."

Jack choked, turning redder as he took another drink of his vodka and tonic and then smiled, feeling silly.

"I don't know where it all began to unravel, but once you marry someone you find out one hell of a lot about them in short order. He's forgotten about me and our marriage and fallen in love with that goddamned Stone Bridge Inn and I suspect he's screwing that little bitch, Melissa Jenkins, whom he hired without board approval. Peter's a very vain man and has no breeding. He's the son of a Baltimore waterfront saloon keeper and he's a selfish son-of-a-bitch. Those goddamned insider trading charges I am sure were true, even though he never confided in me."

"So you think Peter was guilty?"

"I don't really know," she retracted. "If he was, I never saw any of the money."

"I see," said the lawyer, drinking.

"I'm bored with life, Jackie, or do you still let me call you that?"

"Sure, fine."

"I'm bored shitless with Peter Slade, just sitting here alone day in and day out with no one to share my life with. I'm not living! It's bygod time for a change. Would you..."

"Charlotte, please! I really need to be going," Jack Spencer interrupted, feeling very uneasy with the conversation.

Charlotte turned quickly, rising up on her knees before him on the large leather couch, skillfully unbuttoning her one goldtone button at the waist and letting the wrap dress fall off her shoulders and onto the couch. Her tits swung lightly, their round dark nipples erect, leaving her only in white lace-front bikini panties. She smiled seductively. "Now what is your hurry, Jackie? You don't have to get home to your wife and kids for supper, so come on, Jack, just sit back and relax for a while. I remember the way you used to gawk at me back in the days of the Newport Jazz Festival."

Jack Spencer was left speechless as his mouth fell open in disbelief. 'God, I'm dreaming,' he thought. She reached down and began massaging his cock, snuggling up against him, her warm flesh feeling wonderful against his arm. She began nibbling on his neck with the sensuous fragrance of her perfume driving him insane. "Charlotte! God, Charlotte, what are you doing? God, what are..."

Charlotte's lips were moist and hot. He tasted gin in her mouth. Their tongues, lashed together, darted inside their mouths. She ever so gently pushed him back on the cool leather; her hands groped his crotch, skillfully unzipped his pants.

"Jesus Christ," he panted, pushing her back, taking off his shirt and kicking down his trousers.

She reached down and untied his shoes to free his trousers. Spencer was speechless, glaring at the beautiful naked body that he had dreamed of since he was a boy. She looked down at his erection. "Oh, what have we here?" she laughed, stroking it lightly as it turned into blue steel, ready for action. Their breaths were hot and heavy. His trembling hands eased down her warm smooth naked body as he tenderly felt his way between her spread legs and begin to slowly caress her full bush through her panties. She arched her back upwards as he skillfully slid them off. His heart pounded harder with each breath as he slid inside her. She was screaming, "Oh, darling! That's it, goddamn you Jackie. Faster, now! Harder! Fuck me harder!"

Jack gave it one last thrust culminating in a tremendous explosion. His face reddened as the veins on his neck nearly ruptured. "Now!" he cried, shuddering, collapsing on top of her, gasping for breath. 'God what have I gotten myself into? John's cousin; Peter's wife. Oh God, I'm in love with this woman.'

Charlotte giggled, reading his mind, rubbing the hair on his chest. "So, Counselor, that's what you've been after for all these years. How was that pussy? Was it as good or better than you thought it would be?" she teased, grabbing his withering cock.

Jack blushed wildly. "Am I dreaming?" he asked, still massaging her breast with the glee of a teenager as her head slid downward.

An hour later, after dressing, he asked, "Can I get you another martini?" He walked around admiring the splendor of the great hall of the mansion, remembering her trust fund and thinking, 'just maybe, at forty-seven, I've found the woman I want to settle down with at this address.'

# Chapter XI

## Intercontinental Hotel, New York
### November 14, 1984

P aul Ferris awoke with an apprehensive feeling about his ten o'clock meeting with the vice-chairman of the International Monetary Fund. He felt guilty, hungover, and wished he had gotten to bed earlier. He slipped on his robe and answered his door at the Intercontinental Hotel on East 48th Street. The waiter placed his breakfast tray and morning paper on the coffee table, making small talk while Paul signed the room service check and then wished him a good day.

Glancing at the paper without his glasses, his face turned ashen gray at the *New York Post* headlines: 'BLUE-BLOODED MADAM'S LAWYERS TO BARE BLACK BOOK'.

"Oh my God," he whispered, his hand trembling, rattling the cup in its saucer as he poured. 'I have got to get the bloody hell out of here and back to Bermuda before this goes any further,' he thought, fumbling around on the dresser, searching for his glasses.

"Oh, my God, I'm not believing it," he mumbled, reading the article carefully, getting sicker as he read until suddenly he rushed to the toilet and threw up.

Rinsing his face with cold water, Paul Ferris gargled, spat in the sink then dried his face with a fresh towel. He looked in the mirror at his bloodshot eyes, glowing like two cherries atop blobs of dough rising in Cynthia's blackened cookie pan, staring pathetically back at him. 'God, I look like I was in the ring at Madison Square Garden last night,' he thought, the taste of stale Scotch and vomit still foul in his mouth. He ran his thin fingers through his matted graying hair, feeling self-pity as he regarded the face of a man looking fifty who had not yet turned forty. Now that he was awake he was thinking more clearly. 'If this gets back to Bermuda you're ruined, you goddamned whoremonger idiot, and if it does I'll kill myself.'

Paul Ferris reluctantly switched on the television, growing terrified at ABC's eight o'clock morning report showing footage of a beautiful young woman in handcuffs being placed in the back of a black sedan, trying unsuccessfully to hide her face from the camera.

"A new development this morning in the Madam Blue Blood international prostitution case. A roster of wealthy and influential clients may possibly be made public today, ABC News has learned. The New York socialite, Carolina Barrington, arraigned yesterday in an alleged call girl ring in upper Manhattan, will reveal the list according to Miss Barrington's lawyers. The 'black book' listing contains the names of prominent New York business leaders and public officials, along with the names of numerous foreign business clients, we have been told.

'The lawyers for Carolina Barrington, the wealthy young

socialite arrested by the FBI Monday, stated that unless the prosecution dropped the case against Miss Barrington they would make the list public, revealing the names and sexual preferences of over three hundred clients. Now, stayed tuned. We will be right back after this message...."

Paul Ferris ran to the shower, stopping abruptly. 'I've got to get the bloody hell out of New York before my name comes out,' he thought. 'Oh, my God, what about my ten o'clock appointment with the vice-chairman? The hell with him, I've got to catch the next flight.' He grabbed the phone and dialed Delta Airlines.

"Hello, my name's Paul Ferris and I have an emergency and would like to change my reservation from Friday's ten o'clock flight to Bermuda to your next available flight this morning, please."

"I'm sorry, Mr. Ferris, our next flight is at ten o'clock this morning, but I'm afraid we're sold out in first class."

Paul glanced down at five after eight on his watch. 'I haven't got much time,' he was thinking. "What about coach then?"

"Yes sir. We have a seat in coach if you would like or we have first class available at four this afternoon."

"No! Please, give me a coach seat on this morning's flight!" he pleaded.

An hour and a half later the frail little man was running like a madman through John F. Kennedy International airport, trying to catch his plane.

'Thank God, I made it!' His heart was pounding when he finally settled down after having a difficult time finding a place for his carry-on luggage in the overhead. It was ten o'clock. He should be at his meeting. What excuses would he give his board of directors for canceling with the vice chairman of the International Monetary

Fund? He would have to come up with something, being sick maybe. He sure felt sick as hell now, as the plane's wheels lifted off the ground. He gave a momentary sigh of relief. For the first time in his life the managing director of the Bank of Bermuda Limited felt like a fleeing fugitive as he sat in his cramped seat on Delta Flight 2365, homeward bound. His hands were shaking as he unfolded the *New York Times*, cringing at the headlines: 'JUDGE GETS A LOOK AT MADAM BLUE BLOOD'S BLACK BOOK.' He began to read. 'The FBI spokesman in charge of the investigation, Special Agent Oden Terry of the Manhattan office of the Federal Bureau of Investigation, revealed that Miss Barrington has violated federal laws prohibiting the interstate transport of women for prostitution and the corruption of minors as prostitutes ....'

'The FBI! Oh my God, not the bloody FBI doing the investigation!' Ferris slumped down in his seat, hiding, hearing his wife, Cynthia, screaming at him when he got home, 'Paul Ferris, how could you have done this appalling deed to me and your girls??'

'Yes, Paul Ferris, you're finished,' he thought, as the service cart came rolling down the aisle.

"What would you like, sir? Coffee or tea?" asked the stewardess with a smile, handing him a paper napkin and a pack of peanuts.

"Chivas Scotch, on ice," he managed to stammer, struggling for the money clip in his pocket. The fat American tourist seated next to him laughed and made some wisecrack remark that it was five o'clock somewhere.

On an empty stomach, the Scotch rushed to Paul Ferris's head and he liked that feeling, the light-headed feeling that calmed his nerves as he drank to get a grip on himself. He drank out of fear that his reputation was ruined. His name being associated with the New York whores was the nightmare that would be awaiting him in the headlines of the *Bermuda Herald Tribune* when he stepped off the plane: 'BANK OF BERMUDA LIMITED MANAGING DIREC-TOR MAKES MADAM BLUE BLOOD'S INTERNATIONAL LIST'.

The thought of it all left a hollow feeling inside. The Scotch was working fine. He drank, reminding himself, 'damn it, Paul, the list hasn't been released yet, so don't panic, man.' It was a comforting thought. 'For Christ sake, Paul, get control of yourself.' He reached up and pulled the flight attendant's button. Catching the stewardess's eye he held up his empty miniature, signaling for two more with his fingers. The fat American chuckled, "After five somewhere in this world."

Well out over the Atlantic, the Boeing 737 suddenly hit rough air. The pilot made the usual 'stay buckled-up and seated' announcement. The turbulence sent Cynthia's angry cries screaming back at him again now. "Paul! how could you have done this to us?" he kept hearing over and over and over in his head.

The plane jolted sharply, hitting another air pocket, and sending Paul Ferris back to the beginning of his secret life in New York. His guilt concerning his unfaithfulness to Cynthia had been terrible when he first started, but had dissipated as time passed without his getting caught. His appetite for sexual encounters with the Madam's beautiful young girls had grown into an obsession, his thoughts of unfaithfulness long ago vanished.

He took a sip of Scotch. The peat-smoked taste of reinforcing courage went down smoothly as he poured his third miniature into the plastic cup. He suddenly felt anger at his own stupidity and the goddamn self-righteous, sanctimonious Americans for even considering making public the fact that he had gotten an occasional strange piece of ass. What a fucked up sense of values the Americans have anyway.

'Damn Siegfried Dassler, too, for introducing me to Carolina Barrington in the first place,' he thought.

The third Scotch was working nicely, calming his failed nerves, bringing back his first international meeting of the World Bank's Conference on Third World Debt in New York in the fall of 1981. Ronald Reagan had just been elected president, inheriting an international monetary crisis from the Carter Administration whose human rights policy had flooded third world countries with easy credit, leaving them billions of dollars in debt. The default of these loans by the developing countries had been the agenda for the World Monetary Fund's crisis. Brazil and other South American countries faced default, threatening a collapse of the international monetary system. He was a senior vice president of the oldest and most prestigious bank on the island. The bank had sent him to represent them at the New York accord.

'Damn Herr Siegfried Dassler,' he thought again, his anger returning to the man whose family owned the largest private bank in West Germany. The Dassler name was associated throughout the world with international banking and financial power. He could clearly see the German president of the Dassler Deutsche Bank, walking over and introducing himself at the morning coffee break. "*Guten tag*, Herr Ferris. *Wie geht es ihnen*?" began the tall stately German with graying temples, in his heavy guttural accent.

"*Guten tag*," Paul replied, smiling.

"*Nehmen SIE, bitte, meine KARTE*," the German had said, handing Paul his business card.

"I'm very sorry, Herr Dassler, I do not speak Deutsche."

"*Das ist schade*. I would be verry pleazzed for you to be my guestt for dinner thiss evening if you have no plans, Herr Ferris from Bermuda."

"Why, why certainly, Herr Dassler, I'd be honored."

"*Danke schon*, Herr Ferris. Verry welll dhen, I will meet you at de River Cafe in Brooklyn Heights at eight o'clock, yes?" he had said sternly.

"Eight o'clock. Very well then."

"*Auf wiedersehen.*"

"*Auf wiedersehen*," Paul had replied, rushing to the nearest pay phone and telephoning Cynthia with the news, thinking, 'why in this world would Herr Dassler, a wealthy and powerful world financial leader, be inviting a nobody of a vice president Bermuda bank executive to dinner?'

"Hello, Cynthia, how are the girls? ... Guess what! I've been invited to dinner tonight with Herr Dassler, ...Yes, the German Banker.... I'm not sure, but it should be very interesting...."

"Oh, Paul. How very exciting. I'm sure he wants to interview you for a position with his bank, or something," Cynthia's eager voice had responded. "But, do we really want to leave Bermuda, Paul?"

Paul Ferris remembered looking out of the cab window at lower Manhattan that night as they had crossed the Brooklyn Bridge, arriving at the River Cafe an hour early and being seated at the bar. He remembered ordering a Scotch on the rocks as a cold breeze blew off the East River through the revolving door. From the sweeping semicircular bar, he had absorbed the subdued atmosphere and gentle murmur of the wavelets lapping against the foundations of the restaurant. He had gazed at the beauty of the Brooklyn Bridge swooping across to lower Manhattan which was covered with a light mist of rain and he was caught up in the mystique of it all.

He remembered staring at the bridge's silhouette against the Manhattan skyline when Herr Dassler's heavy German accent sounded from behind, "*Guten abend*, Herr Paul Ferris, I would like to introduce you..."

Dassler's voice had vanished into thin air as Paul stood dumbfounded, fully engrossed in the beauty and charm of Herr Dassler's guest, Carolina Barrington. The sophisticated young New Yorker, whose family could be traced to the arrival of the Mayflower, had held Paul spellbound with her knowledge of world affairs, banking and international business throughout dinner. She had skillfully massaged Paul's ego with compliments concerning his accomplishments with the Bank of Bermuda Limited and being their representative at such an important international banking conference. Herr Dassler had sat back and said little, speaking to the woman occasionally in German and receiving in return her undivided attention and a quick answer in German, always followed by laughter. 'Perhaps they are making fun of me,' Paul Ferris had thought at the time.

The stately German, his gray hair shining in the candlelight, kept ordering bottles of Schloss Vollrads QmP '71 Mosel, and as the evening progressed to Fonseca '48 at midnight, the finest ruby Bin '27 vintage port. It had been an evening of unparalleled finery as Paul said, "*Gute Nacht and auf wiedersehen*," to his host and bid good night to the lady before catching a cab uptown to the Intercontinental Hotel.

The next morning, Paul had just stepped out of the shower and was reading the morning *New York Post* when his telephone rang. He had been startled to hear the electrifying voice of Carolina

Barrington. "Paul, dear, I hate to disturb you at such an early hour, but I have a young friend from Albany, a lovely young woman named Melissa Jenkins, from an affluent family, who is pursuing a modeling career. I had planned on taking her to dinner tonight but I have a conflict. I wonder if it would be too much to ask if you could have dinner with her for me? Siegfried has asked that I join him for dinner with the German ambassador and the secretary of state, or I would not impose on you, and she is such a lovely girl. I thought you might enjoy her company."

Paul was shocked but flattered at the request. "Well I... I guess so..." he had stammered, having already surmised that Carolina was Dassler's mistress. By accepting her request, he could become part of Herr Dassler's inner circle, and befriending Carolina Barrington could certainly be a feather in his hat and help his banking connections.

"Yes, I would be delighted to, Carolina."

"Thank you, Paul," Carolina had replied. "What is your room number?... Her name is Melissa Jenkins, and thanks for being a sweetheart and helping me out."

Paul Ferris had nicked himself twice shaving. He nervously got dressed for his blind date with Carolina's friend and was feeling guilty. He had his suit pressed and put on a fresh shirt and plenty of aftershave. He was practicing introducing himself in the mirror when at precisely seven-thirty his phone rang. "Good evening, Mr. Ferris. This is Melissa Jenkins, Carolina's friend. I do hope it is still convenient to have dinner tonight." Her voice had been so sweet and innocent that Paul had felt at ease for the first time.

"Yes. Yes, Melissa, it is my pleasure. Where are you now?"

"I'm downstairs, calling from the house phone. Shall I meet you in the bar?"

"Yes, of course, excellent idea, that would be fine. Should have thought of it myself," he had chuckled. "How will I recognize you?"

"Well, Mr. Ferris, I hope it won't be too difficult. I'm a redhead wearing a blue dress," came a seductive giggle.

Sweat had been forming in the palms of his hands as he got off the elevator and walked across the Intercontinental lobby. Passing the tropical bird cage in the center, he had flinched at the sudden shrill cry of a cockatiel as he passed, his guilty conscience reminding him of Cynthia and the girls back home. 'Why the hell am I doing this?' he had asked himself as he walked into the bar and spotted Melissa Jenkins. His question had answered itself.

'Jesus Christ!' he had smiled. The pale-skinned beauty, appearing to be twenty-one, was just sixteen. She had glided towards him, wearing a low-cut dress that exposed electrifying cleavage of her firm, young, ample breasts. She had grasped his hand tightly, leading him to a discreet booth in the corner. She had slid in, smiling, her hazel green eyes directing him beside her. He caught the fragrance of her alluring perfume. The waiter, dressed in a black tux, took their order, while Melissa's soft hand rested on Paul Ferris's thigh, bringing forth an instant erection that led them to spend the rest of the evening in his hotel room.

On his return flight to Bermuda, the smug young banker had it all figured out. He had been right. Carolina Barrington was Dassler's mistress and she had used him to introduce her to new clients in return for her personal services. She had developed a distinguished list of clients: corporate executives, politicians, international businessmen, all living or visiting New York on liberal expense accounts. That list now included the name of Paul Ferris, the next managing director of the Bank of Bermuda Limited, and like all the rest he had become addicted to the sweet pleasure of young whores and kinky sex.

The plane jolted. Paul took up the *Times*, rereading very carefully the story, especially the part about Carolina having developed a two million dollar prostitution ring requiring a staff of forty other young girls besides Melissa Jenkins. 'At a thousand dollars a night or more, no wonder she was making millions,' he thought. 'God, I must know ten or twelve of them personally.'

Then it hit him like a bolt of lightening. 'Oh my God! The bank auditors will scrutinize my expense reports after this all gets out! Why in the hell was I so stupid as to falsify my expense vouchers as entertaining New York bankers, when I was screwing the Blue-Blooded Madam's call girls? How damn stupid of me. I'll get fired, lose my pension and get indicted for embezzlement by the authorities as well!' His mind filled with terror as the stewardess gave the 'buckle-up' announcement and the plane made its final approach to the Bermuda Airport.

Paul glanced around nervously as he disembarked from the plane, passing quickly through customs before rushing to the newsstand for the the *Bermuda Herald*. In a stall in the men's room he nervously read only of Russian troops in Afghanistan, Japanese investment in the United States, Prince Andrew's involvement with a soft porno actress, much to the Queen's disapproval, etc. Nothing appeared regarding Madam Blue Blood or her 'Black Book' that would possibly list Paul Ferris's name, not even an obscure article on the back pages, as he gave a sigh of relief. 'Oh Lord, if I can only get out of this mess, I'll stay the hell out of New York forever,' he thought, going home that night to his family and a fine dinner at seven.

Back in New York it was a few minutes before six o'clock at Harry's Bar in the basement of the Woolworth Building. Oden Terry couldn't wait to tell his drinking buddy the latest on the Carolina Barrington case. He loved working prostitution cases, especially ones with whores as beautiful and sophisticated as Carolina Barrington's girls were. The S.E.C. investigator arrived a few minutes later and the bartender, Wolfgang, sent over his usual Four Roses. The thin man sat down at the table against the subway train wall and pulled out a pack of Camels.

"How you and dem whores doing, Ode?" Flynn O'Grady asked out of the side of his mouth.

"Man, Flynn, I nailed the Madam today!" the FBI agent exclaimed, excited as a schoolboy on holiday, looking around, making sure no one could hear. "We got this one young thing who started hooking for the Madam at sixteen and has agreed to testify against her. Can you believe it?"

"Naw! Sixteen, Ode, you kiddin' me? That young?"

"Yeah, beautiful young redhead named Melissa something-or-other, who's stacked like a brick shit house. Her testimony is going to put the Madam away for a long time."

In the days that followed, Paul Ferris was a nervous wreck, praying to God each day that his past wouldn't be discovered. He read an article about Madam Blue Blood that appeared in the 'People Section' of *Time Magazine*. No names were revealed, just a small story about the prostitution ring. He arose earlier than usual each morning, scrutinizing the Bermuda paper for any news about the case. Nothing happened until one day in January, 1985 Paul was reading the Sunday edition of the *New York Times* when his eyes fell on a small article that read, 'Barrington Offers Plea In

Prostitution Case'. His heart stopped as he read that one of her former prostitutes, Melissa Jenkins, had testified on behalf of the government. Evidently no names had been disclosed, thank God, and the article concluded by saying that Carolina Barrington had been placed on five years probation and required to pay over a million dollars in back taxes and fines.

With the passage of time, Paul Ferris gradually forgot about his past transgressions and the whores in New York. He felt as though he had been tested by the Almighty, and turned extremely religious in repentance of his past sins. On Sundays he became a regular lay reader of scripture at St. Peter's Church, the oldest Anglican place of worship in the western hemisphere.

Bank of Bermuda Limited, under Ferris's leadership' flourished. He avoided New York if possible by delegating business trips there to associates whenever possible. In fact he traveled hardly at all. His last trip off the island was in December 1988 to attend the Group of Ten nations central bankers conference in Basel, Switzerland as a key speaker for establishing principles to which world bankers should adhere to deter money laundering.

Being the new managing director of the bank gave him access to all the accounts. One day he noticed a confidential discretionary trust belonging to an American named Peter M. Slade that had experienced exceptional growth since it had opened in early 1980. It was new on the 'Over Ten Million Asset Report' that he reviewed each week for investment performance. 'Now this guy, Slade, has got to be getting insider tips on Wall Street! He's a rich American trying to dodge the IRS. I'll duplicate some of Mr. Slade's trades which is legal under Bermuda banking laws.' Paul Ferris was disappointed when Slade's trust account suddenly became dormant in the summer of 1985 after making him a lot of money.

Paul Ferris's professional and personal fortunes flourished. His life could not have been better until his phone rang at ten o'clock on the morning of Tuesday, June 19, 1990. It was the long forgotten, but familiar voice of Carolina Barrington on the line.

# Chapter XII

St. David's Head Light, Bermuda
June 18, 1990

All hands were hiked over the rail in the early morning light as the *Encounter* raced across the Atlantic searching for Bermuda hidden in the dark and rain. The wind was out of the northwest at twenty knots, not the usual prevailing southwesterly winds that blow at this time of year, and Moffett was thankful for such good air. The five-foot seas made the boat surf, then wallow as the bow burrowed down into the trough. Sailing was rough as the waves washed over the side, soaking the men in their foul weather gear who were trying to keep the boat on an even keel.

They were all exhausted but hung on the windward rail with their feet securely hooked into the toe straps. He knew his crew was taking a beating with each wave. John Moffett appreciated their efforts as he watched them work. He strained his ears for the feared sound of breakers crashing on the deadly coral reefs that extended ten miles out from the island.

Tony was below, hanging onto the chart table, adjusting the radio directional finder, fine tuning frequency 323 Khz for the St. David's radio beacon. The direction finder's piercing frequency came and went. "Keep steering on a heading of 185 degrees, Skipper. That is our strongest signal from St. David's," came his troubled voice up through the open companionway hatch.

"Here, take the helm a second, Bob," Moffett said, sticking his head down the hatch. "Do you think we are east of the North East Breakers buoy, Tony, or not?"

That was a tough question for the Englishman to answer, sitting there pondering over his chart and worried sick that they were off course. It was critical that they stay well north of the North East Breakers buoy and then turn south and approach St. David's Head from a heading of 226 degrees to keep from running aground. They had to be east of the northernmost reef; if not, they were destined to be shipwrecked. In this weather it was impossible to take a sighting at daybreak to be certain of their exact position. Moffett was waiting for an answer. "I say we are to the east of the North East Breakers buoy all right, Captain, but keep keen ears topside. Very keen ears, indeed, I say, for the sound of the bloody breakers."

John Moffett took the helm again and was thinking about what his navigator had just said. The way he had said it meant that he wasn't too damn sure if they were to the east or not. That worried him immensely. If they were to the west or too far south they were headed straight into the Great Breaker Ledge Flat and the certain disaster that had sent many mariners to a watery gave. He had already endangered the lives of his crew once during this race, and he damn well didn't want to do it again.

The minutes seemed like hours as the *Encounter* fought her way on a southeasterly course toward the island, her crew tense and in pain as they continued to hike over the rail. The skipper was very pleased with the exceptional speed they were making, but it was hard to concentrate on speed when he knew at any moment he could run aground.

Below, Tony checked his watch for the elapsed time since his last sighting at dusk yesterday before the weather turned foul. He plotted their position using the wind speeds and boat speed at a position of 64 degrees 85 minutes north latitude and 32 degrees 80 minutes west longitude. Twenty minutes later he made a final calculation that put them to the east of the North East Breakers buoy and, he hoped, out of harms way, but he wasn't confident he had plotted accurately. He shouted topside to the skipper, "Captain, the Kitchen Shoals buoy should be off our starboard bow anytime now."

"Men," John bellowed, "our brilliant navigator says keep a keen eye for the Kitchen Shoals buoy off our starboard bow."

John Moffett's face wore the pressure of sailing his yacht into the treacherous Bermuda waters filled with rocks and coral reefs. He knew in this weather that the only safe approach to the island would have been from the southeast, but that would have added hours to his elapsed time. 'Had he been stupid to risk the reefs,' he wondered, once again putting victory ahead of the safety of his yacht and crew? He had weighed and considered the risk when he made his initial decision to sail northward when the weather turned. Now he was having second thoughts as the real possibility of being lost and hitting a reef sank in.

Peter Slade was hanging on the rail with the rest, wearing his long underwear and sweat suit under his foul weather gear. 'This is really a lot of fucking fun,' he told himself in his miserable state as he strained his ear to the windward at the faint distant sound of a bell. The sound carried in again with a powerful gust of wind, and yes, by God, it was distinctly the right sound. From which buoy though? The Kitchen Shoals buoy marking the final approach to the finish line at Bermuda's eastern extremity or the Breakers buoy, which meant they were sailing straight into jaws of hell? He struggled for the sounds of the surf on reefs which would mean just that.

"I hear a bell, Skipper, off the starboard bow!" Slade shouted aft. All eyes peered into the thick fog while the distinct clanging grew louder.

"There it is!" shouted Tony, who was now on deck standing by the captain, with a sigh of relief at the sighting of the bobbing light of the buoy jutting out of the stormy waters. The crew cheered loudly.

'Thank God,' thought John Moffett, 'we have safely found Bermuda and I was by God lucky not to get shipwrecked. Thank God for Tony Stevenson, too. Now all we have to do is get to the finish line ahead of Flint Firestone, who I hope to hell runs aground.'

"You got me a new course, Tony?"

"I say steer on a heading of 145 degrees, Skipper, until we observe the Mills Breaker buoy," Tony replied, as he made his entry in the log.

"Now's our chance, men. Let's get up some canvas," John ordered, his broad forehead reddened from the weather as he grasped the helm on the *Encounter*.

The fog was lifting as the sky grew lighter and the sun began to break through the clouds. "Sail ahoy off our port quarter, Skipper! Can't make it out, though," Bob Ganloff shouted.

John grabbed his binoculars just as the sail vanished into a squall. "Well I'll be goddamned," he said a few minutes later. "It's Firestone and the *Martinis* all right. The son-of-a-bitch must be two or so miles astern so let's get the lead out."

"Give the devil his due," Doc Pearson smirked, "Flint's a damned fine sailor and is bearing down on us really fast it looks like."

"Shall we raise the Finish Line Committee on the radio and identify ourselves?" Tony asked, sticking his head up the companionway to have a look.

"Hell no, let's keep quiet and don't let Firestone know where we are. Wait until we have to at the five-mile mark," Moffett replied, just as the *Encounter* disappeared into a squall.

"That's where we are now, Captain."

"OK, make contact on VHF Channel 72 then."

"Aye, aye, skipper. Finish Line Committee, this is the sailing yacht *Encounter*, sail number US 41639, approaching finish line. Acknowledge. Over."

"Yacht *Encounter*, sail number US 41639, this is the Finish Line Committee boat. We acknowledge your approach to the finish line. Check in with us within two minutes after you have crossed the finish line and guard this channel for thirty minutes after finishing for future instructions. Over."

"Land ho!" John shouted, seeing the first glimpse of Bermuda through the clouds that were lifting, clearing away the fog by the brisk northeasterly wind. "OK, men, the wind's behind us so let's give her a kick in the ass and take her across in style. Port watch, break out the spinnaker and get it stopped below in the cabin. Lively now, every second counts," he barked as the crew hustled below to prepare the large parachute-like red and white sail.

The men's voices drifted up from below. John rethought his decision to hoist a spinnaker under these conditions. 'Once the spinnaker is set free it is difficult to control. If it starts to set halfway up or doesn't set, it will flog about, costing the *Encounter* precious time,' he thought as he looked around and saw the *Martinis'* spinnaker pop perfectly, propelling the competitor forward with a burst of speed. He heard Flint Firestone on the radio to the committee boat.

"Hurry up, guys! Firestone just popped his spinnaker and is making his move on us," John shouted, watching as the men stopped the spinnaker by passing the sail through a bottomless bucket holding rubber bands that were dropped off every two feet to hold the sail together until it was hoisted.

Peter ran up the companionway, holding the spinnaker head and trailed by the other, as he glanced out at the *Martinis* looming larger. "Hustle, guys, we can't let those bastards whip us at the finish line! We've got five thousand dollars riding on the next fifteen minutes!" he shouted as he scurried forward to the bow, running the spinnaker guy through the pole and hooking the snap shackle to the head of the sail.

"Make sure the sheet and lazy spinnaker guy are slack, men," John ordered.

"Slack, Skipper!" Bob shouted back.

"Hoist away!" came the order, as the huge sail shot up the mast with the screaming of the winches. "Take in the sheets," John ordered, as the rubber bands began to break and the beautiful sound of the spinnaker breaking open into its huge parachute-like form filled with wind was heard giving the *Encounter* a sudden power surge to the cheers of her crew. They sailed past the Mills Breaker buoy.

"Come to a course of 226 degrees and hold it, Captain!" Tony shouted, checking the buoy with his binoculars. "Our next buoy will be the Spit. Keep to starboard of it."

There it was at last: St. David's Head, the most easterly point of Bermuda, with the St. David's Head Light appearing now, small on the horizon through the fog and rain. John kept a watchful eye on the spinnaker as well as the *Martinis*, which continued to gain in a dead heat for the finish line.

'How the hell could I have been so stupid?' John thought, wishing he could recover the valuable time lost in the near disaster with the supertanker. 'That damn near cost us our lives and now probably the race, even if we still cheat and don't report it.' The exhaustion of over three days with little or no sleep was taking its toll. The tension built.

'Now, damn it, I've got to make it up to them by winning this race,' he thought, reflecting back on how Peter had comforted him in the cockpit after the near collision. Peter was a damn great friend and he really appreciated his loyalty after he had screwed up.

"I've blown it, Peter, loaded up the bases and pitched a home run ball," John had said in disgust.

"Don't blame yourself, John. It was a judgment call, and besides, there was a mechanical failure when we couldn't get the shaft engaged. We all have sworn oaths never to mention it again, so forget it. No one will ever know, unless you want to log it."

"I hate like hell to have to cheat to win this race, Pete. I've lost the crew's respect and confidence already without having to cheat, too."

"The hell you've lost it. Look, they're just a bunch of goddamn criminals who would be in prison without you anyway, Johnny,"

Slade had said, thinking after his critical remark of O'Grady's half million dollars stashed below.

"Yeah, but I hate to lie and cheat to win, damn it."

"Hell, John, no offense, but that's what the hell you lawyers do for a living: lie, man. All the damn time anyway. Why be so damn sanctimonious and righteous now?"

"Practicing law's one thing. Sportsmanship's another. I've damned well never cheated at anything in my life when it comes to sports, and besides, I nearly got us all killed over my ego and the damn trophy. I've lost their respect. I know that and I hate the hell out of it."

"You haven't lost shit, John, but if you feel that way, win back some respect, goddamn it! Win the trophy for all of us then...."

Peter's words came back again and again to the rhythmic pounding of the *Encounter*'s hull taking on the waves. "Win the race. Win the race," it said, and in the distance the St. David's Head Light loomed larger, and over his shoulder so did the *Martinis*.

"Firestone's gaining on us, Skipper! What the hell should we do?"

"Adjust the spinnaker pole, higher. Trim the sheet, that's it, trim her up some more. That's it! Just stand by you guys!" John voice was hoarse now as the committee boat came into view.

"Jesus, it's going to be close! Too damn close," Peter shouted, as the *Martinis* was now in full view. The tall, imposing figure of Flint Firestone could plainly be seen at the helm wearing a navy blue blazer and his white yachting hat with gold braid.

'Look at that arrogant bastard,' Peter thought. He hung on the rail, his back killing him with strain. His biceps burned with fire, blinded by the stinging salt spray in his face. He riveted his burning eyes to the top of the approaching St. David's Head Light and waited with the rest.

The finish line was in plain view in the distance, marked by a green buoy and white flashing light stretching on an imaginary line seaward four-tenths of a mile to a black buoy with white flashing light. Riding over the crest of the waves and running with the wind under full spinnaker, the *Encounter* was losing to the *Martinis*, which was now making her move.

Peter Slade knew there was nothing else he could do to help win the race except hang there. The sound of the wind brought back the roar of the crowd the afternoon he had intercepted a pass for the winning touchdown in the final seconds of the Maryland-Clemson game. That was football and he had done that alone. He was helpless now, having to stand by and await orders knowing the rest was up to fate and the wind. He kept his eyes glued on the committee boat dead ahead.

"The bastard's still gaining on us, Skipper. Should we try a starboard tack and get a better angle on the seas?" Bob asked.

"No, we will hold our course. Don't want to take a chance on gybing the spinnaker and screwing up!"

"They aren't closing as fast, Skipper. Maybe you're right. Lets don't take a chance of that and hold what we've got."

"There's the committee boat! Off our port bow a quarter or so!" Doc Pearson shouted in a high, shrill, excited voice that cut through the wind. The *Martinis* closed to within a hundred and fifty yards.

"Get out your money, Moffett! Must be that you've lost your guts the way you're sailing that yacht!" Firestone's deep voice carried with astonishing clarity in the wind, trying to demoralize John Moffett and his crew.

"We're still ahead of you, Firestone!" John shouted back, his voice muffled by the wind as he watched the closing seaward black buoy marking the finish line approaching.

"Say again, Skipper! I can't hear you!"

"Screw you, Firestone!" Peter shouted, his eyes still glued to the committee boat and the green buoy, thinking now of the replica trophy of St. David's Head Light in John Moffett's hands.

"Don't let the bastard rattle us, gentlemen. We're holding our own, and he can't hear us against the wind anyway."

From the wheelhouse of the committee boat, the finish line chairman, Sir Edward Swaysland of the Royal Bermuda Yacht Club, stood with binoculars trained on the two approaching yachts bearing down with great speed toward him. "Yes, yes indeed, a thoroughbred race to the finish, those two. It is going to the wire indeed, gentlemen," he turned and said to an American, "just like Churchill Downs."

"The *Encounter* and the *Martinis* are a matched pair of yachts you know, Sir Edward," the American replied. "My God, look at the drag race to the finish."

"Watch closely, gentlemen!" Sir Edward bellowed. "I do believe, by Jove, the *Martinis* is going to overtake her!" The two yachts closed to within a hundred yards of the finish line, white spray jetting from their bows.

"The most astonishing finish in all my years!" screamed Sir Edward to the loud applause of the committeemen as the two yachts shot across the line.

"Jolly sporting finish! Yes! Yes, indeed, the *Encounter* has won by half a boat. Do we all agree?" Sir Edward asked, sounding the siren. Cheers of both crews cannoned across the water as the radio cracked with eager voices of confirmation.

"This is the yacht *Encounter* checking in with the committee boat," John Moffett's voice shouted over the radio just as Flint Firestone broke in.

"Yacht *Encounter*, congratulations, gentlemen! You have won line honors for the first to finish the 1990 Newport-Bermuda Race. Your official time is seventy-one hours, fourteen minutes and twelve seconds," Sir Edward, voice came across loud and clear.

"Impossible!" shouted Firestone.

"Phone call, Mr. Oden," Wolfgang, the bartender at Harry's Bar in the basement of the Woolworth Building in Manhattan shouted above the noisy crowd. The FBI agent stepped forward and took the call.

"Give me that number," Wolfgang heard him say. Oden jotted down the number in his diary before going to the pay phone in the hall to the men's room where it was quiet. The FBI agent dialed Bermuda.

"Where are you, Flynn?"

"Staying at the Naval Air Station Bermuda at the BOQ. Just got word that Slade's boat got here a little while ago."

"Good deal. What about the Madam? She there?"

"Watched her check in at the Princess this afternoon about two. One fine looking chick, Ode."

"Well, I'm drinking to you getting Slade this time, Flynn...."

"I damn sure will. I've been after him for a helluva long time. I'll nail his ass this time, Ode, thanks to you."

"I never could figure why you're so damned determined to get him, Flynn. Doesn't make much sense to me."

"Personal. You don't understand. But, Ode, I appreciate your help on the case. Without it, I'd have never known about the

Madam and I couldn't have set him up without the help of the FBI."

"Nothing to it, man. If you need me give me a call, and while you're in Bermuda, screw the Madam for me if you get a chance," Ode Terry laughed.

"What a piece of ass, Ode!" the skinny man replied out of the corner of his cigarette-dangling mouth. "I can't wait to meet her in the morning and send her and Slade over to see the wimpy ass banker."

# Chapter XIII

## Royal Bermuda Yacht Club
### June 18, 1990

The *Encounter* was welcomed by an excited armada of sailing enthusiasts, mariners and well-wishers as it sailed into Bermuda's Great Sound on its way to Hamilton Harbor. The crowd cheered wildly from sailing yachts, pleasure craft and row boats, to the sounds of the screaming sirens and foghorns. Geysers of water shot skyward from the cannons of the harbor's fireboat that led the parade. It was with such fanfare and celebration that the line honors winner of the 1990 Bermuda Race sailed into Hamilton Harbor.

"Does this mean we've won the Lighthouse Trophy?" Slade shouted, watching the flotilla with utter astonishment and pride.

"No! We have won line honors, mate. The first yacht to finish the race. The Lighthouse Trophy is based upon our correct time under the IMS system. We shall just have to wait and see if another yacht can overtake our corrected time," Tony replied, waving to the well-wishers who had just pulled alongside. "We shall not know the results until the remaining yachts have finished."

"Come over here, you little sawed-off limey!" John shouted, grabbing the Englishman around the neck with his forearm. "You're the world's best navigator as far as I'm concerned. God, you were incredible! Gentlemen, the winner of the Schooner Mistress Trophy award to the navigator of the first yacht to cross the finish line!" he shouted, holding up Tony's hand.

The small Englishman blushed as a wild cheer rang out from his shipmates.

"We were indeed the first to finish. Can you bloody believe it, mates?" Tony screamed, grabbing Moffett around the waist and fighting hard to control his emotions. The jubilant but exhausted crew ecstatically basked in the thrills of victory, waving and shouting to the cheering armada that escorted them triumphantly toward the Royal Bermuda Yacht Club winner's berth.

Flint Firestone, trailing behind in the *Martinis*, was thinking, 'isn't there some way that you can make this come out different? Isn't there anything you can do to make a difference besides just sitting here on your ass and letting Moffett walk away with your trophy? Sometime during the race they had to have screwed up, broken a rule or cheated, or done something wrong. If they did, I know just the man that will spill his guts,' he smiled with a stern face, admiring the breathtaking natural beauty of crystalline blue waters and green hills of the semitropical island.

The *Encounter* sailed past the historical regal pink Hamilton Princess Hotel, an island landmark visited by countless British aristocrats, Hollywood movie stars and wealthy yachtsmen.

Carolina Barrington had just stepped out of a refreshing shower after arriving on her early morning Delta flight from

Boston. Hearing the celebration in the harbor, she grabbed a pink terrycloth robe out of the closet and dashed onto the third floor balcony loggia to investigate. She was listening to FM 89's coverage on the radio. "Yes, ladies and gentlemen, the line honors for the first to finish the 1990 Newport-Bermuda Yacht Race is the yacht *Encounter*, a fifty-foot sloop hailing from the Newport Yacht Club and owned by Captain John Moffett, a prominent New England trial attorney. Captain Moffett and his crew are at this moment very, very happy sailors as the *Encounter* is now entering Hamilton Harbor trailed by the second place winner, her sister yacht the *Martinis*. Now this is a very interesting story, indeed, these two yachts are owned by ex-brothers-in-law who are fierce competitors...."

"The *Encounter* won!" Carolina Barrington exclaimed, running back inside and grabbing her 35 MM camera with a telephoto lens. She sighted in on the *Encounter*, focusing on each crew member, searching for none other than her fellow agent, Peter M. Slade. The *Encounter* was furling her sails while she motored slowly up the harbor below on the way to the Royal Bermuda Yacht Club.

'Oh! That must be Peter Slade. The handsome man with thinning blond hair. That's got to be him, all right. Isn't he gorgeous,' she thought. Her camera's automatic shutter snapped away. 'He's not only handsome, but sexy as well,' she thought watching Slade's broad smile as he put his arm over the shoulder of the captain. The two men were smoking victory cigars and laughing, waving to the crowd and blowing kisses.

'So, Mr. Peter Slade, you're my new partner tomorrow morning, are you? I wonder if his former partner, Herb Gidwitz, has been released from federal prison. What a wonderful customer ole Herb was before the government shut down my social club. I don't think Peter Slade was ever a john of mine or I would have remembered one of the girls talking about a good-looking man like him.'

At thirty-two, the tall, beautiful brunette strained her large dark eyes for one last glimpse of Peter Slade before the *Encounter* motored into its berth at the yacht club, out of view. She gave a sigh, took her camera and went back inside.

Carolina laid her camera down, dropping her robe to the floor, admiring her naked body in the dresser mirror. It was a perfect body, slim, firm and as perfect a body as a woman's body could have been, and she kept it that way by long hours in the gym. She poured a glass of wine from the hotel's welcoming basket which was topped with a big pink bow and filled with fruit that would be good for breakfast. She turned slowly before the mirror, lifting first her firm buttocks and letting them bounce, then her breasts. She was satisfied with the way her body looked as she lay naked across the king-size bed studying the ceiling, thinking of how long she had been without a man.

Her dark eyes slowly closed as she sadly remembered her dead lover, Siegfried Dassler, the incredibly wealthy German banker who had died in her arms last October in Bar Harbor, Maine, on a beautiful moonlit night. Sieg had been her lover, her father, her best friend, and had brought her indescribable happiness for many years. He had also stuck by her through her troubles with the law, hiring the best attorneys in New York for her defense. When she thought about that, Carolina's anger at the Justice Department for forcing her to be in Bermuda was burning deep inside again.

How different would her life have been had she not met Sieg at the tender age of nineteen? She had never finished her undergraduate degree at Wellesley or entered the Harvard Business

School as her father had planned. She had never joined the Peace Corps as she had always dreamed about either. She had sacrificed a lot in those early years by being Dassler's mistress, including being reprimanded by her wealthy parents for seeing a married man who was their age. It had only made Carolina Barrington a rebel when confronted and ordered to stop seeing him. Who the hell needed her family trust fund that was left her by her grandfather, she had shouted. She could make her own fortune in the world's oldest profession and that was where Sieg had been such great help, introducing the likes of poor Paul Ferris who had been just one of her many elite clientele.

Sieg was dead and that was that, all a part of her past. She was close to the end of her federal probation and her enrollment as a Justice Department agent. She was now living well off her inheritance from the trust fund that had kicked in this year. Her parents had failed to have it revoked after her prostitution trial that had made world headlines. Carolina Barrington was alone and lonely, a marked woman, it seemed, for the rest of her life.

'To hell with all this,' she thought, lying there naked in the warm room. Being forced to come to Bermuda was just the beginning of a new chapter in Carolina Barrington's life. Slowly her soft hands with perfectly sculptured nails began to tenderly massage her firm ample breasts, moving deliberately down her lean beautiful body to the sounds of soft classical music on the radio. Her thoughts were no longer of Siegfried Dassler. Her fantasies were instead of the handsome, masculine, mature man whose face had appeared in her camera lens and was now slowly refocusing in her head. Yes, now it was that strong man holding her, sucking her breast, massaging her ass. Her fingers simulated his manhood that slowly sank inside her, exploding in the fabrication of raw, savage sex.

Her hands continued to caress her smooth naked body. Her eyes squinted shut with her head thrust back on the pillow. Breasts rising and falling with each breath as her nipples stood erect on her ribbed torso, expanding and contracting faster with each shortened breath. The tautness of her thigh muscles in her long, shapely legs curled her toes inward. Her fingers played the wonderful pleasures of Peter Slade inside her like a grand concerto by a concert pianist. Slowly she could feel her climax building before erupting magnificently to her whimpered cries of ecstasy. "Oh God, Peter Slade, I can't wait," she whispered to a man she had never met.

Caught up in all the celebration in the harbor, Peter Slade quickly glanced up at the magnificent regal pink Princess Hotel passing in the late afternoon sunshine. He inhaled the sweet fragrance of the island and wished to hell he was somewhere else. 'Well hell,' he thought, 'tomorrow morning that's where I'll be going,' not knowing what was in store for him when he arrived. He was unaware of his fantasy lover and co-agent in Room 300.

The *Encounter* motored into her winner's slip at the Royal Bermuda Yacht Club. Paul Ferris arose from behind his massive mahogany desk in the richly decorated managing director's suite atop the Bank of Bermuda Limited building on the adjacent Alouby's Point. The small but distinguished looking gray-haired executive walked over and focused his tripod telescope on the *Encounter*. It was tying up a short distance away. "Are you going over to the yacht club to welcome the winners, Mr. Ferris?" Margaret Fox, his executive secretary, asked upon entering his office and joining him by the window.

"I'd love to, Margaret, but I'm afraid I must wait on the calls

I'm expecting from New York after the markets close. What is the name of that yacht?"

"The news just announced that line honors go to the *Encounter* from Newport, skippered by a Captain John Moffett," she replied, crossing her arms as Paul Ferris focused his telescope on the yacht and its crew.

"What a triumphant moment for those chaps," he said, amused by their celebration and unaware that the *Encounter* had brought him serious trouble in the name of his own bank's customer, Mr. Peter M. Slade. He snapped his fingers to the rhythm of the welcoming gombey music from the steel band that floated up from the Royal Bermuda Yacht Club dock. He was a happy man returning to his desk.

John Moffett and his navigator were the first members of the crew to be greeted by the commodore of the RBYC when it tied up in the winner's slip of the historic storied pink yacht club. Corks flew as the champagne bottles popped to the wild cheers. The crew was toasted with Moet and Chandon by the commodore to celebrate their lofty accomplishment.

For over an hour the Racing Committee, along with the jubilant club members and the press, congratulated the *Encounter* and her scroungy but happy crew. Flint Firestone kept to himself but was getting his share of attention as the second place winner. The Bermuda Customs Inspectors in their Bermuda shorts waited patiently for the celebration to subside. Peter Slade watched them nervously, thinking more about the half million he had on board than he had before. CBS's Bermuda affiliate, Channel 10 news team cornered John Moffett for an interview. Journalists' cameras flashed under the hot lights of the TV cameras.

Peter Slade was still keeping a close eye on the customs inspectors who seemed to be enjoying the event. When the crowd calmed a bit the chief inspector approached.

"Congratulations, Captain. Welcome to Bermuda. May I please inspect your manifest and crew passports so you can continue your celebration?" His assistant passed out customs cards to the crew that gathered around.

The inspector boarded to complete the documents. His assistant stamped the crew's passports on the dock. "Which one of your crew members will be departing Bermuda on your yacht, Captain?" the inspector asked below.

"Here is my returning crew list comprised of myself, Tony Stevenson, navigator, Bob Ganloff, first mate, and Dr. Duane Pearson and Peter Slade as crew," John replied.

"Very well, Captain, the rest of the crew will need to show a copy of their return airline ticket to my assistant."

Peter Slade fought to stay calm as he filled out his customs card. The thought of the blue sack of O'Grady's money hidden below made him feel like a criminal. Sweat formed in his armpits.

"Have a jolly good stay in Bermuda, gentlemen, and my heartiest congratulations to you all," the inspector said, after completing his processing, checking their passports and making one last review of his documents.

"Oh, Mr. Slade. Where are you, Mr. Peter M. Slade?" the inspector asked, looking over his glasses.

Never let'um see you sweat, Peter thought, having a hard time finding his voice. "Yes, sir, Inspector. I'm Peter Slade."

"Oh yes, Mr. Slade. You forgot to check if you were single or married," he said, handing back the form.

"Married," Slade laughed, making the correction, thinking, 'oh

God, now they are going to search the boat.'

"Congratulations once again, gentlemen," said the chief inspector, taking their customs cards and walking back up the pier.

Peter Slade let out a sigh of relief. He had accomplished his first assignment as an agent by successfully smuggling the money in.

Slade hurried below and grabbed his sea bag, wondering if the money would be safe stuffed deep inside the forward sail locker. He slipped his padlock off his duffel bag and locked the locker just to make sure no one discovered it accidentally. Topside, he grabbed another glass of champagne and headed for a hot shower in the club's locker room.

He emerged thirty minutes later a new man, dressed in his wrinkled navy double-breasted blazer, white slacks and blue and red striped tie. The freshly shaved Slade rushed to the bar for an overdue Glenfiddich with a splash.

'God, this drink tastes great,' Peter thought, drinking his Scotch and looking around at the crowd of journalists and yachtsmen with their ladies. He sucked down his drink and was returning to the bar for a refill when out of the corner of his eye he caught John Moffett coming up the stairs. "Hey, Skipper, how about a Glenfiddich?" he shouted across the room over the applause of the crowd acknowledging John Moffett's entrance.

The celebration grew louder with people screaming at each other to be heard. The hour was getting late and the Glenfiddich made Peter's sea legs wobblier. Finally, he took John aside. "I'm going to hit the sack, Skipper. Got some government work to do in the morning, so I'll see you in the afternoon."

"Thanks, buddy. I'll be at the Waterloo House just down the street, or over here if you need me. Just be careful and don't let those bastards trip you up."

"Congratulations, Skipper! You won your trophy."

"We haven't won the Lighthouse yet, sailor! Do be careful, now."

"Wonder what Doc Pearson's been talking to Firestone about in the corner over there, John?" Slade asked, nodding at the two men engrossed in deep conversation drinking Bacardi rum swizzles.

"Who the hell knows, Pete," John laughed, at the top of his game now as the winner. He turned just as another member introduced himself and his wife.

'The faggot's probably trying to gobble Firestone's goober,' Slade thought, content now after having stuffed himself at the elaborate seafood buffet. The sounds of the celebration faded. He went down the stairs to the locker room to get his duffel bag and headed for the Glencoe Hotel.

Outside the evening was mild and beautiful with the smell of the island sweet in his nostrils. He hurried down Front Street with his duffel bag on his shoulder to catch the seven-twenty Paget-Warwick ferry for Salt Kettle across the harbor.

It had been almost seven years since he had seen the entrance to Bank of Bermuda Limited, which looked just the same as he passed. Peter Slade chuckled, thinking of the millions of dollars he had in his trust account inside, where Paul Ferris had just completed his last call to New York and was tidying up his desk for the day.

Dressed in blue blazer and Bermuda shorts with knee socks, Paul Ferris scampered down the stairs, hurrying to catch the Paget-Warwick ferry home. He accidentally bumped into Slade going up the gangplank of the *Deliverance*.

"Make sure I get off at Salt Kettle," Peter told the ferry captain before settling down behind the wheelhouse.

"We make two landings at Lower and Hobson so just relax, mate," the captain cheerfully replied.

Paul did just that, watching the charming old Bermuda cottages and mansions slip by as the ferry churned across the harbor. Slade inhaled deeply, feeling a little lonely as his thoughts turned to Charlotte and the Stone Bridge Inn. He was feeling very sleepy and tired and a little drunk too.

"Salt Kettle," the skipper announced as Slade shouldered his duffel bag and hiked up the gangplank at the landing. In the twilight of the afternoon he walked the short distance down a narrow alley lined with neatly painted pink cottages to his home for the next week, the Glencoe Hotel.

The small hotel had once been a residence. Built in the 1800s, it overlooked Salt Kettle Bay and was far from the noise and crowds. It awaited him in all the informal elegance and natural serenity that he had imagined when he approached the reception desk. Soft calypso music floated out across the Great Sound Terrace from the bar and he thought briefly about having another drink.

"Welcome to the Glencoe, Mr. Slade," came his warm reception from the desk clerk. Slade registered and followed the bellman to his room.

"Is this your first visit to the Glencoe?" the bellman inquired, opening the drapes onto a private terrace with a view of the harbor from the spacious room which was decorated in bright colors.

"Yes! God, this looks wonderful," Slade replied, testing the mattress, after being on the cramped boat for the last three and a half days.

"Is there anything else I might get you, Mr. Slade?"

"Please fill up the ice bucket, and I want you to get these

clothes pressed and back early tomorrow morning," Peter replied, unpacking his duffel bag.

"Will eight tomorrow morning be soon enough, sir?"

"Eight is fine," he replied, handing him a five dollar bill and bringing an eager smile.

"Enjoy your stay, Mr. Slade. My name is Jerry, and should you need further assistance, please call."

Peter walked over and stood by the telephone, dreading to make his call. He checked his watch. 'Half past eight in Newport,' he thought, wondering if Charlotte was drunk. Probably not, or at least not totally drunk, perhaps just nasty. He held his breath, dialing 1DD to place the international call.

The phone ran once, twice, then just before he was about to get the answering machine, Charlotte's slurred voice came on the line.

"Hello, darling. How are you and things at Beach Mont?"

"Fine, Peter, and yourself?" came Charlotte's cold reply.

He replied, livelier this time, "Well, we made it! And guess what, Charlotte? The *Encounter* won line honors!"

"Well, congratulations...."

Then, without thinking, Peter Slade asked his wife, "Charlotte, please fly out and help us celebrate. I'll meet you at the air..."

"Peter, you have to be kidding!" she snapped and slammed the phone down.

# Chapter XIV

Peter Slade awoke at three-thirty, unable to go back to sleep after a restless night of bad dreams. He lay in the soft bed listening to the silence in the room. 'After days at sea on the pitching boat and the howling wind, this is wonderful,' he thought, fighting to fall back to sleep. After lying there in the dark for an hour, he finally got up and put on his running gear and went down to the Glencoe lobby for a cup of coffee. He was still sore at Charlotte for having hung up on him last night, and even angrier at himself for having asked the bitch to join him in Bermuda.

The rich aroma of the freshly brewed Jamaican filled the small lobby. "Good morning. Spare a cup of that coffee, my friend?" he asked, startling the young clerk who was toiling with his night audit at the register.

"Oh, yes sir, Mr. Slade! It will be my pleasure. Cream or

sugar?" he asked, smiling, springing up and pouring a large styro-foam cup full.

"Black, and how did you know my name?"

"Your picture's on the front page of the morning *Gazette*, Mr. Slade, with the rest of the *Encounter*'s crew. I recognized your name from our guest list, sir. Congratulations on winning."

"You're a very bright young fellow," Slade replied. "Ever wind up in Newport, look me up. I'll have a job waiting for you," he added, turning and walking out onto the dark terrace.

"Yes, sir, Mr. Slade, and you have a good day, sir," replied the young man, thinking: 'Wow, what a nice gentlemen the American is!'

'It will be a good day all right, a really goddamn good day, I imagine,' Slade thought. He took a seat at a table on the Great Sound Terrace with his coffee and waited on daylight. The sounds of the waves off Salt Kettle Bay lapping peacefully against the wharf made Peter Slade relax and, after his restless night, he needed that.

Slade had always been a morning person, loving the early hours before daylight, watching the earth awaken. It reminded him of duck hunting on the Chesapeake Bay, freezing in the blind before daylight, waiting for a flock of green-head mallards to decoy in. He could hear their wings whistling overhead when it was still too early to shoot as he calmed his big yellow Labrador, Dakota. Only this morning it wasn't freezing cold and he felt like the ducks must feel just before they get shot after realizing that the decoys are bogus and they have been screwed.

A thin orange line broke in the distant clouds in the eastern sky, bringing the first traces of daylight which accented the gently white sloping roofs of the houses across the small bay. While drinking his coffee he was thinking he should probably have a silent prayer asking God for guidance. No, that would be hypocritical, praying only at a time when his back was against the wall. He sat there thinking about his religion. The sun slowly broke through the clouds, casting a soft light on the deserted terrace. Sad thoughts of young David came creeping in as they always seemed to do early in the mornings.

'What were the best times that you can ever remember?' Slade asked himself, knowing the answer. It was the early morning hours when David was little and they sat at the kitchen table eating breakfast surrounded by decoys, waders, his Browning shotgun and shells. Dakota had gone wild with anticipation of the hunt, whining and scratching himself. "Why can't I go duck hunting, Dad?" young David would plead.

"You're not old enough yet, son. Next year, when you are five years old, perhaps you can go if it is all right with mother."

"Please, pretty please, Dad? I'm four," the young voice would say, proving the point by holding up four small fingers. "Let me go now!"

"I tell you what we will do, my young soon-to-be-a-duck-hunter son."

"What's that, Dad?" asked the youngster with the same sharp blue eyes like his dad's that danced with excitement.

"You can help me and Dakota clean the ducks when we get back, and next year you can go with us, I promise..."

There had never been a next year for David, and Peter Slade still had a terrible time in the mornings knowing that he had never got to take his son duck hunting. 'In this fucked-up world, perhaps David had been lucky not having to live through it,' Slade thought. He knew it was sad and depressing reasoning that and he had to put it out of his mind if he was going to concentrate on the day that lay ahead.

Watching the seagulls sailing overhead in the light breeze, carrying with it the smell of the sea, reminded Slade of the Stone Bridge Inn. This small, quaint hotel had caught his attention when he read about it in the Bermuda Department of Tourism brochure, and for that reason he had chosen to stay here. The gulls were flying about freely and he wished to hell he could fly, too. He watched the early morning sun reflecting off their white and black tipped wings. Their sad cries broke the peaceful tranquility of the early dawn as they dipped and dove, swooping low over the surface of the water, feeding.

'Well, today's finally the day that I've been dreading,' Slade thought, 'and there is nothing more I can do about that except face up to it the best I can. What the hell will I have to do with O'Grady's half million, anyhow? It's got to be money laundering or perhaps it's a bribe to some Bermuda bank official to get...'

"Well...I'm...a...goddamned...idiot!" Slade said aloud, pausing between words. His government mission suddenly sent a flood of fear tearing into his guts. 'Damn it,' he thought, 'it's just too damn simple for me to have even considered! Why in hell was I so damn stupid not to think of it before I got here? Those bastards are going to make me deposit the half million in Bank of Bermuda Limited into my own trust account! Jesus Christ, Slade!!! You're fixing to dig your own grave before they shoot you, idiot! They are going to nail me for income tax evasion sure as hell once they confirm I got away with millions of untaxed dollars.' With that unsavory thought, Peter Slade sprang to his feet and ran.

He ran across the empty terrace and along the wharf, down the narrow darkened lanes of Salt Kettle. Like an Indy driver coming off a steep, banked turn, he took a hard right onto Harbor Road, sprinting westwardly away from the rising sun. He gasped for air.

His heart pounded and he began to tire. He fell off the pace to catch his second wind and was now running at his normal seven and a half minute miles, sweating Scotch whiskey profusely. The perspiration streamed down his face, soaking his T-shirt as he ran.

Peter Slade's breathing came even and steady, deep from inside his lungs. Running along Harbor Road he noticed a man sitting on the veranda of his large house reading the morning paper as he passed. 'Look at that lucky guy over there,' he thought, 'why in the hell isn't he out running too?'

The man in turn glanced up briefly, thinking what an uncivilized way for anyone to start a day. He watched the runner pass.

Paul Ferris arose that morning at six which was his normal hour. He was sipping his morning tea while reading the *Royal Gazette* on the veranda of his multi-million dollar waterfront mansion on Hamilton Harbor. He had bought the house with profits made by duplicating Peter Slade and other customers' securities trades. This procedure was completely legal under Bermuda banking laws. Foreign bankers scoffed at the prohibition of such acts by United States securities and tax laws. Paul Ferris considered this practice a perk in his position as managing director of Bank of Bermuda Limited where bank-secrecy laws were much more important to the bank's reputation and insider trading was never even given a second thought.

Ferris read about the Newport-Bermuda Race, examining closely the photo of the *Encounter*'s crew. He glanced back at the runner who was now out of sight, rereading the caption under the picture. 'I wonder if that is the same Mr. Peter M. Slade that is a customer of my bank,' he thought, reexamining Slade's photo more closely. 'He does look familiar, very familiar from somewhere, but that would be very coincidental if it was the same man.'

Paul Ferris was watching Channel 10 through the open French doors when the newscaster got his attention. "The *Encounter*, a fifty-foot Racing Division Class Three yacht owned by Captain John Moffett took line honors to finish the 1990 race first with an elapsed time of seventy-one hours, fourteen minutes. However, our news team now at the Royal Bermuda Yacht Club has learned that the challenger, Captain Flint Firestone of the *Martinis*, has apparently filed a protest with the yacht club duty officer at eight o'clock last evening within minutes of the six-hour deadline for doing so. The *Martinis* crossed the finish line only seconds behind the *Encounter*."

"We take you now live to our reporter, Harold Bishop, at the Royal Bermuda Yacht Club for an update and the latest news on the 1990 Newport-Bermuda Race."

Paul Ferris watched as the camera focused on Flint Firestone standing in the main hall of the yacht club. "Captain Firestone, we understand that you filed a protest last evening against the yacht *Encounter* and Captain John Moffett. Is that correct, sir?"

The tall, arrogant Firestone spoke in his deep New England brogue, "Yes, I have in fact filed a protest with the race committee last evening."

"Captain Firestone, on what rules infraction are you, or what incident, might I ask, are your grounds for the protest?"

"It would be inappropriate to comment on that at this time until the protest goes before the International Jury. However, I will add that it is filed in accordance with the International Racing Rules and is well-founded and can be easily proven."

"Please elaborate," a reporter for *Sail World* shouted.

"I have no further comments at this time, gentlemen. Now, please excuse me," Firestone concluded as he turned and walked away from the camera.

"Well, there you have it, ladies and gentlemen. A protest has been filed by Captain Flint Firestone against yesterday's line honors winner, Captain John Moffett and the yacht *Encounter*. We will keep you abreast of the latest developments as they unfold."

Carolina Barrington was just awaking at nine o'clock when the *Deliverance* docked at the Hamilton ferry terminal and both Paul Ferris and Peter Slade disembarked down the gangplank. 'Saw that guy on the ferry yesterday,' Slade recalled, following the banker down the street and watching him disappear through the entrance of the Bank of Bermuda Limited. 'Hope to hell we don't meet again today, buddy,' Peter sighed, stopping to examine his image in the glass door. He was wearing his favorite blue, red and gold striped tie and his navy blue double-breasted blazer and white slacks. 'You are in for some serious shit today, buddy,' he thought as he walked down Front Street to the Royal Bermuda Yacht Club. Flashing his visitor's card at the door, he entered.

The *Encounter* looked rough after the race. She was covered in scum with rusty stains from the wires running in red lines down her blue hull and was covered in salt. 'At least I don't have to clean up this mess,' Slade thought, despising the toxic smell of hull cleaner. He boarded, scampering down the companionway ladder to retrieve the money stowed in the forward sail locker. Doc Pearson was sprawled opened-mouthed in his underwear on the berth directly beneath it. 'Damn it, I'll have to wake the bastard to get the money,' Slade thought, taking a large pan off the stove and slamming it on the deck, KA-WHAM!! The startled doctor sprang up in his berth.

"Dear heavens! What in this world was that???" Doc screamed, rubbing his bloodshot eyes. "Peter??? I could just kill you for doing that..."

"Sorry, Doc, did I awaken you?" Peter asked casually in his usual cheerful voice.

"Peter! You scared me half to death! Oh, God, I feel awful. Those rum swizzles are just terrible!"

"Yeah, you look like hell, too, Doc. Too much celebrating last night, you and Flint Firestone? What was that guy saying, Doc?" Slade asked, kicking an empty champagne bottle out of the way and catching a whiff of the doctor's foul breath as he stumbled around trying to find his pants.

"When was I talking to Firestone?!"

"In the bar, when I was leaving, about seven-thirty."

"I don't... remember.... Yes, I do remember talking to Flint... Oh my God, I'll never drink rum swizzles again, Peter."

"Got pretty fucked up, did you, Doc?"

"I've never been that drunk in my life, Peter. Where's John?"

"Still at the Waterloo House, I guess. Sorry to disturb you, Doc, but if you will excuse me, I'll get the rest of my gear," Peter replied, taking his key and unlocking the sail locker, removing the blue canvas bag and tightening the drawstring.

"Why are you so dressed up this morning, Peter? You look real nice," Doc said, reaching over and brushing lint off Slade's shoulder.

"What was Firestone talking about, Duane?"

"Jesus, I don't know, Peter! The last thing I remember is that he was helping me get out of the bar. He's SOoo strong...."

"Have a good day, Doc," Peter replied disgustedly, scurrying topside and out the front door of the yacht club on his way to the Princess Hotel. He approached the Waterloo House on Pitts Bay Road. 'Should I go ahead and tell John about my secret account, or not?' he wondered.

Peter Slade stopped in front of the pink archway with steps leading up to a flower-filled patio of the Waterloo House. What could he say to his lawyer now after he had lied about the secret trust account in the Bank of Bermuda Limited years ago? 'Hey! Hey, Johnny, forgot to tell you about the millions I got stashed next door in the Bank of Bermuda Limited, ole buddy. By the way, the Feds want me to deposit all this money I smuggled in on your boat into my secret account this morning so they can arrest my stupid ass for income tax evasion this time, since they failed to convict me for trading on inside info. Yeah, John, I'll never lie to you again, my friend, if you can just get me out of this mess.' He snickered and started walking again.

The formidable entrance of the Princess Hotel had not changed in the seven years since Slade had last entered the elegantly colonial lobby. He glanced at a quarter past nine on his watch. 'Better check in with George Henley at the Stone Bridge, this might be my last chance,' he thought, searching for a phone.

"Good morning, Boss! Where you at?" ...Lord God, I'm glad to hear from you and to hear that Mr. Moffett won that race!"

"Yes, George, I'm fine, and how are things at the Inn?"

"Couldn't be no better, Mr. Slade. Mr. Legate's daughter's wedding was a humdinger. Them the drinkinest white folks that I ever served liquor. Liked to work this poor ole man to death!"

Peter laughed. "What was the bar bill, George?"

"You got to give me a raise, Boss. Them white folks drunk up over four thousand dollars worth of my liquor!"

"How wonderful! What about Mrs. Slade? How much has she drunk up?"

"Haven't seen hide nor hair of Mrs. Slade, neither, Boss."

"What about Melissa? Is she there?"

"No, sir. She hasn't come down from her room yet. It's still pretty early here, but Miss Melissa, she doing just fine. What time is it where you're at?"

"A quarter past nine. Are you and the rest of the staff OK, George?"

"Yes sir, Mr. Pete. I've never felt better!"

"OK then, George, keep things on an even keel and tell every-one that Mr. Moffett won the race," Peter said, hanging up, momentarily lifted by George's cheerful voice lingering in his ear.

Slade had another cup of coffee while looking out the large windows of the lobby at the hotel's concrete pier, crowded with competing yachts that had finished the race. The boats' hulls were tarnished from the sea as the crews began to stir outside to clean them up. The sound of the water cascading past the rock-climbing orchids in the lobby was soothing to his frayed nerves. He kicked the money bag securely against the wall and patiently waited.

"Heard the latest?" asked a tall American sailor of his buddy in passing.

"Nope. What's that?"

"Firestone filed a protest last night against the *Encounter*! Can you believe that?"

"No kidding! What in the hell for?"

"Don't know..." the tall man replied, still walking, his voice trailing off.

'Firestone? That son of a bitch,' thought Slade, straining for more of their conversation. 'Protest for what? I better call John,' he thought, glancing up at five till on the wall clock. 'Hell, he will know soon enough, if he doesn't know already.' Peter Slade walked over to the house phones, passing by the Adams Lounge that was just opening. 'I need a drink of Scotch. Hell no, not this morning, no time for drinking, sailor, you got to keep a poker face,' he told himself, picking up the phone and dialing Room 300.

"Good morning, Mr. Slade," the wonderfully refreshing and sophisticated voice of Carolina Barrington answered. "I've been expecting your call."

"Who is this?" Peter inquired firmly.

"Come up to Room 300, Mr. Slade, and we will be introduced."

"Ask him if he's got the money," a distinguishable Brooklyn accent interrupted in the background.

"Have you brought the money, Mr. Slade?"

"Yes, I have it," Slade replied sharply. Feeling mean, he hung up.

On the short walk down the hall from the elevator, Slade could feel his anger rising. 'Stay calm, damn you, stay calm. This is no time to get rattled. Never let them see you sweat,' he was saying to himself as he rapped forcefully on the door.

The door opened widely as Peter Slade stood dumbfounded, peering into the most captivating eyes he could ever remember. The tall slender woman was dressed in a gray business suit draped with a pink scarf to match her expensive jewelry and nail polish.

"Come in, Peter, I am Carolina Barrington," she said, extending her hand.

"Morning, Slade. Heard youse guys got caught cheating on television this morning," smirked O'Grady out of the corner of his mouth. He was slumped in a chair, dressed in Bermuda shorts and smoking a Camel.

Slade didn't answer, his eyes riveted on the beautiful lady standing in the door. "It is a pleasure to meet you, Ms. Barrington...."

"Come in, please, and do call me Carolina, Peter. I understand we will be seeing quite a bit of each other the next few days. By the way, congratulations on the *Encounter*'s victory yesterday," she replied, closing the door.

"Didja hear, Carolina?" O'Grady snarled. "The challenger, Firestone, said they cheated. Doesn't surprise me none, Slade, you and that slick lawyer Moffett of yours."

Peter tried harder to ignore O'Grady's comment, watching Carolina roll her large dark eyes, giving him the hint that whomever she was, she was on his side. He hoped so, anyway. 'Damn she's beautiful,' he was thinking as the name, Carolina Barrington, rang a bell. Could it possibly be? No, surely not Carolina Barrington, the Madam Blue Blood from New York!

Slade entered the room and pitched the money bag on the floor in front of O'Grady's sandaled feet. "Here is your money, O'Grady. Count it."

O'Grady's laughter turned into a hacking cough. He scoffed at Slade, "Geez! It will get counted all right, Slade," he finally managed.

"Now, if you and Carolina don't mind, I will be going. I have a busy schedule today."

O'Grady laughed harder, tears welling up in his eyes as he coughed and laughed, a nasty, high-pitched repulsive laugh, making Slade sick as the skinny man's blood rushed to his freckled face. "Didja ask if I minded, Slade?" he gasped, taking another drag off the cigarette, getting nastier. "You're damn right I mind. So, buddy, you better cancel your social calendar until further notice from me. I'm your and the lady's handler on this undercover assignment and I got your ass on a leash, Mr. Slade. Didja get that? You're following my orders."

"OK, let's get on with it then, O'Grady. What do you want me to do next?"

"Carolina, make your call to Ferris at the bank," ordered O'Grady.

She took a seat next to the phone, crossed her sexy legs and dialed. Slade didn't flinch a muscle. He walked calmly over and looked out the window.

"Good morning. Mr. Paul Ferris, please.

"Yes, this is an old friend of his, Carolina Barrington from New York...."

Covering the receiver with her hand, she said to O'Grady, "Paul's in...."

"Hello, Paul.

"It has been sometime.... Yes, I am doing well, thank you, and yourself?.... All that is behind me now.... No. I am here in Hamilton, Paul, with a business associate of mine and we need to make an appointment to meet with you today.

"I understand, Paul. But it is urgent that we meet.... No, Paul, I want to meet with you, not your assistant, damn it...." Carolina put her hand over the receiver again. "He's stalling, Flynn....

"NO! Tomorrow at eleven o'clock will not be convenient," she replied as Peter Slade's stomach knotted. "Two o'clock this afternoon will be OK unless we can meet sooner.... Fine then, two o'clock."

"Didja get that, Slade? Takes de money there and go with the lady to the Bank of Bermuda Limited this afternoon at two. She knows what to do when youse guys gets there," O'Grady ordered between coughing spells and lighting another Camel.

# Chapter XV

John Moffett ignored the message light on his telephone when he returned from an early morning swim in the Waterloo House pool. 'Probably more damn reporters,' he thought. He was euphoric after winning line honors and being the leading contender for the Lighthouse Trophy with the best corrected time. 'A hot shower will feel great to massage my sore muscles after three days at sea,' he thought, stepping into the shower.

Twenty minutes later he was wearing a terrycloth robe, gazing out at the Hamilton Harbor from the balcony of the white-columned mansion turned hotel. He was wondering how life must have been to have lived there when Napoleon met his Waterloo back in 1815. Ignoring the flashing light, he watched a straggler from the race to the Onion Patch motor his yacht up the harbor. 'Those guys must really be exhausted after being out there over four days,' he thought. The boat joined the impressive racing fleet that had already finished the race. 'God, I hope none of those guys have a better corrected time than I do.' The thrill of winning the Lighthouse Trophy was growing ever stronger.

Moffett could see his yacht tied in the winner's berth at the Royal Bermuda Yacht Club. A huge smile swept across his broad face as his confidence built that he had finally won his trophy. 'Winning that trophy is the most important thing in my life, and considering the class of competition, I'm one hell of a sailor,' he thought, 'especially in whipping that pompous ass, Flint Firestone, at the finish line.'

The prevailing southwesterly wind blew the bright colored signal flags that decorated the hundred or so yachts moored at the Princess Hotel's pier and the Bermuda Dinghy Club in the distance. 'What a grand and glorious feeling to be the winner over all of them,' John Moffett thought, when the telephone broke his reverie.

"Moffett, speaking."

"Captain Moffett, we have a number of messages for you, one of which is urgent. Shall I have them sent up, sir?"

'Probably congratulations from President Bush. Presidents do those sort of things,' he thought. "Yes, send them on up right away."

John Moffett clicked on the television. His scalp prickled at the sight of Flint Firestone being interviewed in the grand hall of the yacht club. The sound quickly followed when the set warmed up. "Yes, I have in fact filed a protest with the race committee...." Firestone was saying, his voice drowned out by John Moffett swearing.

"WHAT ARE YOU PROTESTING? YOU SPINELESS BASTARD!" he screamed, startling the bellman who was knocking at the door.

"Good heavens, sir! Is there anything wrong?"

"No, nothing. Thanks, buddy. Here," Moffett replied handing him a five dollar bill and quickly closing the door.

"Goddamn it! What's this?" he asked, glancing down at the neatly typed white envelope bearing the Race Committee's logo which he grabbed off the top before throwing the stack on the coffee table. He briefly inspected the bold type: PERSONAL AND CONFIDENTIAL, HAND DELIVER. He ripped open the envelope, glancing back at the television to see if Firestone was off the air.

John's hands were trembling. He scanned quickly down the page, 'An official protest has been lodged by the captain of the yacht *Martinis*, Flint Firestone.... An inquiry by the International Jury will be held at one p.m. today in the Prince Albert Room of the RBYC to resolve.... You are not required to attend but we recommend that you do so.... A copy of the protest will be made available to you at ten a.m. this morning...'

"GODDAMN HIM!" Moffett swore again, grabbing the large stack of faxes, telegrams and phone messages, and heaving them against the wall. He grabbed the coffee table and flipped it like a pancake on a griddle before seizing the nearest chair and lifting it over his head in his fit of rage, catching himself just before smashing it against the wall. Moffett stomped around the room, noticing a fax from his law firm, Moffett, Spencer and Grace, on the floor as he put the chair down and stormed into the bathroom and threw cold water on his face to get hold of himself. "Goddamn you, Flint Firestone," he swore quietly, drying his face and looking in the mirror in total disgust. The sick feeling of having a protest filed against him sank in.

John Moffett's brilliant legal mind was instantly at work analyzing the situation, searching for any possible clues as to what race infractions Firestone could possibly be protesting. After a few minutes he came to the conclusion that there was only one possibility: the tanker, the goddamn tanker. Surely to hell it wasn't the tanker situation that Firestone had gotten wind of. 'My crew all sworn an oath of secrecy about the engine, so surely to hell that couldn't possibly be it, or could it? Somebody could've talked,' he was thinking. He ran through his crew list. 'NO! That's impossible,' remembering Peter's remarks and watching Doc Pearson and Flint Firestone engaged in deep conversation, drinking rum swizzles at the yacht club last evening.

John Moffett thought it all over again to make sure. Was it the drag race to the finish line? No, that was not a possibility. The finish line was observed by the Finish Line Committee and nothing had been said. The *Martinis* would have had to protest immediately as required by the racing rules by flying a red triangle Code B flag for any maneuver infractions that might have occurred.

John shaved and quickly dressed, glancing back at the mess he had made of his room. He righted the coffee table and left. Passing through the lobby he grabbed a quick cup of coffee, hurrying next door to the RBYC to face his frustrated crew and the press.

"Captain Moffett!" the reporters screamed as he made his way across the great hall. "Have you gotten a copy of the protest yet?"

"What did you do, Captain?" another shouted as flashes from the cameras lit the room.

"No, I haven't seen the protest," John replied. He kept moving, a trick he had learned after having dealt with the press hundreds of times before and after court. On the dock now he dodged more reporters and was met by Bob and Tony along with the remaining crew who were busy getting the boat shipshape and squared away. From their glum faces, John knew they had already heard the news.

"Anybody seen Pete this morning?" John asked, as they gathered below in the sanctuary of the main saloon, out of sight of the reporters.

"Yes, Captain. Peter came aboard earlier this morning all dressed up. Didn't say where he was going, though," replied Doc Pearson sheepishly, his head pounding as John shot him a nasty look.

'He's the bastard,' John thought, 'the god-damned faggot that's ratted on me. I'll kill the SOB with my bare hands if I get disqualified.'

"What the hell's going on, John?" Tony and Bob asked simultaneously, their voices raspy and harsh with anger.

"Don't know, gentlemen," John replied. "I will be able to pick up a copy of the protest at ten this morning from the International Jury. Bob, I want you and Tony to go with me to get it while the rest of you guys get this boat cleaned up, please."

"What the hell's Firestone protesting anyhow, Skipper?"

"Look, gentlemen, we cannot prepare our defense until we read the complaint. It's like an indictment; you've all been through this process before," John intentionally reminded them of their criminal past. "Let's stay calm and get this mess cleaned up now, and don't discuss it with those reporters out there."

Captain John Moffett and his crew had been nervously waiting for over half an hour in the Prince Albert Room when someone asked, "Where the hell's Slade?"

"I forgot, he has a business appointment," John replied.

The men made idle chitchat in low nervous voices, waiting for the International Jury to enter. John Moffett sat stoned-faced, knowing he had to be his own lawyer, and that was a dangerous thing considering the trophy was at stake.

The door to the Prince Albert room flung open and Flint Firestone and his crew trooped confidently in. The almighty protester and prosecutors had arrived to dethrone him with his captain's hat tucked neatly under his left arm. The two crews exchanged angry glances from across the room as did their captains. Firestone seated himself next to the aisle in front of the jury. He was wearing a double-breasted blazer, white slacks and Harkin sailing shoes.

At precisely one o'clock the International Jury entered from the back of the room. The chairman, vice-chairman and three jurors took their seats behind a large conference table. Mr. Hugh Stewart, the chairman and a distinguished member of the Cruising Club of America, introduced the members of the jury which was comprised of two members from the Royal Bermuda Yacht Club and two representatives from the Cruising Club of America. The judges were chosen by their peers for being men of impeccable character, possessing judicial temperament and a reputation for integrity. They were all recognized as competitors in world-class competition, and had been confirmed by the prestigious U.S. Sailing Committee on Judges.

The proceedings began with a tense silence. Captain Moffett and the crew of the *Encounter* leaned forward in their chairs and waited.

Chairman Stewart spoke. "Gentlemen, for the record, the International Jury was not to be held until Thursday of this week. However, due to the serious nature of the protest lodged against the standing lines honor yacht and current corrected time leader, we have scheduled this hearing early and for obvious reasons."

The tension got thicker in a room of nerves. The chairman continued explaining the rules of protest and the manner in which the jury would conduct the inquiry. "Our decision will be made after we have gathered all the facts. We will either find the *Encounter* guilty or not. If infractions have been made, and depending upon the severity thereof, we will either disqualify the yacht or penalize it by increasing its elapsed time by two hours or her corrected finished position by 20 percent," he concluded.

Doc Pearson's eye began to twitch as the chairman's voice echoed in his aching head. He knew the gravity of what had just been said.

'Firestone's an impressive enough looking guy,' Moffett thought, sizing up his accuser as Firestone stood to address the jury. 'But he's no damn lawyer,' Moffett surmised, as he leaned back in his chair and listened, quietly planning his defense.

"Captain Firestone, we have read your protest, and at this time request that you make your allegations public before the jury and the accused, Captain John Moffett."

Firestone spoke in his deep, rich New England voice. "Gentlemen, I have been told in confidence by a member of the *Encounter*'s crew that during the race John Moffett engaged the engine in direct violation of not only Fundamental Rule C, which states that a yacht shall compete only by sailing, but as specifically addressed in Rule 54, Propulsion, which defines sailing: 'A yacht is sailing when using only the wind and water to increase, maintain or decrease her speed, with her crew adjusting the trim of sails and hull and performing other acts of seamanship.' By engaging the engine, the *Encounter* gained enough advantage to give it the needed seconds to cross the finish line less than half a yacht ahead of the *Martinis*. It is my protest that I am the winner, given the fact that Moffett cheated."

The gray-haired jurors, wearing crested blue blazers and ties, took careful notes, listening intently to Firestone, exercising their years of experience and wisdom. Moffett was impressed. This was his jury that he was looking at. For the first time in his life he was on trial.

Who was the Judas on *Encounter*'s crew? To a man their hostile eyes fell on Dr. Pearson squirming in his chair.

Firestone took a drink of water and began again. "On a much more serious note, I am charging that Captain John Moffett has violated Rule 75, Gross Infringement of Rules of Misconduct by intentional cheating, a deliberate infringement and should, therefore, not only be disqualified from this race but dealt with much more severely by the U.S. Sailing Committee for such a flagrant violation of Rule 75, the most fundamental of International Yacht Racing Rules, gentlemen. John Moffett did not report the incident in his yacht's Certificate of Compliance of the race."

"Captain Firestone, for the record," Chairman Stewart interrupted in his refined New York accent, "for the record one does not protest under Rule 75. You can, however, as a protester suggest that a penalty under Rule 75 be considered by the jury."

"Very well, Mr. Chairman, I amend my original protest to read that I suggest that the International Jury invoke a penalty under Rule 75 for intentional cheating in the Bermuda Race."

Mumbling erupted on the *Encounter*'s side of the room. John shot the crew a dirty look to stay quiet.

The chairman then asked, "What evidence do you have to present to the jury to support your allegations, Captain Firestone?"

"It was confidentially confided to me by a member of the *Encounter*'s crew last night. I would like to keep his name confidential for obvious reasons, gentlemen. The *Encounter*'s engine was run..."

"I'm afraid that you will have to be more specific, Captain. The jury cannot act on hearsay testimony."

Firestone struggled, shifting his tall weight to his other foot, turning now and looking directly at Dr. Pearson.

"It was that man, Dr. Duane Pearson, seated over there. He told me at the bar last night that the *Encounter* had run its engine during the race and for a matter of some time, I was told."

There was a rumble like distant thunder throughout the room. Everyone was looking directly at Doc Pearson's pasty white face. His right eye twitched furiously. Beads of sweat formed on his aching brow.

"Very well, Captain Firestone. Please be seated. Is Dr. Pearson present? Would you please address the jury and, for the record, please state your name, occupation and address."

Standing in front of the jurors, Dr. Pearson closed his twitching eye and grasped his hands before him. He began in a high-pitched feminine voice, "My name is Dr. Duane L. Pearson. I am a non-practicing psychiatrist and I live in Newport, Rhode Island. And... and... Flint Firestone is a pathological...."

"DOCTOR! Please. You will have a chance to make a statement. Just answer my questions and let's not get into any name calling. I see that you are listed on the sail application of the *Encounter* as a member of the crew. Is that correct?"

"Yes, sir, I am," Doc replied, pressing and twitching his body from one side to the other. The *Martinis* crew snickered.

'I'm going to kill the son-of-a-bitch,' Moffett thought. He caught himself starting to object to the questioning of the witness, but remembered, fortunately, that this was not a court of law. He remained silent and outwardly unemotional, fighting hard to keep calm.

"Doctor, did you talk to Captain Firestone last night at the Royal Bermuda Yacht Club?"

"Yes, I remember speaking with Flint Firestone."

"In that conversation did you state that the *Encounter* had engaged its engine while sailing in order to gain unfair advantage and in violation of the Rule 54 and Fundamental Rule C of fair sailing and fail to report the incident on its Certificate of Compliance?"

"I did not!!! Flint Firestone is what we psychiatrists refer to in clinical terms as a pathological liar and I had no conversation..."

"YOU'RE A LYING BASTARD, PEARSON!!!" Firestone erupted, lunging forward. Blood rushed to his face, turning it crimson as the chairman's gavel fell.

"ORDER! ORDER! I shall not tolerate such outbursts, Captain Firestone!"

John Moffett had spent his career in courtrooms and felt relieved when his accuser lost control. He was still very uncomfortable at being the defendant and his own attorney. When he was called, he approached the jury, looking each of them directly in the eye with his sad eyes. He spoke in a firm but relaxed voice.

"Gentlemen, I am John Moffett, captain of the *Encounter*, and I would like to take this opportunity to introduce my first mate, Bob Gangloff, Navigator Tony Stevenson, and the rest of my crew over here."

His voice came righteously forth, soothing to the jury's ears. "Gentlemen, I am here on behalf of my yacht, my crew and the Newport Yacht Club, of which I have had the honor to serve as commodore. As a reputable sailor and a long-standing member of U.S. Sail, I flatly deny the charges brought upon my yacht and its crew in the 1990 Newport-Bermuda Race by Flint Firestone. These false accusations are brought by my ex-brother-in-law. He has had an ax to grind since my firm represented his ex-wife in a recent divorce proceeding in Providence. His ex-wife just happens to be my sister, paralyzed by Captain Firestone while driving under the influence in an automobile accident two years ago. My sister received a four million dollar settlement in her divorce proceedings after Flint Firestone abandoned her for a twenty-five-year-old fashion model, his own daughter's age. I am shocked that this bitterness from the divorce proceeding in April of last year and our past family relationship would enter into the rules of sportsmanship. I uphold as the foundation for competitive sailing..."

"THE GODDAMN DIVORCE DOESN'T HAVE A DAMN THING TO DO WITH IT, JOHN! THAT QUEER DOCTOR..." Firestone shouted to the chairman's gavel pounding on the table once more.

"Silence! Silence! Captain Firestone..." the chairman admonished as order was soon returned and Moffett continued.

"I only tell you this because I am horrified that, under the rule of fair sportsmanship, Flint Firestone would be such a poor loser and hold a grudge against me and my crew to bring up such fictitious charges. You have just heard that the charges were denied by Dr. Pearson, a psychiatrist whom Flint has made such personal insults and slanderous statements against. Flint, you should be ashamed..."

The skilled defense lawyer had done it once again. So quickly and cleverly and without any objections from the stone-faced jury, he knew he had discredited his accuser by skillfully reading the jury's eyes.

"It's all a damn lie, gentlemen...."

Moffett interrupted, "We did not at anytime during the

Bermuda Race engage our engine to gain unfair advantage in violation of Rule 54. And I would like to suggest that the committee consider invoking Rule 75 against Flint Firestone for these unfounded accusations. He is in serious violation of fair sportsmanship."

Firestone's face flushed. The jury sat, expressionless, staring at him.

The chairman asked, "Captain Firestone, do you have anything further to say before your final statement?"

Firestone lost control, screaming, "You're damned right, I do! Dr. Pearson is a bald-faced liar and a faggot. He told me last night when he was drunk that the *Encounter* had run its engine when John damn near got them run down by an oil tanker after he miscalculated who had the right-of-way. Moffett is a rotten attorney and a masterful liar, makes his living doing it. Give the whole damn bunch of criminals a lie detector test and then you will see who is shooting straight...."

"You are absurd."

"Why in hell did Pearson admit it then last night when I was talking to him then?.... If this thing is not taken up further with a lie detector...I'll pay for it, have a damn lie detector team fly out here today from Boston at my expense... I'll by God write you a check. If you let these cheats get away with running their engine there will be a grave injustice that will mar the integrity of international sailing till hell freezes over."

"Is that all, Captain?" Chairman Stewart asked coldly. "They do have lie detectors in Bermuda, for your information, Captain; however, sir, it is not deemed proper to employ such devices in this hearing." He then smiled and nodded to John, "Captain Moffett, do you have a final statement?"

"Only to say it is regrettable that this protest hearing was ever held. I am embarrassed by it all. I trust the jury will find that the *Encounter* has not violated Rule 54 nor have I at any time dishonored myself or my crew or the Newport Yacht Club by violating Rule 75. Thank you, gentlemen," John said soberly, looking once again with his sad eyes directly into the eyes of the jurors.

"Gentlemen, the International Jury will now recess for deliberation. The jury will reconvene at two o'clock this afternoon."

# Chapter XVI

## Bank of Bermuda Limited
### The Morning of June 19, 1990

"What do I do now, O'Grady?" Slade asked, glancing at his watch and getting that nasty, mean feeling back inside again. "There's a lot of time before we go to the bank..."

"Geez, I don't know. Whatever suits ya. Didja understand that youse guys gotta be at the bank at two?"

'Yeah, Joe Camel, I understand,' Slade thought, 'and I'm damn sure not going to sit in this room listening to your blabber, you chain-smoking shithead.' He glanced over at the lovely long-legged woman still sitting by the phone.

"Care to join me for a bite of lunch, Carolina?" Slade asked politely, picking up the money bag and swinging it over his shoulder.

"Hey, I'm hungry too. Where youse guys goin?" O'Grady asked, mashing out his cigarette.

"Nowhere with you, Joe Camel," Slade snapped. "I'll see you back here at one-thirty, lady."

"No, wait, Peter, I'll join you!" Carolina's voice seemed desperate. She dug frantically in her purse for the room key. "Excuse us, Flynn. Should I call you after our two o'clock appointment, or what?"

"I'll call you," O'Grady replied smugly, shooting them a dirty look, thinking, 'everything is working out perfectly, pretty boy. Your ass is grass, Slade, and I'm the lawn mower. You will be my and Ode's guest for dinner on the plane to New York tomorrow night when you're handcuffed.' He waited for them to leave the room before placing a call to the Manhattan office of the FBI.

"Hey, Ode! Don't forget to pack your Bermuda shorts!"

"I've got them packed, Flynn. How's it going out there?"

"Slade showed up with the money and they've got a two o'clock appointment at the bank. Everything's on schedule."

"Good."

"I'll notify you tomorrow after I get an arrest warrant approved by the chief in Washington so you can come out and arrest Slade."

"What about the Madam? She's a tough looking bitch, isn't she?"

"Tough as a garlic milk shake, man."

Outside a bright Bermuda sun glared off the white-tiled roofs of the buildings. Slade donned his Ray Ban sunglasses, saying, "Hey, lady, I don't know what the hell I'm in for here, but I don't like it!"

The two of them started down Pitts Bay Road for the short five-minute walk into Hamilton. She replied, "Can you believe the nerve of that guy, wanting to have lunch?"

"I can believe anything when it comes to the Feds," Slade replied, swinging the bag to his other shoulder.

"Got enough money in that sack to buy my lunch, sailor?" Carolina laughed, touching Slade casually on his arm.

"Hell yes, lady! Enough to buy the whole damn island of Bermuda dinner tonight. Now hear this! NOw HEar THis! Joe the Camel O'Grady will be buying dinner for residents of the island, courtesy of the Securities and Exchange Commission of the United States Government whose regulations state that no Bermuda shorts shall be worn!" Slade shouted, giving Carolina a slight hug around her shoulders, feeling the smooth texture of her tanned skin. The two began laughing hysterically.

"O'Grady does look exactly like Joe Camel in the new Camel cigarette advertisement. I almost cracked up when you called him that to his face, you awful man," Carolina laughed. Her three-inch heels echoed off the sidewalk from a stride that only a slim, beautiful fashion model could take and get away with.

"Joe Camel is an ugly bastard all right, and if he wore glasses, O'Grady would be his twin."

She stopped for a moment at the entrance to Waterloo House and looked him straight in the eye. "Well, Peter, I'm not in Bermuda vacationing with Mr. O'Grady either, you know? You weren't really going to leave me to have lunch with Joe Camel, were you, dear?"

"Do I look like the mean type of guy?" Slade grinned, thinking, I hope to hell Moffett sees me with this foxy chick.'

They began walking again and he said, "Wherever you are, Johnny my boy, good luck with Firestone, the son-of-a-bitch."

"What are you talking about?" she asked, walking quickly past the Bank of Bermuda Limited without comment.

"Like O'Grady said, we had a protest filed against us by a guy named Flint Firestone."

"What for?"

"Beats hell out of me. We had a five grand bet riding on the race, and Firestone had better pay up or I'm going to personally whip his ass," Slade said as they made their way along Front Street, which was crowded with tourists off the cruise ships docked at the Hamilton wharf.

They leisurely window-shopped in the small pastel-colored buildings with snazzy boutiques and shops, making casual conversation. He felt like he had known her for a long time now, while the fresh Bermuda breeze ruffled his thin hair as they strolled along. It was a wonderful feeling for Peter Slade, like being a schoolboy with a crush on a pretty girl for the first time.

The sounds of the steel band playing gombey music made them stop on the wharf to listen. Slade noticed a seagull that had lit on a piling and was watching them, knowing that they both wished to hell they were somewhere else.

When the band stopped playing, he asked, "Where would you like to have lunch, Carolina?"

"Some place out of the way, where Joe the Camel can't possibly find us and you can put that heavy bag down," she replied, feeling his biceps.

"You name it."

"Oh, I know just the place? Let's go to the Hog Penny. Follow me, sailor."

They turned off Front Street onto Burnaby, walking a short distance until they came to an old English pub. Slade glanced up and down the street for O'Grady before ducking quickly inside.

"Can I take the bag for you?" the waiter asked.

"No, thank you," Slade replied, as the woman gave him a big smile. "You can bring us a couple of pints of draft."

The Hog Penny was dark and cool. It was refreshing to be out of the hustle and bustle of the Front Street tourist trap. They were seated in a secluded corner booth in the back of the dark and smoky den. The waiter returned with two pints and menus.

In the dim light, Slade looked into the eyes of the woman he had known for less than two hours and asked, "Carolina, are you, or should I say, were you the Blue-Blooded Madam from New York?"

Carolina didn't hesitate answering in her soft marvelous voice, "That was me, Peter, the Blue-Blooded Madam of New York City who claimed international fame after I got busted by the FBI over five years ago."

"I thought so."

"Are you surprised to find me here?"

"Yeah, I guess. Real damned surprised, actually," Peter said, scratching his forehead. "Pleasantly so, though."

"I wish to hell I wasn't here, but hopefully after today and tomorrow this will be the final chapter in my past."

Peter Slade wondered what her role was in all of this — whatever this was that they were doing — and he needed to ask her that. "I remember reading about it in the *New York Times*."

"You and the rest of the world. But you know, Peter, on the other hand, at times I'm not sure that if I had it all to do over again, I would do it any differently," she said, her voice cracking. She bit her bottom lip and he noticed tears welling up in her eyes as memories of Siegfried Dassler returned.

"Are you OK? I'm sorry I brought it up."

"Yes, I'm fine. Thanks."

"We all have skeletons in our closets, don't we?" Slade asked, captured by her charm, desperate to somehow find out if his hunch was correct and he was going to have to launder the money in his own secret account. 'Is she on their side or mine,' he wondered, hoping to hell Carolina Barrington wasn't trying to set him up. Who in the hell could he trust?

"Yes, we do. I don't recall ever meeting you in New York, Peter," she said seductively. "Did you ever date any of my girls?"

"No, I really didn't. I was married then, but I bet you know my old partner at Porterfield Hartley, Herb Gidwitz," Peter laughed.

"You're right! Herb, 'Junk Bond King of Wall Street'. Wow, what a guy. He arranged for hundreds of engagements between your clients and my social club staff. Herb helped make me a wealthy woman before the goddamn FBI and IRS came along and broke it all up."

"How did they bust you?"

"With a sledgehammer," she sighed, taking a sip of beer.

"No, seriously. How did they?"

"Oh, one of my girls named Melissa was underaged and turned state's evidence on me. That got the ball rolling. Damn that little bitch! I treated her like a daughter, and she screwed me over."

"Carolina, how about leveling with me? Where do you stand in all of this crap with O'Grady? You a government agent now, or what's your deal, may I ask?"

"Yes!" she laughed. "I'm trapped just like you, Peter."

"As part of your plea arrangement?"

"Yeah. I'm repaying my debt to society in a plea-bargain agreement with the Justice Department for running an interstate prostitution ring and for income tax evasion. After this assignment, I'm finished with them forever, I hope."

Income tax evasion. The words made prickly spines run up Slade's back. "What do they want us to do with this at the bank this afternoon?" he asked, cutting his eye to the money bag. Leaning forward in the booth, he watched her reaction, taking a drink of beer and leaving a mustache of suds on his upper lip.

She reached across the table and wiped it away with her warm soft hand. "Peter, I cannot tell you what's next. I would if I could, but that's part of my deal with Joe Camel, the pencil-ass. Please don't ask me again. You've got your job to do and I've got mine. I feel terrible about all of this as it is, damn it."

Slade sat back, looking disappointed. "I understand," he replied, glancing down at his watch, dreading for two o'clock to arrive.

"Not to change the subject, but how are things going at the Stone Bridge Inn, Peter?"

"The Stone Bridge Inn?! How do you know about the Inn?"

"Peter, the FBI briefed me on you at Logan Field yesterday before I left Boston and flew out here to meet O'Grady."

"Oh, yeah. What did the FBI have to say?"

"They were much more flattering than our handler, Joe the Camel. He didn't have anything good to say about you before you showed up this morning. I don't know what it is about him, but he hates your guts."

"Yeah, tell me about it. It's mutual. What did the FBI tell you?"

"Oh, everything about your past: Wall Street, Vietnam, Charlotte, your arrest, everything except your jock size," she grinned.

"Extra large, of course!" he quipped. "You ready to order some lunch?"

The lobby to the Bank of Bermuda Limited was just as Slade had remembered it: cool black marble floors and walls with indirect lighting illuminating the bank's name in big gold letters on the wall. Very conservative and tasteful as one would expect of a Bermuda bank. Carolina Barrington led the way as they took the elevator to the top floor and were greeted by a very plain woman named Margaret Fox sitting at her desk outside the managing director's office. "May I help you?" she asked.

"Yes. I am Carolina Barrington and this is Mr. Peter Slade. We have a two o'clock appointment with Mr. Ferris."

"Please be seated. Can I get you coffee or tea?" Margaret Fox inquired, shooting a skeptical glance at the blue bag Slade was holding behind him. She quietly spoke with her boss on the intercom.

"No, thanks," Carolina replied, taking a seat on the sofa. Slade took a seat in the adjoining armchair, trying to keep the money bag out of sight.

Paul Ferris came from behind a heavy wooden door that bore his name and title. Stepping out with a ghostly plastic smile on his face, he immediately recognized Slade from his picture in the morning paper. "Ms. Barrington, what a surprise," he said, extending his hand and ushering them quickly into his spacious office.

"Paul, this is my business associate, Mr. Peter Slade, from Newport, Rhode Island," Carolina introduced the two men.

"Yes, please be seated," replied the banker, who was dressed in a coat and tie and Bermuda shorts. He nervously extended his cold moist hand, glancing suspensefully at the blue bag. "I think I saw your picture in the morning paper, Mr. Slade, did I not? Congratulations on the race."

"Thank you, Mr. Ferris, I am staying at Salt Kettle and I saw you on the ferry this morning. What a coincidence: we meet again!"

"Can I get anyone anything? Mr. Ferris?" Margaret Fox asked.

"No, thank you. Please hold my calls, Margaret," Ferris replied, fidgeting in a large black leather executive chair that made him appear very small.

'So here's the man I got the letter about from the Securities and Exchange Commission five years ago,' Ferris thought. 'He's the man they were investigating and wanting to know about his trust account when they inquired about the stock transactions that I duplicated. This is all very strange, his showing up now with Carolina. I must be very careful with these two Americans.'

"I am just a member of the *Encounter*'s crew," Peter said, looking around at the elegant office.

"Well congratulations! I had lunch at the yacht club and I do hope things go well for your captain at the protest hearing this afternoon, Mr. Slade."

"Thank you, Mr. Ferris."

"Now, Carolina, how might I be of service to you and Mr. Slade?"

"We would like to open a confidential joint account in mine and Mr. Slade's names," Carolina replied, leaning forward in her chair as the words made Peter Slade cringe, but not flinching a muscle.

"Very well," Ferris replied. "I will need to see both of your passports."

Peter handed over his passport. The banker's hand was trembling, Slade noticed, while Carolina dug in her purse. "We have a minimum of fifty thousand dollars, U.S., to open a new account. How would you like to arrange for the opening balance?"

Carolina pulled out her passport and took the blue canvas bag from Peter and walked over and emptied it on Paul Ferris's desk.

"My god!" Ferris stammered, drawing back in horror at the pile of one hundred dollar bills. "Carolina... what... what is this?"

"One half million, U.S.," she replied. "Count it for yourself, Paul."

"What!" Ferris exclaimed, pushing back from his desk. "We at the Bank of Bermuda Limited are not engaged in the illegal act of money laundering, Ms. Barrington. I am highly insulted that you should ask!" his voice trembled as he reached for a glass of water.

"Now, Paul, just calm down. Peter got the money through customs without any problem...."

"Yes! Yes, I know, but Bermuda has just signed into law the United Nations Convention Against Illicit Traffic in Drugs that also criminalized money laundering.... Here, take all this money back. It's the law in Bermuda now."

"Take it easy, Paul. No one will ever know..."

"No! It's against the law, a criminal act...now. I'm not having anything to do with it."

"Nobody knows it's here but the three of us."

"That...that's...yours and Mr. Slade's affair! I'm not having anything to do with any of this, I tell you. I...I cannot oblige the two of you. It's illegal."

"Please, Paul, don't make it difficult on yourself. Don't make me play hardball with you, dear."

"Hardball? I haven't a clue as to what you are speaking."

Slade was thinking, 'good, the wormy little guy's not going to take it. Why is she opening a joint account? Thank God, I didn't have to make a deposit to my trust account.' His guts wrenched tightly as he sat and watched the blood drain from

Paul Ferris's face. It appeared that he might break down at any moment.

"I'm very sorry I...I...I cannot help you. Now I have another appointment if you will please..."

"Look, Paul, I've got the dates, names, and numbers plus the amount of money that you invested at my social club in New York when you were dating my call girls. Twenty-four thousand dollars in 1983 alone. Now, we open a secret account in my and Mr. Slade's name and make the deposit or your bank directors are going to ask you some pretty embarrassing questions," Carolina said in a mean-spirited voice.

Paul Ferris's jaw fell slack in horror at her words.

'You goddamn blackmailing bitch,' Slade thought to himself. He then remembered that it wasn't Carolina speaking but the United States Justice Department. 'Ferris is going to lose it,' he thought, watching the banker come unglued.

"You wouldn't dare do such a bastardly thing as blackmail me, Carolina..."

"You got it, Paul! Now start counting the money. I don't have all day," she said with grit in her voice.

Ferris started counting the pile of cash on his desk, "There are laws against money laundering and blackmail on this island, and I have a good mind to go to the authorities over this!" Ferris fretted. He counted the money in a neat pile while Slade and Carolina filled out the routine new account application, listing their address, profession, etc. Peter awarded John Moffett his power of attorney. A photocopy of their passports was taken for identification after Ferris stowed the money under his desk and out of sight.

Thirty-five minutes later the whole process was completed

when Ferris handed an envelope containing a temporary hand-written receipt on a piece of bank stationery to Peter. "It will take some internal finagling on my part to get this money deposited and into the vault without raising the suspicions of the head cashier and creating a violation of the internal control procedures which our bank has against money laundering. Give me until tomorrow and I will have the transaction completed and have your account number for you, Carolina."

"Very well. We will drop by tomorrow morning around eleven o'clock and pick it up, Paul."

"Fine," Ferris replied flatly. "Will ...will there be anything else?" he asked coldly, his flushed face expressionless.

"Oh, yes. Just one other thing, dear, that I want you to do for me, Paul," Carolina said in a matter-of-fact voice.

"WHAT?!! What is that?"

"I want a list of every United States citizen and their address-es who have a secret account or trust account in this bank when I arrive to pick up our new account number tomorrow morning. Please put it on a computer diskette, if you don't mind."

"BLOODY IMPOSSIBLE! Bloody damn impossible!!! The Bank of Bermuda Limited would never disclose its customer's names and breach our confidential trust. Never! I can arrange this cash transaction by being blackmailed, but, ladies and gentlemen, I will assure you that Paul Fitzgerald Ferris will not breach the trust of his clients, blackmail or not, Carolina Barrington!" he almost shouted, shaking uncontrollably.

Carolina opened her purse, holding up a six-page computer listing of the names, times and places, along with the amount of money that Paul Ferris had spent in her social club over the peri-od from 1981 to November 2, 1984. The names of the ladies numbered sixty-four and the services came to one hundred and sixty-eight thousand dollars. "Paul, you either prepare me a list of your American clients with secret accounts or I'm going to deliver this list personally to the *Royal Gazette* tomorrow at noon!"

"WHAT??!! I...I... can't do it, Carolina!" Ferris sobbed, tears running down his ashen face, streaming now, dripping on his desk as he covered his face with his hands. "Why are you ruining my life, blackmailing me this way? OH, why? I never harmed you in any way, Carolina, have I? Please tell me what I've done to you to deserve this?" His whole body shook, sobbing, a complete wreck of a man now.

Peter Slade was in shock, almost feeling sorry for the poor guy. He was thinking, 'I've been screwed if the poor miserable son-of-a-bitch agrees to get her a list and the Feds get my name and trust account number. This bitch is ruthless! The fucking United States government is ruthless! Goddamn this bunch of lousy blackmailing bastards!' Slade was still thinking when Carolina stood up and said coldly, "Get hold of yourself, Paul, we are leaving. We will be here for the list of account numbers and our new account number at eleven tomorrow morning, and, for your sake, Paul, please have it ready or I'm going directly to the newspaper."

# Chapter XVII

## Pitts Bay Road, Hamilton
### Afternoon of June 19, 1990

Peter Slade rushed out of the lobby of the Bank of Bermuda Limited ahead of her onto the street. "What the hell's next, Carolina?" he asked in a razor-sharp voice. Thrusting his hands in his pockets he rocked back and forth on his heels. When she didn't answer, he looked at her and saw how shaken she was by it all. 'She looks damn pitiful,' he thought, not knowing what to do or say next.

Blackmail was beyond his comprehension and the very lowest of acts, especially blackmail by his own government. The government he had fought a war for, as had his father and grandfather before him to defend the principles that the government of the United States of America was supposed to stand for. Liberty? Freedom? Justice? What the hell had happened to the blind scales of justice when the United States Justice Department had reverted to turning them into low-life blackmailers to get a goddamn list?

Peter Slade hated having been part of it, and for the moment had hated her for doing it, too. She looked into his quick blue eyes and she knew that from the way he was looking at her that he thought it had been her idea.

She was still hearing Paul Ferris pleading for his life, crying, begging, and it was more than Carolina could take.

Now she was trembling, her eyes shamefully downcast on the street. She looked away, fighting to regain her composure. Her long dark hair caught in the Bermuda breeze and wrapped around her face. She swept it back, putting on sunglasses. "I don't know what to do next, Peter. Nothing until tomorrow morning, I suppose. Meet me at my hotel around ten-thirty."

'God, she's beautiful, and feeling awfully sorry that she had to blackmail the poor bastard,' Slade was now thinking. He watched the sun glistening on her dark hair. He hated the government of the United States more than ever for putting her through this, the rotten blackmailers. He took his hands out of his pockets and looked around feeling sick.

"If O'Grady wants to talk to you, he will call at your hotel."

"Don't look now, but Joe Camel is sitting across the street watching us. Let's walk back toward the Princess Hotel," Peter said, trying to act casual.

"Is he following us?"

"I think so, but don't let him know you see him. Blackmailing that poor pitiful Ferris sucks, as far as I'm concerned," Peter added, feeling sorry for Carolina and afraid she might begin to cry.

She was walking bent forward, her head down and her shoulders, shaking. He knew she was crying silently, and he hated it when women did that. She searched for a Kleenex in her purse. He handed her his handkerchief. The seriousness of O'Grady getting the list of Americans with his name on it made him weak in his knees.

'Damn it,' Slade thought, 'should I ask her to have dinner with me tonight and spill my guts about MY name being on that list? No. Why trust a woman you just met this morning?' He had to come up with a better plan. Looking over at her, he felt a strong urge to hold and console her as she wiped away the tears.

They were at the entrance to the Royal Bermuda Yacht Club when he stopped, reached over and lightly touched her arm. "OK, lady, I'll drop off at the boat and then see you at the hotel in the morning," he was saying, the words coming hard. He wanted to leave her, but at the same time he hated to. He glanced over his shoulder at O'Grady coming down the street.

"All right, Peter. But I hope you understand that none of this was my idea...."

"I know, Carolina, it's not your fault. You and I are just following orders, pawns for that bunch of sick sons-of-bitches," he replied, not looking her in the eye as she handed his handkerchief back.

Slade double-checked the breast pocket of his blazer for Ferris's receipt and said goodbye.

He walked quickly toward the pink arched doorway of the prestigious old club and passed under the massive royal coat of arms. Through the heavy wooden doors flanked by antique brass running lights and into a museum of sailing history he passed. He walked down the long hall past trophy cases, oil paintings of famous sailing yachts and models of the same. Countless portraits of past commodores lined both walls. He came to the bar and took his seat on a tall bar stool at the extreme end so he could look out at the harbor. He watched the seagulls and was very disturbed.

The bartender, a black man named Walter, came over and smiled a genuine smile.

"Give me a draft," Slade ordered, unaware of the International Jury deliberating in the Prince Albert Room. Peter Slade was faced with far greater troubles than getting disqualified from the Newport-Bermuda Race. He drank, thinking about the fateful trap he had fallen into and continued to watch the gulls. For the first time since his arrest in New York, Peter Slade knew that there was an excellent chance that he was going to prison.

'If Paul Ferris gives Carolina the list tomorrow morning, I'm dead. If he does — and there is no reason he won't, considering his whole career and life are at stake — how in the hell can I get my name off the list before she gives it to O'Grady? If I level with Carolina tonight, maybe I could take the diskette to a computer store and erase my name, or hell, buy a laptop and do it myself. Bad plan. O'Grady will be trailing us, so that won't work worth a damn.'

Slade took a long draw of the draft, and now that he knew what O'Grady was after, realized that he had no other choice but to run. 'I'll catch a flight to London tonight, then fly to Switzerland: draw my millions out of my Bank of Bermuda Limited account and open a new account in another Swiss bank, Bank Lou. That's it! It's a piss-poor plan but it's my only choice. I'll take the train from Switzerland to Naples and catch a freighter for South America. Rio perhaps. No, Buenos Aries. Argentina would be better. At least I can *habla espanol* and the Argentine women are beautiful. With my money I can hide out there for the rest of my life and live like a king.'

Peter Slade was thinking about starting his life over again with millions. It was a depressing thought, leaving everything and everybody; however, it was a lot better choice than raking leaves for the next twenty years in Lewisburg. He sat there drinking his beer. 'I wonder if O'Grady has instructed Bermuda Customs to pick me up if I try to leave the island; or should I maybe try to steal Bob Ganloff's passport? We have some resemblances, if the passports aren't checked too closely by Immigration. Hell yes, my plan has got to work.'

He was thinking about the war now, and how important the element of surprise is to catch the enemy off guard. So this was his plan of escape: 'strike quickly and decisively, before O'Grady has time to freeze my account once they know the number and figure out I'm on the run. You will be an international fugitive from justice then, Peter M. Slade, never able to return home to the United States again.

'Fuck it!! This whole crazy idea stinks, running away to South America like that.'

"Do you want another draft, Mr. Slade?" asked Walter, smiling. Slade's mind was made up.

"No, thank you. Walter, it's time to either fish or cut bait, my friend!" He sat the empty mug on the bar and looked out at the lifeless *Encounter* moored at the dock, her pennants flapping in the brisk afternoon breeze. A solitary seagull flew by and, seeing it, he knew fleeing was the way it had to be.

Slade approached the boat. A reporter from the *Royal Gazzette* came out of nowhere. "Mr. Slade. Why aren't you with the rest of the crew at the protest hearing?"

"Have better things to do with my time," Peter replied in an irritated voice as he boarded.

"Mind if I come on board and ask you some questions, Mr...?"

"Sorry, but I am just leaving. Captain Moffett will be glad to talk with you when he returns," Peter snapped.

"Is there any merit to the protest filed by Captain Firestone?" the reporter shouted.

Peter didn't answer. He jotted John a note to call him at Glencoe Hotel when he returned and left it on a nail on the captain's cabin door.

Thirty minutes later he was back at the Glencoe Hotel. The receptionist handed him a fax from Moffett, Spencer and Grace when he got his key. 'Congratulatory note from the lawyers, nice gesture,' he thought. He took out his pocketknife and carefully opened the envelope.

Slade's jaw went slack. He quickly read the notice of a special stockholders meeting of the Stone Bridge Corporation, '...to be held at ten o'clock on the morning of June 29, 1990, for the purpose of replacing Peter Slade as president and chief operating officer of the Stone Bridge Corporation.'

"Goddamn her," he whispered. The message left a sudden bitter loneliness he had not felt since his bad days in New York. It ripped into his heart, leaving a deep pain. He walked in a daze to his room. He was losing the Stone Bridge Inn and all its wonderful people and his wife, too. His marriage was over and the pain got stronger as the reality of it sank in.

Suddenly his heart turned bitter. Peter Slade went into a fit of rage. "YOU GOTTA BE KIDDING, you goddamn bitch! Take the Stone Bridge Inn and cram it up your ass, Charlotte, because Peter Slade's out of here!!!" he screamed.

The phone rang.

"PETE!! By God, we whipped Firestone, son! The International Jury ruled in our favor, thank God! Can you believe it? The

*Encounter* holds line honors and as soon as a handful of the remaining yachts are in we have the Lighthouse Trophy almost wrapped up! Get on your dancing shoes, 'cause we're going to raise some serious hell, my man!"

"Congratulations, Johnny, you smooth-talking son-of-a-gun. I bet Flint Firestone must have shit in his pants!" Slade shouted while thinking he had to capitalize on buying time for his great escape by sounding cool.

"Everything OK, Pete? How did it go today?"

"Hell, it went well with the Feds, Skipper! But now I've got another helluva problem. Did you get the fax from Jack Spencer?"

John read the urgency in Peter's voice. "I got one, but haven't opened it what with the damn protest going on. What's up?"

"Charlotte has called for a special stockholders meeting on the 29th of June to fire me as president and chief operating officer of the Stone Bridge Corporation! She can't do that, can she, John?"

There was a brief pause before John calmly replied, "Yes, Pete, she owns fifty-one percent of the stock and is chairwoman. It will be damn near impossible to make the meeting if you sail back; the awards ceremony is on the 24th."

"What the hell do I do then, John?"

"Well, have you tried calling her?"

"Yesterday I invited Charlotte to fly out here to help celebrate and she flatly refused, hung up in my face."

"OK, Pete, listen. Let's not make the situation worse than it is. I'll call Jack and see what's up. Give me an hour or so to get these reporters out of here and time to get back to Waterloo House. Remember, there's a cocktail party at the U.S. Consul General's at eight-thirty. We are meeting at the bar of the yacht club at eight."

Back at Waterloo House, John opened the fax from his law

firm. He was not surprised by Jack's handwritten note on the first page. "John, Charlotte has requested that I handle her divorce from Peter. Do you have a problem with that, or should she get another attorney?"

'Jesus Christ, Charlotte! What in the hell are you doing?' he asked himself, feeling sorry for his old friend, Peter. 'I had better call Charlotte and Jack and see if I can straighten this mess out without getting caught in the middle.'

His call went directly through to Providence. The firm's receptionist answered. "Mr. Moffett, congratulations, Captain! Does this mean that we get the week off?"

"Heck no!" John laughed. "We've got to cover the overhead. Is Mr. Spencer with a client?"

"No sir. Mr. Spencer has gone on vacation.... No sir, I'm sorry he did not leave word on where he was going....Anne doesn't know either....I tried to call him at home this morning to give him his messages but he didn't answer. I'll try again.... Yes sir, I'll have him call you in Bermuda when we hear from him."

'That's not like Jack Spencer at all,' John thought. 'In all these years, he has never left the office for five minutes without letting his secretary know where he is. He's such an old maid, he would never leave, especially when I am out of town. Better call Charlotte then and see if I can talk any sense into her.'

As usual, it was the voice of the stuffy Englishman, Thomas Terrell, that answered the phone at Beach Mont. "Good afternoon, Captain Moffett, and congratulations, sir."

"Thank you, Thomas. May I please speak to the lady of the house, my dear cousin, Miss Charlotte?"

"Sorry, sir. I am afraid that Mrs. Slade is in New York for the rest of the week.... No sir, she did not leave a number, but I do expect her to call.... May I give her a message, sir?... Very well, my dear Captain, I will have her call.... Your number at the Waterloo House in Bermuda is..."

John hung up the phone. 'This is strange as hell, Jack and Charlotte both out of town. I don't suppose they...?'

It was a much easier decision to make a run for it after receiving the fax. Peter Slade started to pack, then thought better of it. 'I'll leave all my stuff so they will think I am still in Bermuda and hopefully buy some more time when they start looking for me. To fly out, I'll have to use my real name and passport to get a ticket and clear Customs, so it won't make any sense to steal Bob's. Bermuda keeps track of all visitors to make sure they don't have any illegal aliens.'

He checked his wallet, counting twenty-five one hundred dollar bills that he had skimmed out of the cash register at the Stone Bridge Inn to use for pocket money. No more credit cards for Peter M. Slade; he was strictly on the cash basis.

He walked to the lobby and used the pay phone to call British Airways.

"Our direct flight to London's Gatwick Airport is at 8:15 p.m., arriving at 6:50 a.m. Tuesdays and Thursdays.... Flight number 232.... Coach fare is $686.... Yes, we have plenty of seats for tonight's flight. Shall I make you a reservation?"

Peter thought for a moment. It wa really time now to fish or cut bait. "I'll have to get back with you," he said, hanging up and glancing down at a quarter past five on his watch.

He hurriedly returned to his room, pulled out his gym bag and put in his running suit and shoes. He threw in two changes of underwear and socks, a clean shirt, another tie and nothing more.

'If I arrive in London at seven in the morning it will be three o'clock here in Bermuda. I'll catch another flight to Zurich and be in Bank Lou by ten a.m., which will be six a.m. Bermuda time. By noon I'll be on the train to Naples and lay low until I can catch the first freighter for South America. By the time I'm supposed to meet Carolina at ten-thirty tomorrow morning, I'll have the money transferred and be on my way if everything runs smoothly. It's past four now and I'd better get a quick shower. What do I do about telling John?'

Peter put on a clean shirt, gray slacks and his blue blazer. Picking up his passport and gym bag, he hurried to the Salt Kettle landing to catch the six forty-five ferry to Hamilton. From there he could catch a cab to the airport at the far end of the island. The ferry vibrated under him. He felt that sad loneliness returning and it felt worse than it had ever felt before. Not only was he running out on his best friend and lawyer, but the rest of the world he knew. No one could know about this, not even Moffett. Peter Slade would disappear off the face of the earth forever, never to be heard of or seen again.

# Chapter XVIII

United States Naval Lieutenant Rick Sims was just returning to his BOQ at the Bermuda Air Station from a routine twelve-hour antisubmarine patrol in the Atlantic. The twenty-nine-year-old Naval Academy graduate had been flying P-3 aircraft searching for Soviet submarines for six years, and was looking forward to completing his military obligation and returning to civilian life. When he walked into the day-room he caught the irritating smell of cigarette smoke coming from a skinny red-faced stranger talking on the telephone.

"Ode! Didja know they made the deposit?" was all that Lieutenant Sims heard the stranger saying out of the corner of his cigarette-dangling mouth in passing. 'Getting away from these damn weird Department of Navy civilians will be the best part of getting out of the navy,' he was thinking as he walked down the hall to his room.

"Way to go, Flynn. Look's like your blackmail plan's working....Nothing's changed in the Big Apple. Mets lost, Yanks won."

"What about your flight tomorrow, Ode? What time do I need to meet you at the airport?"

"I got an American flight that's leaving tomorrow night at six-thirty from Kennedy. Think you can get the arrest warrant by then, or do I need to wait and come the next morning when it's cleared in Washington?"

"Naw, come de hell on, man. It's a done deal."

"You call me as soon as you get confirmation from Washington to nab Slade then. I'm not getting my ass chewed for flying to Bermuda at taxpayers' expense on a dry run," the FBI agent said as they continued their conversation.


The *Deliverance's* 6:45 departure from Salt Kettle was on time as Slade checked his watch as he boarded. 'We arrive at Hamilton at 7:10 and my flight to London leaves at 8:15. Allowing thirty minutes for the rush hour traffic to get to the airport, this is going to be close, too damn close,' he thought, sitting back and lighting a Macanudo cigar.

The *Deliverance* churned across Hamilton Harbor. 'Come on, damn it, ferry, move,' he sighed as the ferry's engine vibrations kept drumming *Deliverance, Deliverance,* over and over in his mind. Deliverance from what? Deliverance from going to prison was Slade's answer. The seriousness of making a run for his freedom sank in. 'Fleeing is a big, big gamble,' he thought, 'and the stakes are high, but staying and going to the bank with Carolina tomorrow is a hell of a lot worse.'

Once he was on that British Air flight bound for London, there would be no turning back. What if they stopped him going through Customs at the airport? What would he tell O'Grady? 'I've been invited to Buckingham Palace to have tea with the Queen,' would be his answer. He would just have to remain calm and take it one step at a time and deal with O'Grady if he got caught.

'Goodbye forever, you wonderful Stone Bridge Inn and all the great customers and staff,' Slade was sadly thinking. 'Cheerio, United States government, I'm headed for England, you rotten blackmailer. Adios, George Henley Washington,' he sorrowfully thought, 'I'll see you in Argentina someday.' A lone seagull floating overhead in the late afternoon Bermuda sky cried its sad call that echoed off the water back to him.

Peter Slade kept nervously glancing at his watch. 'If I miss this plane there isn't another flight until Thursday and I'll never get the money transferred from Bank of Bermuda Limited to Swiss Bank Lou before my account is frozen by the Feds,' he thought. 'That would be great, trying to start my life over in Argentina, busted, after the Feds confiscate all my money.'

He was smoking his cigar and thinking about what a great life he was leaving behind when George Washington Henley's voice came rolling back like a second conscience, "Peter, I've been looking after you since you was in diapers. So what you doin', runnin' off, boy?" the old black man's southern voice scolded.

'The old man will be dead in a few years,' Peter thought. The loss of his life-long confidant brought tears to his eyes. He quickly wiped them away with his handkerchief, scented still with Carolina's perfume. 'The old man's always been dependent on me, and will be shattered when he finds out that I'm gone. Charlotte will fire him along with Melissa Jenkins and anyone else she thinks is a friend of mine. I hope to hell Pierre quits; that will really screw things up for the bitch in the kitchen, but hell, she couldn't care less about what happens to the place, anyhow.'

'Johnny Moffett,' he chuckled. 'John's going to be really pissed when he finds out I lied about my secret account in the Bank of Bermuda Limited and even madder for my leaving: without counsel or saying goodbye. I can hear him now, "Slade, you are a common criminal, a fugitive of the United States Government! Where in the hell are you so I can kick your ass?" John's really going to be mad since I'm not on his crew for the returning voyage of the *Encounter*.

'O'Grady will check with Bermuda Customs and find out very quickly, very, very quickly where I have gone by checking with British Air. The whole damn world will then know I have gone on the run. O'Grady and the Justice Department will notify the IRS as soon as they confirm my secret account, which will hopefully have a zero balance by tomorrow if everything goes as planned. The blackmailing vultures are after the millions I owe in back taxes, penalties and interest, and are going to be mad as hell since they can't find me and put me in jail. Well, at least George will know I am alive and I'll get word to him where I am in Argentina somehow.'

'Charlotte, you goddamn bitch! Well, my dear, our life together was just never meant to be, my loving wife of four years. You'll have one hell of a mess getting a divorce from a missing felon; lady! My interest in the Stone Bridge Inn will be seized by the government along with all my other assets: the condo in New York, stock portfolio at PaineWebber. So, what the hell. What a wonderfully confusing mess for her and Jack Spencer to have to sort out.'

He took a puff of his cigar and watched blue smoke trailing astern in the wind. Slade chuckled, knowing how embarrassed and angry Charlotte would be. He gazed out across the harbor at the Hamilton Princess, following along the third floor to where he knew Carolina Barrington's room was. 'That beautiful sexy woman's in there and I'll never get to see her again. I wonder what she will think in the morning when I fail to show up at ten-thirty for our appointment with Ferris? How long will O'Grady wait before he starts looking for me? Probably an hour or less, which is time that I desperately need to make it to Zurich and still have a cushion to open my new Swiss bank account.'

The *Deliverance* shuddered underfoot as the starboard engine backed down, the diesels whining as her master docked at the Hamilton Ferry Terminal. Peter Slade moved quickly up the gangplank, rushing to catch a cab to the airport before anyone saw him. He hurried along the wharf to Front Street to the nearest taxi stand.

In the distance he heard sirens and saw flashing blue lights as police cars and an ambulance passed by. He could see a crowd gathering in front of the bank in the distance. 'I wonder what the hell's going on down there,' he thought, jumping into the back seat of the taxi.

"Where to, sir?" the driver asked.

"The airport, and hurry. I've got an 8:15 flight, driver."

"Oh! Eight-fifteen, you say. I do hope we can make it." Peter was watching closely as the cab crept through the congestion in front of the Bank of Bermuda Limited. He saw the television news team fighting their way through the solemn crowd behind the paramedics.

"What's all this commotion about, driver?" Peter casually asked as he nervously glanced at his watch, thinking he was running out of time to make the flight.

"I am not sure, sir. Let's turn on the radio and see if we can find out," the driver replied, switching on the radio to the sounds of soothing calypso music. The late evening breeze felt refreshing on Slade's freshly shaven face as they rode with the windows down.

The cab made its way slowly along North Shore Road, following the Atlantic, as Peter watched the surf breaking, sending the big waves washing white foam up on the pink beach in an endless stream. And on the western horizon a late afternoon thunderstorm was building in the distance, reflecting Slade's innerstorm as the cab crept toward the Civil Air Terminal on St. George Island, still twenty-five minutes away. He glanced nervously at his watch and took a deep breath, counting to ten before slowly exhaling. Perspiration formed on his flanks and he felt it trickling down. He hated Charlotte now more than ever as he watched the surf pounding and the lightning flashing from the approaching storm. He took another deep breath and held it as the beautiful lush green Bermuda landscape draped in long shadows of the late afternoon sun went by.

The cab turned onto the causeway to St. George Island. The terminal came into view and with it the large British Airlines DC-10 parked at the gate. 'How in the hell do those birds fly?' he wondered, looking at the massive plane dwarfing the small terminal building. 'There is the plane that will take me away forever and to a new life,' he hoped. Slade's guts tightened. The taxi veered off Kindley Field Road into the Departures lane of the entrance to the airport terminal.

There was a last minute feeling of desperation to turn back and take his chances. Slade kept asking himself over and over again: 'am I acting prematurely? Will O'Grady have them nab me when I try to board the plane?' Had he been paranoid in thinking that the Feds were after him when they were really after the list of the Bank of Bermuda Limited customers that Ferris hadn't even turned over yet? 'What a wimp that Paul Ferris is, crying like a baby,' Slade thought as the cab pulled up to the entrance to the terminal and came to an abrupt stop.

'This is it! My last chance to turn back,' Slade hesitated before paying the cab driver and glancing at twenty-to-eight on his watch. The flight would leave in thirty-five minutes, and he still had to get his ticket and clear Customs. Slade knew he was running out of time. If he failed to get on this plane then the next one wasn't until Thursday evening, and that would be too late. As he approached the British Air check-in counter there were still three passengers ahead of him. He looked around nervously and decided to hit the men's room before queuing up in line. 'Stay calm, ole boy, stay calm, damn you. This is the most critical part of the mission, so don't blow your cool,' he was thinking. He hurried through the terminal looking for the restroom.

He suddenly caught a glimpse of the Bank of Bermuda Limited out of the corner of his eyes on the television in the bar. A news bulletin was breaking.

"What the hell is this?" he gasped, his heart racing.

The announcer's British accent came across so precisely, "There has been the untimely death of one of Bermuda's outstanding business and civic leaders. Mr. Paul Ferris, managing director of the Bank of Bermuda Limited, was found dead at the bank late this afternoon by the cleaning staff, apparently by his own hand...."

The rest of the report faded. Peter felt his knees buckling under him. He collapsed into the nearest chair in a daze. His mind raced wildly, "Well I'll be goddamned! I can't believe it," was all that he could say.

"What will you have, sir?"

Slade didn't answer.

"Sir, are you all right?" the cocktail waitress asked again, seeing his head thrown back, eyes shut.

"Double Glenfiddich on the rocks," he muttered, not knowing whether to stand up and shout or bury his head on the table and cry for joy. The news of Ferris's death rumbled through the crowd of Bermudians who had gathered around the television.

At the Princess Hotel, Carolina Barrington wept when she saw the news bulletin that Paul Ferris had committed suicide. "My God, how can this have happened? I've murdered poor Paul Ferris! Paul's dead. Dead!" she sobbed, knowing that blackmailing him had caused him to kill himself. She rushed to the telephone and called the Glencoe Hotel and asked for Peter Slade's room. "Answer, damn it, Peter," she said, trying every thirty minutes, not wanting to leave a message for a return call that might cause trouble.

Carolina Barrington had never felt this depressed, unless it was when she was arrested by the FBI, but then she had still had Sieg to fall back on. She sat helplessly by the telephone, recalling that misty November night at the River Cafe when Sieg had introduced them nearly a decade ago. Who would ever imagine Paul Ferris would end up this way? She was young then, full of herself and in love. Invincible from everything and anything, even God it seemed. God would surely punish her now, she was thinking, as deep feelings of guilt settled in.

Carolina would always remember Paul Ferris as the perfect date for her youngest and newest whore, Melissa Jenkins, the woman responsible for her being in Bermuda tonight. She hated Melissa Jenkins and hated herself for introducing her to Paul.

'If they had never met, Paul would still be alive and I wouldn't have this on my conscience,' she cried, remembering what great action Paul had been, spending thousands of dollars, and what a popular john with her girls for his generous tips he had been. Just before her arrest, he had turned into somewhat of a weirdo — dual dates, and some other kinky action — but forget about that now,' she thought, 'poor Paul Ferris is dead. My God, I have committed murder, no less,' she sobbed, anxiously phoning the Glencoe for Peter Slade once again.

Slade left the airport in a taxi after finishing his drink. He headed for the Royal Bermuda Yacht Club to meet his shipmates. Riding along North Shore Road, the thunderstorm was quickly approaching the island. The wind picked up, and he knew it would soon be raining. He was a very different man than twenty minutes before as the shocking news of Paul Ferris's death seemed too good to be true. The Scotch felt warm and mellow inside his belly and he was calm. The endless waves broke upon the beach and the dark and the fog rolled in.

He had plenty of time to reach the Royal Bermuda Yacht Club to meet John for the party at the U.S. Consulate. 'What a break, he thought, what a damn wonderful break, Ferris checking out on us like that. Jesus Christ, what did he do with the half million I gave him this afternoon? Did he deposit it in the new account like he was supposed to? Or did he deposit it in my trust account, out of spite? How will O'Grady know what Ferris did with it? Wherever he deposited it, the Feds will try and get an injunction to get it back and still have a chance of trapping me somehow. But that will not be tonight or even tomorrow and I'm no longer on the run, thank God. Paul Ferris, I love you, you poor miserable dead son-of-a-bitch. I've got to see Carolina tonight.'

"Hey, driver," Slade said, taking out his pen, writing a note on his business card and sealing it in the envelope that had held Ferris's hand receipt. "Want to make twenty bucks tip?" he asked, placing the receipt back in his breast pocket.

"As long as it is honest, certainly! At your service, sir!"

"When you drop me off at the yacht club, have the concierge at the Hamilton Princess get this message to one of their guests, Miss Barrington. Then make dinner reservations for two at Once Upon A Table Restaurant in the name of Peter Slade, at nine-thirty," he said, handing the driver the envelope.

"It will be a pleasure, Mr. Slade! The maitre d' at the restaurant is my good friend and neighbor. I will have him arrange a very nice table for you, Mr. Slade."

"Make it a private one, too," Slade replied, getting out and paying the fare and thinking how wonderfully confident the Bermudians were.

Inside the yacht club, Peter tipped one of the staff in the locker room to take his gym bag and stow it on the *Encounter*. He strolled casually into the bar to arousing cheer from his shipmates who were all drinking heavily. "Slade, where the hell have you been all day?" they shouted, shaking his hand and slapping him on the back. He ordered his usual Scotch, relieved not to see Doc Pearson.

"Knowing Slade, probably out trying to get laid while the rest of us have had to defend our honor before the International Jury and Firestone!" Moffett laughed with a loud roar coming from the men.

Peter grabbed his Glenfiddich, bellowing a toast, "Here's to the crew of the *Encounter*! I've never known a more rotten bunch of bastards! May you be in heaven thirty minutes before the devil knows you're dead!"

Suddenly the bar fell silent. The yacht club commodore, trailed by the Race Committee, rushed excitedly into the bar calling, "Captain John Moffett! Where are you, Captain Moffett?"

"I'm over here, Commodore."

"Congratulations, Captain. It is official. YOU have just won the Lighthouse Trophy!" the commodore shouted, shaking John's hand as a roar went up the bar.

Peter toasted with his Glenfiddich again, "Let's hear it for the ocean's best sailor! Gentlemen, to Captain John Moffett, the 1990 winner of the St. David's Lighthouse Trophy!"

At the Princess Hotel there was a knock at Carolina Barrington's door. "You have a message, Miss Barrington," the bellman said, slipping an envelope under it.

Carolina immediately recognized the envelope from the bank. "Peter, you dear darling," she sobbed. "How wonderful to invite me to have dinner." The fear of being alone tonight disappeared along with her tears. While showering she shaved her legs closely, and afterwards painstakingly applied her makeup after drying her hair. She slipped into a black crepe dress, cut low in front with a sheer stretch mesh bodice and sleeves. Putting on her highest heels she turned in front of the mirror to ensure the above-the-knee hem showed plenty of her lengthy legs. It was 9:25 when she telephoned the restaurant, confirming the reservations before catching a cab to Once Upon a Table to meet a slightly drunk Peter Slade.

# Chapter XIX

## Once Upon A Table Restaurant
### Evening of June 19, 1990

Carolina Barrington arrived a fashionable fifteen minutes late to the restaurant, appearing at the door accompanied by the maitre d'. She lingered for a moment before entering, letting her eyes adjust to the soft candlelight and admiring the handsome gentleman at the table in the intimate parlor of the richly restored eighteenth century home with its priceless antiques. When she entered, Slade got up quickly. The maitre d' helped to seat her and unfolded her napkin. He gave a slight nod of approval to Peter who stood speechless for a moment before managing to say, "Good evening, lady. You look fabulous tonight!"

"Thank you," she replied. They sat in the candlelight staring deeply into each other's eyes. She was wondering if Peter was feeling as terrible about Paul Ferris's death as she was. Slade, on the other hand, was delighted she had come and the suicide was far removed from his thoughts as he admired her in the flickering flame.

Carolina suddenly flinched at the lightning and instant clap of thunder, as the summer storm blew in off the Atlantic. The rain pelted the window which was covered by delicate lace curtains and she raised her voice over the storm, asking, "Have you heard about Paul?"

"Yes," Slade replied flatly, watching her eyes for a reaction.

"I needed desperately to see you. I've called ten times to your hotel, Peter. Thank you, my dear, for inviting me to dinner. This is a wonderful way to end a terribly dreadful day, although I can't remember feeling so rotten about anything before in my life."

"Yes, it's been one helluva bad day for both of us, and especially for your friend, Paul Ferris," Slade said, shaking his head slowly, still watching her closely.

"Do you think that the authorities will question us about Paul's death tomorrow, Peter?"

"Most certainly! Maybe even tonight if they find the money or perhaps a suicide note that implicates us."

"Oh, dear! I had completely forgotten about the money...."

Slade raised his eyebrows. "Well, I only caught a little of the news. What did they say about Paul?"

"Only that he committed suicide and was found by the janitors hanging from the mezzanine in the bank lobby. They didn't give any more details or mention a note. I can't believe it. I've known him for so long."

"From where?"

Carolina drew in her chin, biting her bottom lip before answering him in a slow, painful voice, "I met him through Sieg, who introduced us at the River Cafe in New York one night, maybe ten years or so ago."

"Sieg?"

"Siegfried Dassler was my lover and I suppose, in a way, my pimp, even though I never really looked at it that way. He was an extremely wealthy and influential German banker who helped introduce me to potential clients. I used his contacts to arrange dates for my social staff. The night after I met Paul I introduced him to a sexy young girl named Melissa, the same little bitch that I told you about at lunch today who turned state's evidence and testified against me. If it wasn't for her, I wouldn't be here tonight and Paul would still be alive."

"He just didn't seem like the type that would..."

"Looks are deceiving. Anyhow, Paul went absolutely nuts when he got an affection for the girls...." She hesitated for a moment. "This is SO terrible, darling, I feel like I've murdered Paul, Peter," she said, her quivering voice beginning to break.

"Nonsense, Carolina! The man committed suicide."

"Yes, but only because I blackmailed him."

"YOU did nothing of the sort. The goddamn Justice Department and O'Grady blackmailed him. You were just made to follow orders like a soldier, so don't be so damn rough on the messenger, Carolina, please."

"Yes, dear, but I still feel responsible for blackmailing...."

"Look, the Security and Exchange Commission and the U. S. Attorney's office are the blackmailers in this whole damn rotten mess," Peter replied angrily, glancing at the door to make sure no one could hear him. "What would you like to drink, lady?"

"A glass of white wine would be nice."

Peter inspected the wine list, flagging a waiter who was passing in the hall. "French?" he asked Carolina.

"Yes, dry, very dry, please."

"Waiter, let us try a bottle of Meursault, 1987."

"A very fine selection, sir. An exquisite white from Southern Burgundy. Dry, very nice."

"Yes, I know. Let me try a bottle, please."

The waiter returned, quickly handing Peter the bottle which he inspected before nodding for the waiter to open it. He then inspected the cork before tasting, nodding again his approval as Carolina's glass was filled.

"To a new and brighter tomorrow for both of us, my beautiful lady," Peter toasted. The rain beat against the lace-covered windowpanes and the music from the pianist was Sinatra's "I did it my way..." The music floated down the corridor along with the smell of wonderful food.

"You were saying Paul would go nuts. What do you mean, nuts?"

"Absolutely nuts, like some possessed sex maniac. He would fly to New York, check in at the Intercontinental and date maybe three or four girls in a single week, spending three or four thousand dollars on them. Melissa was his first and favorite, but sometimes he would date two at the same time. They loved him. He was kind and generous and very strange at times, they said."

"You mean, like kinky? That meek little guy in Bermuda shorts, Paul Ferris, kinky?"

"Yes, very kinky and they say he was far from little, huge, if you know what I mean. Like he would... oh hell, Peter, lets not go into it. He's dead now so there is no need to go into it...."

"Yes, of course not. One must show respect for the dead."

"Oh, by the way, congratulations. The *Encounter* was officially declared the winner of the Bermuda Race. The cab driver told me on the way over here."

"Thank you," Slade replied. "Captain John Moffett's a very happy man, winning the race and getting out of the protest. You should have seen him at the U.S. Consul's cocktail party a little while ago. He looked like a victorious Julius Caesar returning to Rome. Did you see our handler, Joe the Camel, after you got back to your hotel this afternoon?"

"No, I was surprised that I didn't. I thought I would at least hear from him. I feel guilty keeping you from your shipmates' celebration tonight, dear."

"Are you kidding? You're a lot more appealing than that bunch of outlaws!"

"Thank you, I guess. It *is* strange that O'Grady didn't call or come by when I got back to the hotel. I wonder if he has heard about Paul's death yet?"

"I don't know, but he will by tomorrow morning when we tell him. Do you think Ferris deposited the money as you instructed?"

"I would say not. He probably killed himself to keep from doing it and providing us with the customer list. Why go to the trouble to deposit it and violate your code of ethics and International and Bermuda law by being part of a money laundering operation when you can simply hang yourself?"

"God, Carolina, you're awful."

"No, really, I was only kidding about the hanging bit. Please, dear, don't make me feel worse than I already feel...."

"I think the police will question us when their investigators find the money. His secretary, Miss Fox, gave me the once-over when I took it into his office, and I know full well she will tell the police about our visit..."

"Yes, you are right. I feel very uncomfortable about that. What do we tell the police?"

"Tell them the truth. The United States Justice Department ordered us to do it, and then we sick'em on our handler, O'Grady. That son-of-a-bitch will deny he knows us!" Peter said, shaking his head. "This thing could really turn into a bigger mess now that Ferris is dead."

"God, do you think that we could get arrested for blackmail or money laundering?"

"Do you trust Joe Camel to bail us out?"

"You're right! Those sneaks will say they never heard of us. I don't know about you, Peter, but I'm getting the hell out of here in the morning...."

"Don't forget you have to have authorization from your handler, pooch."

"Let's not talk about it anymore, Peter. It's upset me. I just hate it. So, how was your afternoon?"

Peter grinned. 'If she only knew what an afternoon I had been through,' he thought. "Wonderful!!! Absolutely wonderful!! I had a lovely surprise from my wife when I returned to the Glencoe."

Carolina smiled weakly, anticipating the worst, that Mrs. Slade might be coming to Bermuda. "Yes, and what was that?" she asked timidly.

"A fax from her lawyer. My lovely wife has called a stockholders' meeting of the Stone Bridge Corporation to terminate me as president and chief operating officer on the 29th of June."

"You've got to be kidding!"

"I am afraid not. I knew we were sailing in troubled waters, but I had no idea she felt this way," Peter replied, casting his eyes down into his wineglass.

"You poor, poor darling. God, how terrible, Peter."

"Yes, the Stone Bridge Inn has been the love of my life. I have worked my ass off to turn it into a first-class establishment. However, she is the majority stockholder and holds the first mortgage. The goddamn bitch. I'm sorry, Carolina, I just get a little emotional when it comes to this."

"Of course you do, my dear," she said, leaning forward so that he had a good view of her cleavage. "What does your lawyer say?"

"My lawyer is John Moffett, Charlotte's first cousin! He told me a little while ago that he was unable to get in touch with her, and that everything would be fine."

"Moffett! John Moffett, the captain of the *Encounter*, is your lawyer?"

"Yeah. He's been my best friend since we met in college. Kept me out of jail with the Feds. Now he's caught in the middle between the two of us, I guess."

"Does it mean you're getting a divorce, Peter?"

"As sure as I'm sitting here. I didn't think she would do it, though, not rough like this. Mean-spirited, trying to kick me out of my own inn that I worked so hard to build. Low blow, real low blow. That woman's got problems."

Carolina leaned further over the table. Peter poured her another glass of wine, his eyes having a wonderful feast looking down the front of her dress. "I don't want to pry, but what kind of problems?"

"No, it's OK. Drinking problems, for one thing. Her first husband was an alcoholic, and I'm afraid she has gotten caught by the bottle and gin martinis."

"Why would she get into the sauce so?"

"Boredom, that's part of it. Sometimes big money is a damning luxury. People lose self-worth or challenges in their lives if they have never had to work for anything. I tried to get her interested in helping with the Inn, but it interfered with her tennis games and horseback riding."

"You poor dear, man. What a lousy day we are having..."

"Not from this moment on, damn it!" said Peter, flashing his radiant smile as he reached across the table and lightly squeezed her hand. "Would you like to order? I'm starving."

Flynn O'Grady caught news of Paul Ferris's death on the news bulletin while watching television in the BOQ guest quarters at the U.S. Naval Air Station. The bachelor officers' quarters cost eight dollars a night. Up until now he had been thoroughly enjoying his Bermuda assignment, especially the fact that he was pocketing almost one hundred and ten bucks of his travel per diem by staying in government quarters and eating fast foods from the snack bar on the installation, after getting special permission from Washington that he was on an undercover assignment.

When the news hit him, he panicked, double-lighting cigarettes and pacing around in the deserted day room, mumbling to himself, trying to muster the guts to call his boss before he left for the day. He finally got the courage to place the call to the assistance chief of enforcement's office, William Dowling at the Security and Exchange Commission office in Manhattan. "Goddamn it, Chief, you aren't goin' to believe what's just done happened out here," he said out of the corner of his mouth.

"Shoot, Flynn, it's past six here. I've got a train to catch."

"Didja hear the goddamn banker, Ferris at Bank of Bermuda, done hisself in this afternoon, and..."

"What do you mean, Flynn?!! Done himself in?!!"

"I mean, like killed hisself."

"What? You got that list of customers we're after, Flynn?"

"Hell no, I ain't got de list, Chief Dowling. They was supposed to get it tomorrow morning. Had it all set up for Barrington and Slade to get it at eleven...."

"What about the cash? Has Ferris got the money, or what?" an irritated voice barked back.

"They dropped the money with the banker, Chief. He's got it, I seen dem guys when they come out of the bank this afternoon and the bank's got de money."

"What about a suicide note?"

"Don't know of any note, Chief."

"Damn, I've got to talk to the U.S. Attorney and the FBI. If he left a note that he was blackmailed and they find out that we were behind it... Hell, these guys in Bermuda aren't a bunch of spicks that you can easily bribe like that bunch in Nassau.... The Bermuda government is going to create a hell of a problem for us if they find out what you've done, especially now that one of their outstanding citizens has killed himself."

"Yeah, Chief, I understand..."

"Hell, you better! You still at the Naval Air Station number?"

"Yeah, Chief."

"I've got to call and notify the chief in Washington to see where we stand on this, then get back to you. Don't make any moves. Don't do one damn thing until I tell you, O'Grady. Understand? Damn it, I'm going to miss my train."

"What do I tell Barrington and Slade to do tomorrow about their appointment at the bank, Chief?"

"Nothing! What the hell they going to do, man? Go meet with the stiff at the morgue, dumb-ass? Don't do anything until you hear from me. You hear? If this hare-brained plan of yours back-fires on us now, your ass is in deep shit, O'Grady. We're talking about a real diplomatic boondoggle: U. S. government tampering with Bermuda's banking system by blackmailing bank executive who hangs himself. What the hell will Congress say with us screwing with the internal affairs of one of our oldest allies? You want to testify before the Foreign Relations Committee, Flynn?"

"No sir, Chief," O'Grady replied. His ear rang from the slamming of the receiver by his boss. He lit another Camel, pondering to himself, 'that goddamned Slade, damn it to hell, I almost got him nailed with his foreign bank account and now this shit happens. If this operation boomerangs, those assholes are going to blame me and I can kiss my government retirement goodbye.'

Ron DiLorenzo's phone rang just as he was putting on his coat to leave for the day from the U.S. Attorney's office at St. Andrews Plaza in Manhattan. The recently appointed U. S. Attorney was delighted with his new position as the head of the most prestigious and powerful outpost in the United State Justice Department. He was responsible for all federal litigation filed in Manhattan, the hub of the world's financial center. The 'Plaza', as it was known and feared by New York lawyers, was the host of the nation's most sophisticated and complicated financial cases, in addition to prosecuting New York's organized crime and drug cases. He hesitated, then took the conference call from Jason Hard, chief of enforcement for the S.E.C. in Washington, DC, and his assistant, William Dowling, whose office was nearby in the World Trade Center.

"We've got a slight problem in Bermuda, Ron, that I feel compelled to inform you about. I got Bill Dowling on the line with us," the chief said as greetings were exchanged.

"Ron, we better get together first thing in the morning with the FBI. Our Bermuda operation just got screwed up. The Bermudian banker hanged himself after our agent O'Grady blackmailed him."

"What?!" DiLorenzo shouted over the phone. "This can't wait until in the morning, for God's sakes! If we're implicated as being part of a blackmail scheme, then somebody's head is going to roll, and it's not going to be mine."

"Well, your office approved the plan, Ron."

"You get that damn FBI agent on the horn, Hard, and have him notify Washington to put it on the computer that if any inquiries by the Bermudian authorities are made, have them forward them to Ode Terry here in New York as the agent in charge, and instruct Terry to squash it. Is that clear?"

"Yes, sir. What about O'Grady in Bermuda?"

"Get his skinny ass out of there and tell the son-of-a-bitch he knew nothing about the blackmail, absolutely nothing! He never heard of nor has seen Peter Slade after his arrest in 1986 or the Madam either. As far as we are concerned they acted on their own, two felons trying to launder money, and we will pick them up under a probation violation if they want us to. Am I understood, gentlemen?"

# Chapter XX

## Bank of Bermuda Limited
### June 20, 1990

nspector Wendell Whitehall of the Hamilton Police Department was at the bank by eight o'clock to question Paul Ferris's secretary, Miss Margaret Fox, before the bank opened at nine. He had been up most of the night investigating the shocking death of one of Bermuda's most prominent bankers. He had called Interpol, the international police agency in London, who instructed him to call the FBI in Washington immediately to notify them of Paul Ferris's mysterious death. Ferris's suicide seemed very suspicious to the veteran Inspector and came as a tragic shock to Ferris's family and business colleagues. Why would the managing director of a major Bermuda financial institution suddenly and mysteriously kill himself? Could his death be connected in some way to the breaking Bank of Credit and Commerce International bank scandal?

Waiting for Miss Fox, the veteran inspector was mulling over his conversation with FBI Special Agent Ode Terry whom he had spoken with that morning in New York. The agent had been very cooperative and had informed the inspector that he was in charge of the BCCI investigation and would keep Ferris's death in mind and inform him of any leads that might develop. Whitehall was puzzled. Why had the FBI agent asked on three occasions during the brief conversation if there had been a suicide note and if any American citizens were involved? Was there any possible connection to Ferris's death with the BCCI and the American Government, he wondered. Why all the questions about the Americans?

Inspector Whitehall was knowledgeable of the BCCI situation. He had been approached several years ago by the bank's founder, the Sultan of Brunei, while he was vacationing in Bermuda, to serve on his international investigative team. Thank heavens, he thought, that he had not taken the position, for later it turned out that the bank, known for its clientele of dictators, terrorists and drug lords, became the largest bank failure in history and also the world's largest fraud. Why was the FBI investigating a foreign bank in the first place, he wondered.

Unbeknown to Inspector Whitehall, the Justice Department had opened an extensive and high priority investigation of the BCCI. How had the bank gotten controlling interest of First American Metro, the holding company in Washington, DC, for First American Bankshares in Washington, Atlanta, and San Francisco, that was operating under United States bank charters? When the BCCI, along with all of its affiliate banks, had become insolvent, costing its investors and depositors throughout the world billions of dollars, the investigation lead to Clark Clifford, the BCCI's former American legal counsel and former United

States Attorney General and advisor to Presidents Truman, Eisenhower, Kennedy and Nixon.

Mr. Clifford was the first chairman of First American and was under investigation for having arranged for the approval of BCCI's charter application with Comptroller of the Currency, which while serving as their attorney stated the three failed institutions had no foreign ownership. Congress was pressuring both the Justice and Treasury Departments for answers on how three United States chartered banks failed when in fact they were foreign owned and operated by the BCCI. It was rumored that the BCCI was actually a part of the Central Intelligence Agency's international network to finance covert activities throughout the world.

Arriving at her office on the third floor of the bank, Miss Fox smiled sadly at the inspector. A plain-looking woman in her early thirties, she was exhausted from the events that had transpired since last evening. "May I get you a cup of tea?" she asked.

The inspector looked at the woman who was holding a white handkerchief to wipe away her tears. "No thank you, Miss Fox. How long have you worked for Mr. Ferris?" he asked, beginning his questioning.

An hour later, Inspector Whitehall had finished interviewing Miss Fox and had accepted her offer of a cup of tea in the boardroom before being introduced to the others.

"Good morning, Inspector Whitehall," Mr. Stanley Giffin, the bank's chairman said, extending his hand. "Sad affair we have here, Inspector. This is our auditor, Mr. John Thornton who is a partner at Price Waterhouse & Co., Chartered Accountants, in London, and this is the bank's solicitor, whom of course you know, Mr. William Jordan from Hamilton. Mr. Thornton has flown all night by chartered jet from London to attend the funeral and be of assistance to us."

"Good morning, gentlemen. This is a grave and tragic event, Paul Ferris's suicide. Like most Bermudians, I only knew Mr. Ferris casually. I investigated an embezzlement by one of the bank's tellers a few years ago. Remember that, Miss Fox? That sort of thing, yes. Not knowing him personally, I need your assistance in answering some questions. I hope not to be a nuisance or offend any of you in doing so. Thank you."

"Yes, yes we understand, Inspector. You have a job to do and, as sad as it shall be, we need to get on with it and put this dreadful event behind us once and for all," replied the solicitor. "We will assist you in any way we can."

"Indeed," chimed in the chairman. "This is not the sort of thing that is particularly good for the bank's image. Though Paul Ferris's untimely death is a terrible shock to all of us personally, the sooner we clear the air the better off the bank will be," he concluded, getting a blank stare from Miss Fox standing across the table.

"Yes, shall we get on with it then? I spoke with Mrs. Ferris last evening and was given this apparent suicide note." He held up a piece of personal stationery with the envelope addressed in Paul Ferris's handwriting to his wife. "It appears that Mr. Ferris was having a runner deliver this note to his home in Warwick at approximately the same time he jumped off the mezzanine attached to a rope. Rather odd, I'd say, from my previous experience in investigating."

"So that's how he did it, Inspector, hanged himself, did he?" asked the auditor, Mr. Thornton from London, who had spoken for the first time.

"Yes, I am afraid he did, indeed. Took a piece of rope and then jumped from the second floor mezzanine into the lobby of the bank. That is where the cleaning staff found him hanging at approximately ten until six last evening. They notified the police."

"Oh dear, I still cannot believe he's dead," sighed Miss Fox, dressed in a conservative black dress, low heels and wearing only a touch of makeup. "It's not his character at all to commit suicide! He had everything in the world a man would want: money, prestige, family, health. So why would he hang himself, Inspector?" She broke down and began to sob, dropping into a chair at the large conference table around which the group was standing. She wiped away her tears before asking in a quivering voice, "What on earth did the note say?"

"Yes, what does it say?" the chairman, an aristocratic white-haired Bermudian in shorts asked, taking a seat at the head of the table and motioning for the men to join him. When everyone was seated, he continued, "I've known Paul for over thirty years and I doubt very seriously that he would take his own life unless something very dreadful had happened to this bank."

"Here, I shall read you the note then, if you wish. If there is anything, as Miss Fox mentioned, that seems out of character in the note, please say so. You know people have been known to be forced to sign their own death warrants as a disguise for murder."

"Murder? Murder, for heavens sakes!" they all gasped.

"I'm not saying that Paul Ferris was murdered, gentlemen, but that's why we have to investigate all suspicious, untimely deaths. This is especially true now, with the BCCI bank failure and scandal that has shocked the world's financial community. You would know more about that Mr. Thornton, wouldn't you? The BCCI is a client of Price Waterhouse, isn't it?"

"Yes, I am afraid so," the Englishman blushed. "But for god's sakes, does that have anything to do with Mr. Ferris's death?"

The inspector shrugged at the question and began in a low, respectful voice to read:

"My Dearest Cynthia,
I have lived a good full life, the most wonderful part of which has been sharing my love for you and the girls. I trust that you will be fixed since I have provided handsomely for your financial security. I will be awaiting your arrival in heaven, for my work on this earth is done.
Please forgive me.
I love all of you,
Paul"

They just sat there at the conference table. The haunting words lingered in their ears and Miss Fox began to sob loudly. The men looked around at each other nervously, shaking their heads and not knowing what to do or say next. The inspector broke the silence. "Would there be any reason why Mr. Ferris would be under any financial pressure, either personally or from the bank, or perhaps from outsiders?"

The chairman spoke up. "No, not from the bank. The bank has been very successful under Paul's leadership. I will assure you, Inspector, if there has been any involvement with the BCCI, then we shall know it after Mr. Thornton conducts his audit."

"Yes. Yes indeed," replied Mr. Thornton. "We will start our audit within the hour, as soon as my audit staff arrives from London. We will leave no stones unturned, Mr. Chairman, I will assure you. My auditors have been instructed to look at everything to assure Mr. Giffen and his bank directors that Mr. Ferris's death had nothing to do with the bank's involvement with the BCCI affair or anything illegal. We will also certify that his suicide was not motivated by any bank irregularities or improprieties on his behalf as the bank's managing director, such as violations of Bermuda banking laws, deception or money laundering, etc., etc."

"What are you talking about, Mr. Thornton?" Miss Fox almost shouted. "Deception?"

"You know, deception, like embezzlement and the likes thereto, Miss Fox," the auditor untactfully answered in an irritated voice.

"You are exactly on point, Mr. Thornton," the lawyer chimed in, looking quickly at the chairman and Inspector Whitehall. "WE must insure that Paul's suicide does not blemish further this bank's reputation and has no connection to this BCCI affair or any misappropriations of funds which will affect our shares price or shareholder confidence in the board."

'Damn this bunch of bloody vultures, insulting Mr. Ferris's integrity,' thought Miss Fox. 'They don't give a damn about poor Paul Ferris at all. It's the bank's assets and reputation that they are concerned about, and now they are speculating that Mr. Ferris might have been an embezzler?'

"Miss Fox, I have already asked you once, but may I start with you? Has anything unusual surfaced in the last few days that was out of the ordinary? Unusual events, behavioral changes? Anything that would have made Paul Ferris commit suicide?"

Margaret Fox looked around the table as all their eyes were glaring at her. 'You bunch of bloody vultures, I hate you,' she thought, then Peter Slade's blue bag with a half million dollars surfaced in her mind. She wiped her eyes with the handkerchief.

'Should I tell them about the two American visitors yesterday,' she pondered. Her deep devotion and respect for Mr. Ferris's reputation and his family prevailed. "No. Nothing whatsoever, sir," she replied flatly.

"No indication of blackmail, threats, angry investors, suspicious calls or visitors?"

"I worked as Mr. Ferris's secretary for six years. He was the same calm, collected gentleman yesterday afternoon when I left the bank at five as he was the day I first met him," she lied, thinking now of what to do with Slade's money that she had hidden in the coat closet in her office.

Flynn O'Grady was summoned to the phone by the BOQ CQ at seven that morning. It was the unwelcome voice of his boss, William Dowling, assistant chief of enforcement of the S.E.C., calling from New York. "Flynn, I've been up half the night trying to get this Bank of Bermuda mess that you got your ass into squashed before the shit hits the fan. Chief Hard and Ron DiLorenzo are both plenty pissed that you talked us into getting involved in this blackmail deal. I got off the phone last night with the U.S. Attorney and he ordered me to abort the Bermuda operation and for you to get the hell out of there immediately. The FBI Director in Washington has been notified by some Bermuda cop investigating Ferris's suicide that it might be connected to this goddamn BCCI bank failure. What the hell do you think will happen if Congress finds out that we put a hooker and inside trader up to blackmailing Ferris?"

"OK, Chief Hard. What about the money?"

"The hell with the money! If this thing breaks, it's going to cost the government a helluva lot more that a half million in diplomatic embarrassment! We will deal with the money later through channels. But now, just you, Barrington and Slade get the hell out of Bermuda on the next flight. Do you understand?"

"Yeah, Chief, I'll get right with it," O'Grady replied.

"One other thing, O'Grady. You don't know a damn thing about the money or and you haven't talked to Slade or the Madam if they get arrested by the Bermuda Police. Understood??."

"Yeah," O'Grady chuckled, hanging up the phone and searching for a fresh pack of Camels. He lit a cigarette and stood smoking, listening to the phone ringing off the hook in Room 300 at the Princess Hotel.

Slade and Carolina were having coffee in bed at the Glencoe Hotel when Slade's phone rang. Slade reached over and nibbled at her breast as he answered it.

"Slade, this is Flynn O'Grady. I want you out of Bermuda immediately. The operation has been aborted, so pack up and catch the next flight back to the States — that's orders from the U.S. Attorney hisself. Didja get it?"

"No shit, Flynn," Slade snapped. "Well, I don't have a goddamn airplane ticket, and if I did I wouldn't use it, because I'm on the crew of the *Encounter* and we are not sailing until Sunday morning," Peter snarled. Carolina jumped up on her knees wearing nothing but a rattled look on her face.

Peter continued, "Her?...no. How in the hell would I know where Carolina is?" he replied, as he reached over and lightly patted her buttocks.

"Flynn, I'm not leaving until Sunday, I don't give a shit what the U.S. Attorney ordered. If the police ask me any questions I'm going to tell them to talk to my handler, Flynn O'Grady of the S.E.C.

"Yeah, I got a receipt for the money. What do you want me to do with it?... OK, I'll hold onto it, but I'm not leaving on the plane," Slade replied, slamming down the phone.

Carolina's long messy hair partially covered her firm, rigid nipples. She asked, "What the hell is that all about, dear?"

"Flynn. He's looking for you. Said for us to get the hell out of Bermuda... This job's been called off, thank God."

Carolina leaped out of bed and slipped on her panties. "You can stick around if you wish, Peter, but I'm getting the hell out of here, and now, before we get questioned by the police. You had better get rid of that receipt."

"Are you crazy?"

"Call me a cab, please," she said, slipping on her black dress without taking time to put on her bra.

"God, get back in this bed, woman. Let's do it once more before you leave..."

"Are you crazy, mister? My pussy is so sore I won't be able to sit down for a week. Now, hurry. Call me a cab, dear."

"I'll walk you down to the ferry. It's quicker. Or is it so sore that I need to carry you over my shoulder?" Slade snickered. He slipped on a pair of Bermuda shorts, kissing her passionately one last time.

"Peter, how will I ever be able to contact you?" she asked, clinging to him.

"I'll be at the Stone Bridge Inn on the twenty-ninth of June, you can damn well count on it. Call me there."

"Will it be all right?"

"Sure, why not?"

"Do be careful, my dear. Oh, please, don't be foolish. Leave with me now and get rid of that damn receipt before the police find you with it."

"Hell, no! It's the only proof I have that I gave the money to Ferris, besides you...."

"I don't like it. It's too incriminating. Please, Peter, get rid of it! I'm your witness."

"It's fine, love. Kiss me."

"Go with me. We can go to my place in Boston and hang out for a while..."

"Sorry, love. I have to sail back with John and the rest of the guys. It's a principle, so get moving."

# Chapter XXI

## Salt Kettle Landing
### Thursday June 21, 1990

A strong gust of wind struck the woman when she disembarked from the *Deliverance*. She leaned into the wind and fought her way up the gangplank to shelter in the reception hall. She nervously glanced around the empty white stucco building, then entered and took a seat on the wooden bench that ran along the wall facing the door. Margaret Fox waited, staring at the white plaster walls which were broken by an open doorway and flanked by two glass block windows that provided a dim light. Out of the storm now, she had found a welcome refuge and was glad her hectic day with the police and auditors at Bank of Bermuda Limited was over. In the peaceful serenity of the hall she waited and prayed for the soul of her dead boss and mentor, Paul Ferris. She would miss him dearly and felt a deep bitterness for the Americans she felt had killed him.

Earlier that afternoon Peter Slade had received a brief but

puzzling phone call from a familiar voice who refused to identify herself, a voice sincere but desperate, carrying with it an extreme sense of urgency, almost panic. "It is critical that we meet alone at the Salt Kettle ferry landing at six forty-five this afternoon," she had said before hanging up.

'Now who in the hell could that be,' a curious and apprehensive Peter Slade had thought, pouring a single malt Scotch and wondering whether to go or not.

The Salt Kettle landing was deserted except for the seagulls that were seeking shelter in the lee of the landing when Slade came running up from the Glencoe Hotel in the rain. Standing under the porch of the reception hall with water dripping off his thinning sandy hair and running down his granite face, he watched the departing ferry splitting whitecaps as it churned out toward Hinson's Island. 'Damn it,' he thought, 'where is this person? I'm supposed to be at the yacht club meeting the crew for the cocktail party at the Naval Air Station tonight.' He examined the ferry schedule neatly secured under glass on the wall, impatiently glanced down at his watch and was just about to leave when it occurred to him to check inside. The woman was sitting quietly with a neatly wrapped parcel in her lap.

"Mr. Slade?" asked the woman, wearing a scarf and a black raincoat, as she stood up.

"Yes."

"I am Margaret Fox from the bank," she said, loosening the scarf and letting it fall around her neck.

"Yes. Why, yes, Miss Fox, how are you?" Slade asked, barely recognizing Paul Ferris's secretary from his brief visit at the bank yesterday afternoon. The woman flinched as lightening flashed, chased by a deadly rap of thunder as they stood facing each other.

'What the hell does she want,' Slade was wondering. The wind-driven rain beat against the hall in a roar. She began speaking, her voice drowned out by the storm.

"I'm sorry, I can't hear you, Miss Fox," Slade shouted, raising his hand to his ear and shaking his head. She stepped closer.

"Mr. Slade," she began again, her voice cold and sharp against the weather. "I'm glad you came. Here, you left this in Mr. Ferris's office yesterday afternoon and I am returning it to you," she said, thrusting the package into his hands.

"What is this?!" Slade sputtered, examining the neatly wrapped brown paper package, taped at the corners and along the seams and bound tightly with heavy twine. He felt an instant sigh of relief, realizing from its weight that the package could only contain O'Grady's half million dollars.

"Please, Mr. Slade. It is the money that you tried to get Mr. Ferris to launder for you and Miss Barrington yesterday. It's there if you would like to count it."

"No," Slade frowned, "that won't be necessary."

"I don't know who you are, sir, but I am sure you are aware of Mr. Ferris's death."

"Yes, Miss Fox, I truly am sorry...." Peter tried to say, sensing the woman's hostility as her angry eyes riveted his.

"Sorry!" she sarcastically laughed. "You Americans never cease to amaze me, Mr. Slade. You have the gall to try to launder your drug money with Bank of Bermuda Limited. You did attempt to blackmail Mr. Ferris into doing it, didn't you now? I'm positive you did, or he would never have accepted your money in the first place. I hold you and that woman responsible for his suicide," her shrill voice cracked above the weather.

She stood glaring at Slade. He let her get it off her chest. Then she caught herself, regaining her composure and saying, "The police inspector came to the bank this morning, investigating Mr. Ferris's death, and the bank auditors also arrived today from London to conduct an audit..."

"Do the police know about this?" Peter asked abruptly, dropping his eyes to the package.

"No, nor do the auditors. Mr. Ferris had hidden the money last evening in my coat closet and left me a note to return it to you without a word to anyone. I sneaked it out of the bank after closing hours. Now, Mr. Slade, I suggest that you take your dirty money and return to the United States immediately just in case the authorities do get onto something and want to question you. If they should inquire, we never met. Understand? Or else we will both be co-conspirators in this dreadful affair."

"Why are you taking this risk of returning it to me then?"

"As I said, Mr. Ferris's final orders.... I feel I have his reputation to uphold, or at least his dignity, if he has any left. That should not be any concern of yours, Mr. Slade. No one but you and I know about this, and if you are wise you will keep it that way and leave Bermuda on the next flight to the mainland."

Slade looked out the open door at the cold sheets of rain dancing off the whitecaps on Hamilton Harbor. The excitement of at last knowing that the Feds wouldn't get the list of Bank of Bermuda Limited's U.S. customers was overwhelming. Momentarily it appeared that the identity of his secret trust account was safe from detection, and the very thought of it made him want to scream and shout with joy. He hid his emotions, looking now in pity at the distrusting woman standing before him. He wanted to tell her the whole damn truth about the money, Flynn O'Grady, the blackmail scheme by the Securities and Exchange

Commission. He wanted to tell her about being forced along with Carolina into being the messengers. He wanted to tell her about Paul Ferris, the wimp she admired so much, the whoremonger and hypocrite that she held in such high esteem. Peter knew there was nothing he could say to Margaret Fox that would change things or her feelings toward him. So he smiled weakly, saying in a small voice, as he was backing toward the door, "Miss Fox all I can say is that I am terribly sorry that things turned out this way.... I'll be going now. Sorry for your troubles... and thank you..." his voice trailed off as he turned and started for the door with the package under his arm.

"Mr. Slade," cracked her bitter voice once more.

"Yes," Peter replied, not turning around.

"I do hope Mr. Ferris's death weighs heavily on your and Miss Barrington's conscience. God pity your souls on Judgment Day for forcing a wonderful Christian man to take his own life," her voice broke now as it echoed off the plaster walls of the hall, while the wind died down and there was only a light drizzle falling.

"Sorry," mumbled Slade as he kept walking out into the freshness of the rain and the sea in the air, with her voice still echoing from the hall. The seagulls flushed off the water, crying loudly as they flew. A few minutes later, back in his room at the Glencoe Hotel, Peter dried off the package and placed it in the closet. He took Ferris's bank receipt out of the breast pocket of his blazer and inspected it carefully. He reached for a Macanudo cigar, biting off the end and spitting it on the floor before striking a wooden match. 'Should he burn the receipt,' he thought. 'Thank God it's in Paul Ferris's handwriting and on a piece of the Bank of Bermuda Limited stationery that would be impossible for the auditors to trace in the accounting system.' The end of the fine premium cigar turned into an amber glow above the flame of the match as he turned it.

Slade took a piece of stationery out of the drawer and wrote a note to John Moffett explaining the receipt which was enclosed along with instructions for him to hold it in safekeeping. He intentionally didn't mention that he had gotten the money back from Miss Fox. He quickly addressed an envelope to John's law firm in Providence, walked to the front desk, got a stamp, and dropped the letter into the mail slot at the front desk.

Slade poured another Scotch when he returned and took a long draw off the cigar, the rich blue cedar-aged aroma lingering in the air and spiraling upward to his sudden hysterical burst of laughter. "Well I'll be damned," he bellowed. "Slade, here you are, you son-of-a-bitch, with a dead banker's receipt in the mail and a half million dollars cash in your closet.... The goddamn Feds have called off your case. Kiss my ass, Flynn O'Grady! Kiss my ass, sweet Charlotte Slade! Now, how in the hell am I going to get the money back into the States without anyone finding out?"

He was pouring another drink as the *Encounter*'s crew caught a cab at the Royal Bermuda Yacht Club for the U.S. Naval Air Station. He would catch up with them later. He began dancing around the room like a man just released from prison, savoring the taste of the Scotch and the moment along with the fine cigar. He thumbed through the yellow pages, dialing. The party on the other end answered.

"Hello, Airborne Express? Can you pick up a parcel at the Glencoe Hotel for me?"

At the Ritz Carlton Hotel on Central Park South in New York, Charlotte Slade was having her first martini on this beautiful summer afternoon, having just descended to the Jockey Club Bar from her suite on the top floor overlooking Central Park. Her lawyer, Jack Spencer, was by her side in one of the city's plushest restaurants.

'Jesus Christ,' Jack Spencer thought, his head still throbbing from last night, 'I've drunk more in the past week than I've drunk in the past ten years.' He stood, stirring his martini, searching for the courage to begin again. He swirled the olive, watching the vermouth and gin blending together. 'How stupid of me.' He was thinking of what a sheltered conservative life he had been living before he got mixed up with Peter Slade's soon- to-be ex-wife.

The two of them had been discussing Peter Slade for three days, not calling him by name, but giving reference to "HIM" in their plans for the future.

"What do you think I should ask HIM for, Jack?" Charlotte asked in a quick voice, not yet mean from the liquor.

"You own the controlling interest in the Inn, plus you hold the first mortgage on the property," the attorney replied. "Do you want to continue to operate the Inn after we fire HIM, or would you want to buy HIM out?"

"Buy HIM out?!! What the hell for?" she snapped, feeling the martini. "I've bought the property, renovated it and have paid him a salary to run it. So why in the hell do I have to buy HIM anything?"

"Yes, dear, in theory you are quite correct, but the law does not look at it that way. The Stone Bridge is a corporation and he owns forty-eight percent of the stock which you gave HIM at the time of incorporation when you married HIM. So we have the business appraised and he either has to buy us out or we buy HIM out."

Charlotte polished off the last of her first and ordered the second martini, even though Jack had not begun to drink. "Get with it, Jack, when are you going to learn to drink, man?" she asked, glaring at his first martini still untouched on the bar.

That's offensive, Spencer thought, smiling back at her as he took the martini. "To the long lost love of my childhood," he said, throwing the martini down. The gin made him shudder, stammering, "I'm...I'm up with you, now darling. Let's have another round."

"How the hell is he going to buy me out? He doesn't have that kind of money," Charlotte asked, drinking on her second one now.

"Well, we could have HIM arrange for financing, or perhaps you could hold a note for your interest and let the Inn pay for itself over the next ten to fifteen years if the cash flow will handle it. I'll say this for HIM, he is certainly a very fine restaurateur."

Sipping on the second martini, she responded, "Take a note from HIM? Are you kidding, Counselor?! Have to fool with HIM for the next fifteen years of my life waiting for a check each month? Hell, I'd rather give HIM the goddamn place, or better yet, burn the son-of-a-bitch down, rather than have to deal with that bullshit."

While the two drank and plotted at the Jockey Club Bar, Melissa Jenkins was walking up Fifth Avenue. She was in New York on her day off from the Stone Bridge Inn and was now passing through Grand Army Plaza, past the Plaza Hotel. Melissa was dressed in a single-breasted black silk jacket worn over the ivory dots of her crewneck and short navy blue skirt. She turned onto Central Park South, walking the two short blocks to the Ritz. Shading her eyes from the bright sun with a wide-brim white hat and designer sunglasses she entered the hotel. The young woman was in New York shopping for her new fall wardrobe even though she could ill afford one on the two thousand dollars a month Peter Slade was paying her.

Melissa's pale blue eyes adjusted to the weak light, searching for a girlfriend from her working days for Carolina Barrington. She removed her glasses and walked through the small, plush lobby into the bar, stopping abruptly after spotting Mrs. Slade and Mr. Spencer drinking martinis, engrossed in conversation. She discreetly turned and slipped on her sunglasses. Pulling her hat down she walked slowly past them in time to overhear Jack Spencer saying, "First things first. Let's fire HIM first, Charlotte, and then I'll file your divorce immediately after that."

# Chapter XXII

Government House
Friday, June 22, 1990

The crowd was mingling quietly around the reviewing stand erected in front of the Governor's Mansion. John Moffett and his crew waited patiently for the Newport-Bermuda Race ceremonies to commence.

From his vantage point high atop Langton Hill, John gazed out over North Shore Road to the blue Atlantic Ocean, and the thought of sailing home on Sunday with his trophy gave him that wonderful feeling of being on top of the world. A balmy prevailing southwesterly breeze swayed the palm trees briskly as their long shadows cast by the late afternoon sun danced on the manicured lawn. He glanced nervously at his watch. 'Just fifteen minutes more,' he thought.

Suddenly he was stricken with a felonious feeling about cheating to win. Looking up he saw Flint Firestone walking up the long drive with his crew. The sight of the man made the feeling of guilt vanish. If the truth was known, John rationalized, Firestone probably cheated, too.

The crowd grew and with it grew the triumphant exhilaration of being the recipient of the Lighthouse Trophy as people came up and shook John's hand. He felt ecstatic glancing around at the remainder of his crew, Bob Ganloff, Tony Stevenson, Dr. Pearson and his old and loyal friend, Peter Slade, mixing and mingling, shaking hands with the crowd.

He quietly called for them to gather around. "Gentlemen, we did it, thanks to you. I wish the rest of the guys could have stayed for the awards presentation."

"I do, too," Peter responded, "but they had to get back to work or school. They did one hell of a job."

He tried to continue, feeling a lump in his throat. "You all did, and I can't tell you how appreciative I am...."

"Come, come now, Skipper, don't get sappy on us," Peter laughed, when he saw John's emotions breaking.

Doc Pearson stood back, unusually reserved, keeping to himself. He had done so since the hearing with the jury. 'I probably should take a plane back. These guys hate my guts,' he thought, approaching John. "John, I feel terrible about the hearing and the suspicion Flint cast on me for ratting on you guys. Do you still want me as a member of the crew on the return voyage, Captain?"

"Absolutely, Duane. We had our day in court and by God we won it. So forget it, Doc. Don't mention it again."

"Are you sure it's all right with the rest of the guys? I feel so embarrassed and chastised...."

"Everything is just fine, so forget it happened," John said again, looking up at Government House which stood before them. Upstairs in the austere Victorian mansion, with its three massive archways supporting a balcony that connected two wings of the house, was the governor of Bermuda who at any moment would be coming down to present his trophy.

"This place is just SO gorgeous, isn't it?" Doc asked, following John's eyes as they surveyed the mansion. Then he disappeared quietly into the large crowd.

'Well, that's that,' John thought, watching him go. 'I'm glad Doc cleared the air. I won't have to deal with that problem once we get under way, I hope.' He looked around at the crowd. 'What a wonderful sight! All these yachtsmen dressed in white slacks and blue blazers mixing with dignitaries and their fashionable ladies, the naval officers in white uniforms and other honored guests. This is splendid, this is my moment in the sun, you lucky son-of-a-gun.'

Members of the Race Committee were busy quietly placing the thirty-six shiny trophies on a long table that stretched the length of the stage. The onlookers stood and admired the prizes. Moffett's eyes feasted on the St. David's Lighthouse Trophy, the tall replica of the Mount Hill Lighthouse on St. David's Head, the world's most prestigious racing trophy which in ten minutes would be his.

Flint Firestone stood silent, infuriated as his eyes coveted the Lighthouse Trophy that he knew was rightly his. 'Damn a second place finish and being the recipient of the Edul Tankard Trophy,' the imperial looking man was thinking.

'Firestone, you're a rotten loser,' Moffett thought as he watched Flint eyeing his trophy. He intentionally avoided eye contact with his ex-brother-in-law. Both men felt the tension between them building.

"Well, if it isn't Captain Flint Firestone," Slade said sarcastically from behind John. "I think it's time I hit Flint up for the five thousand dollar wager he owes us guys."

"Pete, just a second. Hold it. Don't dare start anything here. Wait until later...after the ceremony."

John's orders were ignored. Slade started walking over to where Firestone and his men were standing.

"Good afternoon, gentlemen. Flint, let me ask, when are we going to settle up on our wager?"

Flint Firestone drew his head back defensively, "Are you kidding, Slade?"

"Hell no, Flint, I'm dead serious. You guys owe us five thousand dollars, and we intend to get paid!"

"Look, Slade, I don't owe you cheating bunch of bastards a goddamn penny. Your suck-buddy, Dr. Pearson, told me you cheated and you all know damn well you cheated. So you cheating bastards owe my crew five thousand dollars if anything. We won this goddamn race and you guys stole it..."

"Wait a minute here, Firestone! You don't understand, son. Who's going to get the Lighthouse Trophy? It sure as hell isn't you guys! The jury settled all of that yesterday, my friend. Now pay up, or are you such a damned chicken-shit loser that you're going to welsh on your bet?"

"Hell no! I pay my bets, by God, unless I'm dealing with a bunch of low-life cheating criminals such as the likes of you guys, Slade!!!" Firestone shouted, his face turning crimson as the crowd began to take notice and separate.

"Watch who the hell you're calling criminals, cock sucker..."

"I'm by God calling you a fucking criminal, Slade..."

"You either pay up, Firestone, or I'm fixing to whip your blue-blooded ass right here and now in front of the Bermuda governor!!! You hear me, Firestone?!" Slade retaliated, while the crowed formed a large circle. The two men squared off.

'Oh my God,' Moffett panicked, rushing forward. 'Peter's going to pick a fight right here in front of the whole damn Race Committee in violation of paragraph 17 of the Race Rules. We will get disqualified sure as hell for a serious breach of conduct by a member of my crew!'

"Hey, cut it out, Pete," John shouted, coming forward.

Firestone was also well aware of paragraph 17. He was suckering Slade into a fistfight. 'This is as easy as reeling in a shark on a line,' he thought. 'I'll win back the trophy by default.'

"Go ahead, bad boy, throw the first punch, shit-head," snarled the bigger man in a low breath.

John was quickly pushing his way through the crowd. The committee members stopped what they were doing and, along with the others, pushed forward, watching, trying to figure out what the disturbance was all about.

"Go ahead, Slade, you fucking inside-trading creep. Go ahead and hit me, you fucking criminal!" Firestone growled, just low enough for the crowd not to hear. The circle tightened around the two men, their fists clinched, blood vessels bursting on their necks and foreheads. They circled in a counterclockwise direction now.

'Firestone's a pretty good-sized fellow, but Slade can take him,' Bob Ganloff thought. "Deck him, Pete!" he shouted. Moffett jumped between them in the nick of time.

"Get the hell out of the way, Johnny!" Peter shouted, pushing John back and fighting to get around him and throw the first punch.

"Stop it, Pete, or you will get us disqualified, goddamn it!" Moffett ordered, quietly pushing Slade backwards into the crowd just as the TV camera focused in on them.

The Royal Bermuda Yacht Club commodore rushed up. "Gentlemen, what seems to be the problem here?"

"No problem, commodore," Tony Stevenson smiled, as John and Bob forced Slade further away.

"That guy over there, Peter Slade, off the *Encounter*, tried to pick a fight, Commodore. I got witnesses. The *Encounter* should be disqualified for a breach of conduct under rule 17..."

"Gentlemen! Please. I'll hear no more of it. Now let's get on with the ceremonies, please, and everyone do try to behave themselves and not mar this affair."

Slade began laughing, still trembling with anger as he tried to calm himself. "I guess I would be pissed off, too, if I was Firestone," he said, "after being screwed out of the trophy by my damn ex-brother-in-law lawyer...."

"Goddamn it, Pete! What in the hell are you doing, man? If you had hit that guy I could kiss the trophy goodbye, you dumb asshole," John barked, grabbing Peter tightly by the arm.

Peter Slade grabbed his hand with vengeance, forcefully removing it. "Don't you ever call me an asshole again or I will whip your goddamn ass, John. The goddamn truth of the matter is that the trophy belongs to Flint anyway...." Peter snarled, just as a hush fell over the crowd and the two men separated.

The governor of Bermuda was ascending down the steps from Government House now as the crowd gathered in. He was a distinguished looking man, middle-aged and fit, dressed in a gray business suit and escorted by his two military aides, their uniforms accentuated by white coats. The governor approached the podium and took his position. On cue the Bermuda Regimental Band broke into the British National Anthem, followed smartly by the Star-Spangled Banner as the two countries' colors were presented by the Color Guard.

John Moffett was visually shaken by Slade's actions and words. He knew what Peter had said was true, but coming so abruptly from his best friend, even though said in anger, it made him furious. 'Trying to rain on my parade, are you, Pete? Who the hell does Slade think he's talking to,' he was thinking just as his name came blaring out over the loudspeaker. "Ladies and Gentlemen, the winner of the Lighthouse Trophy is Captain John Moffett from Providence, Rhode Island, and, for the first time in the history of this race, the sailing yacht *Encounter* also wins line honors...."

Peter Slade watched the fire dance in Firestone's eyes as John stepped forward to receive the Lighthouse Trophy and the crowd went wild with applause.

It was the next morning and Saturday at last which found Peter Slade hungover and packing at the Glencoe Hotel. He felt like hell from single malt Scotch, consumed in great quantities after the Government House awards celebration. He felt low and angry over his run-in with John. 'I'm damn glad to be getting the hell out of here,' he thought, thinking of the long boring voyage back to Newport only to get fired from his job. 'Damn Charlotte to hell. I should catch a flight to Boston and shackup with Carolina for a couple of days instead of sailing back with John. Oh, what a wonderful piece of ass that woman is,' he smiled, looking around the room and thinking about Thursday night. 'Hell no, I'm committed to sail back, even if I have to put up with Moffett's bullshit. Hell, it will give me plenty of time to think about my divorce and a chance to plan for the future.

'Well, life could be a helluva lot worse than it is,' he was thinking as he finished packing his gear in his seabag. 'A hell of a lot worse, for damn sure,' remembering his nightmare of being arrested in New York. 'I could very easily have been arrested by the Justice Department again this week. I can't believe that they called off their Bank of Bermuda Limited operation that quickly. You can bet they haven't given up looking for my bank account, but it does look safe for the moment.'

Peter Slade made one last inspection of his room to make sure he hadn't left anything. Noticing the twine from the package, it suddenly struck him that just maybe Margaret Fox was working for O'Grady and had set him up somehow. 'What a stupid move on my part, shipping the money! Why didn't I just turn it over to O'Grady instead of trying to steal it and smuggle it back into the U.S?'

'How damn dumb can you get, Slade? Doing something stupid just when my plea-bargain agreement with the Justice Department has only eight more days left before it expires. Now I've set my ass up again.' He closed the door and walked to the front desk to pay his bill.

Saying goodbye to the cheerful staff at the Glencoe was not easy. They had all been such wonderful hosts, much like his staff at the Stone Bridge Inn. He felt sad at leaving the strong bond. "I'll be back next year," Slade promised grabbing his seabag and hurrying down the narrow lane to the Salt Kettle landing to catch the Warwick ferry to Hamilton for the last time.

Peter Slade disembarked thirty minutes later in Hamilton, ducking into the tobacconist, Chatham House on Front Street, for a forbidden box of Hoyo De Monterrey Cuban cigars. His next stop was Burrows & Lightbourn for three bottles of Glenfiddich single malt for the voyage home. With these last minute essential provisions, he hurried to the Royal Bermuda Yacht Club and paid his seven hundred and sixty dollar bar bill in cash.

Out on the dock in the bright sunshine there was a large crowd of yachtsmen and well-wishers gathered around the *Encounter* which was preparing to get under way. John, who was busy making last minute preparations for their return, glanced up, giving Peter the cold shoulder. This bothered him some.

The Englishman shouted, "I say, Slade, get along here mate and give me a hand with this gear. We're about to cast off for St. George's to clear Customs, unless you want to swim back to America."

"Hey, you won the Mixer Trophy, Tony, for being the navigator of this boat, and now listen to you, limey, you think you're the skipper ordering this deck hand around!" Slade shouted back, laughing.

"The navigator I am, mate. Now act alive and get aboard before we cast off without you."

"What time did you say that American flight to New York was, Tony?" Peter asked, half-joking, setting his seabag down to the delight of the onlookers' laughter. During the next week, he would wish a thousand times that he had flown.

The *Encounter* sailed out of Hamilton Harbor escorted by a small armada of fans. It reached Ordinary Island in St. George's Harbor on the eastern end of the island by midday and tied up at the pier awaiting clearance from the Bermuda Customs officer. The *Martinis* was tied at the wharf. Firestone and his crew were nowhere to be seen, and that seemed a little strange to John Moffett.

"Bob, will you and Doc go over to Somers Supermarket for

some fresh fruits and vegetables and any other stuff you think we have forgotten?"

"Sure thing. Hey, Tony, how about giving us a hand," Bob said.

"Someone stay with the boat. I have to go to the Customs office and clear and check the weather."

"I'll stay with the boat then, " Peter volunteered, as they left. Sitting alone in the cockpit he was anxious to get under way on their return voyage to Newport.

He watched John walk up to the Customs office to get the boat's manifest and papers stamped and the weather forecast. Moffett stopped outside on the porch. 'I wonder what the hell he's waiting on?' Slade thought.

The warm June sunshine beat down on his hangover which had turned into a dull headache. The fresh salt air was clearing out his sinuses, making his head feel better. He grabbed a cold beer and lit a Hoyo De Monterrey. He smoked, lying back and watching the blue curling smoke from his cigar turn and twist in the breeze, reminding him of Carolina Barrington's naked body on top of him in bed. He had not spoken with her since she left and he was thinking more about her with each passing hour as the reality of going to sea with three guys and Doc Pearson made him squirm.

Peter suddenly felt the urgent need to call the Stone Bridge Inn to check in with George. He had forgotten to tell him his plans and see if the Airborne Express package had arrived.

Hearing the three sailors return down the pier with sacks of groceries, Peter shouted, "Got to make a quick phone call, guys. Be right back."

John Moffett had waited until Flint Firestone was out of the Customs office before entering. 'There was no need for further confrontation with Flint,' he thought. Firestone left without speaking.

John Moffett went inside and got his paperwork processed. The last thing he did before leaving was to check the latest weather map posted on a clipboard. 'Sunday's long-range forecast looks great,' he thought, hanging the clipboard back on its nail. He hesitated to confirm the weather with the Customs officer who had just gotten on the telephone. 'He'll probably talk for an hour,' Moffett thought, and left.

"Where you headed, Pete?" he asked as Slade ran by.

"Got to call the Inn."

"Well make it snappy, Peter. I'm ready to cast off," Moffett barked, coming down the Customs office steps. He was still feeling ill about Peter's near disaster at the awards ceremony.

"Hold your damn horses, John!" Slade shouted back in a flash of anger as he ran past. 'Fuck him! He's gotten the big head over his damn trophy, the cheating bastard.' He direct dialed with a trembling hand. 'Damn it, I'm not putting up with his shit. I'll get my gear off the boat and catch a plane to Boston.'

Melissa Jenkins's refreshing voice answered the phone. "Hello, Mr. Slade. Congratulations! Thank God you called before you left Bermuda," she said in a breathless voice of concern.

"What's wrong? We are just about to cast off, Melissa. May I speak to George, please?"

"Mr. Slade, I tried to call you at the Glencoe, but you had just checked out. We had to put George in the hospital this morning! He was complaining of chest pains..."

"What?! My God, is he all right?"

"Yes, sir, he is resting at the moment. The doctors haven't said if he had a heart attack or not...."

"Which hospital?"

"Fall River General. Room 312."

"Good God! Do you know, Melissa, if he got my Airborne Express package yesterday?"

"Yes, he got it and put it in the wine cellar."

"Good! Don't dare tell anyone it is in there. It's a special present. Get George some flowers, will you? And tell him I'm on the way back. Get him anything he needs, Melissa. I'll be back by the 29th..."

"HURRY UP, Pete!" Moffett shouted. Doc was standing on the pier holding the line to cast off.

"Mr. Slade...."

"Yes, Melissa? What is it? I got to go..."

"Nothing. I'll discuss it with you when you get here. Have a safe passage," she said, thinking of how to break the news that she had seen his wife and her attorney at the Ritz Carlton in New York yesterday.

Peter walked slowly back to the *Encounter*, steaming mad.

Moffett saw that he was angry, and quickly tried to patch things up by saying, "Sorry, Pete, didn't mean to rush you, man. I just want to get past those reefs before it gets dark on us."

"LOOK, John. George is in the hospital. I'm going to have to fly back to Newport and check on him," Slade said angrily. "Let me get my gear off."

"I'm sorry, Peter. What's wrong with him?"

"Heart problem."

"How is he?"

"In the hospital. That's all I was told."

"Damn, Pete, I'm sorry. We really need you, man, but if you have to check on George, I'll round up another crew somewhere. Wouldn't be wise to sail the boat a man short..."

"Aw fuck it then. Let's cast off," Slade replied sharply, jumping on board.

The rest of the crew fell silent. Peter Slade went below, knowing he should have taken time to call George before he left.

"We got clear weather and good sailing, gentlemen," Moffett announced, starting the engine. "Let's get those lines cast off."

The boat drifted away from the Ordinance Island pier and Moffett engaged the shaft. "We'll be taking four-hour watches and take turns cooking. After we get out to sea, Doc, you take the four o'clock watch, then Pete, Tony, and myself. "

The *Encounter* motored across St. George's Harbor, glistening in brilliant afternoon sunshine. Peter had a bad feeling about something, he didn't know exactly what, when they passed through the Town Cut, the narrow channel that leads to the ocean. He laid back in his bunk and fell asleep, hoping some rest would improve his disposition.

Out on the northern Great Plains of the United States, wheat fields were baking in the hot humid air that was suddenly invaded by a blast from the cold Canadian jet stream. A storm was born. It started as a tiny vicious depression producing violent thunderstorms as it traveled eastwardly. It built steadily, closing the airport in Minneapolis, Minnesota, for an hour on Friday afternoon, the 22nd of June. From there it traveled east across northern Lake Michigan before being pushed further by the jet stream and producing tornadoes in Albany, New York. Saturday afternoon its sixty-knot winds blew the roof off a school in Huntington Station, Long Island, and disrupted electrical services for over twenty thousand customers as it traveled at forty knots, fiercely building out over the warm waters of the Gulf Stream.

Flint Firestone stopped and watched the *Encounter* motor down Town Cut Channel. He walked up the steep hill from King's

Square to the St. George's Club where he and his crew had taken up residence until the storm passed. He hoped to get in at least two days of golf on the new golf course designed by Robert Trent Jones before the weather turned sour. 'Moffett took the bait, the stupid guy,' he thought, watching the *Encounter* unfurling her sails. Flint was laughing to himself at having taken the morning's weather map, which clearly showed the approaching storm moving east-ward and switching it with last Sunday's clear forecast. The dates on it had gone unnoticed by John Moffett. 'That will teach you bunch of cheating rogues,' Firestone thought, watching the *Encounter* sail out into the open ocean.

# Chapter XXIII

Melissa Jenkins had been at the Stone Bridge Inn since the first of May and was loving her hostess position. The beautiful young woman's warm personality welcomed the guests with a smile before seating them in the formal dining room, or outside on the veranda off the Marble Bar overlooking the Sakonnet River. The innkeeper, Peter Slade, had treated her more like a daughter than an employee. He was always complimenting her on the fine job she was doing. He was a wonderful man to work for, very professional, always kind and considerate of his staff and eager for suggestions to improve the Inn's operations. Rebounding from her checkered past, this troubled young New Yorker had fallen secretly in love with a man twice her age.

The Stone Bridge Inn was also Melissa Jenkins's new home when Mr. Slade gave her a two-room suite on the third floor of the old Inn to live in. He had caught hell from Charlotte when she found out about it, Melissa had later learned from George Henley.

The large windows framed by green shutters looked out across the manicured lawn to the Sakonnet River and beyond to the emerald shores of Aquidneck Island in the distance.

The parlor and adjoining bedroom were spacious, richly decorated in early American furniture and classic antiques, accented by an array of bright accessories that cost a fortune. There was thick, heavy crown molding around the top of the rooms which gave her a secure feeling when she was in bed at night wishing Peter Slade was there with her.

On this Saturday morning she sat before the mirror combing her long reddish hair, lightly streaked by the sun. It was a traditional bedroom painted rich hunter green, heightened by a classic mahogany four-poster bed with a secretary on one side and a chest of drawers on the other. Melissa had finally found a refuge from her turbulent past, which gave the former prostitute dreams and hopes for a new beginning.

Bright sunshine beamed through the open windows. A light breeze ruffled the drapes, bringing with it the smells of the sea and fresh mowed grass. Melissa had learned to tell time 'the Narragansett way' by the changing wind, which, without exception, was light in the mornings before the arrival of the offshore smoky sou'wester, at noon building to twenty knots on summer afternoons. Before the offshore winds came today, Melissa knew she had to be back from visiting George Washington Henley in time to greet the luncheon guests.

She scampered down the three flights of stairs, greeted by the wonderful aroma of freshly baked bread. She entered the noisy kitchen, filled with cheerful voices and the clamor of pots and pans.

It was a magnificent, large kitchen, full of stainless steel appliances with copper skillets of every size hanging on a rack above the island. Pierre Borochaner moved quickly about in his tall white chef's hat, his white starched apron already soiled. He stood cooking before the great gas stove. His staff of eight assistants was busy preparing for another large June wedding for which the Inn had become renowned, in addition to the regular Saturday yachting guests.

"Pierre, I am taking the van to the hospital to check on George," she shouted, catching her breath and pouring a cup of coffee.

"Yes, of course, Mam'selle," he replied, not looking up from the lime torte filling he was whisking in a metal bowl simmering in water on the stove.

"Are you preparing your scrumptious frozen lime torte with fruit today, Pierre?"

"Yes, of course, Mam'selle! It is the summer time, yes?"

"Hmm, sounds great. Be sure to save me a piece. I'll be back in a couple of hours. Is there anything I need to get while I'm out?"

The young French chef dared not look up, acknowledging Melissa's question by shaking his head, raising the corners of his long handlebar mustache with a smile. "Nothing, Mam'selle. How is Monsieur George this morning?" he asked, still whisking the pale lime filling on the blue gas flame, making sure the bowl didn't touch the water causing the mixture to curdle.

"Not very well, Pierre. The hospital called last night and told me that his heart had weakened and he was on oxygen. They have moved him into intensive care."

"Oh no, Mam'selle! Should we try to contact Monsieur Slade?" he asked, glancing up briefly with concern, still whisking the lime mixture.

"Why? He's out in the middle of the Atlantic somewhere now."

"Yes. Yes of course, you are right, Mam'selle. There is nothing Monsieur Slade can do. Only worry. Only worry, yes?"

The Fall River highway was jammed with summer vacation traffic headed for the beaches. Melissa was listening to the radio as she drove. "Now, a hit from 1983 by the Police, 'Every Breath You Take' for your listening pleasure," the announcer said.

On hearing the title, Melissa suddenly thought, 'oh my God, poor ole George's heart won't last long enough for Peter to get back. What a terrible loss for the boss, his life-long friend dying without his being here. What a crying shame for me, too, losing the only really good, trusted friend I have.' She was saddened at the thought of losing the wonderful old black man who had become her close friend since she arrived.

'If something happens to George, I don't know what I'll do,' she sighed, remembering her secret agenda to capture Peter Slade. 'Without George on my side, it will be difficult, damn near impossible, knowing George's influence over the boss. I wonder if I should tell George this morning that I caught Charlotte shacking up in the Ritz with Mr. Moffett's law partner, Jack Spencer, or wait and tell Peter myself?

'What a deceiving, evil woman Mrs. Slade is, running around on such a wonderful, kind man. She doesn't deserve him, the rich spoiled bitch. I'm beginning to hate her as much as I hate that god-damn Carolina Barrington for turning me into a whore when I was just a child.'

As she drove, the deep psychological scars of her past subconsciously surfaced. Melissa Jenkins reconfirmed her strong-willed determination to regain her self-esteem and make something out of her life. She was by God going to make it at the Stone Bridge Inn and, hopefully, someday share her life with the innkeeper, Peter Slade.

The traffic snarled ahead. She felt that deep anger and resentment she had harbored all of her life for her mother, Julie, and her stepfather, Alvin Jenkins. Alvin told her when she was eight that her mother had been pregnant with her when she married him. Her natural father was a man her mother refused to talk about. She did find out some years later at the Catholic orphanage that her mother had been married for a short time to a man named Flynn O'Grady.

Melissa drove, reminiscing about the early days of her childhood while growing up in the Sunset Park district of Brooklyn. Third Avenue was a drab no-color row of tenements where the sounds of the Gowanus Expressway never ceased, and from the fourth floor kitchen fire escape she could see only the torch of the Statue of Liberty rising above the roofs. "Can I go see the Statue of Liberty, Mommy?" she could still hear her childish voice pleading to Julie, and then the car in front of her stopped at a traffic light.

'Were there any good times back then?' she asked herself, waiting for the light to change. None, except perhaps escaping that cold dirty flat to attend Public School 314 where it was warm in the winter and you could get a free lunch. Summers were hot and terrible, except for swimming in the swimming pool in Sunset Park that was built years ago by the W.P.A. The rest of it was a nightmare, living with alcoholic parents and going to bed hungry most nights and having to listen to their terrible fights.

Melissa Jenkins could not think about all of that now. It had been permanently blocked out of her mind, those years of sexual molestation by her drunken stepfather and the physical violence she had seen her mother go through. "You are nothing but a bastard, Missy, you little slut! I'm not your real daddy. Your mother was knocked up when I married the bitch," Alvin's hot whiskey breath had said when he raped her at twelve while her mother lay passed out on the couch.

"Stop it! Stop it! Alvin," her screams came in the scenes of her frequent nightmares. She would sit up in bed screaming, with the ending always being the principal of P.S. 314 taking her into his office where a lady from the welfare department said, "Your parents have just been killed when your apartment burned this morning, Melissa..."

So that had been the end of Mommy and Alvin on a cold, dark, dreary winter day when they asphyxiated themselves, leaving her as a twelve-year-old ward of the State of New York.

Life at the Catholic orphanage outside of Albany was the first stable life she had ever known. It was a tremendous adjustment for a child with such a troubled past who had always fended for herself. The Sisters were strict and she adjusted rapidly, causing no problems and learning quickly in the school where they taught good manners, personal hygiene and how to get along with others.

Life was good as an orphan until that summer day two months past her sixteenth birthday when Father Patrick took her into his study and tried to kiss her and fondle her breast. 'The hell with this place,' she had thought, remembering her abusive stepfather. She had run away without saying a word on a bus for New York City to start a new life on her own.

Entering the Fall River city limits, Melissa Jenkins vividly recalled the day she had arrived back in New York as a fully developed teenager. It was as if it had happened just yesterday, stepping off that Greyhound from Albany at the Port Authority Bus

Terminal on 8th and 41st alone. She was back in the city at last, and on her own for the first time in her life. Then destiny dealt her another rotten hand when she jumped in the back of a cab on West 42nd Street and came face to face for the first time with a woman named Carolina Barrington.

"Where are you going, young lady?" Carolina had asked as they both laughed in surprise as Melissa started to get out with the paper shopping bag in hand containing her only belongings.

"Brooklyn, lady, what about you?"

"I'm going downtown, too, so get in, let's share. Driver, you can drop me off at the South Street Seaport on your way to Brooklyn."

"Where in Brooklyn you go?" the Vietnamese driver had asked Melissa in his sing song voice, looking at the young woman in his rearview mirror.

"2111 Third Avenue, Sunset Park, between Bay Ridge and Park Slope..."

"Yes, I live near there!" came an oriental smile.

'What a beautiful young redhead,' Carolina had thought, 'and what a sexy young body she has.' "Sunset Park? Is that were your parents live?"

"They're both dead. I used to live there when I was a kid," Melissa had replied confidently.

"Sunset Park. I'm not familiar with it....Is that where you live now?"

"No, I'm just back from Albany. What about you? No, let me guess! You're from the Upper West Side, aren't you?"

"Very good, girl! How did you guess?"

"Easy. You're rich," Melissa had said, nonchalantly.

'I like this spunky little bitch. Clean her up and spend some time with her and she could really do well,' Carolina had thought. 'I have so much demand from my clients for the young ones these days, especially from the older foreigners, and that young stuff is prime billings.' "How old are you?"

"I'm eighteen, almost nineteen. Why?" she had lied as the cab headed down Broadway.

"Just wondering. Albany? Going to college in Albany?"

"No, I'm just back in town looking for a job," she had replied looking out the cab window. They chatted, getting acquainted while riding toward downtown Manhattan.

"By the way, I'm Carolina Barrington..."

"Nice to meet you, Mrs. Barrington, I'm Melissa," she had replied as the cab approached the South Street Seaport.

"Can I invite you to lunch, Melissa?" Carolina had asked. The two ladies got out of the cab and walked into Sloppy Louie's Restaurant. Laughing together, they ordered lunch.

"Do you have a place to stay now that you are back in New York?"

"No, no I don't.... I was going..."

"You poor darling. I tell you what let's do, since you don't have a place. You can stay at my place, Melissa, for a couple of days until you find a job."

"Are you sure, Carolina, I won't be..."

"Heavens no, girl, I have plenty of room. Where's the rest of your stuff?"

And so they had met, Melissa overwhelmed by the beautiful surroundings of Carolina's exclusive West Side apartment and the wonderful clothes that she was given to wear. The phone was always ringing. A steady line of beautiful young women would come by and have coffee each morning before disappearing behind closed doors into the study for fifteen minutes or so.

"What is it that you do, Carolina?" Melissa had naively asked on the second day of her visit.

"Well, Melissa, I own an exclusive escort service for very wealthy men who are lonely and need the companionship of beautiful young women."

"Really?"

"Yes, my staff makes a lot of money going to dinner at expensive restaurants, dancing, seeing New York with some of the city's richest guys. Foreigners, too, sometimes."

"Do they have to sleep with them or stuff like that?"

"Only if they want to and are smart!!" Carolina had laughed, watching Melissa's reaction. "Have you ever been to bed with a man, darling?"

Melissa had blushed at the question. "How much money can one of your girls make in a night?"

"Three or four hundred dollars plus tips. Depends on how romantic she is with her date. Why?"

And so it had happened. Melissa's first date at the Intercontinental Hotel was with a married banker from Bermuda, and how well she remembered Paul Ferris, but now her thoughts turned to George Henley as she drove into the hospital parking lot.

'Dear God, why good ole George? One of the sweetest and kindest persons I have ever known,' she thought, refreshing her makeup in the rearview mirror before entering the hospital and asking directions to the ICU where George had been moved during the night. On the elevator to the sixth floor she searched for the stamina and courage to face George alone in his grave condition.

She asked the nurse at the nurse's station, "Which room is Mr. George Henley in?"

"Who are you? You're not part of his family, are you?"

"No, I'm not. I'm his friend from work."

"I'm very sorry. The patient can receive only his immediate family. He's a very sick man."

"Yes, I know, but he doesn't have any immediate family. I'm as close as it comes besides our boss, Mr. Slade, who is out in the middle of the Atlantic Ocean and won't be home for several days."

The nurse looked up sympathetically before returning to her duties. "You can see him for just a few minutes then, dear, Room 677. He's suffering from congestive heart failure and his situation is very serious, in and out of consciousness, so don't stay long."

George Washington Henley lay dying. Melissa could hear it as he gasped for each breath of oxygen that flowed through the clear tubes in his nose. An IV slowly dripped into the vein in his arm, as his handsome black face rested motionless on the white pillow. The heart monitor screen showed steady, weak blips on the neon-green screen as the line of the graph bumped along. She quietly eased over and took his hand as his eyes slowly opened. He smiled weakly. "Missy, that you?"

"Yes, it's me, George," she smiled, trying to fight back her tears.

"Is our boss man home yet?"

"No, George, I spoke with Mr. Slade yesterday just before he sailed from Bermuda and he said to tell you to hang on. He's on his way and will be here just as soon as he can," she said, gripping the old man's hand tightly as tears welled up in her eyes.

"I'm a-hanging all right, Missy," he gasped with a good-natured chuckle, struggling for breath, "by my finger tips is about all."

"Just rest now, George, don't exert yourself. Mr. Slade will be here as soon as he can."

"Lord, Missy, you tell the boss man that if I don't hang on long enough for him to get back here, then he best change his ways, 'cause I'm right with the Almighty and I'm not going to see Peter Slade no more if he winds up in hell!" he chuckled.

"George, don't talk that way! Everything is going to be just fine. You rest now. Do you need anything or do you have any relatives that I should call?"

"No, Missy, you and Mr. Slade are all the family I got."

Carolina Barrington's phone rang in her exclusive condominium in a converted old warehouse on the wharf on Boston Harbor across from the Marriott Hotel. She instantly recognized Flynn O'Grady's Brooklyn accent calling from the S.E.C. office of Jason Hard, chief of enforcement in Washington, DC. He had been summoned along with William Dowling to explain how the Bank of Bermuda Limited operation had gotten screwed up.

"Carolina, we got to get a statement from you to straighten out this Bermuda thing. I got to have a full accounting from youse guys on what you done over there. What's your schedule look like next Thursday afternoon?"

"What are you doing calling me on a Saturday, Flynn? I didn't think you bureaucrats worked on weekends."

"You and Slade got a problem, lady!!! Don't be giving me no shit...."

"Oh yeah? Like what kind of problem, Flynn?"

"Start with getting this operation screwed up and then telling us what's happened to the half million dollars what's missing."

"No need to come to Boston next Thursday, Flynn, looking for a half million! I sure as hell don't have it. Slade's got the receipt from the bank, and if you want that, call him when he gets back from Bermuda. I can say everything I have to say over the phone, everything...."

"Naw, don't work that way, lady. I gotta get a sworn, signed statement on what youse guys done to get that banker, Ferris, to hang hisself and blow this whole damn operation. Youse guys got my ass in a crack with the chief here in Washington. I got to get a sworn statement from you and Slade..."

Carolina thought for a moment. 'I've got to talk to Peter first so we have our stories straight,' she thought. "All right. I'll be out of town until Monday, July 2nd. Give me a call then and we'll get together in Boston or I'll meet you some place."

"Monday the 2nd ain't gonna get it, lady. Remember, goddamn it, I'm your handler on this job and you best follow orders."

"OK. Thursday then! Don't short circuit..."

"You heard from Slade yet?" Flynn asked out of the side of his mouth, desperate for a Camel in the smoke-free office.

"No. Why would I?" she replied, hanging up the phone, thinking, 'I desperately need to get in touch with Peter so we have the same stories. He was planning to be back a week from today, Saturday the 30th. Perhaps I can get a number from the Newport Yacht Club and call him. No, better yet, I'll go down to the Stone Bridge Inn and get it from the bartender, George, Peter talked so much about. I've been wanting to see the Inn for myself,' she was thinking, dialing National Rental Car's toll-free number and reserving a car for the following Monday, the 25th of June.

Flynn O'Grady was traveling alone in the lounge car of the Metroliner back to New York. He was thinking about his meeting with the U.S. Attorney on Monday morning and how he was going to get raked over the coals for losing the half-a-million in cash that had been used to blackmail Ferris. He was smoking his usual Camel and drinking Four Roses from a flask he had in his breast pocket, listening to the clickity-clack of the rails.

Flynn O'Grady had been given an ultimatum: have a full report in the chief's office in Washington explaining everything, including the missing money, by Monday, July 2, or he would be fired. 'I got to talk to Slade when he gets back next Saturday, after I talk to the Madam on Thursday,' he thought, carefully drafting his report on a yellow tablet as he rode the rails. 'Then I will finish it up on Sunday in the office and take the train back to Washington for a meeting with the chief on Monday, July 2nd. His thirty-year career with the S.E.C. was hanging by a thread. "I've got one last chance to nail Slade, the son of a bitch," he said out of the corner of his mouth as the train approached Penn Station.

# Chapter XXIV

## The Atlantic
### Monday, June 25, 1990

I t was during the early morning watch of the second day that Captain Moffett first noticed signs of bad weather. He watched the needle on the barometer slowly sinking from 1022 to 1020 millibars. An hour later he observed that it had dropped even further to 1017. He knew that this depression was being pushed west to east by the prevailing westerlies, and a rapid drop in the atmospheric pressure indicated big trouble. Why in the world had he not been given a warning about the storm before he sailed?

The very thought of a storm sent a chill up his spine, after recalling Tony's stories of surviving the Fastnet '79 disaster. 'Atlantic storms can be fatal,' he was thinking as he logged in his watch.

The dark silhouette of his relief appeared in the companion-way hatch. "Good morning, Skipper. Steady as she goes?"

"Steady as she goes, Pete. You got the helm, Mister, she's all yours. Hold on 315 degrees with this wind. If it changes let me know. It more than likely will change at daybreak."

"Aye, aye, Captain, almighty winner of the coveted Lighthouse Trophy, SIR!"

"Cut it out and get up here, Slade!" Moffett laughed, delighted that Peter had recovered his sense of humor. John had been worried about their run-in on Ordinance Island.

"Are there any ship's lights on the horizon?"

"None, but keep a keen eye for those supertankers! I'm going to my cabin and get some rest now. Call if anything happens."

John was having a hard time falling asleep, which was unusual. He lay listening to the bubbling of the sea running in the boat's wake. Tossing and turning in the dark, he worried about the approaching storm. Why in the hell didn't the weather map at the custom office indicate a problem? His small sailboat was caught out in the middle of the vast Atlantic and what should he do? Should he alert his crew? 'No, not yet,' he thought, 'I don't feel any signs of the long rolling swells yet, and from the barometric pressure, the storm could still be hours or perhaps days away.'

"Damn it," he swore at his insomnia, as he reached over and tuned in FM 89 Bermuda on his radio, listing patiently for a weather report. The gombey music brought it all back for a moment: Bermuda, Government House, and the thrill and excitement of winning the Lighthouse Trophy. He felt for a brief moment the excitement of his victory over Firestone.

'The crew has been at it for ten days now, nonstop, and I know they're exhausted. I'm glad they have settled down into a daily routine. Now we can all relax and enjoy ourselves unless this depression turns into a storm. Pete's feeling better after our argument. First problem we ever had. I guess I really pissed him off, but damn it, he almost cost me the trophy when he got into it with Firestone. I need to find the right time to discuss the Stone Bridge Inn and Charlotte with him, to see if I can help. I know he's worried about George, too. I was stupid for not asking more about the Fed's mission, but he didn't seem to want to talk about it. It must have gone OK. He's got a hell of a lot on his mind, and I've got to sit down with him and help him get his head screwed on straight.'

Above, Slade held ten degrees off the rhumb line of 315 degrees, a straight shot to Newport, adjusting for the northwesterly wind. The stainless steel wheel was cold to his hands, so he slipped on his gloves. His eyes darted between the glowing fluorescent needle of the compass, mounted in its binnacle squarely in front of the wheel, and the dark, distant horizon. A westerly wind blew lightly across his unshaven face, bringing the clean fresh smell of the ocean. He waited for first light. Looking up into the heavens of the star-filled night, he forgot about his troubles for a moment. Remembering Carolina's naked body wrapped a grin on his face and he wished that he could reach out and touch her now.

'What a nightmare the last few months have been,' he thought. 'Life's a bitch if you let it be, what with George in the hospital and nobody managing the Inn except Pierre and Melissa. I should have at least called him before we cast off, damn it. His birthday is tomorrow. I need to be at the Stone Bridge instead of fooling around out here in the middle of the ocean. Hurry up, you slow sailing son-of-a-bitch.'

Slade was chilled from the cold night air and the wind. 'When is sunrise,' he thought, glancing at his watch. 'I wonder how George is feeling? Never been sick a day in his life that I can remember. If I lose the Stone Bridge Inn, we are headed back to Baltimore, ole timer.' The very thought of it turned his heart cold for Charlotte. 'Did I ever love the goddamn bitch? Yes, I loved her very much back when. Well, do you still love her now?' he asked as the distant running lights of a ship appeared on the horizon, barely visible in the distance, much like his feelings for her now, only a glimmer, too far and distant to really matter anymore.

Was it Charlotte's money that had attracted him when he was desperate and headed for prison? It was a hard question to answer, and the feeling that he had used her returned from deep inside again. Should he admit her to the Betty Ford Clinic and see if they could sober her up? Should he try one last time to salvage the marriage? 'God knows I drink too damn much,' he was thinking, inhaling the sobering ocean air and suddenly feeling thirsty. 'That goddamn bitch has hit drunk city; she's really into that rotten slop.' He pounded the wheel at the thought of her filing for a divorce. 'God, I can't lose the Stone Bridge Inn!'

Peter Slade's heart turned colder, pierced with anger and hurt. 'I *am* the goddamn Stone Bridge Inn, you gin-sucking bitch. I put the whole thing together, resurrected her from the dead, and this is what I get from you, you ungrateful spoiled little girl. Slade, if you're going to keep the Stone Bridge Inn, you have one of two choices: sober Charlotte up and save the marriage, or kill her.'

Peter Slade flinched at his first thought of murdering his wife. 'Jesus, that's taking this thing way too far,' he thought.

Off the starboard quarter, a faint tinge of pink on the eastern horizon announced a new day. His anger was suddenly broken by the Englishman's voice. "Top of the morning, mate! How about a cup of coffee for the old seadog?" Tony asked, handing him a steaming hot mug.

"Thanks, Tony," Peter replied, glad for some company. The two sailors watched the new light softening the hard edges of the boat in the predawn darkness. They sat silently in the cockpit sipping coffee, each with his own thoughts, watching the vast horizon and listening to the keening of the wind in the rigging.

"Sorry to hear about your man George, ole chap. I know you are pretty buggered over it. Captain said he's the best bloody bartender in America, and from the drinking man he is, that says a lot for your chap."

"Right, Tony, and thanks. George will be all right, I hope. He's seventy tomorrow."

"You could have flogged Firestone easily, I say, Pete. Just the wrong time to set out about doing it, wasn't it?"

"Pretty dumb of me to create a scene like that right in front of the Racing Committee. Didn't realize it could have gotten us disqualified. I just lost it when Flint called us criminals...."

"Flint's bloody right, calling us criminals...wasn't he?"

"Hell no! None of us are in jail, are we?"

"Bloody shrink, Doc Pearson, damn nearly did us in. Running off at the mouth like that with Firestone! Don't you say, Pete?"

"No question about it in my mind, Tony, that he told Firestone we cheated by running our engine. I'm not sure he did it on purpose, though, probably just got drunk and was suckered in by Flint."

"Bloody doctor gives me the willies, he does. Just like this weather. Damn fortunate to have survived Fastnet '79, when the boat I was on got knocked down," Tony said. Both men could now make out in the weak light the underlining waves from a great storm as the boat rode slowly over the low rolling swells.

"Yeah, I've never been in a storm, neither has John. What was it like when she turned upside down? Where were you?"

"In the bloody cockpit, I was, Pete, just like we are now. Thrown overboard when she flipped. Dangling by me safety tethers. Hundred and fifty pound bloke like meself generates a force of more than three thousand pounds when he is thrown twelve feet, I later calculated. Wonder the jackwires withstood those loads, mate. Imagine what it did to me. Force alone was enough to kill me, not to mention drowning."

"How long did it take for her to right herself?"

"Rolls on over. An eternity if you're pinned under her. More likely than not you shall be drowned. Damn lucky I wasn't!"

Below, Moffett fought to get some sleep, feeling the *Encounter* rising and falling easily beneath him. He finally got up and dressed and went to check the barometer which had fallen to 1011 millibars. A frown of anxiety creased his broad forehead as he went forward into the main saloon. He turned on the navigation table light and tuned to 3243.5 frequency on Bermuda BBC for the shipping bulletin and listened to the dry sympathetic voice of the announcer's bad news. "Gale conditions... increasing 8 locally gale 6, becoming mainly northeasterly later tomorrow, approaching Bermuda. Mariners, immediate gale warnings in effect for Bermuda waters."

He poured a cup of coffee and stuck his bare head up the companionway, studying the swells closely. They confirmed his fear of the closing storm, watching them roll in from the northwest, much larger now than he first thought. "Gentlemen," he said, stepping into the cockpit, "we are in for some bad weather; real bad weather, I'm afraid. I just got gale warnings on the Bermuda BBC shipping bulletin."

The Englishman spoke rapidly. "Yes indeed, quite certainly we are, Skipper! The bloody barometer's been falling all night. I mean to say, did you know any of this when you checked the weather map at Customs before we left Bermuda?"

"The last thing I did was check the latest weather satellite map on the clipboard just as I walked out of the Customs office. It indicated clear sailing or we sure as hell wouldn't have sailed."

"Yeah, John, we're headed into a little storm. From the looks of those clouds, it doesn't look as though it's going to be too bad," Peter replied, pointing to the rippled cirrocumulus clouds that were clearly visible on the horizon, reflecting off the early morning sun. "Mare's tails and mackerel scales make tall ships carry short sails. What do you think we're in for, really?"

John Moffett now realized he had made a terrible mistake by not confirming the weather forecast with the Custom's officer who was on the telephone when he left his office. 'I was too damned wrapped up in this Lighthouse Trophy to get the long-range forecast, I guess. We should have never left Bermuda,' he thought, wondering if Firestone had also sailed. 'Damn stupid of me to endanger the lives of my crew and the safety of the yacht this way.' "I don't know, gentlemen. I've been watching the barometer falling. Let's get a plot on where this baby's headed and see if we can dodge it, Tony, or maybe make a run for Bermuda if we have to."

The two sailors went below to the nav station table and listened intently to the shipping bulletin on the radio. Tony wrote down the latest storm coordinates from the broadcast and carefully plotted them on the maneuvering board. John turned on the loran and got the *Encounter*'s exact position that was also plotted. Tony removed his glasses, rubbed his tired eyes and said, "I do say, John, we are on a collision course with the bloody storm. It must be traveling at an incredible speed, this one. I mean to say, we are in for a hell of a blow."

Moffett studied the chart carefully. "No way in hell to outmaneuver it is there, Tony?"

"No indeed, afraid not."

"Can't we turn back and make a run for safety in Bermuda without being overtaken by the storm and getting caught on the outer reefs?"

"There is absolutely no way, I say, to achieve that. We will, however, get hit later today by its bloody dangerous quadrant, the exceptionally violent part of the bugger, as you well know, mate."

"What precautions do you recommend then, besides preparing the boat for bad weather?"

"Batten down the hatches and get everything above and below decks secure. I've been through this sort of thing before, remember, in Fastnet '79 off Ireland when we lost fifteen blokes...."

"Good to have you on board, because I haven't been through anything like that, Tony," Moffett matter-of-factly replied.

Four hundred and fifty nautical miles to the northwest a tremendous storm was building seas of sixteen to twenty feet. Forty-knot sustained winds blew white foam in well-marked streaks along its direction. The barometric pressure slipped into a deep depression. The swirling violent air created by the high and low pressure continued to build with the earth's counterclockwise rotation. The storm grew to eight hundred miles in diameter.

The crew continued to monitor the storm on the BBC. They were helpless as the *Encounter* sailed into the jaws of a violent storm that had traveled nearly three thousand miles in four days.

The Englishman was at the helm and it was well into the forenoon watch. The morning skies that had begun clear and sunny had turned hazy, fading the sun into a dim light in the dark gray sky. The wind had stiffened a bit as long rollers were visible on the surface of the ocean. The *Encounter* picked up speed with a brisk northwesterly wind that white-capped the seas.

Suddenly the horizon turned pitch-dark ahead as a black wall of the approaching storm's front bore down on the *Encounter* with incredible speed.

"Waterspouts!!! I say! All hands topside! Look at those bloody bastards dance across the water!" Tony shouted.

The crew scrambled on deck, horrified by a dozen black funneled clouds dropping out of the sky, sweeping across the ocean and forming huge clouds of white spray as they skipped and danced two miles ahead. The *Encounter* reeled as the force of the sixty-knot winds sent blinding sheets of rain into her. The sailors hung on in terror.

"Reef down the mainsail!" Moffett shouted, taking the wheel and swinging the *Encounter* into the wind, letting fly the jib sheet while starting the engine. The boat responded as the sails lost wind and luffed wildly. All hands snapped their safety harness hooks onto the jackwire that ran along the dangerously pitching deck, drenched by the cold sheets of rain. Tony locked his arm around the mast, cranking furiously on the halyard winch, lowering the mainsail. The others, with orange sailstop ties dangling from their teeth, wrestled to bring the violently flapping sail under control.

"Reef her down to the third reef line, Tony!" Moffett ordered. His crew fought the sail, drawing it into the reef band, a reinforced strip of canvas parallel to the boom, reducing the mainsail's area substantially.

Slade took a tie and laced it through the reef eyelet in the mainsail and brought it under the boom and secured it with a square knot, gathering in the bunt of the sail. A strong, powerful gust struck the *Encounter* as he struggled to keep his footing on the pitching deck. They labored with the arm-weary task of making two dozen ties, fighting to keep from being thrown overboard. The frigid rain driven by the gale force winds stung their faces, froze their fingers. Finally, all ties were secure, and the reefed mainsail was hoisted up the mast.

"Now, break out the storm jib, and hurry," Moffett ordered. The small, heavy triangular headsail was brought out of the sail locker into the main saloon. "Make damn sure your safety harness is secure, guys, before you go forward. We've got enough problems without having a man overboard."

"Get on some more power, John, and make sure you hold us into the wind. It's dangerous as hell on the bow!" Bob yelled, going forward.

The diesel engine groaned when Moffett engaged the shaft and shoved the throttle open, steadying the *Encounter* into the wind. The men hunkered low, almost crawling forward on the deck now, fighting the forces of nature, laboring to set the storm jib. The waves broke over the pitching bow, submerging the deck in white water. Minutes seemed like hours until, at last, Ganloff shouted from the pulpit, "OK, guys, that should do it! Let's get the hell back to the cockpit, and be careful!"

Moffett turned the *Encounter* back into the wind. The sails snapped full of air to the scream of the whining winches as the sheets were adjusted. The *Encounter* leaped forward under sail.

"There, that's looking good, men." Moffett yelled, glancing upward at the canvas, squinting his eyes from the driving rain pelting in the face. "Good job, guys! Damn fine seamanship. Now, let's see if the sails hold!"

In the rigging directly above the cockpit, the octahedral-shaped radar reflector strained under the force of the gale. The three squares of triangular metal, which reflect radar signals of passing ships that would otherwise go undetected against the fiberglass hull of the *Encounter*, CRACKED with the report of a high-powered rifle. A mighty gust of wind snapped the fitting, leaving the reflector dangling dangerously overhead, suspended by a single thin wire.

"WATCH OUT!!" came their screams simultaneously, every man throwing his hands over their heads. The forty-pound sphere swung hazardously overhead, oscillating with the force of the wind and the pitching boat. "We've got to get that damn thing down before it kills us!" Moffett barked, watching the clinometer register forty-five degree rolls of the *Encounter*'s hull. He swung the bow back into the wind, giving the engine full throttle. The sails luffed with the radar reflector still dangling above, the thin wire fraying.

"Break out the bo'sun's chair. I need a volunteer to go up and cut that damn down thing down!"

"I'll go up, John," Slade volunteered without thinking. "Hurry and get the bo'sun's chair rigged up," his words came cold and clear over the screaming wind as he kept an eye on the reflector swinging fifty feet up. 'Jesus, what have I got myself into,' he suddenly thought when the danger of being hoisted aloft sank in.

"Here, take this line up with you, Pete. We will have to lower it down and rerig it or we are screwed for sure without it! For God's sake, Pete, get a line on it and don't let it go overboard or fall on us either!"

Slade grabbed a line and a pair of wire cutters. He slipped quickly into the seat and fastened his safety strap. "Here, put on a life jacket, Pete, just in case you get thrown overboard," Moffett ordered. "Doc, you and Bob man the winch and hoist away."

Moffett fought the wheel, gunning the engine to keep the *Encounter* headed into the wind as Slade was quickly hoisted aloft. All eyes followed skyward, knowing that at any second the wire could snap, sending the reflector crashing down.

The bo'sun's chair swung fifty feet above the deck like a circus trapeze. Back and forth Slade swung, grabbing, missing, grabbing again, trying not to look down at the pitching deck fifty feet below. The driving rain pelted him in his eyes as he gritted his teeth. He lunged for the dangling reflector just as the *Encounter* took a thirty-degree roll to starboard. "WATCH OUT!!" he screamed, his voice carried away by the wind. He watched the reflector sailing overboard to be lost forever in the dark waters of the Atlantic. 'Damn it to hell! I screwed that up,' he thought, knowing that without the reflector they were sitting ducks to get run down by a passing ship. He swung for a moment thinking, 'thank God it didn't hit anybody,' feeling sick now as he waved his hand.

"Bring him down," John ordered. The faces of his crew wore a hollow frown, realizing that the seriousness of losing the radar reflector added another grave peril to their already desperate situation.

Flint Firestone was a man born without a conscience into one of New England's wealthiest families. He prided himself in saying, "Never, never show remorse, no matter how bad the deed," and he stuck by his word. He watched the CNN weather forecast on the television on the nineteenth hole of the St. George's Golf Club after he had just finished playing thirty-six holes and had shot extremely well. "We will be able to get in at least eighteen tomorrow morning, gentlemen, before the storm hits," he said to his crew and golfing partners.

"Look at the magnitude of that storm, Skipper. Can you believe Moffett was dumb enough to chance getting the *Encounter* caught out in the middle of that?"

"One's fashion for celebrating victory sometimes overpowers one's common sense," replied his authoritative voice to loud laughter from the men sitting at the bar.

# Chapter XXV

## The Atlantic
### Monday, June, 25, 1990

Within hours after the storm hit, Doc Pearson announced in his feminine voice, "Oh, this storm is making me SO sick. For heaven's sake, I hope I'm not getting seasick, guys!"

'The last thing we need now,' Slade thought, 'is a queer shrink puking all over the goddamn boat. The bastard almost cost John the Lighthouse Trophy after getting drunk and trying to put a move on Firestone. I don't know why in the hell Moffett didn't buy him a plane ticket home after that.' Slade lay in his bunk watching Dr. Pearson across the main salon getting sicker. "Hey, Doc, get topside and get some fresh air. Make damn sure you don't puke down here, man."

"Now, Peter! That's mean of you to say. AAUGhhee," Doc gagged. He rushed forward, almost running over Tony Stevenson coming down the companionway ladder.

"I do say, I'm feeling badly as well, Peter," Tony remarked, passing though the main salon on the way to his forward cabin.

What? Was it possible for the Englishman with all his years of offshore sailing to get seasick too? Slade bounced around on his bunk. Minutes seemed like hours as he braced himself against the violent beating the *Encounter* was taking from the heavy seas.

With his medical training, Dr. Pearson diagnosed his illness: 'the violent motion of the boat is interrupting my brain's ability to maintain its balance. So what? How silly; I'm a psychiatrist. It's only mind over matter. I'll psych my way out of it, stay in the cockpit and breathe fresh salt air until this silly, dreadful feeling goes away.'

But he got sicker, unable to sit up, and there was no room to lie down in the cockpit. The *Encounter* continued to be tossed around by the violent storm. He reluctantly went below feeling giddy, sweating, crawling into his bunk across the salon from Slade. He was miserable and apathetic, scared to death by the storm, paranoid about Slade and the others hating him for running his mouth to Firestone and causing trouble. 'What have I gotten myself into?' he thought, lying there fighting back the nausea. Suddenly his stomach wrenched. He bolted for the companionway hatch, heaving his guts out, splattering vomit across the galley deck. He heaved again, grabbing in desperation for anything to keep from being knocked down by the jolting boat. The vomit washed across the deck, painting its way back and forth, covering it completely. He vomited again, bent at the waist, holding weakly onto the nav table.

"Goddamn it, Doc! Get a bucket. Secure it to your bunk and quit puking all over the fucking place. Jesus, clean that damn mess up, man! It stinks like hell," Slade yelled from across the salon. He was sitting up and putting on his boots and foul weather gear. Watching his step, he slipped on the vomit. Quickly grabbing the ladder, he went topside to escape the hell.

'You mean, uncompassionate man,' Doc thought when Peter Slade passed. 'I hope you get sick, too, mister smarty-pants.'

From the forward cabin Tony was listening, and the sounds of Doc's puking made him feel ill. The experienced deep-water sailor and physicist respected the force of the storm and knew it could easily kill them. 'Almighty God, why me?' he groaned. 'Why am I sick after all my years at sea? I understand relative motion, the power of the wind and seas upon this sailboat and the brutal forces of the ocean that can easily destroy it. Dear God, it is interrupting my mind's ability to interpret the motion of the boat. Bloody hell, if it would only stop for a minute, I could steady myself.' In his mathematical mind he made rough calculations on the stress the boat was taking. 'Luckily she's a strong boat, custom built for deep water,' he thought, hearing the *Encounter* creak and groan with each wave.

The Englishman was stricken by an anxiety attack, a helpless empty feeling of letting his crew down, leaving only three to get through this terrible storm, complicated now by the added danger of no radar reflector. The smell of vomit reeked in the stale air. Diesel fuel had spilled out of the forward tank and had mixed with the overflow from the head to add to the pungent aroma. The smell filtered forward to where Tony had turned green. He lost it, scrambling in time to throw up in the head.

"Sad lot, those two, Skipper," Peter shouted, hooking up his safety harness and coming up the companionway ladder into the dark cockpit.

"Take it easy on them, Pete. They will get over it soon, I hope, or the three of us who are left are going to be tired sailors by the time we get to Newport," he shouted back.

"I feel sorry for Tony, but the shrink can go to hell..."

Moffett held up his hand, shook his head, saying he didn't want to hear it. "Get them some seasickness patches out of the First Aid Kit, will you? Make sure their leecloths are rigged to the bunks so they won't fall out of them when she rolls."

Slade took a deep breath and went below to find Doc Pearson down on all fours with a towel. The bucket slid back and forth on the rolling deck as he struggled to clean up his mess. His head, bent low, was wobbling, seeking stability within the pitching boat. He looked pathetic to Peter Slade, like a wounded deer shot in the guts, staggering, struggling before falling. He tried to wipe with the towel and hold the bucket as they all slid. Slade felt a sudden urge to kick him hard, square in the ass.

"Here, stick this patch behind your ear, Doc," Peter ordered, taking out a seasick patch and throwing it on his bunk. Watching the doctor floundering about on the deck, it was hard for him to keep from laughing. He breathed through his mouth and made his way to the forward cabin, calculating each roll of the boat as he went.

"Fee-fie-foe-fum, I see a sick Englishman," he began in a nursery-rhyme voice, looking down and grinning at green-faced Tony Stevenson, trying to get a laugh.

"I do say," Tony replied, weakly grinning a little.

"If you think you're sick, Tony, you should see the shrink! He's puked all over the galley and it smells like hell."

"Poor miserable chap. Know how he feels."

"Here, put his patch behind your ear, Tony. Captain's orders. I'll help you get your leecloth rigged. Can I get you anything?"

"A Coke would be nice. Yes, very nice of you, indeed, Peter, to fetch me a Coke."

Slade made his way back through the salon. Doc was back in his bunk lying on his back, ghostly in the dim light with his eyes closed, moaning and groaning, "I'm so sick, so sick. God, I'm so sick."

"You want a Coke, Doc? You're got to keep some fluids down or you will dehydrate."

No answer came from Doc, just a quick shake of the head and constant moaning. 'Go to hell, Peter, you mean nasty man,' he was thinking. 'I hope you get sick and drown.'

Peter grabbed a leecloth out of the locker and attached the heavy canvas to each end of the cabinetwork of the berth. 'At least I won't have to watch Doc die,' he thought, securing the leecloth.

He went topside.

"How they doing?"

"Sick. Sick as hell."

Slade was looking out at the angry seas that blew white foam with the wind. The boat's running lights had been switched on. Dark was quickly approaching and Peter Slade felt responsible for not saving the radar reflector. He searched the dark waters, remembering the *Encounter*'s close call with the supertanker. The storm was intensifying. Fifty-knot winds and powerful seas bashed the *Encounter* as she broke into them. This was going to be one long, miserable and dangerous night.

Bob Ganloff slid back the hatch cover and stuck his head out into the wind. "Jesus, it's brutal down here! I feel like I'm the metal ball in an aerosol puke can being shaken by the Jolly Green Giant! What a smell. Goddamn, what an awful smell!" he shouted over the storm.

It was dark now, and the Last Dog Watch change: 'Twenty hundred hours. Two crew members seasick. Slade's watch,' Captain Moffett wrote in the *Encounter's* log.

The three sailors huddled in the cockpit dressed in their yellow foul weather slickers.

"Gentlemen, it's left up to the three of us now to get through this storm. We are in for one helluva long night tonight," John bellowed. "Pete, keep a close lookout for passing ships. When you spot one, we will try to raise them on the radio to let them know we are out here. Keep the flares handy if we need to signal them and also the searchlight."

"Damn betya, Skipper. Now, let's get the washboards in the companionway hatch; the seas will be breaking over us anytime now," Peter shouted as they placed the wooden slats in the grooves in the hatch.

Slade watched the vertical dashboard of instruments directly in front of him. The anemometer was recording fifty to fifty-five-knot winds, force 10 gale conditions that drove the *Encounter* into the thirty-five to forty-foot waves that fell with long overhanging crests. The surface of the sea was white from, great patches of foam that blew with the deafening northwesterly wind.

"Bear off, and hold her at 280 degrees, Peter," John ordered as the *Encounter* took a close-hauled windward port tack. She heeled over at an uncomfortable thirty degrees, racing forward at incredible speed and running across the huge seas, making steering tricky. Even closed reefed she was going too fast. Peter kept his eyes glued to the dark breaking seas, fighting the helm all the way.

"This shit ain't gettin' it! Skipper," Peter screamed after an hour of fighting the wheel. The three able-bodied sailors remained in the cockpit, holding on for dear life. "We're either going to get knocked down or lose our steering if we get hit with one of these breaking crests and she broaches on us."

Moffett knew he was right. He recalled hearing and reading of accounts of yachts that had been capsized in just such dangerous conditions. This was a scary new experience that scared the hell out of him. He leaned forward, holding on tightly, weighing his other alternatives for dealing with the situation.

"Our only other choice is to turn and run before the storm. That will require that we rig a drag off the stern to slow down the boat so we won't exceed the wave speed and broach and capsize," Moffett yelled. His quick mind was planning what would be required in getting the cone of canvas and line over the stern to act as a sea anchor.

"The other alternative is to rig a sea anchor off the bow and lie a-hull with bare poles and ride this damn thing out like a cork on a fish pole. But without a radar reflector that would be suicide by taking a chance of getting run down by a freighter," Bob screamed.

'What a night! What a lousy night to die,' Slade was thinking as the men silently pondered their alternatives to survive the storm. The storm was getting worse, much worse than anyone had expected. He watched the speedometer's digital display flash twelve knots, as the *Encounter* raced down the back of a forty-footer, disappearing in the trough. 'No way in hell a ship would spot us in these seas,' he cringed, looking up at the approaching forty-foot white-capped crest of the oncoming wave. He watched for the big ones out of the corner of his eye, sensing them approaching by the motion of the boat and the increased volume of their roar. Like moving walls of water they came as he tried to steer at an angle down their faces, fighting to keep from letting them break on board.

"Should we bring down the mainsail and try it with just the storm jib?" Peter asked.

"Possibly, but first let's trail some line astern to see if it slows us down any," Bob said.

"Good idea. Let's get a full charge on the batteries before we put any line overboard. I don't want to take any chances and foul the propeller with the line," Moffett replied. "Start the engine, Peter, while Bob and I go below and see about rigging a drag."

Alone in the dark now, Peter turned on the ignition, adjusted the throttle and hit the starter. The diesel engine came to life, which gave a comforting sound of rumbling security beneath him.

Suddenly, without warning, the engine alarm blared. The alarm came blasting from below relentlessly. "WHAT THE HELL?" Slade shouted, at one of the most terrifying sounds that pierced the roar of the storm. No one answered, but he heard men shouting, cursing, scrambling below him. He stood helpless, holding the wheel, listening in horror to the wailing alarm screaming from beneath him.

Moffett's heart stopped at the sight of white smoke boiling out of the engine compartment. "CUT THE ENGINE! CUT IT, PETE! WE'VE GOT A FIRE!" he screamed. Slade hit the ignition switch, silencing the security of the engine. Slade was left with only the howling winds and rumbling ocean; sounds of footsteps scrambling below in desperation. 'Now we're dead men,' he thought, 'What a lousy rotten-ass way to have to die.'

Flynn O'Grady awoke this Monday, like all Mondays, with a Four Roses hangover in his dump of a suite at the St. George Hotel. This Monday morning was different in that he had until next Monday, July 2nd, to prepare a report on the Bermuda operation that could save his job or, better yet, come up with a plan that would nail Peter Slade. 'Fuck em,' he thought, 'the chiefs are making me the fall guy.' He lit a Camel while still lying in bed and stared up at the spider-webbed cracks in the plaster ceiling. It was seven-thirty and he had to be in the U.S. Attorney's office by nine.

O'Grady got up and dressed and took the Fourth and Broad train from the Clark Street Station in the bowels of the St. George, arriving a few minutes later at St. Andrews Plaza across from City Hall.

William Dowling, S.E.C. Chief of Enforcement for the Northeast, was already in the receptionist office when O'Grady arrived. The two men barely spoke, waiting for the U.S. Attorney, Ron DiLorenzo, to arrive when suddenly to O'Grady's surprise, Ode Terry of the Manhattan office of the FBI walked in. "Good morning, gentlemen," he said, shooting Flynn O'Grady a frown and shake of his head.

Ron DiLorenzo waltzed arrogantly into his office ten minutes late, never acknowledging his tardiness. The four men joined him. Another assistant U.S. Attorney from the fraud division, whom O'Grady didn't know, was also present and went without introduction to the others. DiLorenzo got right to his point. "Can't you fucking guys at the S.E.C. get anything right?" he shouted, pounding on his desk.

"I loaned you a half-mill from our confiscated drug money to use in blackmailing some damn Bermuda banker to get the list of all the American white-collar criminals who are hiding money in the Bank of Bermuda Limited, and what the hell have I got in return? One dead banker, a missing half-mil that you guys owe me, and some damn Inspector Whitehall of the Bermuda police demanding information that this might be part of the BCCI's operations while my counterparts in Washington are hot on an indictment of the former Secretary of Defense, Clark Clifford, in that case."

"Having said that, I want my goddamn money back, and I want you, Mr. Terry, to tell us what the hell's going on with Inspector Whitehall."

"I've gotten two calls from Inspector Whitehall. So far, he has not mentioned any blackmail money, or any implication regarding our two agents that were handled by Mr. O'Grady."

"Good, keep it squashed. Now, gentlemen, from the Securities and Exchange Commission, I went out on a limb to give you approval for this harebrained plan and I want my goddamn money back pronto. Hopefully, this whole damn thing will disappear without getting out to the press that we are using drug money to blackmail foreign bankers."

"And does anyone have a suggestion on how we do that?" William Dowling asked.

"I've got a plan, but I need some help...."

"Shut the hell up, O'Grady! If it wasn't for you, we wouldn't be in this goddamn meeting. Jesus, I've got a press conference in ten minutes, gentlemen. Remember, you have until Monday, July 2nd to get it worked out."

# Chapter XXVI

eorge Henley Washington died as he had lived, peacefully and with dignity, late on the afternoon of Tuesday, the 26th day of June. "It was his seventieth birthday," Melissa said after thanking the attending physician at Fall River General. She begin crying, held by the young chef, Pierre, who let her tears flow. "I've got to go to the hospital and take care of his things," she said finally, drying her eyes.

"It is so sad. He was a good man, yes?"

"I'm really glad that I've already made arrangements with the funeral home to prepare the body and hold it until Mr. Slade returns," she said on her way out the door.

'The doctor was right when he told me yesterday that he wouldn't last another day. Peter, oh where are you now that we need you?"

After signing the insurance and hospital release forms, Melissa

341

was given a large white envelope containing George's watch, wallet and keys to the Inn.

"The old gentleman put up a good fight, but his heart just finally gave out. It was all a very peaceful way to go and he experienced no pain," the attending physician consoled her.

"Thank you, Doctor, for providing him with such fine care," Melissa replied, wandering out into the waiting room, carrying the envelope with that sudden-loss feeling one gets when someone close to you dies.

'What do I do next?' she wondered. She dried away her tears and dug deep in her purse for a crumpled piece of paper with Peter Slade's home telephone number written on it. She then walked bravely over to the pay phone and deposited a quarter, dreading to make this call.


The sun broke through the clouds late that afternoon, bathing Beach Mont in prisms of bright sunlight. It had been raining for three days. The awful storm had finally broken and passed out to sea, leaving behind it crisp, clear air. 'I hope the *Encounter* doesn't get caught in this storm,' Charlotte Slade was thinking when she tuned to the Weather Channel, feeling strangely uneasy about her husband.

Charlotte was sitting in the den on the second floor, watching the storm surf that tore at the shore with huge white breakers that were rumbling in the distance. She had been monitoring the weather on and off all day for updates on the storm's progress, hoping it would clear up in time for her tennis match tomorrow morning at nine. In the grand hall below, the great clock majestically struck five o'clock, propelling her automatically toward the wet bar in the corner of the room. She suddenly stopping short in her tracks.

'You told yourself, enough's enough, yesterday and the day before that. Last week, too, Charlotte. This damn booze has gotten to you, so enough's enough,' she was thinking. Her hands began trembling for a drink of gin. 'Damn it, I've got to stop it,' she thought, clasping her hands and sitting down again. She stared at the fresh bottles of Bombay Gin and vermouth on the bar next to the sterling silver ice bucket. Thomas Terrell had followed her instructions for the last four years by placing them there daily.

'It is past five o'clock,' she thought. 'Time for just one short martini, just one, only one,' she thought, as her guts tightened with that terrible feeling that she was coming unglued inside. It was the nasty, shaky feeling that came every afternoon that gin instantly chased away. 'What the hell, I'll have just one short one,' she promised herself, walking quickly back to the bar.

Charlotte Slade inhaled the sweet aroma of gin and vermouth blending over ice in the crystal glass as she poured. She placed two large green olives on a plastic sword, their red pimentos contrasting nicely in the sunlight. She stirred the martini. 'This is absolutely it for tonight,' she thought, holding it up gingerly to the afternoon sun and toasting: "Here's to Jack Spencer, you stupid son-of-a-bitch."

Charlotte was drinking and thinking, watching the beautiful sunset and listening to the surf. That afternoon, meeting at Moffett, Spencer was a damn waste of time and money. 'These damn lawyers make everything so difficult. If I want to fire Peter Slade on Friday, then why in the hell does it take four hours with a lawyer to get ready for the stockholders' meeting?'

She sipped her martini, getting that warm resolve back inside that ended her shaky feeling. She relaxed now on the sofa, looking out at the huge surf. 'What a mess I have gotten myself into,' she thought. 'Jack is still the same goofy nerd that I knew as a teenager, and now he's fallen in love with me. He's such a conservative old maid, set in his ways, meticulous, and really not very bright. I don't know how in the hell he got out of Harvard Law School. He's got the charisma of a corpse, and is a lousy drinker and lover, too. Oh, what have you gotten yourself into, you stupid bitch, screwing around with your cousin's law partner?' Charlotte drained her martini dry.

The Weather Channel got her attention. "The severe summer storm that has been pounding New England and the eastern seaboard this week has finally moved off the coast and out into the Atlantic. It is presently stalled by a Bermuda high that has moved in from the south."

'My heavens,' Charlotte cringed at the sight of the satellite photographs of the large swirling cloud mass rotating counterclockwise on the screen. 'How terrible it would be if the *Encounter* is caught in that mess,' Charlotte thought, sucking the ice in her empty martini and gazing out the window at the heavy surf pounding on the beach below her.

Charlotte Slade felt a sudden uneasiness of remorse, guilt and anger. Her conscience gripped at her for getting involved with Jack Spencer in the first damn place. She imagined with horror the *Encounter* stuck right in the center of the massive storm.

'I'LL have to get this all sorted out,' she was thinking. 'I have got to get Jack Spencer out of my life, once and for all.' She set down her empty martini glass and stared at the gin bottle on the bar. 'If the bastard touches me one more time, I think I'll scream. How do I do it gracefully without Peter finding out? I'll have to do it before cousin John returns on Saturday,' she thought, recalling conversations that afternoon in the lawyer's office. The bottle of

Bombay Gin on the bar only a few steps away was staring back at her. Why not just one more shorty? She walked over and fixed her second one, pouring heavily from the bottle with no jigger this time, recalling her conversation at the lawyer's office that afternoon.

"Mrs. Slade, we are so concerned that your husband and Mr. Moffett might be out in the Atlantic in this weather. Have you heard from them?" Jack's secretary, Anne, had asked as they sat at the small conference table in his office.

"No. Peter hasn't phoned and said that they had left Bermuda yet..."

"Have you heard from Mr. Moffett, Mr. Spencer?" Anne asked.

"I tried to return John's call at the Waterloo House Saturday when I got back from vacation. He'd checked out and I assume he is staying on the boat until the weather clears. John's too cautious a sailor to ever venture out in that storm, I'll assure you. They've held in Bermuda until the weather clears," Jack replied, reaching his hand under the table and squeezing Charlotte's thigh.

Stop it, you stupid schoolboy, she said with her eyes. "I'm not worried about John and Peter after all those two have been through together."

"That will be all, Anne," John's voice had seemed to say in a possessive sort of way as though jealousy of Peter Slade had set in.

Charlotte's thoughts were now interrupted by the ringing telephone. She sipped her drink and waited for the butler to answer it. "There is a phone call for you, Madam," the old Englishman called over the intercom.

'Wonderful,' she thought, reaching for the phone, hoping to hear her husband's voice.

"Mrs. Slade, this is Melissa Jenkins at the Inn. I am sorry to bother you at home, but I'm at the Fall River General Hospital. George Henley died this afternoon. I wonder if you would like to see if you can reach Mr. Slade on the *Encounter* or do you think we should...?"

The shock of hearing Melissa Jenkins's voice bearing the bad news of George's death caught Charlotte totally off guard. 'Good God, how terrible,' she thought, still unable to comprehend the news. 'What a terrible blow this will be to Peter.' "Well...Well, I...I don't know what to do, Melissa. I don't know how to contact Peter or even if they have set sail yet, no one seems to know..."

"Yes, Mrs. Slade, the *Encounter* sailed on Saturday afternoon...."

"How do you know that?"

"Peter called.., excuse me, I mean Mr. Slade called, and I spoke with him just as they were about to cast off..."

"Oh my God," Charlotte gasped, "that means they are caught out in the middle of the Atlantic in this terrible storm...."

"WHAT?? What storm are you talking about? Is Peter, I mean Mr. Slade O.K?!! What in the hell's going on?...Please tell me!...Oh..."

"The same goddamn storm that's ravaged the east coast all this week, Melissa. Don't you watch the news?" Charlotte snapped.

"I'm terribly sorry, Mrs. Slade, I've just been so busy," Melissa said apologetically, sounding almost hysterical. "It's just been hectic these last few days with Mr. Slade being gone and having to deal with George's illness and trying to run this place. I'm terribly sorry to..."

"Are you going back to the Inn, now?" Charlotte asked in a cold voice. 'I'm going to show you a real storm, you little bimbo bitch, when I meet you there,' she thought!

"Yes, Mrs. Slade. I should be back there in a couple of hours or so, I have to drop by the funeral home. I apologize for my outburst..."

"I'll call you when you get there and give you your instructions on what you should do," Charlotte coldly replied, hanging up.

Carolina Barrington was driving south on Route 24 from Boston, enjoying the freshness of the lovely New England countryside which was bathed in the afternoon sunshine after the passing storm. She had waited for the Boston rush hour traffic to clear and was thinking how wonderful daylight savings time was. She listen to the Boston Pops on the FM public radio. She was feeling a little apprehensive about her surprise visit to the Stone Bridge Inn. 'I'll just have a drink at the bar and talk to George without his knowing who I am. I can find out a lot about Peter's life and the Inn that way and hopefully get a number for the *Encounter's* ship to shore and tell him about O'Grady. Oh hell, what do I do if Charlotte Slade should be there? Wouldn't that be an interesting meeting!'

Charlotte ate her olives out of the martini before walking back to the bar for another. She stopped short, thinking it would be best not to show up drunk at the Inn, especially as angry as she was getting over Melissa Jenkins's call. She quickly changed into a crewneck white linen blouse with short apron wrap skirt, putting on her new one-button black slouch linen jacket after brushing her hair and putting on fresh makeup. She smiled at her image in the full-length mirror, still beautiful and impressive, before descending the steep, dark servant stairs from the bedroom to the kitchen. She drove toward the Stone Bridge Inn, designing a plan for dealing with this young bitch, Melissa Jenkins, whom she was more confident now than ever was having an affair with her husband.

There were now three automobiles converging on the Stone Bridge Inn. The women drivers all had one thing in common: they were after Peter Slade. Carolina Barrington, driving a blue Buick rental, passed Fall River General as the ambulance was removing George Washington Henley's body to the funeral home. At the stoplight she didn't notice the white Ford van, with the Stone Bridge Inn's crest stenciled on the door, in the next lane before she pulled into a shopping center to get a pack of cigarettes.

Melissa, knowing she had screwed up by calling Mrs. Slade, sped ahead when the light changed. 'Oh God, I don't think I can deal with life if Peter gets killed in the storm,' she was thinking on her way back to the Inn. 'How stupid can you get, girl, spouting off at Mrs. Slade that way. That bitch will fire me for sure when she calls. No one but you, Melissa, is dumb enough to cross that woman, not even her own husband, Peter Slade.'

After taking a hot shower, Melissa just wanted to stay in her room and be by herself and cry, but that was impossible with the reservations that were already booked. She put on her black, low-cut hostess dress after redoing her makeup. She placed the large white envelope containing George's belongings in her dresser, then hurried downstairs to greet the dinner guests.

Melissa was lost in her thoughts while looking out the Inn's front door when a red Bentley came to a sharp stop. 'Holy shit! Mrs. Slade is here to fire me!' She immediately spread the alarm amongst the staff that the Holy Terror was on the premises. Gathering her composure, she put forth her best face, concentrating on not appearing nervous or plastic. "Good Evening, Mrs.

Slade, welcome to the Stone Bridge Inn. It's good to see you," she said, smiling.

"Thank you," Charlotte, replied, not smiling, glancing toward the bar, feeling very dry inside now for another martini, glancing down at six-thirty on her watch.

"You look wonderful this evening, Mrs. Slade," Melissa said, smiling. "I love linen in summer, and that outfit looks wonderful on you."

Charlotte was a little taken aback, and thought, 'don't try to placate me, you little bitch.' Coyly, she replied, "Thank you, Melissa."

'Oh dear, this is not working,' Melissa sighed, reaching out to touch Charlotte's arm. "Please accept my apology for the phone call. Please!" Melissa implored, catching Charlotte's eyes glancing into the Marble Bar again, needing a drink.

'This beautiful little bitch sure knows how to beg. I'll have a martini, then fire her,' she thought, her hands feeling shaky, guts tightening from the need for gin.

"Would you like a table for dinner, Mrs. Slade, or perhaps a cocktail in the bar before dinner?"

"Yes, a table in the bar would be nice so that you and I can have a little friendly chat, darling. IN private."

"Oh, I would love to, Mrs. Slade, but I must seat our guests. We are packed solid tonight...."

"Get someone to cover for you then," Charlotte snapped, walking into the Marble Bar.

'Oh, shit, here it comes now. Why doesn't the bitch just come out and fire me straightaway?

"Walter," Melissa called, motioning for the head waiter to come over, "will you please seat the guests? I'll be in conference in the bar with Mrs. Slade if you need me," she said, cutting her eyes to the ceiling.

Walter shrugged.

Charlotte had already seated herself in the distant corner of the Marble Bar by the veranda, facing the door to the dining room. Ed, the assistant barman, was serving her a martini when Melissa approached the table, her back to the door. "I'll have a cup of coffee, please, Ed," she ordered.

Charlotte's hand shook when she reached for the glass, but she managed it, sipping the martini without spilling a drop.

'You fucking lush, fire me now, and don't make me sit here and watch you get soused,' Melissa thought. 'Just go ahead and fire me, you bitch, and it will be a real pleasure to tell Peter you've been fucking Jack Spencer while he was gone.'

"Mr. Slade will be devastated when he finds out about George," Melissa remarked, looking Charlotte directly in the eyes.

'I'm smarter than you are, you little tramp,' Charlotte's mind was clicking and getting mean from the gin. 'I'll play along with you've because you been screwing my husband and that will give me grounds for a divorce. Then all this bullshit about a stockholder meeting that Jack Spencer has been planning won't be necessary. I'll have you both then, both of you thrown out of here in a New York second.' She smiled warmly. "Yes, I know, Melissa. They have been very close ever since Peter was a child. I appreciate your concern. Now tell me, Melissa, how have things been going here at the Inn?"

"Rather hectic. Without Mr. Slade and George, this place is just not the same. Our patrons are really going to miss George. Actually, the staff has done a good job taking care of business, but our receipts have fallen off since Mr. Slade has been gone...." she rambled, trying to read Charlotte's mind and figure out her angle when Charlotte's mouth suddenly dropped open, a blank stare filling her eyes.

Melissa instantly followed them, turning her head to catch a glimpse of Carolina Barrington coming into the bar. She walked to the tall bar stool at the Marble Bar, carrying a large shopping bag of items she had purchased at the boutique down the street from where she had been casing the Inn.

She gave Ed one of her sexy smiles that made the middle-aged man act foolish. Ed smiled back watching her ease her shapely hips up onto the stool, revealing a lot of thigh, pulling down her skirt as she went. "A vodka and tonic with lime, please," she ordered, taking out a pack of Virginia Slims.

'My God,' Charlotte gasped to herself, 'isn't that the Blue-Blooded Madam from New York? What's her name? Barrington? Yes, Carolina Barrington, that's her, sure as this world,' she stared in disbelief. 'What in the hell is she doing here?'

Watching Charlotte's eyes, Melissa glanced around again, snapping her head back in confirmed horror. 'My God! It is Carolina?!!! Where in the hell did she come from? OH God!' Melissa shuddered. 'She's tracked me down to have me killed for testifying against her at her trial! God, I never thought it would come to this.' Melissa cringed as her heart pounded, glancing around for hit men in her fright.

Carolina's flirtations made Ed look as silly as a schoolboy. She took a sip of her vodka and tonic, her eyes glancing around the bar, falling suddenly on the two women at the far table. Her face flushed. Her voice trailed off, her look tense and stern as she glared down into her drink, "Who IS that woman with Melissa?" she asked Ed.

"Oh! You're a friend of Melissa's? She lives here. Isn't she great?" Ed asked, smiling, turning his head to admire her, then realizing that she was sitting with Mrs. Slade.

"Yes, I know her. Who is the woman she's with?"

"That's the boss's wife, Mrs. Slade," he replied, reminding himself once more that he had better get with it, polishing glasses feverishly with the white bar towel as they talked.

"Melissa! Melissa, look! That's the New York Blue-Blooded Madam at the bar. Do you remember her? She had the call girl ring in...."

"Mrs. Slade, will you excuse me, please? It's getting very busy in the front. I'll save you our best table for dinner," she whispered, getting up from the table and heading straight for the door.

Carolina stared angrily at Melissa crossing the bar, trying to catch her eye. 'That little tramp's supposed to be in California! How in the hell did she wind up at the Stone Bridge Inn, I wonder? Oh hell, no! Now I see...! She's Peter's mistress, the little whore. No wonder his damn marriage is falling apart. That low-down bastard, taking up with a slut like Melissa.' Her shaky hand reached for her drink.

Charlotte downed her third martini and walked slowly toward the bar. Carolina's eyes caught her coming in horror. 'Oh my god, here comes Peter Slade's wife.'

# Chapter XXVII

## The Atlantic
### Night of June 26, 1990

"**A**RE WE ON FIRE?!!!" Peter Slade screamed, his words swept away by the screeching wind and the alarm blaring below in the engine compartment. "Come on, goddamn it! Somebody answer me!" Slade shouted again, steering with one hand, cupping his other to his ear, listening and waiting for an answer. The answer came in muffled, panicky confusion from below him and above the roar of the storm. 'Oh my God, if she's on fire, there's nothing I can do about it,' he thought. A disgusted feeling of helplessness wrenched his guts, traumatized by the blaring alarm.

The *Encounter* surfed down a huge wave, burying its bow in the trough, sending tons of seawater flooding over the deck. 'Her rigging won't take another lick like that without losing our mast,' Slade thought, catching his breath. He glanced aloft at the mainsail, wiping salt spray out of his burning eyes. The terror of the fire remained.

There was a tremendous gust of wind and blinding rain, followed by a momentary lull. Slade's cries for an answer went unanswered through the howling wind. The panic in the engine compartment seemed to have suddenly stopped as did the alarm. He stomped on the cockpit deck, calling again, "ARE WE ON FIRE, GODDAMN IT?!!!"

The companionway hatch thrust open. John Moffett's oversized head emerged from a white cloud of foul steam. "Goddamn it, Pete! We've blown the exhaust manifold hose on the engine and I thought we were on fire. It was the water on the manifold causing the steam. Now the engine will overheat!"

"Thank God. For a minute I thought that was the fire alarm!" Peter shouted back, shaking his head. "Manifold hose, you can fix that."

The Captain hooked the heavy stainless steel mountain climber's hook on the end of the eight-foot tether and climbed out into the storm, leaving the hatch cover open to let the steam bellow out. Looking downwind to keep the spray out of his face, he sat beside Slade, bracing himself for the *Encounter* to crash into the deep trough of the oncoming wave.

"If we have a spare, we can; if not, the engine will overheat and we lose power. Then we won't be able to run the generator and recharge our batteries. Let's shut off all the current except for the running lights to conserve the batteries."

"Have Tony get a fix with the loran first."

"Good idea. Hey, Bob, have Tony get our position if he is able. We're shutting off the juice," Moffett shouted down the open hatch.

"You're putting too much pressure on the rudder, Pete! Ease

her off and hold her on the quarter on these seas or we will lose our steering," John shouted, watching Peter struggle with the wheel, whose king spoke was marked with a bit of line that hung vertically when the rudder was centered. The line was now horizontal. Tons of water pushed against the rudder, making steering nearly impossible. Moffett knew that the rudder could collapse at any moment under the terrific pressure, causing the *Encounter* to broach and capsize.

"Roger, Johnny! I've been trying to, man, but if we crest with a rough wave on the quarter, we'll capsize, sure as hell."

"I know, but ease her off some anyway...."

"You had better come up with something else, then, pretty damn quick! We're either going to get knocked down or lose it, Skipper!" Slade shouted back, spinning the helm to take the next monstrous wave on the quarter as ordered. "I don't know what is going to break first, me or the goddamn rudder."

"Hang in there, Pete! Let me get below and help Bob get the manifold hose fixed," Moffett shouted, disappearing down the hatch, leaving Slade to be tortured by the unrelenting, shrieking wind that was fraying away at his nerves.

'This goddamn storm is tearing me apart like those filthy vultures slashing the flesh off the dead, bloated gooks' corpses outside of Hue during the war,' he thought, remembering the terrible stench. He was thinking about Vietnam now and how many times he could have been killed and wasn't killed, but deserved to or maybe should have been killed. He thought about the Wall, the black marble Vietnam Memorial where Peter Slade had never had the guts to go, and then he heard the rumbling roar of a rogue wave building instantly off his port quarter. "Holy shit!" he screamed, spinning the wheel hard to starboard, trying to keep the

*Encounter* from broaching. The boiling white foam of the cresting monster lifted the *Encounter* and sent her skidding at a fifty-degree list downward. Slade felt his knees buckling, knowing the boat remained out of control. Fighting with all his strength to get her back again, he swore.

Now the boat was steady and on course again. 'What the hell's taking them so damn long with the engine?'

An hour later, he was still wondering the same thing. The muscles in his back and arms knotted and burned with fire from the strain and tension of three hours at the helm. 'I've got to get some relief soon,' he thought, cringing, bending at the knees to absorb the impact of yet another wave that sent the *Encounter* over hard on her side. 'Jesus, I damn near lost her again that time,' he cried. Cold water trickled down his chest from the opening in his foul weather gear. His strength was fading fast after hours of physical exertion. He knew Peter Slade would never quit until it killed him.

The hatch flew open and Bob Ganloff barked the order, "Start the engine, Pete."

'Thank God, at last, and let's hope she holds,' he was thinking, hitting the ignition. The engine sprang to life, rumbling reassuringly beneath him. 'What a wonderful sound that engine makes!' His spirits lifted, making him forget about his misery with the sweet rumble of the diesel vibrating the deck. 'By God, they have done it! Got her fixed,' he grinned. Just then his jubilation was shattered by a miniature explosion in the engine compartment.

"GODDAMN IT!" Ganloff swore, standing in the hatch. "CUT THE ENGINE, PETE!!!"

'Oh HELL!' Slade sighed. He quickly switched off the ignition, causing the reassuring vibrations to cease and leaving only the terrifying wind.

John Moffett, gasping for fresh air, stumbled up the ladder out of a cloud of white steam.

"What the hell's happened now?" Slade asked.

Gasping for fresh air, he wiped his broad forehead in disgust, "We don't have a spare hose, so we jury-rigged a beer can for a hose and it couldn't hold the pressure!"

"Can't you rig up something else, Johnny?"

"Hell no! That was our only hope, man. We're really fucked now, Pete!"

Peter Slade knew it, too. The white frothing foam on the surface of the ocean reminded him of a rabid fox he had once shot from his duck blind on the Chesapeake Bay. The fox had attacked his Lab, Dakota. Same slobbering, white froth that had scared the hell out of him when the fox snarled and charged the dog. This goddamn storm was the same...just like the fox and just as insane! Slade's guts wrenched in dismay, his arms trembling from the strain as the dark mountains of monstrous white-capped waves marched relentlessly onward. He realized now for the first time that the storm would probably kill him tonight. He wouldn't roll over and die easily. Struggling defiantly at the helm, he fought for his life with all his might.

His inner soul felt a sinking reverence that God's almighty wrath had unleashed its fury and was punishing him for his past transgressions. Praying for God's mercy and forgiveness briefly entered his mind, but was instantly erased by a sudden lightning strike. 'You hypocritical bastard, Slade, why should God show mercy on you now? You got your ass into this mess, and now you either fight your way out of it or you're headed for a cold, watery grave.'

Beside him, John Moffett was thinking his own thoughts.

'What rotten damn luck having the engine crap out on me like this when we must have it to survive. No engine, no generator, no batteries to run the running lights. No radio, no loran, no lights and no way out of this mess except to either capsize and drown or get run down by a big ship. I'll never enjoy the prestige of my Lighthouse Trophy at the Newport and New York Yacht Clubs, and that's a crying damn shame. How could I have been so stupid not to confirm the weather before we sailed?'

"How long will the batteries last?" Peter shouted, dreading the answer.

"We can get twenty to twenty-four hours out of them if we use only our running lights at night. They had almost a full charge when the engine crapped out on us."

The pale-faced Englishman appeared in the hatch and hooked on his harness, stumbling weakly into the cockpit. "Captain, I've piloted our position on the loran, so you can now turn off the power. I regret to report that we are making little if any headway against this bloody storm. The latest BBC weather report has stated that the storm is stalled by a Bermuda high, I say, and along with it, so have we."

"Thanks, Tony. You feeling any better?"

"No, mate, I feel bloody rotten."

"It's OK. Now get back below and keep drinking fluids so you won't dehydrate. Keep warm. We're going to need you as soon as you're up to it, Pete's running out of steam."

"Aye, aye, Captain. Hope to bear up under the shame of it. The likes of an ole salt like me getting seasick like a bloody landlubber..."

"Nonsense, Tony. Now get the hell below and rest," John ordered. The Englishman weakly smiled and then disappeared.

"Hey, Bob! Get topside, will you?" John shouted down the open hatch when Tony had left.

The three able-bodied sailors huddled around the captain to block the wind and try to keep warm. "Gentlemen," the captain screamed, "we have only one choice now without our engine, from the way I see it. We are either going to sail her out of here or tear this boat all to hell and die trying. That's our only hope for survival, my friends."

The men hunkered in the cockpit, silhouetted against the white foam. The *Encounter* disappeared down into a deep trough and then reappeared, climbing a mountainous fifty-foot wave on the other side.

"You're right, John, we either have to sail out of this shit or die here in it. Let's get the drogue over the stern to slow us down and give her some control," Bob Ganloff said in a stern voice. They all three agreed. "Well, gentlemen, there is an old German sailor's song I remember my grandfather used to sing, 'No roses bloom on a seaman's tomb, only the seagulls cry...'"

"What a shitty song that one is, Bob," Slade interrupted, laughing to keep from crying.

"Let's get below, John, and rig this coffin with a sea anchor, and if we don't talk again, Pete my friend, I'll see your rotten ass in Davy Jones's locker!"

Thirty minutes later, an opened-ended cone made of stout canvas attached to a heavy line was lowered off the stern to slow the *Encounter* down. John knew the disputed theories of using a drogue and now he had to test them for himself. Would it slow her enough, reducing the forces on the rudder and preventing the boat from surfing down the front of the waves? 'I have to keep her from surfing,' John thought, 'yet go fast enough so these oncoming waves don't hit her at full speed, knocking us down so we capsize. We have to have minimum speed for good rudder control to steer across the waves, not up and down them. When it gets light I can see about carrying more sail to stabilize this beautiful seaworthy boat of mine.'

With the drogue trailing astern, the *Encounter* slowed and her steering improved. The mate had the helm. Peter Slade was in his bunk being battered by the constant pounding the boat was taking from the ocean. Sleep was impossible in these miserable conditions. He wearily braced himself against the hull with the blankets and cushions and tried to rest. He laid there in the dark eating a Hershey Bar, listening to Doc moaning across the cabin. 'If I don't get some fluids in the poor bastard, he's going to die,' he thought. The stench of the mixture of vomit, diesel fuel and urine washed up and down the deck as the boat rolled, leaving a terrible smell. 'The shrink sounds like he's being tortured on a rack,' Slade thought, as the other man's groans came in cadence as each brutal wave hammered against the boat's hull. 'You poor damn miserable bastard, Dr. Pearson, you'll never see daylight or New York City again, my seasick friend.'

A blinding flash of light illuminated the cabin for a split second, projecting a fluorescent image of George Henley Washington on the bulkhead. "My god!" Peter Slade gasped not believing what he thought he had seen. The instantaneous clap of thunder made him flinch. 'Was George coming to say goodbye?' Peter wondered, his heart feeling empty with an eerie, spooky feeling that George Washington Henley was dead. 'He's checking on me one last time.'

The boat took a savage lick from a monstrous wave that broke over her deck, slamming Slade's head against the bulkhead. Damn it! How much more could she possibly take? He was rubbing his head, irritated as hell that Dr. Pearson was now gaging with the dry heaves.

"Heave your fucking guts out, Doc. We're all dead men tonight anyway," Slade muttered, shivering under a wet blanket. He was feeling the throbbing knot on his forehead. 'I might as well put the poor bastard out of his misery.' Reaching for his razor-sharp Gerber knife on his hip, secured by the Englishman's lanyard to keep from losing it overboard. 'I'll cut the queer fucker's goddamn throat. It will only take a second. Then I won't have to listen to him suffer anymore.'

Doc Pearson was lying on his back, gagging, too weak to sit up. Slobber drooled down from his chin and he couldn't wipe it off. 'Thank God for the leecloth,' he was thinking, 'at least it gives me some privacy and I don't have to look at that psychopath, Peter Slade.' He stared up helplessly at the dark, overhead. His mind wandered in its delirious state. 'Peter Slade! you are just a beast and I hate you for being so unsympathetic. We are all going to die and I don't care if I do hate you, you bastard. I have been SO-O afraid of catching AIDS and now I'm going to die in this damn storm with a terrible man like you. Oh, heavens, if only I could die...if only I had the strength to get topside and jump into the ocean. Yes, if only I could drown myself now. That would be so-o nice....'

Slade was beginning to shiver. He threw his wet blanket aside, knowing he needed to get some more clothes on to fight the first signs of hypothermia. He lunged forward with a sudden roll of the boat, balancing himself, and found his sweater. 'I'll get the good Doctor to sit up straight. It will be easier slitting his throat that way.'

"Hey Doc, sit up, man! Here, have some Coke...."

Dr. Pearson was too weak to move or answer. 'Maybe he died,'

Slade speculated, drawing the knife from its sheath with his right hand and stepping forward, balancing himself against the jerking boat as he went.

Suddenly the hatch cover flew open just as a wave sent cold salt water flooding into the dark galley. "Pete, get ready! It's time for your watch," Bob Ganloff, shouted, quickly slamming the hatch.

Slade's hand was trembling, holding the razor-sharp knife. He slipped the Gerber back into its sheath. 'So it is, Dr. Pearson, you get to lie there and suffer a little longer, you poor pitiful bastard. I don't know what's worse, being topside at the helm or down here listening to your suffering,' he thought pulling on the wool sweater and feeling in the dark for his coat.

"Hey, Doc! You want some Coke, man?" Slade shouted as he started to leave, answered only by moans from the dark. 'Shut up, then, cocksucker!!!' A tingling rage ran up Slade's spine as he snatched the Gerber out of its sheath. 'Go ahead, goddamn you Slade, cut the bastard's throat!'

"PETER! Get the hell up here, man, I'm frozen!"

Slade's hand shook uncontrollably. He tried to slide the Gerber back into its sheath and it stuck. "I'm coming! Hold your damn horses," he shouted back, hooking on his harness and climbing into the cockpit.

"She's steering with a bit of the stern quarter to the sea, and plenty tricky," Bob reported. "I hope the drogue keeps us from getting knocked down and rolled. God, man, what I'd give for a cup of hot coffee."

"It's too damn rough to boil water. There's lots of Cokes, and Doc's plenty sick. You had better try and get some fluid in him or he is going to die, Bob."

"Who the fuck cares?"

"Check on Tony, then," Peter shouted, as Ganloff went below, leaving him alone at the helm to fight the miserable rain and cold. He hated for Ganloff to go.

Peter Slade could feel exhaustion slowly overtaking him. Thirty-six hours without sleep and nothing hot to eat was taking its toll. He knew the survival of the *Encounter* and its crew depended on his endurance and skill with the wheel on this critical four-hour watch. If they could make it until daybreak, then they had a chance, he sighed, flinching from the lightning and staring out into the blinding rain.

He was thinking of Charlotte and the Stone Bridge Inn again. The electrical storm intensified, illuminating the boiling black nimbostratus clouds with jagged jolts of electricity, five times hotter than the surface of the sun, followed by deafening claps of thunder. Slade flinched at a blinding strike, cringed from the whip-crack of the thunder, and hardened his resolve. 'To hell with Charlotte and the Stone Bridge Inn, just try to make it until daylight, take it one hour at the time, and just stay alive, man.' Deep from his inner-soul came a resurgence of his will to live, a feeling to survive not experienced since the war. He cried out above the roar of the ocean, "THIS FUCKING STORM WON'T KILL PETER SLADE!" His words were swept away by the wind in his morale-lifting testament to live. Damn it! He flinched, just when another spectacular lightning flash struck the ocean.

The *Encounter* was responding surprisingly well to the drogue, but still cresting on the seas at a dangerous angle. Slade anticipated each breaking wave, whipping the wheel at the last moment to keep the boat from being knocked down. Sliding down the back side of the wave he shuddered at the close calls, knowing that he would be drowned before she righted herself again if she rolled.

'If you have to die, and we all do,' Peter Slade wondered, 'would you rather drown or take a lightening strike?'

'Are those two pretty shitty choices?' he was thinking, just when a blinding spectrum of multiple tentacles of electricity lit up the boiling black clouds of the heavens. It was instantly followed by the harsh crash of thunder just as the air heated to twenty thousand degrees. Another blinding flash, followed by a sonic boom of thunder, illuminated the foaming white ocean as the *Encounter* crested a wave. It was closer, much closer this time. Slade delicately grasped the stainless steel wheel, thinking now that electrocution was his most likely fate.

Peter Slade felt the electricity in the air raising the hair on the back of his neck. The lightning turned the night into day with a relentless barrage of multiple strikes and thunder. It was like Vietnam all over again. Flashes of incoming, flashes of outbound, as the artillery duels had once illuminated the night. The barrages of high explosives shattered the earth with their percussion as they bracketed in on them. There was no high-pitched screaming whistle to warn you of the incoming mail. Just a blinding lightning bolt reechoing nearby off the ocean.

In a tenth-of-a-second a streak of electricity five times hotter than the surface of the sun left Peter Slade in darkness. Silence, peace at last, removing the harsh screaming wind, calming the waves and driving out the wet and cold of the storm. It was a painless, peaceful feeling of tranquil bliss that his life was finally over and there was nothing more to fear. Only a spiritual silence. Death at last had found Peter Slade in a blinding instant. 'So this is it,' his soul was thinking, and if he could just find young David and George, everything was going to be just dandy.

# Chapter XXVIII

## Stone Bridge Inn
### Evening of June 26, 1990

"Oh God... here she comes now," Carolina Barrington sighed, sitting erect at the Marble Bar. She had just finished staring holes through Melissa Jenkins rushing out the door. Carolina gazed casually out at the Sakonnet River and beyond, watching the late afternoon sun glistening on the white wings of the seagulls gliding with the strong smoky sou'wester of a wind. She was hoping and praying Charlotte Slade would pass her by.

"Good evening," Charlotte's sophisticated New England voice echoed in the empty bar. Soft music floated in from the Steinway playing in the dining room. Charlotte extended her diamond-clad hand. "My name is Charlotte Slade. I'm the innkeeper. Welcome to the Stone Bridge Inn, Ms....?"

"Thank you, Mrs. Slade," Carolina replied, shaking hands, nervously wondering, 'God, what the hell does this woman want?'

"I'm Carol and it's nice to meet you. Lovely place you have here, Mrs. Slade."

"I don't think we have had the pleasure of having you as our guest before, Carol. You are not from Newport, are you?"

"No, Boston. Just on my way to Newport, though, to see an old friend. I read your write-up in the Travel Section of the *Boston Globe* a few months ago and just decided to drop in for a cocktail. Lovely place, just lovely!"

"Thank you, Carol. I appreciate your thinking of us. It was a lovely article, if I do say so. Boston, what a wonderful city!"

"Yes, it is...."

"Ed, fix our guest another gin, or is it vodka and tonic? On the house," Charlotte ordered, catching Ed's eye for another martini.

"Why, thank you, Mrs. Slade. How very nice, what wonderful hospitality, just like the article said..."

"For heaven's sake, darling, please call me Charlotte! May I join you?" she asked, seating herself on the adjoining bar stool, giving the younger woman the once-over while Ed fixed their drinks. 'For a Madam, she sure has a lot of class,' Charlotte was thinking, watching Ed place their drinks on the bar.

"Oh, yes, of course, Charlotte. It's a pleasure."

"Carol, darling, you do look so very familiar. Haven't I seen you somewhere before? Perhaps New York?"

'That goddamn little tramp Melissa told her who I am,' Carolina thought, flinching at the question and taking a long, slow deliberate drink of her vodka and tonic. 'So what if she does know who the hell I am? I wonder just what Melissa did tell this sophisticated bitch about my past? So what? Why the hell should I care anyhow? "Yes. Yes, I am originally from the Upper East Side. Was it a guess or did Melissa tell you?"

"Melissa Jenkins? You know Melissa?!" Charlotte gasped as Carolina nodded suspiciously. "Really! Small world, isn't it Carol? How do you know Melissa, may I ask?"

"From New York. She sort of worked for a modeling agency, back when I first met her..."

"Really now? How interesting...please tell me, Carol, it wasn't your agency, was it?" Charlotte asked, peering down into her drink, wearing the smirk of a gin martini grin on her face.

"WHAT do you mean?"

"Oh come, darling, aren't you the Blue-Blooded Madam, Carolina Barrington, I have heard so much about?"

Carolina's face turned crimson. 'That goddamn Melissa DID tell her,' she thought, 'and what a nerve she has to ask that. Yeah I'm Madam Blue Blood and I just got through screwing your husband, you insulting bitch! Now take that,' she huffed, fumbling for a cigarette. "Yes, Mrs. Slade, I am Carolina Barrington, and rather shocked that you would be so impolite as to ask such a personal question, especially of your guest and a total stranger..."

"Oh! I'm sorry, Carolina, I didn't mean to insult you...."

"Well, you certainly did! Bartender, give me my check!" Carolina snapped, reaching in her purse and flipping her American Express card onto the bar.

"Please, darling! For heaven's sakes, Carolina, I really meant no offense. I was just curious...."

"That little tramp, Melissa, had to tell you. What did she say about me?"

"Calm down, please, darling! Nothing, I swear! I recognized you from the newspaper articles, television... *Time* wrote an article about you.... You do have a very beautiful and unforgettable face that became quite famous around the world. You do know that, darling?"

Carolina seemed flattered by the remark. "Yes, I know, but I would just as soon forget about it, if you don't mind," she replied, signing the credit card voucher. Ed nervously shuffled his feet and tore off her receipt.

"I do understand your sensitivity to the past, darling. Really, Melissa didn't mention a thing. Just the opposite. She got up and ran out of here when she saw you, like she had seen a ghost or something...."

"Really? Now, that is interesting.... Why?"

"I don't know, darling. She's new on the staff. Peter — that's my husband — hired her as the hostess without discussing it with me or getting board approval after she answered an ad in the *New York Times*. Here, let's get a table, darling. Since you know Melissa Jenkins, we have LOTS to talk about. Please...?!"

Carolina Barrington had Charlotte Slade under her thumb. Taking the American Express receipt, she gathered up her purse and shopping bag and followed Charlotte to the same table across the bar, so Ed couldn't hear. 'If nothing else, this will give me a wonderful chance to screw Melissa up and to find out more about this lush Peter Slade is married to,' she thought, with a smile of sweet, vindictive revenge painted on her face.

"Please, do tell me more about Melissa Jenkins, Carolina, darling. I have a suspicion that she might be having an affair with my husband, just between us girls. Peter had some nerve moving her into a suite upstairs...."

"WHAT??!! Peter has that bitch living here at the Inn?!" Carolina snapped, quickly trying to conceal her emotional outburst and hoping she hadn't blown her cover.

"YES!" Charlotte replied, not seeming to have noticed, her

mind preoccupied and furious at the thought of Peter in bed with that young, beautiful redhead.

Carolina was also trying hard to conceal her frustrations, saying in a calm but cool voice, "She is a deceitful little tramp if there ever was one. Worked as one of my girls..."

"What? She was a prostitute? Melissa Jenkins?!" Charlotte gasped, clasping her hand over her mouth.

"I prefer to use the term 'social escort'.... Yes, she did, and a damn fine little whore at that!" Carolina smirked, blinking her eyes in a la-de-da fashion. Ed glanced over, straining to hear what they were saying. Carolina's eyes narrowed into a squint. Her lips protruded in a catty matter-of-fact manner, saying, "The Judas little bitch turned state's evidence and testified against me at my trial after all I had done for her, mind you. I took her off the streets, gave her a home, bought her beautiful clothes and treated her like she was my own daughter! Without her testimony, the Feds didn't have a case....and she was the only one of my girls that ratted on me, damn it."

"Heaven forbid, I can't believe it!" Charlotte cried, downing her martini, thinking only of her wounded pride. "Peter's hired him a hooker as the hostess of the Stone Bridge Inn and has moved the little bitch into the corner suite on the third floor that I decorated with my money!"

Carolina Barrington cut her dark eyes at the ceiling, saying, "Reallllly?!"

"Bartender, another round over here."

"No, thank you, Charlotte, I am just fine. Your husband has some nerve, doesn't he?" Carolina asked, having a hard time concealing her excitement at playing tantalizing tricks on these two bitches. She was loving every moment of it. She could also feel herself getting angrier by the moment at Peter Slade for leading her on the way he had in Bermuda.

"Well, I will give Peter the benefit of the doubt. I'm sure he doesn't have a clue about her past, and how could he?"

"Well... I'm sure he doesn't, but I'm telling you, lady, I wouldn't trust that little bitch as far as I could throw her, much less have her working and living here with MY husband, if I were you," Carolina replied, almost laughing at the thought of how stupid and naive Charlotte Slade must be, thinking of the wonderfully sexy night she had spent with Peter at the Glencoe Hotel. 'Your so-trusted husband, Peter Slade, just screwed my lights out in Bermuda last week, you dumb bitch.'

"Are you married, Carolina?"

"No, I'm not."

"Well, if you have never been married, you don't really know what...."

"Being married has nothing to do with anything," Carolina said in a huff. "You're damn naive or stupid if you don't think Melissa Jenkins is living here and isn't trying to screw Peter Slade, lady..."

'Wait just a goddamned frigging minute here,' Charlotte was thinking, as she drank. Something about this conversation was not adding up. No, it wasn't at all, so playing dumb, she continued, "You are exactly right. I've been very suspicious about those two, especially when Peter moved her into a suite upstairs."

Now both women were thinking conspiring thoughts. Charlotte Slade was getting real suspicious of this New York Madam, and a very sophisticated and beautiful madam she was at that. 'Peter Slade, you no-good son-of-a-bitch, sleeping with that little tramp and me, too!' Both women were now thinking: 'Peter Slade is nothing but a no-good whoremonger.'

Suddenly, Charlotte cocked her head to one side. Sitting erect, she thrust out her chest in an arrogant, dominating way. "I'll attend to Miss Jenkins tonight after closing, darling, you can COUNT on that!"

"Well, I would certainly hope so...."

Charlotte's face flushed. 'Now listen to this slut from New York, would you, trying to act so goddamn innocent and giving me such sisterly advice. She came down here for some ulterior motive, and it certainly wasn't an article in the *Globe*.' "Won't you have another, darling?"

"No, thank you, I have to be running, but thank you anyway, Charlotte. You are on the right track firing that little bitch."

"I thank you, darling, for filling me in on Melissa. I can't wait to see the expression on Peter's face when he gets home, THAT IS, if he does get home, so I can tell him I met you and I've fired his little slut," she cackled in a high, shrill voice that got Ed's attention.

"Your husband's away on business?" Carolina asked, searching for information on how she might get in touch with Peter.

"Oh, no! Not business. He is evidently sailing back from Bermuda on my cousin John Moffett's yacht, the *Encounter*, this year's Newport-Bermuda Race winner. Haven't you heard, darling? Or are you into yacht racing?"

"No, I'm not," Carolina lied.

"Well, let me tell you, they are evidently caught out in that terrible storm that just passed...."

"Are you kidding?!"

"No, and at the moment, I have been unable to reach Peter and to tell him George, our head bartender, died. I'm getting a little concerned...."

Carolina's face flushed, her voice turning harsh with excitement. "How awful. When was the last time you heard from him?"

"Last Saturday."

"God! Have you tried calling on the ship to shore radio?"

"Yes, this afternoon, but no answer, I am afraid...."

"What about notifying the coast guard?"

"No, but I'm considered it."

"Well, what in the hell are you waiting for, for God's sakes? This is terrible!"

Charlotte's eyes drove daggers through Carolina Barrington, sitting across the table. 'Who are you kidding, bitch?' she thought, 'and from what you just said, you certainly have a hidden agenda by showing that much concern for my husband! God, is Peter screwing the Blue-Blooded Madam too? I'll check out what Melissa knows about her tonight before I fire her. I have her address from her American Express card, so I can have a private eye follow-up and see if Peter is involved with her. That should be ample grounds for divorce, having an affair with the world's most renowned madam.'

"Thank you for you concern, Carolina," Charlotte said coyly. "I appreciate your concerns for my husband, and THANK YOU very much for dropping by, darling. It has been a verrry interesting afternoon!" her voice trailed off coldly.

Ed rushed over from the bar. "Excuse me! Mrs. Slade, you have an urgent phone call. Would you like to take it in the office?"

"Yes! Goodbye, Carolina," Charlotte replied, leaving the other women sitting alone at the table, feeling stupid and worried to death about Peter.

'God, could that be him on the telephone?' Carolina thought. 'How could I have been so damn careless to make

Charlotte suspicious of me? What a damn mess I've gotten myself into this time,' she was thinking, picking up her shopping bag and heading for the side entrance, avoiding Melissa Jenkins at the hostess desk.

Jack Spencer's voice came across loud and irritated over the phone. "Charlotte. What are you doing at the Inn? Where have you been? I've been worried and looking all over for you..."

"Look, Jack, you're not my daddy, damn it," Charlotte began very matter-of-factly, her voice slightly slurred. "I have business to attend to here and can't be bothered at the moment...."

"No! Don't you dare come down here...."

"I'm perfectly capable of driving home, damn it...."

"Look, if you want to do something constructive, get over to the Newport Yacht Club and see if they can raise the *Encounter* on the radio and have Peter call me..."

She slammed down the receiver. What a wimp,' she thought, walking from the office and down the hall to the kitchen. "Pierre, what is your 'catch of the day'?"

"We have very nice swordfish, Madame."

"Good. Have a waiter bring my dinner to the office. I'll have a salad with blue cheese. Pick me out a nice bottle of dry white French wine, will you?"

"My pleasure, Madame. A bottle of Muscadet '76 we have. It is very nice, Madame, dry. From the Sevre-et Maine, the very inner best district of Muscadet," the young Frenchman replied. He began preparing her meal personally.

It was now eleven o'clock and the last of the guests were leaving for the night. Charlotte had just finished dinner when the office phone rang.

"Charlotte, I'm at the yacht club, and we can't get through to the *Encounter* yet.... No, we have been trying for several hours, half the club's down here and everyone is worried. The commodore and I have just contacted the coast guard, and the good news is that they have not received any distress signals. They will now be on the alert and keep us advised as the situation develops..."

"Have they heard anything from Flint Firestone?"

"Yes, we called his wife and got hold of him at the St. George Golf Club in Bermuda. He held up there until the weather cleared."

"Did he say anything about the *Encounter*?"

"Yes, it's very strange. He told the commodore that he could not believe that John sailed on Saturday, knowing the weather forecast. What time are you going to Beach Mont?"

"Later. Stay at the club and keep trying to get in touch with them. Call me if you hear anything, and don't bother to come by Beach Mont tonight; I'm exhausted."

Charlotte felt nauseated while tuning in the Weather Channel on the television in the office. The massive, whirling storm was still stalled as it continued to churn the Atlantic exactly in the vicinity of where the *Encounter* should be.

Melissa was in the kitchen with Pierre watching the same channel when Charlotte rang on the intercom summoning her to the office at midnight.

Melissa Jenkins's heart was in her throat. She walked quickly down the corridor, knowing that she was about to get fired after Ed had tipped her off on the bits and pieces of Mrs. Slade and Carolina's conversation he had overheard earlier in the Marble Bar. 'Well, that bitch, Carolina, has finally screwed me by telling Mrs. Slade that I was one of her whores. Should I blackmail Charlotte Slade about seeing her shacked up in New York with Jack Spencer or wait until Peter gets back and tell him myself? What if Peter gets lost at sea and never returns? Where does that leave me? God, I'm nearly broke and need money, and besides, if the Slades are getting a divorce, who will be running the Inn anyhow? Peter doesn't seem to notice a damn thing I do to get his attention. I don't believe if I showed up for work naked he would notice me. Hell, he's probably been screwing Carolina Barrington, or why in the hell would she have shown up at the Inn this evening? She has to be after Peter, because she had no way of knowing I was here. Well, what the hell? This place would never be the same without good ole George Henley anyway. Besides, if I have to, I still got a powerful young pussy that will get me a ticket to anywhere,' Melissa Jenkins was thinking as she knocked.

She knocked a second time. 'I won't let Mrs. Slade have the satisfaction of knowing that she can rattle my cage for damn sure.' Melissa Jenkins politely called, "Mrs. Slade, may I come in?"

"Yes? Who in hell is it? Come in," came a stern but slurred voice from within. Melissa opened the door and briskly stepped in, noticing the empty bottle of Muscadet on the desk, thinking, 'this damn woman's drunk.'

"Mrs. Slade, you wanted to see me?"

"Yes, Melissa, have a seat. What... what do you know about the woman in the bar this afternoon, Carolina Barrington, or whatever in hell her name was?"

"It has all been reported in the newspapers and on television. You know her story as well as I do."

"Yes, but have you ever seen her around here before? Is she a regular customer, or does she come for dinner since you have been here?"

"No. Why do you ask? Did she run out on her check?"

"Don't be silly, I was just curious. When was the last time you saw her?"

"Tonight was the first time I've seen her in years."

"Yes, she said that you were one of her callgirls in New York."

"That was a LONG time ago, Mrs. Slade."

"It was, but I cannot have someone with your reputation in my employment. I want you to pack your belongings and be out of the Inn by tomorrow at three p.m. Do you understand?"

Melissa felt blood rushing to her face, but, remaining true to word, she stayed calm, "Yes, I understand. As a matter of policy, do I get any severance pay?"

Charlotte, a woman who never in her life had to think of money, was muddled by the question. "Why sure, of course. What is your salary?"

"Two thousand dollars a month plus a percentage of the bonus pool for the bar and restaurant that we split among the staff. I usually get around four thousand a month," she lied.

"Fine," Charlotte replied, reaching in the drawer and writing a check and handing it to her. "Here is your four weeks' pay and two thousand dollars severance. Have your belongings out of here by three o'clock tomorrow. Is that understood?"

"I understand, Mrs. Slade," she replied, inspecting the four thousand dollar check. "This is very generous of you. Thank you. I wish you and Peter continued success with the Inn. I'll be gone by three," she smiled sweetly, turning and heading for the door. "One more thing, Mrs. Slade...."

"Yes, what is it?"

"I saw Carolina Barrington in action for a long time. You can bet your sweet royal ass, lady, she didn't drop by without a special purpose..."

"What? What in the hell are you talking about?"

"Good night, Mrs. Slade. Oh, you did talk to Mr. Spencer? He's been calling all night."

Charlotte moaned as the door closed. 'That little whore is on to me and Jack. I should have taken the satisfaction of slapping the hell out of her, damn it,' Charlotte was thinking, drunk now. Firing Melissa hadn't been such fun after all. The room was tilting and she felt hollow and guilty, but furious. Really needing another now, she picked up her keys and headed to the Marble Bar, which was deserted except for Ed who was closing up for the night.

"Yes, Mrs. Slade. Your usual?"

"A double in a to-go cup with extra olives," she replied, leaning unsteadily against the bar. "Let me see the credit card charges. You ever seen this lady — where in hell is it? — this lady, Carolina Barrington, before? Ed?"

"Only tonight, Mrs. Slade. She knows Melissa."

"Damn right she does, who the hell doesn't?" Charlotte slurred, stumbling and nearly falling on the floor.

"Mrs. Slade...."

"Yeah, Ed.... What de...what de hell iss-it?"

"I need to call you a cab, or I will be glad to have Melissa drive you home."

"To hell with Melissa. She's fired...."

Melissa left the office and went running up the stairs to her room, falling on the bed. She burst into tears. "You goddamned bitch, I wish you were dead," she sobbed, tears streaming down her face. She laid there and watched the oversized headlights of the Bentley pulling out of the drive. "Now, what do I do?" she cried, when her phone rang with Pierre's heavy French accent making her feel all the worse.

"Melissa, what is wrong?"

"Oh, Pierre, I've just been FIRED! That bitch ordered me to move out of the Inn by three tomorrow afternoon...."

"Fired! You are fired? Why did Madam Slade fire you?"

"Pierre, I don't know...."

"I quit then! They fire you and I quit. Yes?!!"

"No, Pierre, that will only hurt you and Mr. Slade. Peter will be back in a couple of days and straighten everything out."

"Would you like something to eat, Mam'selle? I fix the beautiful rose something very special, my..."

"No thanks, just run me up some clean boxes and leave them in the hall. I just need to be left alone. I've got to get my stuff packed."

"Yes, of course, Mam'selle Melissa, I am so sorry for us all. If you need help, I will be called, yes?"

"You're such a sweetheart, Pierre. I will call if I need anything. Good night."

Melissa dried her eyes and started getting organized. She opened the dresser drawer and saw the envelope with George's keys and wallet. 'I'll have a bottle of Dom Perignon on the house while I pack, Mrs. Slade.' She grabbed George's keys and walked down four flights of stairs to the wine cellar in the basement. The third key she tried fit the lock as she entered and flipped on the light. 'God what a magnificent cellar, there must be ten thousand bottles of wine down here,' she gasped. 'Now, where is the champagne stored? Oh, here it is,' as she stumbled over the Air Express package from Bermuda addressed to George Henley Washington on the floor.

'Well, what do we have here? George and Peter wouldn't want me to leave this package lying around like this. I'll take it up and give it to Peter if I ever get to see him again.' Placing the heavy parcel under her left arm, Melissa selected a bottle of Dom Perignon '69 and switched off the light on the way up to her room.

# Chapter XXIX

## New York
### Wednesday, June 27, 1990

W hen the Bermuda operation was aborted by the S.E.C., Flynn O'Grady had given up on getting Slade's secret bank account, but he had no idea that his own agency would turn on him. He had one last shot to redeem himself by arresting Peter Slade and getting back the blackmail money, and if his plan didn't work, he knew his career was over. Thirty years of bureaucratic hassle would be shot to hell, leaving him unemployed and unemployable. All he would have to show for it would be his dilapidated suite in the St. George Hotel and a life savings of just over thirty-four thousand dollars to live on. At fifty-six, what could he do for a living? Go on welfare like the rest of the St. George derelicts and drink and smoke up his savings account, he was thinking, reaching for the phone and turning once more to his only friend, Ode Terry.

Oden Terry was sitting behind the White Collar Crime Desk of the FBI's Manhattan office, toiling over a mound of highly sensitive reports on the Bank of Commerce and Credit International that had just come in from the field with a priority deadline. He was the agent-in-charge of the preliminary investigation into one of the world's largest bank frauds. In his twenty-nine year career, never had he seen anything that was this involved after reading the investigation's "Executive Summary".

Agha Hasan Abedi, a sheik from the United Arab Emirates, had founded the BCCI in 1972 with two and a half million dollars and a dream of creating the Third World's largest financial empire. The bank's downfall had been predicated by the arrest of its officials on drug laundering charges when the prosecution had revealed that it illegally and secretly owned First America Bankshares, a Washington, DC, bank holding company, in violation of the Federal Banking Laws. The Justice Department's investigation was casting deep suspicion on the Central Intelligence Agency's involvement with the BCCI in an international money laundering ring used to fund covert operations in South America and the Middle East.

'The goddamn CIA is completely out of control and this is only the tip of the iceberg,' Terry thought, knowing from his Interpol intelligence reports that Abedi had relinquished control of the bank and was in hiding in Pakistan. 'I'll be here all night and not even make a dent in this pile.' He sighed, glancing at quitting time on his watch as his phone rang. "Terry, speaking."

"Ode, man, I'm glad I caught you. Gotta have some help, guy. Can you meet me for a drink after work?"

"Not tonight, Flynn. I'm up to my ass in paperwork..."

"Ode, we got to TALK, man. You was at the meeting last

Monday; my job's on the line."

The agent looked at the huge pile of reports and knew he would never finish reviewing them tonight anyway. "OK. Where 'bouts?" he asked, reading the urgency in O'Grady's voice.

"Our usual place," Flynn replied, sounding much relieved. He started clearing off his desk.

"I could damn sure use a drink after today. See you in twenty minutes."

Flynn O'Grady left his office in the World Trade Center, walking the short distance to the Woolworth Building on Broadway.

Oden Terry signed out and caught the Lexington Express downtown, getting off at City Hall Station. Fifteen minutes later he was walking past City Hall on his way to the Woolworth Building across the street. Passing through the magnificent gold-leafed lobby of the former headquarters for the Woolworth 5&10 Cent Store chain, O'Grady took the stairs down to Harry's Bar and Restaurant in the basement. The bartender Wolfgang's heavy German accent rang out over the noise of the drinkers and the rumble of the subway trains. "Vhas vill it be tonight, Mr. O'Grady?"

"Four Roses," Flynn replied, propping his skinny frame against the bar and lighting up a Camel. He took a strong drink and shuddered, smoking nervously. He waited for Ode Terry to arrive by grabbing the bar and rocking back and forth impatiently, submerging himself in a cloud of smoke.

Ode slipped up from behind him, jabbing him sharply in the ribs.

"Damn it!" O'Grady grunted, shaking hands. Wolfgang laughed and poured a stiff vodka and tonic in a tall glass with a large slice of lime on the lip for his friend.

"Let's grab that table in the corner against the wall so we can talk," Flynn said out of the side of his mouth.

"Goddamn it, Ode, you know that half million cash we got from the U.S. Attorney?" Flynn began once they were seated.

"Yeah, what about it?"

"We got to find that money, and in the process I've..."

"Wait just a fucking minute here. What you mean, WE got to find the money, Flynn?"

"After Slade gave the money to the banker, the banker commits suicide on me, right? Slade and the Madam still got the half million...."

"How do you know that?"

"When Chief Dowling got nervous over this bullshit BCCI scandal and aborted the Bermuda operation after Ferris hung himself...."

"Son, this BCCI's not bullshit..."

"OK. Well listen to this. You was at the meeting with DiLorenzo and Dowling. You heard them bastards blaming my ass for getting this thing screwed up! HOW the hell did I know the banker would stretch his neck or this BCCI crap would break?"

"Well, just what the hell you want me to do, Flynn? I've done about all I can do when I arranged for the Justice Department to provide the Madam and her customer list to blackmail Ferris with."

"Ode, you got to help me get the half million back. Slade's got it," Flynn whined, lighting another Camel off the butt, searching his old friend's eyes for an answer.

"Flynn, you was the guy who masterminded the whole plan after I told you about Carolina Barrington. So when it got screwed up, why shouldn't they blame you? I thought it was a dumb idea, anyway, but the U.S. Attorney bought into it, thinking he could nab some big-time drug dealers and further his political aspirations. Blackmailing a foreign banker was kinda stupid and risky, if you ask me."

"Whose damn side you on here, Ode?"

"Look, Flynn, this isn't good! Especially since they told you specifically to get the hell out of Bermuda and drop it after this BCCI investigation has gotten the bastards in Washington more spooked than Watergate ever did."

"How the hell did I know this BCCI bank case was fixing to break?" Flynn asked again.

"Well you didn't, but by God it did! Something this sensitive... man we're talking about politicians, Treasury Department personnel, the CIA and the former Secretary of Defense that are under investigation...who the hell knows who else is involved? Serious stuff, this BCCI investigation. You came up with the bright idea of blackmailing a foreign bank official, didn't you?"

"Sure I did, with your help! They thought I was brilliant when I told them about the Madam's list with Ferris's name on it to get the secret accounts..."

"Flynn, look, my desk is covered up with this BCCI investigation, stuff so sensitive I can't even begin to tell you about it. Look, goddamn it, I got one more year and I get full retirement and then I'm out of this horseshit. As much as you're my ole drinking buddy, Flynn, my retirement isn't getting screwed up trying to get your ass out of hot water."

"Sure, Ode! I understand that. But what about me, man? My ass is about to get axed after thirty years! They are using losing the blackmail money as an excuse to fire me."

The agent looked blankly at his friend and said nothing.

"Look, Ode, I got a strong hunch Slade's got the money and I need your help to prove it."

"Well, how do you figure that?"

"Just listen to me. All you got to do is have your contacts in Bermuda check and see if any of the air freight carriers picked up a package from the Princess or Glencoe Hotel on June 19th to the 23rd from either the Madam or Slade and track it down for me. Carolina said they ain't got the money, see? So, if they got it, they had to get it out of Bermuda somehow, and air freight, that's the logical way to do it. Ain't no way the Madam would risk going through Customs with it, and I can have the *Encounter* checked by Customs in Newport if they didn't air freight it back. If I can prove Slade took the money, I got his ass on defrauding the United States Government out of a half million and we get the money back to Ron DiLorenzo!"

"What makes you think they got the money?"

"I trailed Paul Ferris's secretary leaving the bank with a brown package under her arm the afternoon after Ferris hung hisself. She jumped on the ferry just as it pulled out of Hamilton for Salt Kettle before I could get on board....I know full goddamn well Slade's got it, because when the secretary came back an hour and a half later, she didn't have it, and the ferry captain told me she had gotten off at Salt Kettle where Slade was staying ...."

The FBI agent sat silently, drinking his second vodka and tonic. He looked around. Harry's was filling with stockbrokers and lawyers, their ties undone, drinking and laughing, talking baseball and stock tips. A short Italian waiter passed around hot pizza and rank franks for hors d'oeuvres.

"Ode, did that Bermuda police inspector who called you about Ferris say anything about finding any money?"

"Never mentioned it, but why should he?"

"If they had found the half million, you can damn well bet your ass them guys would have been asking some questions. Right?"

"Maybe."

"Now, for a man with your connections, Ode, checking out the air freight companies, that's not much to ask from all the shit we done been though."

Agent Terry finished his vodka and tonic in a hurry, swirling the ice and holding up the empty glass for Wolfer to see. "Flynn, I never could figure why de hell you've been so damned hell-bent to get this guy, Slade, anyhow. All it's done is get your skinny ass in a crack. It's not normal, you acting that way about this guy for as long as I can remember. What's your vendetta against Peter Slade anyhow, Flynn?"

"Let's just say it's something real personal that happened over twenty years ago and leave it at that," O'Grady replied, dropping his eyes to his drink and reaching for his lighter just as the wall rumbled from a passing subway train.

"Come on, goddamn it, Flynn! If I'm going to stick my neck out on a limb, level with me, damn it, or else forget it. I got to know the facts, man. Why are you so determined to get this guy, Slade?"

O'Grady took a long drag off his cigarette and held the smoke as if he was smoking a joint. He knew his old friend was right for asking a question he had never been asked before. It had been a long time now since that night in Brooklyn Heights, and a lot of water has passed over the dam, he was thinking.

It was still too painful to think about, much less tell your best friend, who would probably think it was silly anyhow. O'Grady's heart was in his throat, his mouth tasting sour, like foul vomit was caught up in it as he spoke. "I ain't never told nobody this before, Ode, and goddamn it, if you ever mention it to anybody, I'll kill your ass, understand?"

"Take it easy, buddy! You're talking to the FBI, man, and the only friend you got," Terry snapped back.

"Sorry, Ode," Flynn replied, realizing his mistake as he began to speak in a low, hushed voice out of the corner of his mouth. "Right after I was first married to Julie, I was down in Washington at a two-week enforcement training course, see?"

Agent Terry nodded, drinking now, not looking at Flynn O'Grady, and not really wanting to hear this story that he had heard a hundred times before from Flynn's ex-wife, Julie. "Yeah, what about it?" he finally asked.

"Well, this huge snowstorm hit DC that spring, and they turned us out of class early on Thursday for the weekend. I caught a train to Penn Station, took the subway to Brooklyn Heights. Remember, me and Julie was living in that brownstone across from the St. George back then?"

Oden Terry nodded, thinking back on how well he did remember that small fourth floor apartment on Clark Street where he had often visited. He could remember Julie's high-pitched voice ridiculing O'Grady for divorcing her when she was pregnant.

Flynn O'Grady's face exploded with anger and embarrassment. He was sucking hard on his cigarette. Just as another train passed, he blurted out, "It was that goddamn Slade who done knocked up my wife, Julie, man. I caught 'em in the sack that night and chased his ass down the fire escape, buck-naked with his pants and shirt in his hand, threw his shoes at him. He left his coat with his business cards in it, so I knew who the hell he was, the son-of-a-bitch. Two months later to de day after we got back together, Julie tells me she's pregnant, tellin' me it was my kid!"

He took a long drink. His head hung down as sweat popped out on his red-freckled forehead. "I loved that woman. God, I loved her more than anything else in this whole rotten-ass world, man," Flynn's voice began cracking as tears welled up in his eyes. "I...I..." his voice broke. He took time to take another drink and a drag off the cigarette. Regaining his composure, he then said, "I swore to hell, if it was the last thing I ever done, I'd get even with Peter Slade."

"How the hell do you know Julie wasn't pregnant with your kid?"

"The fucking mumps, Ode! I caught 'em when I was fifteen and my balls swole up the size of a basketball, Ode. Made me as sterile as a cut tomcat." Flynn's voice cracked with anger as he blew his nose, really angry at this whole disgusting conversation and his breaking down in front of the FBI.

The FBI agent sat thinking. 'You poor miserable, pitiful bastard, fucked up your whole life over one woman getting knocked up by some son-of-a-bitch on a one-night stand.' But man, was Julie O'Grady beautiful, really something special for this homely-looking bastard to be married to. He finally looked around out of embarrassment and said out of pity, "OK, Flynn. Man, now I understand why you got to get Slade. Take it easy, buddy. Gimme more details on what you want me to do and I will see if I can help out."

"OK, Ode, I appreciate it. All you got to do is find out about the package and then trace it back to Slade or the Madam. We will need a search warrant for the Stone Bridge Inn and one for the Madam's condo in Boston."

"I'll contact my man in Hamilton, see what I can find out. The search warrants, now that's more tricky, but I got some favors I can call in. No guarantees, and remember, we never had this conversation."

Earlier that afternoon at the Stone Bridge Inn a moving van arrived to pick up Melissa Jenkins's modest belongings that had been stored in the basement. Her clothes were all packed neatly in boxes and were loaded into the truck. It was a tearful farewell for the staff as she climbed into the cab, surprising the two husky young movers.

"You don't have a car, lady?" the driver asked, feeling a little uncomfortable for breaking a company rule.

The truck's diesel engine was rumbling. Melissa took one last look at the beautiful old inn as Pierre and the rest of the staff waved goodbye. "Nope, I need a ride with you guys to Yarmouth, Mass," she replied, looking straight ahead, fighting back her tears.

"That's fine with me, but don't tell anybody. We're licensed to transport furniture and stuff, not people," he smiled, cutting his eyes at the beautiful young woman beside him, glancing back quickly seeing her wipe away the tears.

"Right on, brother! This rig got a radio?" Melissa asked, leaning back on the seat, shutting her eyes, listening to the changing gears and the sounds of Simple Red's. "If You Don't Know Me By Now" playing on the radio.

The driver doubled-clutched into high gear, patting the accelerator. It was with the windows down and the soothing whine of tires on pavement that the countryside passed to the sweet smell of summer.

Melissa felt guilty for lying to Pierre about where she was

going. She had thought about leaving a note for Peter but felt a call would be better. She had left George's belongings with Pierre and the Air Express package from Bermuda was packed safely in back of the truck.

The driver was athletic, handsome and strong, with veins that stuck up on his muscular arms. He asked her, "What ya doing in Yarmouth, babe?"

"Same thing I was doing back there. Running the Yarmouth Inn for an old lady I know. Better job, won't have to put up with a drunk boss's wife. What about you, dude? You going to double-clutch this mother, moving people's junk for the rest of your life?"

"Only for the summer. Back to Dartmouth for my senior year this fall. Football practice starts in a month or so."

"You look like a jock. Good luck."

The percussion from the lightning strike blasted John Moffett out of his berth on a dead run into his smoke-filled dark cabin. He scrambled forward into the cockpit, dazed and half-blinded.

"MY GOD!" he screamed, seeing Peter slumped face down on the deck.

The boat had broached on the crest of a mountainous wave, taking on a frightening sixty degrees port list as she slid sideways. He lunged over Peter's body for the wheel, spinning it hard to port just in time to keep the boat from being knocked down. The monstrous roaring white wave broke over them. 'Holy shit, I'm not strapped!' he panicked seeing the powerful surge of water washing into the cockpit.

Moffett dropped to the deck, locking his arms and legs around the steering pedestal, the upright pillar upon which the wheel is mounted, and held on for dear life. He watched in horror as Peter

Slade's limp body was washed out of the cockpit by the wave. He shut his eyes and held his breath, submerged in the icy sea water that tore away his breath. He came up coughing. "HELP!! MAN OVERBOARD!!!" he screamed at seeing Slade's body missing. The boat wallowed out of control.

In the forward cabin, Bob Ganloff knocked Tony down as both men scrambled aft through the smoke-filled salon on hearing the distress call. They choked on the pungent smell of electronics burning as they ran, their pasty white faces gripped in fear. They hooked up their harness and scampered up the companionway ladder to find the captain back on his feet, fighting to regain control of the yacht.

"SLADE! PORT QUARTER, GET HIM!!!" Moffett shouted, pointing. He fought the wheel. The boat was responding; he was slowly regaining control of his crippled boat.

"PETE," Bob yelled in the dark at the silhouette of Peter's body dangling face down on the catwalk, caught by the standing rigging. He lay motionless, his safety line taut around his waist saving him from the ocean. "Give me a hand, Tony! Get him back on board and below." The two men manhandled the limp body back into the cockpit.

"Is he alive?" Moffett screamed above the wind.

Bob grabbed Slade's wrist as they passed. "Don't have a pulse, Skipper!"

"Damn it! Get him below and give him give him resuscitation! Hurry, damn it, and give me his safety line and harness. Somebody check the goddamn boat and see if we are taking on water and get me a damage report!" he barked, flinching at a blinding flash of 20,000 amps of electricity and deafening thunder that just missed them.

The lightning strike had knocked Doc Pearson out of his semi-conciousness. He struggled up to help lay Slade on his bunk as Bob grabbed a light and started checking the boat for damage. "Get back! I've got to give him pulmonary resuscitation," Doctor Pearson screamed in a high shrill voice, checking Slade's throat for blockage. He pounded on his chest under the flashlight beam the Englishman held.

The burnt electrical smell was rancid. "Are we taking on water?" Tony shouted, watching the doctor pound rhythmically away on Peter's chest. The boat was being badly battered, throwing the men about inside.

"See if he has a pulse," Doc ordered.

Tony shined the light on the right side of Slade's badly burned face, dropping down on his knees, grabbing his wrist. "Nothing, Doc! Damn well don't you let the bloke die," he solemnly screamed over the fury of the storm.

The doctor pounded harder, rhythmically heaving down with all his weight on Slade's chest cavity, just above the heart.

"Damn it to bloody hell, I say, Doc. Don't let him die!"

Peter Slade could hear faint voices, familiar voices that came in and then went away. Were they voices from the hereafter? he wondered in his unconscious state. Tony's voice came clearer this time and he felt the heaving forces crushing his chest cavity, pounding away. 'My God,' he thought, 'am I returning from the dead?'

He heard Bob shouting to the skipper, "John, it knocked out all our electronics, no fires. As far as I can tell we still have watertight integrity in the hull."

"PETE? PETE? CAN YOU HEAR ME?" Tony yelled, feeling a faint pulse now on his badly burned left hand.

"What? What the hell?" Peter mumbled. The searing anguish of his burns erupted.

"He's coming around, Doc, I got a pulse on the bugger!" Tony shouted as the doctor collapsed in exhaustion on the deck. "Bob, help me get a blanket over him, I say!"

The two men struggled to lift Peter, the beam of the flashlight rolling around the deck.

"Just take it easy, Pete. Here, let me get some blankets on him. Hey Doc! Goddamn it, will you get up and give us a hand, man? Pete's got some pretty serious burns! Doc, do you hear me?" Bob shouted, grabbing the light and shining it on his greenish-white face on the deck.

"Hey, Tony, Doc is unconscious! Let's get him in his bunk!" The two of them struggled to lift the doctor off the pitching deck.

Slade was breathing erratically, struggling for breath.

"What in the bloody hell do I do now, Bob, since Doc passed out?" Tony asked.

"Is he still breathing?"

"PETE? PETE, DO YOU HEAR ME?"

"I hear you.... What the hell's happening?" Slade whispered, trying to open his burning eyes to a dark world, darker than the darkest cave, darker than death itself. He panicked at the first thought of blindness. "Tony, where are you, man? Goddamn it, I can't see!"

"You got struck by lightning. Just take it easy," Bob ordered, watching Slade shiver, soaked to the bone.

Slade lay there, staring into the pitch black, his face and hand blistered, knowing it would only be a matter of time before it would all be over, anyway. Then the boat took another tremendous wave. He heard Tony shouting that they were taking on water. The sharp pungent smell of burnt electronics stung his nose, and his eyes felt like they had been doused with acid. 'It is better to be dead than blinded and burnt to hell,' he was thinking, as the pain from his burns turned unbearable.

# Chapter XXX

## Beach Mont
### Friday, June 29, 1990

I n the early morning hours a light breeze blew through the open windows of the carriage house bringing with it the sounds and smell of the ocean. At six o'clock, Thomas Terrell arose. He had done so each morning for over fifty years now as the butler at Beach Mont, a position he had inherited from his father who was recruited for the job in 1895. The aging Englishman put on his freshly starched white shirt and bow tie, and a pair of black trousers with a black stripe running down the side. He placed his hat and black jacket with gold buttons on the chair until he left for the 'big house', which he had fondly referred to Beach Mont since childhood.

Beach Mont was indeed a big house, built in 1895 by the New York shipping magnate, Hunter Jason Harrington, who had recruited Thomas's father from London to be the first butler. It had been Thomas's only employment. Under the late Dr. Harriman

Harris's will he had been given a position and pension for life by the estate.

The old bachelor tidied his modest quarters on the second floor of the carriage house which now served as the garage for the Slades' cars and Mr. Harrington's 1932 Rolls Royce Phantom II Continental Touring Saloon. He put on his coat and hat before walking down the long wooded drive to the mansion, passing through the dew-dripped gardens with marble statues of Greek gods standing naked in the roses or hiding in the perfectly trimmed hedges.

Thomas inhaled the fragrance of the flowers, speaking formally to the gardeners already long at work manicuring the gardens to perfection. He missed old Mr. Tim Doudell, the last full-time gardener, who had died twelve years ago and been replaced by a landscape contractor whose staff were mostly Mexicans. Tim Doudell had arrived from England on the same day his father was hired as butler, August 6, 1895. 'Mr. Doudell would turn over in his grave seeing these Mexicans,' Thomas sighed, walking briskly for a man of eighty who worked six days a week and had never once in all these years been sick. 'Now, that Missy', he was thinking, referring to Charlotte as he strolled along, 'is a bit of a spoiled child, and why shouldn't she be, her father killed by the Germans and being pampered all her life by her mother and grandmother. She married Mr. Robert Cocknell who was a classy gentleman to my way of thinking. I always was deeply concerned about their marriage ending in a divorce because of that man's drinking.'

'Now Missy is married to Mr. Peter Slade, a very nice chap who knows the hospitality industry. He is a fellow with a quick wit, but, like me, a commoner, marrying out of his social class.'

Thomas smiled with affection, thinking of how within two

weeks of Peter Slade's arrival at Beach Mont he had grown fond of Missy's new husband, the only member of the household who had ever gone out of the way to treat him other than as a servant. Never thought he would cross that invisible line of the universal code of butlerhood, "We can be friendly but not familiar," that he had been taught by his father. 'Should I dare mention that Mr. Jack Spencer has been seen quite frequently around Beach Mont since Mr. Slade has been gone?' he pondered.

Gathering up the newspapers at the service entrance, Thomas slowly climbed the back steps, and unlocked the kitchen door, wondering how Missy was feeling this morning after getting home very late last night. The old man was concerned about her increasing appetite for gin. Inside, he placed the papers neatly on the table and put the kettle on for his morning tea. He unfolded the *New York Times*, being extraordinarily careful not to ruffle the pages before he delivered it up the steep servant stairs to Mrs. Slade along with her breakfast. The elderly butler read the paper as the tea kettle slowly rumbled, vibrating softly until the escaping steam created a high shrill whistle that went unnoticed.

Reaching the sports page, his half-moon spectacled eyes abruptly read the headlines: *Encounter*, **Winner of New Port-Bermuda Race, Missing in Atlantic Storm**.

"Dear heavens!" he whispered, carefully reading the article that reported the United States Coast Guard had begun its search for the missing *Encounter* on Thursday night and no sign of the boat or its crew had been found. The governor of Rhode Island had sent an urgent message to Washington asking that the navy's P3 antisubmarine squadron stationed in Bermuda join the search for the missing sailors. The article concluded by saying that the bad weather had hampered the search effort but was now improving as the storm began to move off the Bermuda high that had stalled it for the past four days.

"My God, I do hope and pray Mr. Moffett and Mr. Slade are not dead," the elderly butler whispered, laying the paper aside, tending to the steaming kettle. "Must I go straightaway to inform Missy of this tragic news, or wait until she has breakfast? I mean to say, should I go straightaway...?" He walked slowly over and poured his morning tea, still fretting. "Should I go straightaway or wait for her call? Should I now, or shouldn't I? Dear God, I pray Mr. Moffett and Mr. Slade are not dead."

He sipped the tea, pacing about the floor, wishing that the cook and maid, Mrs. Elkins and Tresia, would hurry up and arrive so that he could seek their counsel. He set his teacup on the table and put out the silver serving tray with fresh linen and silverware. He poured a glass of freshly squeezed orange juice, placing it on the tray beside the cup and saucer and silver coffee service. Thomas fretted, almost forgetting the vase with a single long-stem red rose. He carefully refolded the newspaper and stuck it under his arm. It was a quarter to eight, time to go upstairs to awake the lady of the house.

He walked down the narrow hall to the foot of the steep servant stairs leading up to Mrs. Slade's chambers on the second floor. Balancing the tray as he went, his mind was preoccupied with the *Encounter's* fate when he stumbled over Charlotte Slade's outstretched body sprawled at the foot of the stairs.

"MY GOD'S NAME IN HEAVEN, MADAM!!" he screamed at the top of his lungs, his voice echoing over the sounds of breaking glass as the silver serving tray crashed on the marble floor. "DEAR LADY!!! WHAT IN HEAVEN'S NAME IS WRONG???" he gasped, dropping to Charlotte's side and placing his fingers on her neck for a pulse. The old man stood, switched on the light and stared in disbelief at the body lying face down in a huge puddle of blood, her left wrist still lodged in the broken windowpane at the bottom of the stairs. "Gad! Missy's dead! She must have fallen down these stairs and slit her wrist," he muttered, noticing a broken martini glass among all the mess on the floor. "I must go straightaway and call the authorities at once! What a sad pity, my lady, and what a dreadful way to pass. If Mr. Slade's dead, what the bloody hell will happen to Beach Mont?"

Friday at noon Flynn O'Grady and FBI Agent Oden Terry arrived at the Stone Bridge Inn in a black Ford sedan they had driven up from New York. They had passed time along the way discussing the whereabouts of the missing yacht, *Encounter*, and Peter Slade. "Damned place looks closed to me Flynn. Did you call before we left?" Oden Terry asked when they pulled into the empty parking lot.

Both agents simultaneously saw the closed sign and the white wreath of carnations on the front door. "Goddamn, they must have found Slade's body!" O'Grady exclaimed, jumping out of the car and fumbling nervously for his pack of Camels.

"If he's dead, Ode, I'm fucked and we might as well head back to New York and tie on a drunk."

Armed with a federal search warrant and an Airborne Express receiving slip signed by G. W. Henley, O'Grady ran up the steps and rang the bell, waiting impatiently for an answer. He rang again, leaning on the bell this time but was answered only by the solitary sounds of the seagulls. Cupping his hands to his eyes, he peered into the dark entrance, ringing the bell again. "Goddamn it, somebody answer this door! The FBI is out here!" O'Grady shouted, knocking loudly on the door with his fist. "Somebody please answer the door," he implored.

Oden Terry joined him on the porch, reading the note attached to the wreath. "Ha, Flynn, Slade's not dead after all!" Oden said with surprise.

"Who the hell is it that's dead then?!" O'Grady asked, exhaling smoke as he reached for the note.

"Charlotte Slade?! That's Slade's wife isn't it?"

"REEeally! Yeah that's her, rich bitch from Newport out of the Harrington shipping clan. Thank God it's not Slade what's dead, Ode."

"Not dead as of yet, he isn't. Now, let's get the hell out of here and come back after the funeral. This place is closed up tighter than a drum."

"The hell you say, Ode! We got a search warrant here, and we're going to take this place apart and get our money."

"Now just what do you suggest we do, Flynn? Bust down the goddamn door?" the FBI asked sarcastically.

"Stay put, wise guy," Flynn replied. He ran down the steps and around back to the service drive to the kitchen. Thank God, he sighed, taking time to finish his cigarette and catch his breath before walking up the steps to serve the search warrant on the French chef, Pierre, who was preparing his lunch.

Carolina Barrington was frustrated about her stupid unannounced visit to the Stone Bridge Inn on Tuesday evening. 'It was a dumb thing to do,' she thought, thinking more and more about the suspicion she had created with Peter Slade's wife. She was watching the afternoon soap operas in the den of her Boston condo overlooking the harbor, trying to sort out her turbulent and confused feelings for the man. Oh yes, she was in love with Peter Slade all right, evident by her deep concern for his safety, while at the same time bitter and hurt at the thought that he was also having an affair with Melissa Jenkins. She felt used and the thought of the two of them in bed made her insanely jealous, while thoughts of Charlotte didn't; after all, she was older and Peter's wife.

She was applying the second coat of red nail polish when the soap was interrupted by a news bulletin: "There is a new turn of events in the tragic story of the missing yacht *Encounter*, the winner of the Newport-Bermuda Race which has been missing in the Atlantic since Thursday. The prominent socialite, Mrs. Charlotte Slade, was found dead this morning by her butler in her Beach Mont mansion on Newport's prestigious Ocean Avenue. The Newport authorities are investigating and will neither deny nor confirm foul play. Mrs. Slade's husband, Peter Slade, is a member of the missing crew of the *Encounter* which is owned by her cousin, Captain John Moffett, a prominent Providence lawyer. The search for the missing yacht continues in the Atlantic off Bermuda and has now been joined by the navy patrol planes stationed there."

"Oh my God, Charlotte Slade's dead!" Carolina gasped. "I can't believe it! I was just with her last Tuesday night! God, I bet Melissa Jenkins has murdered her! Yes, I know it was Melissa. The little bitch was damn well capable of it, especially if Charlotte fired her the other night like she said. Ha, ha, what wonderful news for me, this eliminates both of those bitches!" Then the harsh reality of the *Encounter* and Peter Slade being lost at sea jolted her again.

"Oh, where are you, darling?" she sighed as the wrenching, empty helplessness plummeted to the pit of her stomach. "God, please help Peter," she cried, tears streaming from her dark eyes just as a startling knock came at her front door. Wiping away the tears, she called, "Who is it?"

"Flynn O'Grady, with the Securities and Exchange Commission, Carolina. Open up."

"I'm not dressed, Flynn. Do you mind? Go away," Carolina replied, her voice piercing and angry.

"I have a federal search warrant here, lady, and the FBI. Open up, or do you want us to bust down the door?"

The agents heard footsteps inside as the deadbolt lock was turning, then the sound of the chain going taut as the door partially opened. Carolina peered through the crack. Both agents flashed their badges simultaneously. O'Grady handed Carolina the search warrant. She glanced at it and unlatched the chain. O'Grady pushed his way inside.

"What in the hell is this all about?"

"We're looking for the half million dollars you and Slade brought back from Bermuda."

"Flynn, have you gone nuts? Peter has the receipt Paul Ferris gave us when you had us blackmail him in his office. I told you Ferris took the money. He has it, or the bank's got the damn money. Not us."

"We'll see about that. Start in the back, Ode, I'll take the kitchen."

"I don't have the money and Peter sure as hell doesn't...."

Oden Terry walked to the bedroom and she heard drawers being opened. Flynn pulled out a Camel and his lighter.

"Don't you dare light that damn cigarette in here," Carolina snapped just to be contrary.

"Look, I got this signed air cargo receipt from Airborne Express for a package picked up in Bermuda on June 21st from the

Glencoe Hotel and delivered to the Stone Bridge Inn. Signed for by Slade's bartender, black fellow named George Washington Henley who just died, see? Package weighs eighteen pounds, same as half a million in hundred dollar bills."

"Yes, so what about it?"

"I saw Ferris's secretary take a package out of the bank after work on Thursday, June 21st, the day after Ferris hung hisself. That's how I know you two conspired to steal the money. We're talking major fraud here, lady, and you are a co-conspirator and fixing to go to jail."

"Jail? What the hell are you talking about?" Carolina cracked, questioning for the first time the reality of Slade having the money and trying to get her trapped in the heist somehow.

"You was seen at the Stone Bridge Inn on Tuesday night, the twenty-sixth, drinking with Mrs. Slade in the bar, weren't you?"

"Yes, I was. I dropped..."

"Do you know she's dead?"

"Yes, I just heard the news on the television. I dropped by the Stone Bridge Inn and was having a drink at the bar when Mrs. Slade walked in. It was just by coincidence I met her," Carolina replied, thinking, 'God no, they don't think I'm a suspect in Charlotte's death, do they?'

"Look here, lady, you're on probation, right?"

"You know damn well I am, Flynn."

"OK, Pierre, the French chef at the Stone Bridge said he saw you leaving out the side entrance of the Inn with a shopping bag which had a package in it after dark...."

"That's a lie! I had a shopping bag all right, items I purchased at the shop down the street," Carolina almost shouted, panicking, thinking now that Slade might just really have taken the money and she was about to get arrested for somehow being involved with him.

"Carolina," Flynn O'Grady said out of the corner of his mouth in a nasty voice, feeling that he had stumbled onto something good, "you're goddamn lying to me! You better fess up here. Pretty lady like you got no business getting busted for defrauding the government out of a half million and going to prison over helping Slade steal the government's money. Shoot straight with me, Carolina, and I'll make sure you aren't implicated when we place Slade under arrest."

"I'd... tell you if I knew anything, but I don't," she replied with fear in her voice.

"Come on! Carolina, you're lying like hell! Where's our goddamn money at?"

"Look all the hell you want, O'Grady, but don't make a mess of this place. I'm telling you I don't have it or know one goddamn thing about it," she said, her voice turning angry. She returned to her nails and the television.

The program changed at the hour and after an extensive search the FBI agent walked into the den and shrugged. "Let's go, Flynn. There's nothing here, man. Sorry to bother you, Miss Barrington."

Carolina stood with her arms crossed, furious at such an intrusion on her privacy. She was also now thinking, 'how in the hell did that damn con-artist, Peter Slade, get the money? He has got to have it or the FBI wouldn't be involved and have gone to all of this trouble to search my place. Man, Slade's a rotten no-good son-of-a-bitching bastard and to hell with him.'

O'Grady grudgingly agreed. "Yeah. Let's go then. This case is still open, Carolina, and when we arrest Slade I'm coming after you next for lying to us. So you better think about what I said, see? Better think damn hard and give me a call."

O'Grady followed Ode down the hall to the elevator, hearing the door slam behind him. 'Damn it,' he was thinking, 'my time's running out. I've only got until tomorrow night to nail Slade before our agreement expires. But if he's got the money and isn't dead, now that's another story,' he thought lighting a cigarette.

Melissa Jenkins had been hustling to fill her drink orders as she waited at the service stand at the Yarmouth Inn bar where she was now working as a waitress, living in a small room upstairs. Mrs. Planky, an elderly widow and old friend she had spent a vacation with one summer while she was in the orphanage, had no children and was delighted to have her there. Melissa also felt very fortunate, especially since she was getting her room and board free and making nice tips.

It was the beginning of a long Fourth of July weekend on the Cape and the restaurant was already packed with noisy patrons full of the holiday spirit. The six o'clock news came on Boston's Channel 13. Melissa caught the commentator mentioning the *Encounter*. She quickly reached across the bar and grabbed the changer, turning up the volume.

"....Charlotte Slade is dead of apparently accidental causes. She was found this morning by her butler in her Newport mansion, Beach Mont. Mrs. Slade was the wife of Peter Slade and cousin of the captain of the missing yacht *Encounter*...." She turned the volume down, elated by the sudden glee that consumed her heart.

'Serves the bitch right,' she thought. The bartender placed the last of her drink order on the tray. She was terribly distressed for Peter's safety, yet ecstatic at the news of Charlotte's demise. 'God, it's wrong to feel this way, it's terribly wrong. What the hell,' she shrugged, 'it's a hell of an ending to another chapter in my screwed up life.'

Flint Firestone felt no remorse at having sent the *Encounter* and its crew off into the storm and possibly to their deaths. He watched the Weather Channel in the St. George's Club pub with his crew. "One questions John Moffett's judgment, sailing off into that," was all he said as the force of the storm closed in on Bermuda.

In the Atlantic, five hundred miles to the northwest, the barometer was rising again for the first time since Monday. Tony Stevenson made his entry in the *Encounter's* log: '30 June 1990. 0001 hour. Storm beginning to break, barometric pressure rising. Winds out of northwest sustained at twenty, gusting to thirty knots. Heavy seas, no electronics, boat still intact but no engine. Crew is exhausted. Doc Pearson very ill, unconscious. Slade back on his feet after receiving burns and temporary blindness from lightning strike.'

'Bloody damn miracle we are still alive,' Tony thought, checking the sextant with his flashlight, hoping for the skies to clear so he could get a fix. 'As soon as it is daybreak, I'll go straightaway and take a fix and see just what the bloody hell our position is. I'd better check on those two blokes,' he thought, turning the beam of light on the side of the Dr. Pearson's head. He reached down and felt his neck for a pulse. "What the bloody hell?" he exclaimed, bracing himself against the boat's rolls. He jerked three Dramamine seasick patches from behind the doctor's ear.

"Captain!" Tony shouted through the hatch. "I do say I have just discovered why the good Dr. Pearson has been acting odd. He's bloody well overdosed!"

"What the hell are you talking about, Tony?"

"I say, the bugger has applied three Dramamine patches behind his ear for the seasickness. Must of bloody well not read the directions. Very dangerous, more than one, that is. Should of known more than one at a time would knock his knickers off. Him a doctor!"

"Jesus, three Dramamine patches! No wonder he's screwed up; that stuff's powerful as hell. Get him up and get some fluids in him quickly, before he goes into a coma."

"Aye, aye, sir!" Tony replied. "I say here, Doctor," he shouted, slapping Doc's face with a whack that woke up Peter Slade.

The burns on Slade's face and hands still hurt. "What the hell you doing to the poor bastard, Tony?" Peter asked as he pulled back his blanket with his bandaged hand.

Whack! Whack! Tony hit the Doctor harder this time, saying, "We got to get the bloke awake, Pete, he overdosed on Dramamine." Whack! Whack! "Wake up, Doc, I say," he shouted.

"Stop it!" Dr. Pearson mumbled, shaking his head. Tony slapped him again, harder this time. "Stop it!" Doc cried loudly.

"Drink this, my good Doctor," Tony ordered, pulling him up and shoving a bottle of water to his lips.

He drank slowly, coming around a little at a time. He shook his head and continued to drink on his own.

"Is Peter OK?" the doctor finally asked after half an hour, remembering now that Peter had been electrocuted.

"Peter is mending quite nicely, Doctor. I say, thanks to you for resuscitating the poor bloke or I am afraid he would be quite dead!"

"What the hell you saying, Tony? Doc saved my life?" Peter asked, swinging his feet off the bunk and onto the deck, looking rough with the white bandages and a week's growth on his face.

The *Encounter* sailed northward into clearing skies on its homeward voyage, crippled but proud. The storm began to slowly subside and for the first time Peter Slade knew they were going to make it now. Looking across the cabin at the man he had almost murdered with his Gerber knife, he shook his head. He stared at Dr. Duane L. Pearson for a long time, the homosexual psychiatrist from New York City that he hated had saved his life. He broke the silence, "Thanks, Dr. Pearson, I owe you my life, my friend."

# Chapter XXXI

## The Gulf Stream
### Saturday, June 30, 1990

t was past midnight. Peter Slade lay in the dark cabin listening to the ocean rushing past the *Encounter's* hull and ignoring his pain. It seemed to be easing some and he was glad about that. The pain had been much worse than his shrapnel wound during the war if he was remembering right. He had been given morphine then and wished he had some now.

'Well, I've cheated death again. Now it's time to close out this last chapter of my life,' he thought. 'To hell with Charlotte Slade, to hell with her. To hell with the Stone Bridge Inn and to hell with money. I'm just lucky to be alive. These scars will make for great drinking conversation at the Marble Bar. But there won't be a Marble Bar,' Peter Slade thought, 'unless I can screw Charlotte out of it in the divorce.'

'At least my plea-bargain agreement with the Feds terminates at midnight. After four long years I'm finally finished with all that.

There is nothing Flynn O'Grady can do to get to my account after the Feds aborted their Bermuda operation. George has the half million and I'll hand it over to O'Grady when I get back to Newport.'

Peter Slade's burns still hurt. The suffering brought with it the remorse he was feeling over Charlotte and his marriage breaking up. He wished somehow now he could have straightened things out before it had gotten this far. He had a sick feeling that it was far too late for that now.

Their days back in New York provided memories of good times. During worst times in that terrible winter of 1986, Charlotte had stuck by him. She had given him the moral support he so desperately needed when he was headed for jail and he would always love her for it.

From the sounds of the ocean came Chris de Burgh's 'Lady in Red" song, bringing back memories of that wonderful December night at the "21" Club, Charlotte dancing in a red wisp of a sexy dress with its elegant georgette straps over her bare shoulders. Her blond hair and blue eyes were sparkling like the champagne they were drinking. They had never been more in love than dancing away that night. "Damn it," he swore, remembering how good it was then.

Slade asked himself once more, 'Do you care anything about anything anymore?' He lay quietly thinking about that, feeling the boat smacking into the waves with a whoosh, listening to the sounds of the wind in her sails. 'She's a damn fine boat,' he thought, 'or we wouldn't be here.'

"You're damn right I care a lot," he said out loud. It sounded funny to hear his own voice. 'I'm damn lucky to be alive and having a new lease on life. It's time to put it all in the past and get on with life.

'After what you have just gone through, Slade, all this other bullshit doesn't really matter anymore. It's time, by God, to live a new life now after cheating death. Live fast and hard, before time runs out on you. It will be September soon and the bullfights in Madrid's Plaza de Toros Monumental will begin. I'll take a room at the Ritz and drink *vino tinto* in the smoke-filled bars on the Calle San Vicente Ferrer until dawn. I'm fishing in October off Venezuela for the great marlins and swords on the La Guaira Banks. Smoke Hoyo De Monterrey double coronas at the bar in Madam La Chuleta's in Caracas and screw her Latin whores until I drop. Glenfiddich after breakfast and to hell with this screwy world. Now, man, that's what I call living!'

'I'll get another Dakota and duck hunt from my old blind on the Chesapeake in November after pheasant hunting in Minor County, South Dakota. Damn it! Slade, you're damn lucky to be alive,' he was thinking, after the eerie experience of returning from the dead.

The wind held steady from the northwest. He could feel the boat making good headway toward home. 'You're the luckiest bastard in the world, Slade, having been dealt another hand,' he thought, reminded so by the dull aching feeling from his burns.

'Your renewed zest for life is just fine and dandy,' Peter Slade was thinking, 'but it takes money, a lot of money, to live a lifestyle like that. The millions stashed in Bermuda are as worthless as tits on a boar hog if you can't spend it. What about Flynn O'Grady's half million?' he thought. 'I could let George keep the money instead of returning it to the Feds. George could buy a bar back in Baltimore as soon as he gets out of the hospital. I'll help George get a minority enterprise loan from Uncle Sam and open up 'George's Home Plate Sports Bar and Grill' across from the new Camden

Yard that they are building. I'm the bartender this time, George, and you are in charge.'

'No, I'll wait and see how the divorce turns out to decide about all of that.' He glanced down at the fluorescent glow of his watch, then got up and dressed.

After striking a favorable meander in the Gulf Stream, the northwardly flow of the current significantly increased the *Encounter's* speed. Warmed by the stream, the strong northwesterly wind felt good on Peter Slade's face when he climbed into the cockpit to take his watch for the first time since being struck by lightning.

"Pete, you sure you're up to taking her?" John Moffett asked, examining Peter's bandaged hand with his flashlight. "Let me see your face."

"Hell yeah, Coach, I'm fine. Sometimes you just got to play hurt."

"Seriously. Does your hand bother you?"

"Hell yeah, but when is the last damn time you heard of a 30 million volt lightning strike keeping Peter Slade off the playing field, Johnny?"

"You're tough, Pete, you are tough as nails, but if you're not up to it, I can take the helm."

"No, not tough, Johnny, just lucky. Lucky as hell. We all are lucky as hell to have survived that storm...."

"You're right. We would never have made it, Pete, if we hadn't had you on board...."

"Bullshit! Forget that. It just wasn't our time to die, Johnny, and that's all there is to it."

On the eastern horizon, the first tinge of pink announced the

*Encounter's* last day at sea, and what a beautiful day Peter Slade knew it was going to be. Bob Ganloff handed up a cup of hot coffee as the smell of Dr. Pearson's bacon cooking filtered up from the galley's stove through the open hatch. Tony had just shot the morning star.

Slade sipped his coffee, starving for his first hot meal in five days. He was thinking that tomorrow at this time he would be back at the Stone Bridge Inn, thank God. 'I'll get George and Thomas to move my clothes over from Beach Mont. I'll take the master suite at the Inn down the hall from Melissa on the third floor. Now won't that be sweet? I'll live at the Stone Bridge until my divorce is final, then, depending on how things shake out, head for Baltimore if things don't work out.'

He could almost hear ole George's southern voice laughing with the wind, "About time, Boss Man, that you drug in!" Peter Slade smiled affectionately and missed his old friend. He sat back and held his course, anxious for the voyage of the *Encounter* to end.

Below, the captain was asking, "What's our position, Tony?"

The sextant lay on the table beside the Englishman after he had plotted their position on the plotting board, making calculations on his sight-reduction worksheet, referencing the *Nautical Almanac* for the currents and winds. He took a sip of tea, laying down his parallel rules and pencil and smiled confidently. "I say, 40 degrees 16.7 minutes North and 71 degrees 8 minutes West. Dead on the rhumb line to Brenton Reef Tower, Captain."

"How far is my yacht club?"

"Hundred or so miles, I say."

"Great. We must be making ten knots hull speed," Moffett replied. "Let's see, it's four-thirty now. Can we make landfall before dark?"

"Midnight or later, to be realistic with the current and tides."

"We'll have to replace the batteries in our jackass-rigged running lights then."

Topside, Peter squinted at a dot just above the surface of the ocean, closing in fast from the east. "Hey, Johnny, we got some company off our starboard bow!"

"What the hell you got up there, Pete? A ship?"

"Approaching aircraft, close to the deck, barreling in on us, Skipper," Slade replied, pointing toward the aircraft's flashing lights in the distance.

"Give me the binoculars," John ordered, coming up the ladder, followed by the navigator.

The aircraft was closing in swiftly on the *Encounter* at two hundred feet off the water. "Hm, looks like a navy patrol aircraft of some kind to me," John muttered, as the roar of the engines grew louder.

The Navy P3 antisub patrol plane passed directly overhead, its turbo jets deafening to the crew as Bob and Doc excitedly scurried up the ladder. The plane made a sharp turn to the south before returning astern this time with its powerful searchlight blinding the sailors as it roared past in the early morning light. Passing overhead, the plane dipped its wings under the tremendous roar of its engines.

"Break out the signal flags, Tony! Hurry, these guys are trying to tell us something."

"What do they want?"

"I don't know!" John shouted, as the plane banked hard to the left and circled for another run on the *Encounter*. "I'll signal them to let them know what the hell we're doing!"

Bob and Tony rummaged under the cockpit seat, sorting out the signal flags. "Quick, give me a halyard," Moffett ordered, snapping on the yellow and blue Kilo flag followed by the solid yellow Quebec to the halyard. "Hoist away," he ordered, as Tony ran the flags quickly up the mast. The crew sat back and watched the plane circling.

"Jesus Christ, Tony! You sure about our position?"

"I say. Absolutely sure!"

"Good God! You don't think we've wandered off course into the navy's target practice range off Norfolk, do you?"

"No way, absolutely not."

"Do you think the lightning screwed up our compass and we are coming into Norfolk by chance?"

"No sir! We are bloody hundreds of miles from Norfolk."

"You're sure the strike didn't screw up our compass?"

"Took a fix at dawn! She checks out."

The radioman on the P3 grabbed the intercom in the observation bubble, "Lieutenant Sims, it's a positive confirmation on the yacht *Encounter*. Read it clearly on her transom, plain as day, sir."

"WE found the *Encounter*, men!" Rick Sims shouted. "Great, what's she signaling?"

"She's signaling Kilo, Quebec, Sir."

"She wishes to communicate. The vessel is healthy and requests free pratique?"

"Yes, sir, that's confirmed."

"Roger," Lieutenant Sims replied, "she has evidently lost her radio. We can't raise her. I'll make another pass. See if we can confirm the number of crewmen on deck."

The plane made another long, slow pass, flying dead to starboard beam at a hundred and fifty knots. The radioman counted,

"One, two, three, four, five crewmen on deck, Lieutenant."

"Five confirmed?"

"Yes sir. Five crew, confirmed."

"Hot damn, get a message to the NavCom," the pilot shouted over his cheering crew. "Pay Window has located the missing yacht, *Encounter*, winner of the Newport-Bermuda Race. Give our position and time. All five crew accounted for and the vessel has signaled that it is not in any apparent danger and is proceeding on a course 350 degrees for Newport. Good job, men, we'll get a commendation medal for finding these guys. What a great way to ship out on."

"Damn fine job, Rick," the copilot replied. "Pay Window has beaten the coast guard once again at their own game! What you say, let's make one more pass and wave off and head for home!"

"Hey, John, we're not in any target range. Those guys were looking for us," Bob Ganloff said, looking up as the plane grew smaller, its engines fainter, disappearing off into the horizon to the southeast.

"I guess Anna or Charlotte must have gotten concerned about us and called the coast guard. Don't worry, we'll be home by tomorrow in time for breakfast, ladies," John laughed.

John caught Peter Slade's eyes, shrugging as if to say, 'what the hell, man, I know what you're thinking. To hell with my cousin, Charlotte Slade.'

'So to hell with Charlotte,' Peter Slade was thinking. 'Things will work out.' The two old friends had spoken as John Moffett went below.

The *Encounter* sailed on into the early morning of the final day of her voyage home, bathed in brilliant sunshine and maintaining a good speed with a strong southwesterly wind. After a hearty breakfast of hotcakes and bacon, the captain shouted, "Break out the Scotch whiskey and some of those Cuban cigars, Pete. Let's light up a Cuban Monterrey and pour up a stiff drink of that Glenfiddich you got stashed."

"To the winners of the 1990 Onion Patch Race!" Ganloff shouted.

Peter Slade followed orders. "Here's to a damn fine skipper, gentlemen! Captain Johnny Moffett, Esquire, man of the world, and one slick-ass lawyer!" Peter shouted back, holding up his bandaged hand.

Moffett drank to the toast. He was caught up in his victory, drafting a speech for the television camera when he docked in Newport Yacht later that night. John Moffett felt the glory of having won the race and survived the storm.

In the early afternoon, CNN News flashed the live footage of the *Encounter* on the world news that was taken from a plane sixty miles off Newport earlier that day. The camera caught John Moffett smoking his cigar at the helm. Bob and Doc lounged around the cockpit drinking beer. All three men waved excitedly at the plane that flew within yards of the boat. Tony and Peter scrambled on deck, easily reading the CNN letters on the jackets of the film crew. The newscaster reported the significance of the signal flags that were still flying from the halyard.

"Thank God!" Carolina screamed, having been glued to the television for hours in her Boston condo. "He's safe, oh my God, Peter's alive!" she gasped, clasping her hands and jumping up with excitement, getting closer to the screen, searching for Peter Slade on deck.

The commentator's report concluded by saying the *Encounter* would arrive in Newport at approximately two a.m., Sunday morning, "and what a sad homecoming it will be for two members of the crew, Mr. Peter Slade, the husband of the late Newport socialite, Charlotte Slade, and her first cousin....

Carolina clicked off the television, her hands shaking with excitement. 'God, I've got to warn Peter that O'Grady and the FBI are looking for him,' she nervously thought. 'What should I do? Go down to the Newport Yacht Club and meet him? Or wait and give him a call early in the morning at the Inn? With Charlotte's death, it wouldn't be appropriate to go to the yacht club, not in this situation, and what good would it do to tell him about O'Grady if I did? I'll just have to wait and see if Peter Slade calls me tomorrow,' she decided. Second thoughts of whether on not he would entered her mind for the first time.

'With Charlotte's death, how different Peter Slade's life will be,' Carolina thought, lighting a cigarette. 'He'll get to keep his Stone Bridge Inn and probably inherit Beach Mont and all Charlotte's money if she didn't specify otherwise in her will. I wonder where that leaves me? I wonder what the hell happens to Peter Slade if Flynn O'Grady finds him with the stolen cash? O'Grady's desperate and he's got the FBI after Peter Slade. If he stole the money he sure as hell had better not say I had anything to do with it! I'm not getting involved in this mess. To hell with Peter Slade,' Carolina Barrington was thinking as she picked up the telephone and called an old girlfriend in New York to arrange a visit.

Melissa Jenkins was in her room at the Yarmouth Inn unpacking from her move. She was singing along with the lyrics of, "It Must Have Been Love," that was playing on her portable radio. The song was from her favorite movie "Pretty Woman" that she had seen three times. She had memorized the words and was fantasizing about how wonderful it would be to take acting lessons some day.

She picked up the package from Bermuda addressed to George Washington Henley. 'I wonder what's in here,' she thought, hesitating, then shaking the box before laying it aside. 'What the hell? George is dead and Peter Slade sure might be, too,' she thought, reaching for a pair of scissors lying on the dresser. She cut the string and tore away the brown wrapping paper that Martgaret Fox had so carefully wrapped.

"OH MY GOD!!!" she screamed, cupping her hand over her mouth, staring in disbelief at the box full of neatly packaged one hundred dollar bills. "There must be a million dollars in here," she gasped, running over and locking her door. 'What in the hell do I do with all Peter Slade's money,' she wondered, quickly closing the blinds even though she was on the third floor.

She glanced at her watch, it was three-fifteen and the bank was closed, before remembering it was Saturday. She slammed the box closed and then opened it again, fanning a stack of hundreds to make sure it was real. She neatly repacked the box, tying it tightly with the string before locking it inside her suitcase and hiding it under her bed. She quickly grabbed the brown wrapping paper and stuffed it along with the rest of the trash in a plastic garbage bag and locked her door, scampering down to the dumpster in the alley. 'No, Melissa! Somebody might find it if you throw it in here. I'll burn it,' she thought, taking it around to the kitchen and throwing it in the Inn's incinerator.

Melissa Jenkins's hands were trembling as she ran up the kitchen steps. She ran up three flights of stairs and unlocked her room quickly and checked under the bed. 'What in the hell do I do with all that cash,' she wondered, replacing the suitcase under the bed. Melissa flipped on the television just in time to hear the CNN news report that the *Encounter* had been found. "Thank God!" she screamed, "Peter Slade is alive!" She broke down with joy, tears streaming down her face. Suddenly she stopped.

Melissa dried her bloodshot eyes, getting the suitcase out again, her mind racing wildly. She began counting hundred dollar bills with all sorts of wild thoughts racing through her mind. 'God, do I go down to Newport tonight after we close to meet Pete and tell him I have his money and about George's death? Now that Charlotte is dead, I can get my old job back at the Stone Bridge Inn,' she thought, just for a moment, looking back down at the box of cash lying on the bed.

Melissa Jenkins was thinking about where life had taken her from her tragic beginning in New York to where she was now. She would soon be twenty-four and had nothing to show for it, no education, no money, only her beauty and great personality and a suitcase full of one hundred dollar bills. 'Peter Slade has got to be a multimillionaire now that Charlotte is dead, so what the hell? This money is just petty cash to him.'

It was time for Melissa Jenkins to be thinking about her future after all her years of conflict and sorrow. Lying there on the bed was her great escape from her past in a neat stack of green one hundred dollar bills.

'To hell with you, Peter Slade, find me if you can, because Melissa Jenkins will be a hell of a long way from Yarmouth, Massachusetts, by tomorrow morning.' She repacked the money and went downstairs to reluctantly tell old Mrs. Planky she was leaving, but not to where.

On Sunday morning, July 1, 1990, a beautiful young redhead

stepped off the Northwest flight form Boston at the Los Angeles International Airport wearing tight fitting designer jeans, sunglasses and no bra. At the Northwest LAX baggage claim, Melissa Jenkins waited nervously for her suitcase to come out of the chute onto the conveyer belt. 'This is my one real break in life,' she was thinking with no remorse just as her suitcase popped out of the chute, sliding down on its side. She grabbed it, clutching it tightly in her hand and walked confidently out into the bright California sunshine to the taxi stand.

"Where to, lady?" the cabby smiled, jumping out to leer at the beautiful young woman's body.

"The Beverly Hills Hotel, driver," Melissa Jenkins replied with an air of importance, sliding her sunglasses down off her forehead, knowing her fantasies of living in Hollywood, California, had unbelievably come true.

# Chapter XXXII

## St. George Hotel
### Labor Day Weekend, 1995

F lynn O'Grady was drinking and smoking Camels, living off his welfare check and still residing in Suite 8813 of the St. George Hotel. His rent was being subsidized by the Social Services Agency of the City of New York. He had not eaten in two days, sustaining himself on nicotine, Four Roses and Coke and a terrible cough. On the afternoon of Saturday, August 26, 1995, Flynn O'Grady was stone broke and nearly out of Camels and without a bite to eat in his hotel room.

'Well, it's time for another trip to the scrap heap to cut up enough copper tubing to make it to the end of the month,' he thought. He was looking out the open window of the hotel, and wiping sweat from the stifling heat.

Flynn O'Grady's eyes were sunken into his head. His scruffy gray matted beard hid his homely face. He hadn't had a haircut in months, giving him the appearance of the Grim Reaper in a New

Year's Eve cartoon. It had been over five years now since he was fired by the S.E.C. His only friend, Oden Terry, had been stricken with prostate cancer and died the year after he retired from the FBI.

O'Grady still harbored an angry grudge for a man named Peter Slade. More so now than ever before after his failed attempt to get Slade's Bermuda bank account backfired on him and he got fired without a pension. 'Ten years ago today, Ode and I arrested Slade,' O'Grady chuckled, remembering taking the handcuffed investment banker out of his plush offices in disgrace. 'I guess in a way I won,' he thought, 'but that's all past history now.' He smoked his Camel, realizing he had only two packs left to make it to next Friday when his welfare check came.

It would be dark soon and time to go to work. He lifted his rail-thin frame off the corduroy couch and went to his cluttered bedroom closet and dug out an old blowtorch. He filled the torch with gasoline and lit the nozzle. A blue-white flame erupted with a hot whoosh. Flynn O'Grady smiled, turned off the torch and checked the batteries in his head lamp. The light was dim, but would have to do since he was broke and didn't have money to buy cigarettes, much less new batteries. He checked the large burlap bag to insure he had his crowbar, hammer, hacksaw and vise-grip pliers along with an extra burlap sack and a sixty-foot nylon rope. 'This is hard damn work,' he thought, returning to the couch to rest. He began to cough.

It was now past midnight. Flynn O'Grady stood up and lit a cigarette in the dark. He had been dozing in and out of sleep since seven and it was now time to go to the scrap heap. He threw the burlap bag full of tools over his shoulder and walked down the deserted hallway to the fire escape on the inside of the building.

He climbed up to the roof and made his way silently along the huge hotel to its vacant building on Clark Street. Reentering from the fire escape he turned his head lamp on and walked down the tenth floor hallway to the mechanical room. Inside he went to work. First with the crowbar and hammer, knocking away the crumbling plaster and exposing the copper water pipes. 'Now it's time for some heat,' he thought, lighting the torch and melting the soldering that held the tubing together. It was a slow process, but he was making headway. After an hour he had salvaged forty pounds of copper tubing worth a dollar ten cents a pound at the scrap dealer off the promenade in Brooklyn.

Flynn O'Grady took a smoke break, cutting off the torch and head lamp to save his batteries. Sitting in the dark he lit a Camel and suddenly smelled smoke. "Jesus Christ!" he muttered, jumping up and switching on his light. 'Where the hell is the smoke coming from,' he wondered, looking down in the hole he had knocked in the wall. To his horror he saw a small red glow in the wall on the floor directly below.

O'Grady grabbed his crowbar and hammer and ran down the dusty hall to the stairs. He bolted down the steps and ran up the hall to the mechanical room on the ninth floor that he had mined the month before. The room was filling with smoke when he entered and started beating out the small flames with his crowbar, thinking, 'I got here just in time to get this goddamn fire under control.'

He suddenly heard a terrifying rumbling coming from below on the eighth floor. "OH MY GOD!" he shouted at the sight of the huge flames that were spreading rapidly in the old building. 'I've got to get my stuff and get the hell out of here, and fast,' he thought, not panicking. He ran back up the smoke-filled hallway to the tenth floor, coughing loudly from the smoke and feeling short of breath.

Back on the tenth now, Flynn O'Grady grabbed his tools and placed them in the sack. He started for the door just as his head lamp went out.

The sad lonely cries of the seagulls always fascinated Peter Slade. He wondered why they sounded that way if they were in fact as happy as they appeared. He watched them flying in the brisk smoky sou'westerly wind as they soared high above the Stone Bridge Inn into a perfect blue sky. The wind carried in it the trace of an early fall and Peter Slade was now fifty. His thin sandy hair, turning gray at the temples, ruffled in the breeze. The nasty scar running down the left side of his face gave him a macho look, disguising the deep lines etched in his granite face. His ice-cold blue eyes read without glasses the Sunday edition of the *New York Times* on the veranda off the Marble Bar where he sat smoking his favorite Macanudo cigar.

It was Sunday, September 3, 1995, the tenth anniversary of the Labor Day weekend that he had met Charlotte in the Benton Point State Park parking lot. It had been exactly ten years since Charlotte had introduced him to the true love of his life, the Stone Bridge Inn.

For Peter Slade it had been a long week of sad memories. He had been thinking about Charlotte as he always did on Labor Day. Suddenly he was wondering if she had gone to heaven and was looking down at him through the eyes of one of the gulls. 'Now, that's a weird thought,' he was thinking, listening to their sad cries ringing out from above. Was that Charlotte crying? He watched the gulls soaring overhead for a long time, wondering if he still loved her.

Charlotte had been a lovely person, even though she was cursed by her wealth and tormented by alcohol in the end. He had loved her once and at times like this he still did. The thought of her being dead made him think of what credentials he needed to make it past St. Peter at the Pearly Gates. He sure didn't want to go to hell.

He was still reminiscing about the past when Ed passed by. "Bring me my usual," Peter Slade ordered.

In a jiffy he had a Glenfiddich, neat, with a glass of water on the side sitting on his table. He was now ready for his Sunday ritual, smoking the cigar and reading the newspaper on the veranda of the Stone Bridge Inn. It was a very fine afternoon for doing that.

The Sunday edition of the *Times* was unusually small, but it was a holiday weekend he remembered. He read the headlines, turning the pages until midway through Section A, when something about the S.E.C. caught his eye. He stopped and read carefully.

"Well I'll be damned!" Peter Slade exclaimed aloud, reading an article's caption: FORMER S.E.C. INVESTIGATOR RESPONSIBLE FOR WALL STREET CLEAN-UP CAUSED ST. GEORGE HOTEL FIRE.

> The body of a former S.E.C. Investigator, Flynn O'Grady, the agent responsible for initiating the investigation of the investment banking firm of Porterfield Hartley & Co. during the inside-trading scandal of the mid-eighties, was found in the St. George Hotel yesterday. Mr. O'Grady was credited with the beginning of the clean up of Wall Street and the financial markets by Democratic Senator Ron DiLorenzo of New York. The former U.S. Attorney responsible for the securities fraud investigations stated that through Mr.

O'Grady's persistence and determination his office had been able to restore investors' confidence in the securities industry. The Senator also stated that Flynn O'Grady was a dedicated investigator and a legend at the Securities and Exchange Commission.

Mr. O'Grady, a long-time resident of the hotel, was an alcoholic and welfare resident and had lived the life of a pauper after being fired by the S.E.C. in 1990. The resident had evidently set the blaze with a blowtorch he was using to steal copper tubing out of the vacant part of the hotel to sell to supplement his welfare check.

The landmark St. George Hotel was gutted by fire, miraculously claiming only Mr. O'Grady's life. Hundreds of people from the surrounding brownstones and apartment buildings were forced to evacuate in blankets, bathrobes and their T-shirts and shorts. Over five hundred firefighters from 50 engine companies and 27 ladder companies responded to the equivalent of a 16-alarm blaze that was reported at 3:31 a.m. that left only the exterior walls where the once grand staircase led to the front desk of the largest hotel in New York City.

The fire marshal reported that the fire had originated in a vacant section of the 110-year-old hotel where none of the eighty residents lived. Half the residents are permanent with the rest being welfare cases housed there by city agencies. The cause of the blaze was determined after a thorough investigation by the fire marshal, police and Federal Bureau of Alcohol, Tobacco and Firearms who found Mr. O'Grady's body in the rubble on the tenth floor.

'What a deserving way for the rotten bastard to die,' thought Peter Slade, laying the paper aside. He shook his head slowly and took a drink of Scotch, thinking back on what an asshole Flynn O'Grady had been. He had often wondered what had happened to O'Grady after he showed up threatening to have Slade arrested for stealing the government's money on the morning of Monday, July 1, 1990, the day of Charlotte's and George's funerals.

Peter had leveled with the FBI that he had shipped the money to the Stone Bridge Inn. From there the investigation seemed to have been dropped. Without legal assistance from John Moffett, Peter Slade had threatened to reveal the Justice Department's Bermuda blackmail scheme to the *Washington Post* with a telephone call to Ron DiLorenzo.

Peter Slade took another drink of Scotch and a long draw of the cigar, blowing smoke with a smile. "Well, here's to Flynn O'Grady. May your soul roast in hell ten years to the day after you arrested me. George Washington Henley used to say, 'Everything that goes around, comes around, and the sun don't shine up the same dog's ass everyday, nohow!'"

Peter Slade took another deep draw off the Macanudo. He now knew that he would never know why Flynn O'Grady had been so hell-bent to do him in. All of a sudden, he didn't really care. It was all over now.

The breeze caught the blue smoke of the cigar and carried it along with the sad cries of the passing seagulls. Slade's mind fast-forwarded over the last ten years now that he knew Flynn O'Grady was dead.

He thought sadly about Charlotte and George Washington Henley, his old friend. He was glad that Thomas Terrell, the last of the true English butlers, was still serving him breakfast at Beach Mont where he now lived. Under Charlotte's will Peter Slade could still live there. In accordance with the provisions of Charlotte's grandfather's will, the mansion would be donated to the Newport Historical Society to become part of the Cliff Walk Tour of Homes after the spouse of the last living heir either remarried or died.

Dr. Duane Pearson's obituary had been in the *New York Times* last December. The cause of death was AIDS at forty-three, it had read. Peter Slade had made a fifty thousand dollar memorial to the AIDS Foundation of New York City in memory of the homosexual doctor who had once saved his life. He took a sip of the Glenfiddich and felt good about having done that.

Peter Slade thought often about Melissa Jenkins. He knew she must be happy in Hollywood as a star going by the name of Beverly Blevins. All this time he had suspected that she had stolen Flynn O'Grady's money, but for some reason he never told the FBI. When he heard she was a soft-core porno star, he had thought about getting her video, but for some reason it just didn't seem right. He was glad she had gotten her name in the bright lights. When she never called after Charlotte's death, it confirmed his suspicions and hurt his feelings. "Money does strange things to people sometimes," Peter Slade had said.

Carolina Barrington had married a Boston lawyer by the name of Charles O'Grady, of all things, and they had a kid. Slade read her book, entitled *The Blue-Blooded Madam of Manhattan*. He had seen her late one night on the Merv Griffin Show and later at Grill 23 & Bar in Boston. He had taken his date to the restaurant in what was once the commodities trading floor of the old Salada Tea Company on Berkeley Street and a cigar-friendly place. They had exchanged glances, but neither spoke.

Tony Stevenson had returned to England and founded TSFusion, Ltd, which produced cameo encrustations of gold on crystal that he had patented. The new company was revolutionizing the jewelry industry and Tony was now getting rich.

Bob Ganloff dropped by occasionally to get away from his Miller Beer Distribution Company. He still remained a hard man to converse with.

United States Senator John Moffett was the freshman Republican from Rhode Island. He had resigned from partnership with Jack Spencer, who would remain a confirmed bachelor to the end.

Flint Firestone still sailed daily in good weather on the Sakonnet River. He would tie up at the pier in front of the Stone Bridge Inn for a late lunch and cocktails. Firestone and the innkeeper frequently laughed and joked about his unpaid wager from the 1990 Onion Patch Race as the two men sat at the Marble Bar and smoked cigars and drank vodka and tonics. It seemed ironical to Peter Slade, remembering what George Washington Henley used to say, 'What goes around comes around,' when Flint Firestone reentered the *Martinis* in the 1994 Newport-Bermuda Race and won the Lighthouse Trophy fair and square.

Peter Slade was sitting in the bright sunshine thinking about all that had happened to him over the past ten years. It suddenly dawned on him that he must have close to twenty-five million dollars in his secret trust account in the Bank of Bermuda Limited. A smile painted his scarred face. He picked up the portable phone and dialed Delta Airline's flight reservations office.

"This is Peter Slade. Book me a first class reservation on your next flight for Bermuda tomorrow morning out of Boston, please.... Yes, I will be traveling alone...."

The End